W9-BNE-551

GREAT OR NOTHING

JOY McCULLOUGH
CAROLINE TUNG RICHMOND
TESS SHARPE
JESSICA SPOTSWOOD

DELACORTE PRESS

Text copyright © 2022 by Joy McCullough, Caroline Tung Richmond, Tess Sharpe, and Jessica Spotswood
Jacket art copyright © 2022 by Louisa Cannell
Jacket lettering copyright © 2022 by Ann Chen

GetUnderlined.com

Educators and librarians, for a variety of teaching tools,
visit us at RHTeachersLibrarians.com

Library of Congress Cataloging-in-Publication Data
Names: McCullough, Joy, author. | Richmond, Caroline Tung, author. |
Sharpe, Tess, author. | Spotswood, Jessica, author.
Title: Great or nothing / Joy McCullough, Caroline Tung Richmond,
Tess Sharpe, Jessica Spotswood.
Description: First edition. | New York : Delacorte Press, 2021. | Audience: Ages 12 and up. |
Summary: "A reimagining of *Little Women* set in the spring of 1942, when the United States is suddenly embroiled in the Second World War, this story, told from each March sister's point of view, is one of grief, love, and self-discovery"— Provided by publisher.
Identifiers: LCCN 2021005587 (print) | LCCN 2021005588 (ebook) |
ISBN 978-0-593-37259-3 (hardcover) | ISBN 978-0-593-37260-9 (library binding) |
ISBN 978-0-593-37261-6 (ebook)
Subjects: CYAC: Sisters—Fiction. | World War, 1939–1945—Fiction.
Classification: LCC PZ7.1.M43412 Gr 2021 (print) | LCC PZ7.1.M43412 (ebook) |
DDC [E]—dc23

The text of this book is set in 11-point Adobe Caslon.
Interior design by Ken Crossland

Printed in the United States of America
10 9 8 7 6 5 4 3 2 1
First Edition

For Jim McCarthy

Tide

The water turns
at the moon's insistence.

Wild storms rock the surface
but the waves are pulled
by a stronger force.

Jo at the page
Amy at the easel
Meg at the hearth.

Dramatic as lightning,
but this turning, this force
is also the caress of a sister's hand

soft slow gentle
and certain as death.

CHAPTER 1

JO

There was a moment in each day where she forgot.

It never came at the same time; if it had, perhaps then Jo could have prepared for it. But how could you prepare for forgetting, just for a moment, that what once was a quartet had been reduced to a trio?

There was no rhyme or reason to the moments she stumbled. She had found that there was no rhyme or reason to any of this; grief and war, they were intertwined. Bedfellows in the truest sense. The only way to defeat them was the same: battle.

But there was no way to win hers. Jo was Sisyphus, rolling that boulder up the hill, only to lose her grip right before she reached the top. Because there was no way to bring her back.

Beth was gone. Not the way Laurie or Father was gone or how Amy was gone. But really, truly gone.

It still felt so wrong. Like Jo had tripped into a nightmare she couldn't wrench herself from. Was that why she forgot? Was her mind simply ill prepared for the new world she'd woken to that terrible day?

After, staying home had been unbearable, but she had borne it as long as she could—for Meg's sake, for Marmee's, even for Amy's, though her little sister always seemed to soldier through. But when the attack on Pearl Harbor shocked America, the war that had been knocking at their doors finally burst through in the cruelest, bloodiest way. Grief had no place in the aftermath (grief made its home in her heart, dug a burrow and set up for good) when action was so badly needed. The March sisters—the broken, out-of-tune trio that was left—had scattered. Meg had stayed with Marmee; the good daughter, who'd never rock the boat too much. Amy had done what she did best: put on a smile and sought a way out and found it. And Jo had run.

There was no polite way of putting it, and she wasn't the most polite in the first place. She wouldn't lie and deny it to herself, at least. She had run, as far and as fast as she could. The war effort needed women, capable women who could handle explosives and build planes, with steady hands and a smile on their faces for the newsreels.

She would've preferred Laurie's path: a uniform, and a gun in her hands, and a boat overseas and some Nazis to defeat. She'd told him to punch Hitler for her as she straightened the wool lapels of his uniform before he shipped out. He'd let out a laugh, but it hadn't reached his eyes. He'd been so upset with her, still, but there had been nothing to do but put the sting of her rejection aside. There were much more important things now.

He had shipped out, and she thought she might die, because she may not have loved him the way he wanted, but she did love him—more fiercely than anyone but her sisters and her parents. Jo had never been one to give her love lightly, and now so many pieces of her were missing. Laurie hadn't taken her heart, but part of her laughter, her joy, her mischief and adventure, for that was what she thought of when she thought of him.

And all she could do was run from her sisters, from her grieving mother who had thrown herself into distraction after distraction, from the memory of her father's hand cupping her cheek as he said goodbye.

From Beth, in that bed, so, so pale and still.

Was it any wonder that Jo lived for those moments she forgot Beth was gone? She craved them like a drunk craved whiskey. But the crash of remembering: that was worse than the shakes the men too far gone got when they didn't just want drink but needed it.

Even the sweet things had their bitterness these days: A kiss witnessed on the street could be the last. A love letter sent could end up being unread. A knock at the door and two soldiers outside could destroy an entire family. *We regret to inform you* . . .

They all knew the words now. The girls on the line didn't dare even speak them, like it'd conjure up a curse. But when the news of someone's husband or father or brother rippled through the factory, it was what ran through everyone's minds. Those words, that telegram. *We regret to inform you* . . .

Jo turned over on her narrow mattress, checking the clock on the rickety table that held her lamp and the stack of *Life* magazines she'd borrowed from Anna, two doors down. It was still dark out—not even five yet. The boardinghouse should be quiet, yet she heard the unmistakable click of oxfords in the hallway. Mrs. Wilson, who owned the boardinghouse, liked to say that wood floors kept her girls from getting up to no good. Mrs. Wilson hadn't figured out they'd all just learned how to tiptoe.

Some new girl hadn't gotten the message.

Six weeks ago, Jo had been the new girl, the rules of the boardinghouse a mystery to her. But she'd grown up in a house full of women: she knew to stake out her territory . . . and how. Soon enough, she'd be ruling the roost.

She pulled on her robe—plaid and stitched with love by Meg, something that used to make her feel warm, inside and out, and now just made her feel guilty and mad, still so damned *mad* at her—and padded across the creaky floors of her room. Swinging open her door, she expected to catch Anna or Evelyn, or maybe even Molly, who liked to play at being a good girl but who all the girls knew was up to *something* with the late nights she kept.

Secrets were hard to keep in the boardinghouse, almost as hard as keeping quiet. But the early-morning visitor was doing nothing to muffle her steps or the thump of her suitcase as she set it down in front of the door across from Jo's. Her back was to her, red curls that couldn't be called anything but *unkempt* swaying, as she tried to get the door to open. Jo could hardly blame her for not keeping up her hair—in these parts, women kept their hair tucked safely under cotton turbans more often than it was styled into pageboys and pin curls.

"I thought the rookies were coming in on Wednesday," Jo said, her voice hushed in the silence that came before the din that seemed to hum over the boardinghouse at most hours.

Instead of startling like Jo half expected the girl to do, she just cast a look over her shoulder. "Oh, doll," she said. "If you think I'm fresh meat, *you've* got to be new. I'm just back from my stint in Texas, training the new batch of WASPs."

Jo had a feeling she wasn't talking about the insects, but she wasn't about to ask. The world was full of new words, acronyms, and slang she had never learned and was still trying to. She hated feeling out of the know, and suddenly she was wishing she hadn't been so eager for distraction she'd flung her door open or spoken at all.

"I'm Peg," said the girl—woman, really—pressing a hand against the breast of her practical navy gabardine jacket. "You must be the Jo that Mrs. Wilson mentioned when I called. She had to move me to this room because you have my old one."

"Are you the one who rigged the window with the corkscrew so it'd close properly?"

A smile crept across Peg's face. "That was me. I'm also the gal to come to if the hot water's coming out in drips. Me and that rickety hot-water heater have a special bond."

"The girls'll be glad to have you back, then. We haven't had more than five minutes' worth of hot water for weeks."

"I arrived just in time."

"Are you working the line?" Jo asked.

Peg's smile widened. "I don't make the planes. I fly them."

"You're a pilot?"

"I am."

Jo had heard of them: the aviatrixes that had been trained to fly the planes she and the other girls built. They ferried them from the factory to the air bases mostly, but there were murmurs that some did more. Secret missions. Flygirls towing targets for the boys' anti-artillery training. The kind of flying and danger that could get a girl killed. That may already have gotten girls killed.

Once, the thought of that kind of adventure might've thrilled her, but now, all Jo could think of was the loss. Most of the girls who lived at the boardinghouse worked at the factory with her, with a few exceptions. But there were other working women streaming in and out of the boardinghouses across the state and the country: girls working in offices, in factories of all kinds, not just munitions and aircraft—plus the girls who stayed at home to take over farming, or teaching like Meg. Everyone had been thrust into new worlds, but Jo felt like she was the only one unmoored from the shift. Surely that couldn't be true.

"Peg!" A squeal broke out. "You're back!" Anna came flying out of her room, throwing her arms around Peg. "I want to hear absolutely everything about Texas."

Inside her room, Jo's alarm went off and she retreated as Anna's excited voice rose and, through the hall, muffled clanging—the other girls' alarms—began. The silence of the morning was broken: it was time to come alive.

Jo closed her door and pressed her back against it for a moment, letting the alarm run to an abrupt halt, the echo hanging there. The murmur of voices in the hall, the rush of water down the way, the giggles and yawns: it was like every morning of her childhood, just more. Mornings always reminded her the most of what she'd left behind. The girls joked about it: *Jo needs a cup of joe in the morning, or she's a bear.* They all had their quirks: Anna spent much too long on her hair, and Evelyn tracked in mud wherever she went, because that girl preferred spending time in the Victory Gardens over spending time with people. Jo was grumpy in the morning, and Molly was just plain secretive. Mrs. Wilson looked over them all, extending her benevolent sternness like a quilt to cover them and this hodgepodge place they'd come to call home.

It should have been enough.

It was not. Nothing ever was for Jo. That was the thing, wasn't it? Laurie wasn't enough, yet she was for him, somehow. Meg had taken one closer look at John, it seemed, and given up everything she'd ever dreamed of—because, somehow, *he* had been enough. Jo didn't know what had changed in Meg: she had known John for ages; he'd been Laurie's tutor, after all. But suddenly, things were different. At least Jo could understand Amy's choices more than Meg's; she'd stepped into the unknown, her little sister. Jo had begrudging admiration for her nerve. Meg had just stepped toward a man. An uninspired, staid one at that. How could she be happy?

And, more importantly, how could Jo *not* be happy for her? That was the question Meg had hurled during their fight, before Amy had come upstairs like gasoline thrown on an already furious fire.

After everything, Meg had said, *how can you not be happy for me?*

And how can you not understand me? Jo had shot back.

Meg had no answer, but maybe just as damning—neither did Jo. She'd been trying to find one ever since. All these months, and she'd failed each time.

Jo crossed the room to the vanity crammed underneath the drafty window that was kept shut by Peg's clever corkscrew trick. Jo's one good pair of stockings was draped over the mirror. Once she wore holes in this pair, she wasn't sure where she'd find the money to afford another. She found it hard to care. It

7

seemed ridiculous to dress for the ride to the factory and back, but she couldn't exactly walk around in the coveralls she wore at work, even if they were damned comfortable.

She plucked her crumpled slip from its place on the edge of the vanity, disrupting the pile of letters underneath.

Were they letters if they never got finished or sent? Now, that was a question for the philosophers and thinkers of the world. Not for a girl who had slept badly and hadn't had any coffee yet.

Yet she found herself picking up the top one.

> Dear Meg,
> ~~I KNOW that I said some awful . . .~~
> ~~Leaving home was one of the hardest . . .~~
> ~~I had to get out of that house, Meg.~~
> ~~Sometimes I'm so angry at you I could spit.~~
>
> I miss her, Meg.

Jo's fingers lingered on the only words left that weren't crossed out. Eyes burning, she caught sight of herself in the beveled mirror. She set her jaw as the boardinghouse din rose to its normal daytime hum.

She had a job to do. They all did. She had to pull herself together.

I miss her, Meg.

She *had* to.

Feathers

You are the gull, Jo,
strong and wild,
hurtling headlong
into the squall.

Meg, the turtledove
bonding fiercely
to those she chooses,
devotion undeterred.

Amy, the lark
ever straining toward
the clouds, the nest
awaiting her return.

I love
to watch
you fly.

Beth

Each time you
took flight, my sisters,
I felt a ruffling
in my own feathers.

But I stayed in my nest,
wings tightly tucked.

There are so many
lurking dangers
in the great, wide world
and a bird
is so tiny
so frail.

But the twigs of my nest
the bits of twine and hope
began to fall away, the natural
course of things, inevitable

until there was
nothing left to hold me
and I had to fly
                away.

CHAPTER 2

MEG

When the bell finally rang to signal the end of the school day, Meg grabbed her gray wool trench coat and her little red cloche hat and scrammed. Usually she enjoyed a gossip with the other teachers, but Frankie was crowing about her engagement, and Meg couldn't bear it somehow. The other girls were positively pea green with envy, crowding around to ooh and aah over Frankie's ring. Meg gave Frankie a squeeze and said she was over the moon for her, but to be honest, the words stuck in her throat a little.

Was that who she was now—someone who begrudged her friend's happiness?

She felt like a real heel about it.

The other girls were going for pie and coffee—sugar was rationed, and there were rumors coffee would be next, so they wanted to get it while they still could—but Meg begged off, claiming papers to grade. She did have papers to grade, and she ought to go home and make herself a nice cup of tea and get to it. But the themes of *The Scarlet Letter* hardly seemed important now. All the boys could talk about was how they were going to fight Hitler just as soon as they turned eighteen: *Don't you know there's a war on, miss?* And the girls were no better, abuzz with letters from beaus, brothers, or neighbors, and plans to do their part as nurses or WAACs or factory workers after graduation. *The Scarlet Letter* didn't stand a chance.

Meg walked alone through the woolly gray October afternoon, craving the comforts of home. But home offered poor comfort these days. She let herself in and looked around the empty parlor, crowded with memories: Jo, sprawled on the rug, reading one of her stories aloud in between crunches of a ripe red apple. Laurie banging through the kitchen door, a baseball in his hands, inviting Jo for a game of catch. Father snoring in his armchair, the newspaper (USS KEARNY TORPEDOED! 11 SAILORS KILLED!) drooping across his chest like a wilted flower. Marmee bustling about in the kitchen, the sweet cinnamon scent of a freshly baked pie drifting out. Amy turning the radio on, rolling up the rug, and dancing in her stockinged feet to the latest Tommy Dorsey. Beth playing along on the piano, her face tired but aglow with happiness because they were all together.

Had it really only been a year?

Meg ran a hand over the dusty lid of Beth's piano. No one had touched it for months. She could hardly stand to look at the blasted thing.

Marmee wasn't home yet. Probably she was at one of her committee meetings. Marmee led half a dozen different committees these days. Ever since Father had enlisted as a navy chaplain, she kept herself so busy Meg hardly saw her. Sometimes, Meg wondered if it was on purpose, if Marmee was avoiding her, if she blamed her for the way things had fallen apart. She couldn't bring herself to ask. Marmee came home late, ate egg-salad sandwiches standing up in the kitchen, and then practically fell into bed every night, exhausted. Meg suspected it was the only way she could sleep.

Outside, someone was whistling Glenn Miller's "Don't Sit Under the Apple Tree (With Anyone Else but Me)." Meg's pulse kicked into a gallop. She rushed to the window in time to see the postman, Mr. Hargreaves, shove something into their mailbox. Meg was out the door in a flurry, without coat or hat or gloves, her block heels clicking against the sidewalk as she *sprinted* for the mailbox.

Mail! This was the best part of her day. Sometimes the *hope* of a letter was even better than the letter itself: Maybe Jo regretted her harsh words. Maybe she had finally written to apologize and tell Meg about the factory where she was working and the boardinghouse where she was living. Maybe she missed Meg. Maybe she forgave her.

Meg was having trouble forgiving herself.

"Thank you, Mr. Hargreaves!" she shouted as the elderly postman crossed the lawn to the Laurences'. He was about as popular as Bing Crosby these days.

Meg shoved her hand into the mailbox, her eyes closed with anticipation. She drew out a single letter. It was addressed to her—but it wasn't from Jo; it was from John Brooke. She hugged it to her chest, but her heart sank a little. She loved getting letters from John; of course she did. But it had been almost two months since her sisters had left home: Jo to work in an airplane factory in Connecticut, and Amy to study art in Montreal. They hadn't parted on good terms, and Meg missed them desperately.

Meg and John, on the other hand . . . they had parted on *marvelous* terms. She blushed, remembering it. The night before he'd caught the train down to Fort Monmouth for officer training, John had taken Meg to the pictures. They'd seen Greer Garson in *Mrs. Miniver* and gone for Cokes after. Then, sitting in his old Buick Special in the Marches' driveway, John had asked if she'd be his girl. If she'd wait for him while he was away. Meg had said yes, of course she would, and he'd kissed her till she was dizzy. Till he saw Amy peering out the window at them, the little snoop! Meg had kissed him one last time, then practically floated inside, flushed and happy.

The Marches had had precious little happiness that year, spring and summer passing in a haze of grief and work and a series of anxious goodbyes as they'd waved off Laurie and then Father and then John. Meg had expected her sisters to be happy for her. When they hadn't been able to manage that, it stung.

She ripped open John's envelope right there on the sidewalk. When she'd skimmed its contents, she let out a contented little sigh. He missed her. The army was treating him well, and the food was all right. After chow, he played gin rummy with some of the guys, or they watched pictures like *A Yank in the R.A.F.* He said Betty Grable couldn't hold a candle to Meg.

He hoped to get home and see her when his training was finished, before he went overseas. Meg's teeth chattered as she hurried inside. Would he give her a pin? Or a *ring*? Lots of girls were getting engaged before their fellas shipped out; half of them had whirlwind weddings weeks or even *days* later.

Was that what Meg wanted—a ring?

She imagined the other teachers crowding around her like

they had around Frankie, but the image fell flat. The people she'd want to celebrate with most wouldn't be happy for her. No man would be good enough in Jo's eyes, and all Amy cared about in a suitor was money, the little snob; she would never deign to marry a poor schoolteacher like John.

Meg was a schoolteacher herself. Why would she scorn John for it? She and her sisters had had such silly dreams when they were children: that Meg would be a famous actress on Broadway, her name in lights, and Jo would write a Great American Novel. They'd live together at the Waldorf Astoria hotel in New York City and have all the most fascinating bohemian friends. Amy would marry an English lord and paint in Paris, and, she promised, she'd absolutely shower them with presents.

They hadn't imagined another war.

Meg shook off her gloomy thoughts. She'd write to John straightaway, so he wouldn't have to wait and wonder. She filled the kettle and threw another log on the woodstove to thwart the chill. Marmee was trying not to use the furnace in order to preserve fuel (*Use less so they can have more!*).

Meg settled in at the kitchen table. "Darling" was the fashionable term of address, but it seemed so . . . jaunty. Meg didn't feel very jaunty these days. She didn't want to be too forward, either, lest John think she was—what had Amy called her friend Mae Chalfont?—*khaki-wacky*. Boy-crazy.

John had written, *My dearest Meg*. It couldn't hurt to return the endearment, could it?

My dearest John,

It was wonderful to get your letter. I'd just arrived home from school, and as soon as I heard the postman's whistle I was outside—in a flash! I didn't even bother with my coat. I'm glad the army is treating you well. Did you get the package I sent last week? I remembered you liked my maple candies. The first batch was a mess— you'd have broken a tooth!—but Marmee and I had a good laugh about it, and I think the next batch turned out all right. Please let me know if there's anything else you're missing from home, and I'll send it right away. We took some candies over to Mr. Laurence, and he asked after you.

John had been Laurie's math tutor; that was how he and Meg had met. Laurie and Jo and Meg and John had gone to the pictures and the theater and out for Cokes as a friendly four-some. Laurie had hoped for more than friendship from Jo. Everyone—including Meg—had assumed the two of them would wind up together, when Jo was ready.

Meg winced, remembering Jo's fury over that.

It hadn't been love at first sight for Meg, either. John had seemed terribly serious compared to Laurie and his playful the-atrics. Meg had been focused on her classes at Framingham State Teachers College, which didn't leave much time for dat-ing. But John had encouraged her in her studies. When she was hired to teach English at the high school in Concord last year, he had been right down the hall in the math department:

a steadying presence, always ready with a listening ear. He became the first person she turned to with her troubles.

They had become friends, and gradually, something more. Meg found herself looking forward to seeing him in the halls, or at lunch in the teachers' room, or at assemblies—just like a schoolgirl with a crush. Amy had been telling her for ages that John Brooke was sweet on her, but her own feelings had snuck up on Meg.

The students ask after you, too, though I think it's mostly to tease me! she wrote. That mischievous Dorothy Scott, in her third-period English class and the Junior Red Cross, was always slyly asking if Meg had heard how Mr. Brooke was getting on. Then all the girls would burst into giggles, and Doro would say, "Why, Miss March, you're blushing!"

Maybe she did blush a little. She had been living on the memory of those kisses for months now.

Things are well here at home, Meg wrote, then hesitated.

It wasn't a lie, exactly. *Well* was relative now; they all graded on a curve. Just that morning, Meg had come across a handkerchief Beth had embroidered for her, languishing in the pocket of last winter's plaid skirt. She had dissolved into tears, remembering her sister's shy smile.

I am still missing Beth terribly, of course. She was the glue that held us all together.

Despite their bickering, the March sisters had found balance as a foursome, often pairing off: Meg and Amy, Jo and Beth. Without Beth, it felt all wrong. They had had a few months of wary peace, and then everything had shattered and Meg hadn't been able to fix it. She *should* have been able to fix it; she was the oldest and the customary referee for their

17

squabbles. But something had broken, and Meg was afraid it might be irreparable.

They certainly weren't going to mend anything with Jo in Connecticut and Amy off in Montreal. Meg couldn't see why they'd both had to leave! She supposed Concord had never been grand enough for Amy, and at least her baby sister was painting again. But there was plenty to do for the war effort right here, no matter what Jo said. (She'd said planting Victory Gardens wasn't enough—which had felt like a slap in the face to Meg's efforts.)

How are your sisters? John had asked, and Meg loved him for asking. But the truth was that, for the first time in her life, she didn't know. Not really. They'd had an enormous row right before Jo left. Maybe it was even *why* Jo left. Jo's news had taken her by surprise, and Meg responded all wrong. Jo had been furious. She'd expected Meg, of all people, to know what was (or wasn't) in her heart. Then Amy stormed in, wanting to know why they were shouting, and Jo refused to tell her. Amy had felt—and rightly so—that they were shutting her out. It'd gotten ugly between the two of them. Meg tried to intervene, but then Amy called John a fuddy-duddy, and she had lost her temper, too.

Why couldn't her sisters see how happy John made her? Jo thought that agreeing to be John's girl was a mistake, that it would lead to marriage and motherhood, and that would be the end of all Meg's adventures forever. Somehow Jo couldn't see that it was just a different kind of adventure. And despite the thousands of times Meg had defended her from Jo, Amy sided with Jo on this! John wasn't dashing or elegant—or rich!— enough for her taste.

In the end, they had all said terrible things. Meg had told her sisters they were being selfish and childish. She'd told Amy to grow up, that real romance wasn't like the movies. She had said even worse to Jo. She winced as she remembered.

I haven't heard from Jo. Amy's letters are cheerful but brief. I imagine they're both awfully busy, she wrote. There. That was honest without being pathetic. After all, her job was to keep her soldier's spirits up; all the women's magazines said so. And Marmee never complained; Marmee always kept her chin up.

I'm keeping plenty busy, too. The Junior Red Cross is helping with the blood drive next Saturday, and we're organizing a scrap drive at school. We're determined that Concord will beat Bedford and Lincoln and Maynard! Do you know how much iron is required for a single tank, much less a navy ship? I imagine you do! Marmee and I ripped out the wrought-iron fence around the yard, and then she went through our pots and pans and found some to donate. I heard the town plans to give up some of the Civil War cannons. You should see all the junk people are bringing to the schoolyard: tin cans, old license plates, bed frames, bicycles, even old bathtubs!

It had felt good to knock that old fence down. To hit something. The world was unfair; Beth's death and this damned war had taught Meg that. She had never been the March sister with the temper, but lately . . . well, lately Meg was angry, and didn't she have a right to be? She was tired of feeling like what she wanted didn't matter, that she was small and insignificant—not only to her sisters but to God, whom she had begged not to let Beth die.

I wish you were here, John. I'm sure I'd feel less blue if I were in your arms.

Doro Scott was right; she was blushing, as red as one of Marmee's prize tomatoes.

Well, that stack of papers to grade is calling my name, so I must close. Please take care, and write again soon, and know that I am thinking of you always.

They hadn't said those three little words yet. John had couched his regard for her in terms like *respect* and *admire* and *care for you very much*. Meg ran her fingers over the imprint of his signature on his last letter. Somehow, such a little thing made her feel closer to him. But was that love? Her sisters thought love should be full of romantic words and grand gestures, not this quiet intimacy.

She took a deep breath and put her pen back to the paper.

Fondly,
Meg

My Dearest Meg

Forgive me.
When I gave you
that handkerchief, I never
meant it only for your tears.

I meant it for the Meg
who always knows
the proper thing to say or do,
who offers what is needed, always.

For that, I'm sorry, too.

I didn't see the weight
you carried, how doing what's expected
is harder than it looks. I failed
to see the rest of you.

Forgive me, but also understand
how well you play your part, forever on a stage.
But do you know what I think?
Jo doesn't always have to be the bard.

Perhaps this is foolish,
but hear me out: What if
you penned your lines yourself?

What might you write for the role
you want to play, and not the one
your audience expects?

And sometimes?
Oh, Meg, imagine!
What if you toss aside the script,
and instead of reciting lines,
you stand in the light
and simply bare your heart?

Weed

Oh, to see you
ripping out a fence of iron,
yanking it from the ground
like a weed that has taken root.

For the cause, of course.
But did you also feel powerful?

Did you
hurl the metal
on a pile that grew
with each bead of sweat?

Did you
just for a moment
let loose the anger
that's taken root inside your heart?

Did you know
Marmee has been angry
every day of her life?

CHAPTER 3

AMY

Dear Marmee,

Please don't be too disappointed in me. I'm not sure I can stomach that, but I don't think I can keep this from you any longer.

The truth is, I'm not attending art school in Montreal like I told you and Father. Don't blame Flo. None of this was her fault. What happened was—

"Land ho, ladies!"

Amy's eyes snapped up to find one of her bunkmates standing in the doorway. There were nine girls piled inside their metal box of a room, with their creaky beds bolted to the walls and stacked three high on top of each other. They were all newly minted Red Cross workers, and they had a similar look about them, too—healthy, attractive, and with a youthful glow upon their cheeks—but Amy was the youngest by far. Of course, none of the others knew just how young she was at seventeen. She had been careful to keep her age very quiet.

"We're ahead of schedule? You've got to be kidding!" said

Edie Barnett, a petite brunette from Baltimore with a friendly face like Joan Leslie's.

"Captain Townley must've gunned the engines hard overnight," said the girl in the threshold. "Looks like we'll be in Belfast in no time!"

Amy stowed her letter in her breast pocket, telling herself she'd finish her confession later. Land ho, indeed! She couldn't wait to escape this enormous sardine can. With a swing of her legs, she hopped down to the floor and landed right by Edie, who was tossing aside her copy of *Woman's Day* magazine.

"Maybe we'll finally get some new reading material," Edie quipped. The two of them had read the magazine over a dozen times since there wasn't much else to do on board the RMS *Queen Elizabeth*, except keeping their fingers crossed that they wouldn't run into a German U-boat until they reached port.

"Race you topside?" Amy said with a grin.

In under a minute flat, all nine of the girls had laced up their boots, donned their caps, and gunned it themselves into the corridor. It might've been October, but the air below deck felt warm and thick, like chicken soup. Amy would've given her left pinky toe to open up one of the portholes—the smell of sweat and bodies could've gagged a skunk—but the windows had been blacked out and sealed up when the ship was commissioned for wartime service.

As soon as she stepped onto the sundeck, Amy breathed in the salty air. The wind whistled through her hair, threatening to knock off her cap, but she clamped a hand over it as she moved toward the railing. They'd left Brooklyn over a week ago, zigzagging their way across the Atlantic, and for days on end they'd been surrounded by nothing but the sea. But now Amy spotted rolling hills on the horizon, as green as the clovers that sprouted in Concord every spring.

Amy threw her arms into the air and cheered. Edie joined in, too, but their relief was short-lived, because their supervisor, a stern woman by the name of Owens, told them to quiet down. The girls immediately lowered their voices.

"I call dibs on a hot shower," Edie whispered.

"With plenty of shampoo and soap," Amy added, although both of those items were probably rationed where they were headed.

The Brits had been fighting for three years and counting— the lone guard left standing against Hitler's forces in western Europe—but now the Yanks had arrived to the brawl. Soon, the *Queen Elizabeth* would drop anchor and its passengers would splinter off, with the Red Cross girls fanning all over the UK. Some would work as nurses while others like Amy and Edie would join the new Clubmobile program, where they would serve up coffee and doughnuts for the soldiers, always delivered with a cheerful smile.

Amy had already spent six weeks of training at American University in Washington, DC. There she attended lectures on Red Cross history and military policy, which were so dull that she and Edie had to take turns keeping each other awake. Now the real adventure would begin, but Amy felt her stomach pinch. The Red Cross might have been a humanitarian organization, but that couldn't guarantee her safety over in London. If the worst happened to her—if a German bomb landed square over her billet—then her family would never know what had really happened to her. They'd be searching the streets of Montreal for who knows how long, and Amy couldn't do that to

Marmee. As soon as she returned to her bunk, she really needed to finish that letter.

The wind gusted again, and this time it snatched off Amy's cap, sending it cartwheeling through the air and beyond her fingertips. It would've gone straight over the railing too if Edie hadn't reached out and caught it.

"You're a doll. Have I told you that?" Amy said gratefully as Edie handed the cap to her.

"We can't have you losing your hat now, can we?" Edie got a mischievous look in her eye, and she dropped her voice an octave to mimic Supervisor Owens. *A Red Cross employee without her cap? Highly unprofessional! Were you raised by swine?*"

Amy giggled despite herself. She knew she shouldn't laugh at their boss's expense, but Edie was only joking around.

"No more of that snickering," Edie went on, with a dramatic wag of her finger. *"We shan't have you tainting our soldiers with such impropriety!"*

"Shh, someone will hear you," Amy whispered.

"Indeed, someone just might," said a low voice behind them, which turned out to be Supervisor Owens herself. She was a towering woman with a bun of gray hair, and her own cap was pinned in place with an army of bobby pins. "That's quite enough from you, Captain Barnett."

Edie quickly schooled her features. "Sorry, ma'am. It won't happen again."

The older woman set her eyes on Amy. "The same goes for you, Captain Pace."

Amy sucked in a sharp breath. Hearing that name still took her by surprise, even though she'd been using it for months now. "Yes, ma'am."

"There's no place for such *impropriety* in the Red Cross," Supervisor Owens warned them before taking her leave. "Am I clear?"

Edie waited until Owens was out of earshot before leaning toward Amy. "Someone ought to teach Supervisor Sour Face how to have a little fun," she murmured before gesturing at Amy's hair. "Here, let me help you with your cap. We shan't have you looking so improper, my dear Rosie!"

Amy forced out a laugh. Sometimes she felt she had adjusted to her new life quite swimmingly—until someone called her Rosie and then she was reminded all over again about the lies she had spun to get here. Nobody on board the ship knew her as a March girl. She had left that name behind when she decided to sneak her way into the Red Cross, becoming Rosemary Ann Pace, aged twenty-two, with a widower father and one younger brother and no sisters at all.

Here, where she stood, there was no Marmee.

No Meg or Jo.

No Beth.

It was the sneakiest thing she had ever done—even beating out that time when she'd set Jo's manuscript alight with a single match—and somehow she had pulled it off.

It had all started back in late August. An ordinary Wednesday. Amy was supposed to take a quiz that day about the Teapot Dome Scandal, but she'd skipped class instead and hopped a bus downtown. From there, she had stridden toward the office of the local American Red Cross, where a sign out front proclaimed FIGHTING MEN NEED NURSES. VOLUNTEER TODAY!

Amy had hummed the national anthem under her breath

as she swung the door open. She had come prepared. She had made an appointment three days prior and had made sure to look the part for the interview, even stealing a shirtwaist dress from Meg's wardrobe that was the color of vanilla ice cream and that made her appear a couple years older. Amy thought that she looked quite smart and mature, but as soon as she had taken a seat in the little room beyond the receptionist's desk, the dour recruiter had all but dismissed her.

"How old are you, Miss March?" the woman asked. "Nineteen? Twenty?"

Amy straightened her shoulders, determined to exude confidence. "I'll be seventeen in a couple months."

"I see." The woman's lips pulled tight. "You must be unaware that our volunteers are required to hold a collegiate degree and must be over twenty-two years in age. I'm afraid—"

"I'm a hard worker!" Amy was quick to interject, sensing her dismissal. "And the Red Cross needs nurses, doesn't it? Isn't that what your sign says out front?"

The woman's face softened, but not by much. "Here's my advice. Finish school and get a degree. Have you heard of our new Clubmobile program? You'd be a decent candidate for that." She gestured at a poster on the wall, which depicted a trio of pretty young white women passing out doughnuts and coffee to waiting soldiers. The words BOOSTING MORALE ONE CUP AT A TIME were splayed above them. "You've got the spunk and you fit the bill physically, but you do need a college education to qualify."

"Th-that's years from now," Amy stammered, feeling this opportunity slip away.

I can't stay home, she thought. Not with bits of Beth everywhere—her dolls on the shelves and her bed still neatly made. Those reminders still gutted her every day, and yet they paled in comparison to the gnawing shame that ate holes in her heart—because Amy had failed Beth when her sister had needed her the most.

Last summer, when Beth's health had started to worsen, Amy had been too busy traveling to notice. It had been her aunt Carrol's idea to head up to Montreal and to take Flo and Amy with her. They had originally intended to fly to Paris, but with the Germans taking over France, Aunt Carrol decided that Quebec would be the next best thing. And, oh, what a summer it had been. The art classes. The galleries. The little cafés serving the tiniest cups of coffee and the crustiest baguettes. Amy had wanted to soak up every second of it, and maybe that was why she hadn't written as often as she should have. And whenever she did get a letter from Beth, she'd give it only a skim before setting it aside because she had to finish a line drawing for class or get dressed for another party.

All the while, Beth had been dying.

Amy hadn't known that, of course. Beth didn't want to spoil her little sister's time abroad, and so she'd given strict orders to their family that they couldn't reveal the severity of her condition. But that hadn't lessened Amy's guilt over it.

You selfish brat. Amy flinched. That was what Jo had called her during a big row they'd had, and the words still stung like salt on a cut. Both Jo and Meg had piled on Amy, telling her to grow up and asking her awful questions like *Where were you when Beth got sick?*

That was why Amy had skipped school and come to the

Red Cross. What could be more selfless and grown-up than volunteering for the war?

She was going to show Jo and Meg just how wrong they were.

Amy got to her feet, desperate for this job. "I could wash dishes! Or mop floors. Clean bathrooms until they shine." She winced as she said that last part because scrubbing tubs and toilets was her least favorite chore at home, but perhaps she could negotiate that later. "Give me a chance, ma'am."

But the recruiter gestured at the door. "Your resolve is quite notable, but rules are rules, I'm afraid."

"Can't you grant an exemption this one time?" Amy pleaded.

"Best of luck to you, Miss March."

Amy managed to keep her chin up until she closed the door behind her and rushed into the bathroom down the hall so that she'd have a quiet place to blink her tears away. Once inside, she let out a choked breath and tried to think. Surely, she had other options. President Roosevelt had recently signed a bill to create the Women's Army Auxiliary Corps, and she could look into their job openings. But chances were that she would have to be at least eighteen years old to join them, too.

"Hang it all," she muttered.

Just then, she heard someone let out a hiccup. Amy whipped around, realizing that there was somebody in the stall behind her. She hadn't bothered to check it when she'd barged in.

Now she heard a whimper and a sniff. Whoever was in there was definitely crying.

Amy leaned toward the stall door. She knew that eavesdropping was an awful habit of hers, but growing up with three older sisters, she had never bothered to kick it.

"You all right in there?" Amy said tentatively.

In reply, the door flung open, and out stepped a poor girl who looked like she had just watched her beloved tabby cat get run over by a Cadillac coupe. Her face was streaked with tears, and she was hugging a fat folder of paperwork against her chest, which she thrust onto the counter so that she could wipe off her thick tortoiseshell glasses.

"I did everything they said!" the girl said with another hiccup. "I brought two copies of my transcript and *three* letters of recommendation. Professor Compton even said that I should get in with flying colors."

Amy glanced at the girl's reflection, noticing how they had similar expressions on their faces. "Let me guess. You got the boot from the recruiter, too?"

"I didn't even get a single toe in the door, all because of these," the girl said miserably as she gestured at her glasses. "I guess you need at least twenty-forty vision to join the Red Cross. The woman didn't even look at my grades." She chewed her lip hard as if to stave off a sob. "I've got a brother down at Fort Bragg and I want to do my part, too."

"Exactly!" Amy said. "Who wants to sit around at home and tend to a little Victory Garden in your mother's backyard?"

"I suppose that's what I've got to look forward to," the girl said before her tears sprang anew. She jammed her glasses onto her face and reached for the doorknob. "I guess I better start planting turnips."

"Wait! What about your folder?"

"Just toss it in the garbage," the girl called out before disappearing down the hallway.

Amy let out a long sigh and glanced at her watch. She'd better head home and change out of her dress before Meg got home from her staff meeting and called her a little thief. With a frown, she tossed the folder toward the trash can, but it didn't quite make it over the lip and the papers scattered everywhere.

"Damn," Amy muttered as she bent down to gather up the mess. Could her day get any worse? There were so many forms to pick up, too. Medical records. Transcripts. Letters of recommendation. She paused as she read over the papers.

"Rosemary Ann Pace," Amy whispered, brushing her thumb against the girl's name on the folder, neatly typed. Miss Pace had gotten straight A's and glowing reviews from her professors. She'd been the treasurer of the Rotary Club, sung in her church choir, and volunteered at the children's hospital to boot. And yet poor Rosie couldn't get herself to the war front because her vision was too poor.

Meanwhile, here was Amy with her perfect 20/20 eyesight, but she was too young and lacked the proper degree to join the Red Cross. If they could have somehow glued themselves together, they would've been a shoo-in, no doubt. Shaking her head, Amy was about to throw the papers away again when a thought struck her and she froze perfectly still. Perhaps she could . . . ?

No, the idea was too preposterous. It would never work. It would be a bald-faced lie.

You selfish brat.

There was Jo's voice again. Taunting her. Tormenting her.

Amy's cheeks flared hot. *Selfish?* She hadn't picked up a

brush since Beth died. She couldn't stomach looking at her charcoals and paints anymore, so she'd given them all away to Marmee's charity group.

But none of that had dulled the pain of failing Beth when it had counted the most.

Amy found herself clutching the folder to her chest and exiting the building lickety-split, this idea of hers spinning itself into a plan and how she might just pull it off.

"Yoo-hoo, have you been daydreaming?" Edie said. She waved a hand in front of Amy's face before tilting her head toward a group of officers on deck. "I've asked you twice if you want to go play cards with Captain Robinson and his pals."

Amy startled as she remembered where she was standing, on the deck of the RMS *Queen Elizabeth*. "That's all right. You go on ahead."

"You sure?" Edie paused. "You look a little blue. What were you thinking about?"

My sisters, Amy thought, but she couldn't admit that to her friend. So she said instead, "Nothing. Just a spot of seasickness."

"Poor thing. You better stay in the fresh air, but join us for a game of rummy when your head clears, hmm? I think Captain Robinson's redheaded friend is sweet on you," Edie said with a wink before bustling away.

Amy leaned against the rail and stared at the ocean, blinking toward where she had come from. Toward home. She'd lied to Edie about feeling queasy. She wasn't nauseous at all, but she sure was homesick. She missed her creaky hand-me-down bed and the smell of Father's pipe. She missed her mother's Sunday roasts and the summer evenings when her sisters would turn up the tabletop radio and they'd jitterbug in the family room.

But home wasn't home anymore, not without Beth. Everything had broken apart after she'd passed. Father had left. Laurie had left. Marmee had disappeared into church and charity work. And as for Meg and Jo, well, they'd made it quite clear that they saw Amy as little more than a nuisance.

That was why Amy had stolen another girl's name and left Concord in the first place. She'd told her family she was going to Montreal—and that was how it would have to stay.

Drawing in a shaky breath, Amy knew what she had to do. She reached into her pocket and took out her unfinished letter to Marmee.

And she let it drop into the cold waters of the Atlantic.

Amy

Remember when you dropped
through the ice into water so cold
it froze your eyelashes?

Jo was there, and Laurie,
and you were saved, soon huddled
by the fire, doted on by all.

Did you know
as you curled your fingers
around Marmee's best mug
filled to the brim with hot cocoa
that Jo cried for days,
raged at herself, blame piling onto
responsibility and fear
that she might lose a sister?

Here you go, running
onto cracked ice again.

Eavesdrop

I always knew when you were lurking

    behind the door
    beneath the window
    in the air around us.

Walls could not contain you.

Your curiosity crept around
corners, your longing to be the center.
I would have given you that,
were it within my power.
I would have been the youngest, left out.

Now I'm the one on the other side.

And you're out there on the ice,
living with reckless abandon.
Don't waste a second.
Give me a reason to grieve the years
I never got. Fill me with such deep envy
I would set fire to my sister's book
and watch it burn to ash.

CHAPTER 4

MEG

"Have a seat, sir, and one of our Junior Red Cross girls will bring you a doughnut. Would you like coffee, too?" Meg asked a tall, dark-haired man as he swaggered into the school cafeteria. His shirtsleeves were rolled up to reveal a neat white bandage wrapped around his arm.

"Sure, I'll take a cup of joe. Thanks, doll." He sat at one of the empty lunch tables.

"Doro, could you get this gentleman some coffee, please?" Meg raised her eyebrows at Doro Scott, who was gossiping with her best friend, Ginny Tanaka, behind the lunch counter. Meg took a deep breath through her nose, praying for patience. It was an honor that the Red Cross mobile unit had decided to hold a blood drive in their school gymnasium. It was an honor to do her part.

It had also been a tremendous amount of work. The Junior Red Cross had gone house to house canvassing, led a campaign for students to urge their families to donate, staffed recruitment booths at Woolworth's, handed out pamphlets, and hung posters all over Concord. They were determined to meet their quota.

Meg looked at the poster taped to the cafeteria wall: a kneeling soldier, bayoneted rifle in hand, helmet off as he clutched his head. It was emblazoned with the message YOUR BLOOD CAN SAVE HIM. It was easy to forget why she was doing this work amidst the day-to-day drudgery of giving lectures, grading papers, disciplining students, tending the Victory Gardens at home and at school, keeping house, writing to Father and John and her derelict sisters, and beginning to sew presents for Christmas. The poster reminded Meg of the realities of war: Father could be the one who needed that blood.

And there *were* ways a schoolteacher in Concord, Massachusetts, could help the war effort, no matter what her sisters thought. The Victory Garden out by the baseball diamond, the ever-growing pile of scrap metal in the parking lot, handing out doughnuts and coffee to folks donating blood—it might not be glamorous, but Meg *was* helping.

"Miss March? We're all out of fresh coffee." Doro held out the empty pot.

"Get more from the kitchen, then," Meg suggested, smoothing her pleated yellow skirt. Goodness, did she have to tell the girls to do every little thing?

Doro rolled her blue eyes with a long-suffering expression that reminded Meg very much of her youngest sister. The girl flipped a brown curl out of her heart-shaped face and stalked toward the kitchen, where volunteers from the Red Cross Canteen Corps were frying dough and warming vats of coffee.

"Hey, sugar, are you rationed?"

Meg looked around the cafeteria. There was no one else within earshot; the dark-haired man must be speaking to her. "Me?" she asked, and he winked at her!

Flustered, she ran a hand over her caramel-colored hair. The Victory rolls she'd arranged so carefully that morning were drooping, and she hadn't had a chance to reapply her cherry-red lipstick for hours. "I've already got a fella."

"Give him the brush-off and come out with me instead," the man said. "My name's Mikey. Jim Michaelson, if we're bein' formal."

"I'm flattered, Mr. Michaelson, but—"

"Miss March is going with Mr. Brooke," Doro said, appearing with a cup of coffee. Ginny followed her with a doughnut. Weren't they eager beavers all of a sudden!

"Yeah? What about you, Jane?" The enterprising Mikey gave Doro and her close-fitting pink sweater a once-over.

"My name isn't Jane," Doro snapped. She linked an arm through Ginny's and stomped back to the lunch counter.

Meg hid a smile as she followed them.

Doro tugged at her keyhole neckline and sighed. "Are you going to give me a hard time for what I said to that old geezer?"

Mikey *was* far too old for Doro. "No, I don't think that's necessary." Meg busied herself rearranging the milk cartons stacked on the counter.

All new teachers were assigned a mentor, and hers was Miss Pennington, the freshman English teacher. Miss Pennington was ancient and as strict as anything; she had been Meg's freshman English teacher and a terror back then, too. She insisted that Meg was too lenient with her students. But with so many of their brothers and sweethearts off to war—with so many of

the kids determined to join up in another year themselves—
Meg couldn't see the harm in a little laughter. Or in telling off
a man who deserved it.

Ginny swiped her black hair out of her eyes. "I can't believe
he made a pass at you, miss!"

Meg suspected that, to the girls, she seemed almost as ancient as Miss Pennington seemed to her.

"I'm not *that* old!" Sometimes, like now, she felt the chasm
between sixteen and twenty-three, but sometimes she felt barely
older than her students at all—especially when Miss Pennington glared at her over her wire-rimmed glasses!

"But you already have a fella. Don't you?" Ginny and Doro
exchanged knowing glances as a patchy red crept across Meg's
cheeks. "You always blush when Doro asks about Mr. Brooke."

Concord wasn't a very big town. Whenever she and John
had gone to the pictures or out for a Coke, they'd inevitably run
into one of their students.

"You're devoted, Miss March, I can tell. Not like that fast
piece of work Martha Ryder," Doro said glumly. "If she writes
my brother a Dear John letter, I swear I'll punch her lights out!"

"Doro!" Meg chided. Doro's brother, Richie, had joined the
navy right after Pearl Harbor. He'd been their first senior to
enlist, and the whole school was fiercely proud of him—no one
more than his younger sister. Still, violence was uncalled for!

Heels clicked down the linoleum hall, and Meg wondered
how things were going over in the gymnasium, where the Red
Cross had set up three dozen folding cots and four portable
refrigerators. Earlier, a line of donors had snaked down the hall
past the cafeteria doors, but now traffic had slowed to a trickle.

"Why, Meg!" a familiar voice cried. "I thought that was you!"

Meg turned, startled. "Sallie?"

Sallie Gardiner stood in the doorway in a tan box coat and a fur stole. They had been friends in school, but Meg hadn't seen her in ages. Since before the war. Before Beth. "What are you doing here?" Meg asked. "Did you come to donate?"

"Oh, not me! You have to be at least a hundred and ten pounds." Sallie laughed, and Meg ran an anxious hand over her own hips. "I'm waiting for Jack. We stopped by on our way to dinner at the club."

Sallie lifted her left hand to adjust her perfect blond page-boy. A diamond winked in the sour cafeteria lighting.

"Wow-ee!" Meg had heard Sallie was getting hitched—to Jack Moffatt, heir to a line of department stores. Meg bent over the enormous ring. "That's gorgeous, Sallie. Congratulations!"

"Thanks! Jack's a real dreamboat," Sallie gushed.

"I'm happy for you." Meg was. She was also suddenly, shrinkingly self-conscious. Sallie had always had that effect on her. The Gardiners hadn't lost their money in the crash in '29 like Father had, and Sallie always found ways to remind Meg of it. Today she looked like a *Mademoiselle* advertisement, in a smart red dress and the most darling brown leather heels tied with a red grosgrain ribbon.

"Have you set a date?" Meg asked.

"Not yet, but Mother and I are thinking next summer. I do love a summer wedding. Of course, that's supposing Jack doesn't get called up." Sallie laughed a trifle nervously. "I don't know what I'd do without him, Meg. I'd be positively lost. Oh, look, here he comes now. Jack! Jack, darling, meet my old school chum, Meg March. Meg, dear, this is my fiancé, Mr. Jack Moffatt."

Jack kissed Sallie's cheek and wrapped one arm around her waist. "It's a pleasure to meet you, Meg." He held out a hand for Meg to shake. He was a grinning, well-dressed, sandy-haired man with broad shoulders and a slightly crooked nose, which looked as though it'd been broken at least once. Meg bet he'd played football in college. There was no reason whatsoever for her to take an instant dislike to him, except that he was standing there in front of her in his civvies, hale and hearty, while John and Laurie and Father weren't.

Meg shook his hand. "How do you do," she said coolly.

"Thanks for your donation, sir," Doro said. "Would you like a cup of joe?"

"Or a doughnut?" Ginny added.

"Thanks, doll." Jack took the steaming cup of coffee from Doro. He ignored the doughnut in Ginny's outstretched hand.

"We also have crackers," Ginny said uncertainly.

Jack smiled down at Doro. "It sure is swell to see a nice American girl doing her part to help our fellas overseas fight those dirty J—"

"Oh goodness, we forgot to offer you cream for your coffee," Meg said, in an attempt to change the subject. "Can we get you anything else, Jack?"

It was too late. Behind the lunch counter, Ginny's smile had faded. Her shoulders hunched in her gray sweater; she tucked her chin toward the Peter Pan collar of her white blouse. As a Japanese American, she had been on the receiving end of glares and nasty remarks like that ever since Pearl Harbor.

"Thanks, mister," Doro said, with a smile that showed her teeth. "My brother Richie's in the navy. He enlisted the day after Pearl Harbor, so I think it's real important to do my part.

I can't abide shirkers. Able-bodied men who ought to have joined up but are just waiting for their number to be called make me sick. I couldn't even look in the mirror if I was a coward like that."

Jack's face went eggplant purple. He strode across the cafeteria in three long-legged strides and was out the door without a word.

"Well, I never!" Sallie said indignantly. "What an insolent little—"

"Girls, why don't you go check on the coffee in the kitchen," Meg suggested.

Doro held out the nearly full pot. "This is fresh."

"It's not the only thing that's fresh," Meg muttered. But to tell the truth, she admired Doro's fierce loyalty. She regretted not telling Jack off herself. There was absolutely no call for embarrassing Ginny like that.

Ginny elbowed Doro, and the girls retreated.

"Jack is plenty patriotic! He's bought a whole stack of war bonds." Sallie was seething.

"I'm sure he has," Meg said, then wondered why her first instinct was always to soothe, to placate, to smooth over any fuss. Jack had been in the wrong. Ginny Tanaka was one of Meg's best students, respectful and kind and every bit as American as anybody else. She had moved to Concord in the seventh grade after her father was hired as a professor of Asian studies at a local college. There had been some ugly remarks from her peers early on, but Doro had put a stop to that, and the girls had been inseparable ever since. They were both in the Junior Red Cross, the Choral Society (Ginny had a lovely

44

soprano, and Doro was . . . enthusiastic), and the Dramatics Club (Doro as a lead actress in their comedies and Ginny on the stage crew).

"What are you doing here, anyhow?" Sallie sniffed, looking around the pea-soup walls of the cafeteria. Meg felt suddenly ashamed: of the school, which needed repairs that had been put off when their janitor enlisted; of her drooping curls; of the scuffs on her well-worn oxfords; even of her new dress, which she'd sewn from a Simplicity pattern. She'd been proud of it this morning—the deep kangaroo pockets, the cheery lemon-yellow buttons that marched in a neat row to the hem, the pleated skirt that swung out right below her knees. Now she felt conscious of every imperfect stitch.

"I teach English here," she explained. "I'm the advisor to the Junior Red Cross. We're helping with the blood drive."

"I heard that you were teaching, but I didn't know it was *here*." Sallie shuddered. Meg was about to protest that she found it quite rewarding, but Sallie plowed on. "Have you got a special fella in your life, at least?"

"Miss March is going with Mr. Brooke," a voice volunteered behind them.

It was Lizzie Talbot, another of Meg's Junior Red Cross students, carrying a box from the kitchen to the gymnasium. The Canteen Corps must have been wrapping up operations for the day.

Lizzie's boyfriend, Theo Harkness—following her and carrying three boxes to her one—made obnoxious kissing noises. "Miss March and Mr. Brooke . . . sitting in a tree . . . k-i-s-s—"

"Theodore Harkness, mind your own beeswax!" Meg yelped.

Sallie smirked. "Meg, you're blushing. Who's Mr. Brooke?"

"John's a math teacher here, but—"

"A *math* teacher?" Sallie's dismay was evident.

"No, he's lovely! He's—" Meg faltered. *Kind. Steady. Clever.* Those weren't attributes that would impress Sallie, though. "He enlisted right after the spring term, and now he's at Fort Monmouth with the Army Signal Corps."

"You poor thing." Sallie's pitying look raised Meg's hackles. "I heard your father is overseas, too. Imagine, at his age! And— well, I was awfully sorry to hear about Beth. She was the sweetest girl."

"She was." Meg swallowed, her irritation vanishing as tears knotted her throat. "Thank you."

Sallie gave her a squeeze. "Look at you. All the worries of the world on your shoulders." She peered up into Meg's face. "You aren't skimping on your beauty routine, are you? I've got an Elizabeth Arden cream that I swear by. You should try it."

Jeepers! Meg's hand flew to her cheek before she could catch herself. Was she getting frown lines? Surely Amy would have told her.

"You've got to get out and have fun while you're still young, Meg. You don't want to end up one of those awful spinsters everyone is terrified of, like Miss Pennington!" Sallie chortled. Meg winced. "Let's see. Who can we set you up with?"

"Oh, I really don't think—"

Sallie snapped her fingers. "Andy Fitzhugh! Andy's swell. Handsome, and from a good family, too. He's an executive down at the electric plant. Why don't you come out with Andy and Jack and me next Saturday? We'll have a blast!"

"Sallie, I don't think—"

"Come on, Meg. I don't see a ring on your finger, do I?" Sallie waved her diamond-clad hand. "What are you going to do, sit home pining for Mr. Brooke and listening to the radio? On a Saturday night?" She sounded aghast.

"Of course not," Meg said, though the truth was that a cup of tea, the latest issue of *Mademoiselle,* and the Voice of America were her plans for that very evening, and she was rather looking forward to it.

"What, then? Charades with your sisters?" Sallie laughed. "I remember those amateur theatricals you used to put on." For such a delicate girl, she had a loud *haw*-haw laugh, like a donkey braying. It had always mortified Meg when it was directed at her.

But Sallie's words made her wonder: What did Jo and Amy do with their Saturday nights? Jo was in a boardinghouse full of girls now; they were bound to get up to some hijinks. And Amy was never one to sit home alone on a Saturday night if she could help it.

"Oh, I don't know," Meg muttered. "I wouldn't like it if John went out with other girls."

"You'd be doing me a real favor. Who knows what awful dud Andy would drag along if we leave him to his own devices? *Please?*" Sallie batted her eyes. "For old times' sake? You work so hard. Don't you deserve to have fun for once?"

I do, Meg thought. *I do work hard, and I do deserve to have fun for once.*

She heard the clatter of pans and running water in the kitchen—it sounded like the Canteen Corps had put the girls to work washing dishes—and she thought of Doro, criticizing her brother's girlfriend. How would it look to her students if Meg went out with somebody who wasn't John?

But this was only a double date, a group of friends. What was the harm in that?

"All right," Meg said finally.

Sallie squealed, squeezed her, then drew back and gave her a quick up-and-down appraisal. "Wear something nice, all right? We'll go to dinner and dancing in Boston. It'll be swell, I promise. Andy's the best. I've got to run. See you!"

"See you," Meg echoed. She felt like she'd been run over by a bus.

A lead weight was settling in her stomach. She already regretted her impulsive yes. Back in school, Sallie had always played on Meg's worst impulses—her vanity and her pride. Was it too late to chase after her and say, oh no, she'd forgotten, she had other plans for next Saturday?

An enormous crash echoed from the kitchen. Meg sighed. She'd have to phone Sallie later. There was work to do.

Two hours later, Meg limped through her front door, exhausted. "Marmee?"

It was nearly suppertime—the cleanup had taken ages—and Meg was hoping rather desperately that Marmee had made something to eat. Maybe they could share a cozy meal in the kitchen while listening to the news. Afterward, Marmee would sew, and Meg would flip through the latest issue of *Mademoiselle* while they sipped tea. She would ask Marmee how to get out of the double date she was already dreading. Marmee believed in honoring one's commitments, but she had never liked Sallie Gardiner.

"Marmee?" Meg called again, heading to the kitchen.

The room was dark, the woodstove down to embers. Meg switched on the lamp.

There was a note on the table.

Meg, dear—

I'm at a meeting at the Lowells, so you'll be on your own for supper. There's leftover ham in the icebox. I hope the blood drive was a roaring success.

Marmee

Meg plopped down at the table, kicking off her oxfords. As she switched on the Crosley tabletop radio, she remembered Sallie's taunt about spending her Saturday nights pining. But it wasn't John she was missing. She remembered all the evenings she and her sisters had crowded around listening to *Beat the Band* while they varnished their nails. Amy was aces at guessing the song, but Jo was fiercely competitive; she got mad when Amy guessed it first. And of course Amy gloated!

Meg missed them so much. Even their silly squabbles. She grabbed a pen and paper. She'd write Jo and describe how Doro had sassed Mr. Michaelson and put Jack Moffatt in his place. Jo would like Doro; the girl had moxie.

Only . . . how many letters had Meg sent now? Jo hadn't responded even *once*. She was a champion grudge holder, it was true, but this was getting ridiculous.

Why didn't she write? They had never in their lives gone this long without speaking.

Meg looked at the note on the table. Was Marmee avoiding her, too?

No. She was being silly. Marmee was busy. That was all.

Meg put pen to paper. She knew at least *one* person who'd be glad to hear from her.

> My dearest John,
>   I've just gotten home from the Red Cross blood drive at school. What a long day it was! Nothing compared to army training, though, I'm sure . . .

Marmee & Father

Marmee's work:
    dinner on the table
    fire in the hearth
    clean-swept floors
    and mended hems.

Father always
coming and going
preaching, proclaiming,
gathering causes like
clouds he could not hold.

One with dreams
spiraling into the sky
while the other
anchored us
to earth, to truth.

And there we were
in between,
grounded and inspired.

Madame Alexander

Do you remember, Meg,
the first time Sallie
dressed you up, her living doll?

You fretted over the borrowed dress,
the charity a too-tight sash around your pride.
All I saw was my elegant sister,
her grace turning formless cloth
                              into beauty.

You never needed Sallie's finery.
You made your own elegance
in every even hem, careful curl.
You were the most glamorous,
the one I yearned to be
in the rare moment I dared
dream of a life in the world,
more than girl in repose on settee.

It wasn't easy glamour. The world saw
the put-together March, composed, refined.
But I know the time you took, intentional, precise.

CHAPTER 5

JO

"Jo, hurry up!" Molly called. "They'll leave without us!"

Jo drained her cup of the last of its precious coffee and grabbed her jacket and purse. "Thanks, Mrs. Wilson," she called over her shoulder.

"Have a good day, girls" was the rallying cry as Jo dashed across the creaky floor of the boardinghouse and through the door Molly was impatiently holding for her.

"Honestly, Jo," she scolded. "You must be pure coffee at this point."

"Keeps a girl on her toes," Jo said.

"Stop lagging!" Anna hollered, half hanging out of her truck.

Several girls were already piled in the truck, Anna behind the wheel, waiting. Anna had inherited the Ford from her grandfather. Rusty and rickety but as reliable as a clock, it was a fitting vehicle for a girl who made Jo think of Shakespeare and Hermia and "though she be but little, she is fierce." Once winter took hold, riding in the truck bed to work might not seem like such a boon, Jo knew, but it was better than the long walk from the boardinghouse.

Jo scrambled up beside the girls, holding out her hand to pull Molly in with her. Crowding against Evelyn and Ruth with an apologetic smile, she gripped the rusted edge of the truck bed in preparation—Anna drove like someone was chasing her.

"Everyone ready back there?" Anna called to the girls.

"We're all good!" Ruth yelled back.

"Onward!" Anna bellowed, and laughter rippled through the air as the truck lurched forward with a shudder and a belch of black smoke.

East Hartford wasn't a terribly large town; Hartford, across the river, was bigger. Jo didn't think she would've ever ventured toward either of them if it weren't for the war. Maybe if things were different . . . If Beth hadn't . . . Or if she had but Jo hadn't just *bolted*, she would've seen East Hartford shown in a newsreel at the movies with her sisters. She would've thought fondly but distantly of the brave women on the line and never known the weight of a drill in her hand or the way her fingers would cramp and her back would ache by the end of a long day.

But East Hartford was not just a scene in a newsreel. It was home, for now. Maybe for a long time, for who knew how much time their world and their lives would revolve around this fight.

She had thrown herself into the deep end to escape another kind of drowning, only to find herself struggling to keep above this surface, too.

Grief, it seemed, could not be left behind like sisters and boys who should've *known* better than to—

"Don't you think, Jo?"

Startled out of her self-pitying reverie, Jo glanced at Ruth, who was waiting expectantly.

"I'm sorry. What was that?"

"I was saying it would be exciting to be a lady pilot, like Peg," Ruth said.

"You're slow to get going this morning," Molly said, a furrow in her brow.

"She was probably up late reading." Ruth gave Jo a sympathetic smile that made Jo wonder if her pacing in the garden at night had been noticed. Was Ruth giving her an out? She'd take it.

"Reading is my greatest vice," Jo said cheerfully.

"I'm so glad Peg's back," Molly said. "Even if she spends most of her time on the airfield. She has the best stories."

"You like that she keeps late nights, like you," Evelyn teased. "I've seen you two cover for each other with Mrs. Wilson."

Molly glared at her.

"What do you get up to at night, Molly?" Evelyn asked, her brows arching delicately.

"None of your business," Molly snapped.

"I didn't realize there were any female pilots working the airfield," Jo said, trying to save Molly the way Ruth had saved her. Luckily, it worked, steering Evelyn back to the subject at hand instead of Molly's late-night comings and goings.

"Peg's the only WASP I've met," Evelyn said, clutching her hat to her head as they rocked along the potholed road. "I think she's got a few friends who fly on the test field, too, but they live across the river."

"Peg's entire family are aviators," Molly said. "Can you

imagine? Her father taught all the girls, just like he taught the boys. My father would *never*. He didn't even want me to learn how to drive."

"And now you're building engines. Joke's on him," Jo cracked.

Molly giggled. "He still thinks I'm sewing parachutes at the Pioneer factory in Manchester."

"Molly!" Ruth's eyes widened. "You shouldn't lie like that."

"Only way I was going to get here." Molly shrugged. "And you've *seen* my stitching. I don't think the parachute factory would take me!"

Ruth tried to hide her smile and failed. "I must admit, that is likely true."

"Are all Peg's sisters WASPs like her?" Jo asked, curious despite herself. Her own father had raised her to be bold; he had kissed her forehead before shipping out and told her he knew she'd be brave for her mother (how sure he'd been of her ability; how she had wanted to be that girl, and how she had failed). But she wasn't sure, as bold and brave as Father thought her, if he would've encouraged one—or all—of his daughters into the danger of being in the Women Airforce Service Pilots.

"No, I don't think so. Her brothers are both flying bombers. But her little sister's still too young. And Charlotte's a reporter."

"Talk about *stories*," Ruth said, followed by a low impressed whistle. "Charlotte Yates has all of them."

"Charlotte writes for *Life*," Molly added. "You've probably read her articles, Jo."

"Probably," Jo echoed, and as the other girls fell into a conversation about plans for Thanksgiving in a few weeks, she tilted her head back into the rushing air, heedless of how it whipped her hair.

An aviatrix and a woman reporter in the same family. She couldn't help but feel a twinge of jealousy, toward one person she barely knew and another she didn't know at all. But to have a sister who *understood* . . .

She knew she was an outlier. An oddity. She had heard tell of it enough, everyone from Aunt March to Amy. She had thought, once, that as strange as she was, she had at least belonged to her sisters. She had thought, for so long, that she had at least been understood by Teddy. She hated that, even now, thinking of Laurie's nickname made her heart twinge, the memories bitter instead of sweet.

Jo didn't feel like she belonged to anyone anymore, and she barely understood herself these days. She'd known herself before: sister, daughter, friend, writer. The north, south, west, and east to her spinning compass point. She'd been sure of herself to the edge of almost cruelty sometimes, because so many kept hoping for her to fall into roles she kept telling them all she wouldn't.

She was still a sister—but it felt muted now, like a radio turned down too low. She was a daughter—but she had failed at doing what Father had asked of her. And the last two . . .

She had lost Teddy. But had she ever truly had him, when they found themselves in such a tangle, wanting each other in such opposite ways and hurting each other so badly because of it?

As for being a writer . . .

The thing she had been most sure of had slipped through her fingers, and instead of fighting tooth and nail for it, she had let it go.

Beth would be ashamed of her.

"Jo, are you sure you got enough coffee?" Molly asked. "You look positively glum."

Jo pasted on a smile. "I just didn't sleep well last night."

"You better stay sharp at work, or you won't get to move off the riveting line," Ruth warned.

"I know, I know."

The factory employed a mix of men and women. The heavy lifting and more dangerous tasks were assigned to the men. But there were girls who did more than fixing rivet after rivet into metal hulls. You just had to work your way up and impress the right people.

Anna finally slowed the truck to a less breakneck speed as they pulled into the Pratt & Whitney factory along the Connecticut River. Clambering out one by one, the girls were wind-tossed and chapped, but it didn't much matter. Coveralls, turbans, and hard work awaited them inside. Vanity didn't have much place in it, no matter how many pretty factory girls were picked for the newsreels across the country.

Arm in arm with Molly and Ruth, Jo marched toward the factory. When she'd first walked the factory floor, she thought the mechanical din coming from all sides would give her a permanent headache. Now, the rhythmic whir of drills was welcome, though the smell of engine oil and chemicals less so.

"I still can't believe you're lying to your entire family about where you're working," Ruth scolded Molly as the girls hurried into the small locker room that all the women—day and night shift—used.

"Not just where she's working. Where she's living," Evelyn tutted at Molly. "Makes a girl wonder what else she's hiding."

"Oh, leave her alone," Anna said.

"It's just a little fib," Jo said, pulling on her trousers. Meg had made them, and her blouse with the mother-of-pearl buttons as well. Meg had made most of her clothes, except for the coveralls, and the scarf, which Jo resolutely reached for like she could use it to banish the memory of her sister. "We all tell fibs to our families to smooth things over." Jo began putting her hair up haphazardly, knowing that no matter how many pins she used, it would work its way loose. Luckily, she'd mastered tying the scarf in a way to catch the errant tendrils that seemed to have a mind of their own.

"What fibs are *you* telling, Miss Jo March?" Ruth's perfectly painted brows were a true work of art when she raised them.

"None," Jo said quickly, and Ruth laughed as she began to pin her hair neatly up, looking in the mirrored compact she'd propped up on a shelf. Ruth was never mussed, no matter how long the day went or how hard the work was, and she worked harder than anyone, being the most experienced woman on the morning shift. Jo rather marveled at the magic of it. Factory work was messy, and Jo couldn't even get out of the locker room before she had some sort of grease on her. If Peg really could fix the hot-water heater like she'd promised this morning, Jo resolved to give the woman her undying devotion, because she ended her days a mess of oil and sweat, and cold baths were just not cutting it.

The locker room was a less-than-ideal situation, with a hole in the ceiling and sagging shelves to store their things. But they had to make do with what little they were given. After all, many of the men hadn't been pleased when the factory started hiring women. Complaining would just cause more trouble, Jo knew, even if it was her nature to go up against injustice with a blunt sword if need be. But if you wanted to move off the riveting line and into cutting and pressing sheet metal, you didn't complain. Her first week, Jo had watched Ruth and Evelyn work a press machine to corrugate long metal sheets. The precision and nimbleness between the two had been like a dance: a dangerous, industrial ballet.

She had immediately wanted to learn how, only to find out that few women were allowed to operate the heavy machinery. Thus, she had thrown herself into proving her worth. So far, no luck. But it gave her something to focus on, other than her many failures.

A bell clanged in the distance. "Shift change," Anna said, grabbing her scarf and tying it hastily over her hair.

"That's us," Jo said, raising her voice over the gaggle of chatter and laughter.

"Come on, girls!" Molly tugged at Evelyn's arm. "Mr. Bates will have my head if I'm late again."

"I'd be more worried about Mrs. Harris," Jo called as they hurried down the hall in a group, passing by the sweaty workers heading off the floor. "She has her eye on you."

Molly scoffed at the mention of the head of the women's division, a stern woman who was more stubborn than Molly herself. "Mrs. Harris has her eye on *everyone*."

"It's her job, Molly," Ruth protested.

"Is it yours to be such a Goody Two-shoes?" Molly shot back, but instead of being offended, Ruth, so good-natured, laughed.

"Absolutely," Ruth said, and no one could scowl in the face of such easy agreement. Molly's toothy grin spread reluctantly across her freckled face.

"You don't make it any fun to fight with you," she told Ruth.

"The lessons learned in a house full of brothers," Ruth said serenely. "Never engage with their nonsense."

"Sounds like the opposite of my life with sisters," Jo said, not thinking it through.

Both Ruth and Molly turned to her, puzzled.

"I didn't know you had sisters, Jo," Molly said.

Heat crawled along Jo's cheeks. "Haven't I mentioned it?" she asked, aiming for airy. "We're all scattered to the wind right now. You know how it is, with all this." Before anyone could respond, she walked past her friends, pushing the doors to the inspection room open. Mrs. Harris was waiting to check them over, in case they forgot a ring or a watch or a stray curl, a welcome distraction.

Her worlds couldn't be kept apart forever. Jo was no juggler. And home—true home—would always be that creaky little house with Marmee and Father and her sisters.

Home would always be where Beth rested.

The idea no longer comforted her.

It haunted her.

Forget

Try to forget me.

Seize those rare moments
when you are not broken
by grief, but fueled by it

    fuse them into your spine of steel
    let me be part of your strength

until one day that grief transforms
to something else entirely.

And then?
Remember me.

Lies

Lies I've told:

> I'm fine.
> Lots better, really.
> It's just a tiny headache.

A good night's sleep
and I'll be right as rain.

> God doesn't give us
> more than we can handle.

This is my lot;
I've made peace with it.

> To Jo
> that I never
> thought of Laurie
> like that.

To Meg
that her special tea
put me right to sleep
and her meatloaf
was better than Marmee's.

To Amy
that I longed
to go to London
when really I knew
it would never be
(not for me)
but I would say anything
to see her brilliant smile.

CHAPTER 6

AMY

After disembarking in Northern Ireland, the Clubmobile girls weren't finished with their travels quite yet. They barely had time to shake off their sea legs before they hopped onto a troop train that chugged south, toward their final destination.

London, Amy thought dreamily.

How many times had she and Beth read the encyclopedia entry on the English capital in Father's study? They had fancied themselves strolling down the Thames and sipping tea at Harrods (with plenty of milk, as the British preferred) and spending hours at the Tate galleries, where Amy would feast her eyes upon the oil paintings by Turner, Sargent, and Waterhouse. She'd always wanted to see *Carnation, Lily, Lily, Rose* in person.

The train whistled, and Amy shook the thought away. She knew she had to stop reminiscing about those rose-colored afternoons that she and Beth had spent together as girls, or else she would start tearing up and make her eyes go red. She was a proper Red Cross worker now and she hadn't come all the way to England to weep.

With a forced pep to her step, Amy headed for the nearest door as the train pulled into the station, pausing only because Edie needed help with her suitcase.

"Think we have time to take a powder?" Edie asked, fishing for her compact. "I swear I can feel the bags under my eyes."

"Oh, you look swell like always." Amy looped her arm through Edie's elbow and they pushed through the crowd together. They had only known each other for a couple months, but they already got along like they were longtime pals. Sure, Edie was a little bit too khaki-wacky, but she was fun and carefree (unlike Meg) and never overly critical (like Jo). She was exactly what Amy needed.

"I can't wait for a proper bath. Let's hurry," said Edie, picking up the pace, but Amy lingered a step behind.

She glanced back at the train and released a tight breath while she was at it. She had done it; she'd made her way across the Atlantic and had finally arrived in London. All her planning—all her lying—had worked. Back in August, she had returned to the Red Cross, but this time to the office in Waltham, where no one would recognize her. Amy had kept her fingers crossed in her pockets while the new recruiter looked over her paperwork (or, rather, Rosie Pace's paperwork), and she'd prayed that he wouldn't notice the thin layer of correction fluid that she had applied on the vision form, effectively changing the 20/200 to 20/20. She was almost certain that she'd get caught and exposed as a fraud, but the recruiter had deemed her "a very fine candidate" and had given her the green light to officially join the Red Cross.

All Amy had had to do was trade her integrity and steal another girl's identity to get here, but she tried not to think about that too much, lest her stomach start hurting.

Amy and Edie made their way to the main road, where a Red Cross truck had been sent to collect them and take them to their billet. Amy claimed a seat toward the back of the vehicle so that she could peek out the canvas flap as they drove, but the London she saw looked very different from the photos in Father's encyclopedia.

"Wow-ee," whispered Edie, whose eyes had grown rounder than Big Ben.

One minute, the city looked perfectly ordinary—cozy shop fronts and wartime canteens serving liver sausages with Woolton salads—but then the whole landscape would shift, like a bomb had gone off. Which had actually happened. Entire buildings lay crumbled, while piles of brick littered the sides of the road, mixed in with bits of porcelain and copper pipes and other remnants of lives torn apart.

"Those Ratzis sure left a mess and a half," Edie said.

"Sure did," Amy replied, her throat dry.

Edie looked a bit green and decided to study her fingernails, but Amy kept staring at the wreckage. For years, the Nazis had dropped bomb after bomb over England, taking bites out of its cities and chipping away at the nation's resolve. Amy remembered how Marmee would listen to the updates on their Crosley radio as she made dinner while Meg would look up from grading papers and say, *I hope they got the children out in time.* But the Brits had hung on by sheer grit and rock-hard guts, and just over a year ago Hitler had moved on to his next target, Russia.

"Don't worry. Those German bombers shouldn't bother us too much," Amy said, mostly for Edie's benefit but maybe for her own as well. The Nazis still ventured over the Channel to keep Churchill on his toes, so the city remained in blackout at night, and now Amy would be living right in the thick of it.

But she tried not to dwell on that as they pulled up to their lodgings. The sign out front declared, in a fancy cursive script, *Hotel Royale*.

"Well, hi-dee-ho," Amy said, hopping out of the truck. "Home, sweet home."

With thousands of American troops streaming through London these days, many hotels across the city had been called upon to open their doors and accommodate the Yanks. But the Hotel Royale didn't give the impression that it served royalty— maybe a knight or two, and a very long time ago at that. The exterior brick looked grimy, while the carpet in the foyer had worn as thin as Swiss cheese, and was that a cigarette burn on the concierge's desk?

"Pace? Barnett? You'll be in room three-oh-three," said Supervisor Owens, who handed them each a silver key. "Meals will be served in the dining room, but remember to bring your ration cards."

Amy barely heard her, because both she and Edie were already racing upstairs to search for their room, which they found two floors up and at the end of the hall. The place looked like something out of Aunt March's house, but more faded and not as well kept, with the floral wallpaper peeling at the corners and the brass chandelier hanging a bit crooked. Still, it was a real room with real beds. Compared to their bunk space on the RMS *Queen Elizabeth*, it felt quite *royale* indeed.

"Looks like we'll have another gal with us," Amy said, noting a set of wooden bunk beds along with a single on the opposite wall. Their mysterious third roommate had claimed the latter by tucking her suitcase underneath the bed frame, but there was no trace of her otherwise.

"Hopefully, she isn't too much of a meatball," said Edie, who had kicked off her shoes and was rubbing her sore heels.

Amy doubted that she would be. The Clubmobile girls whom she'd met so far had all been very accomplished—there'd been teachers and social workers and graduate students among them—and they'd been upbeat and chatty to boot. She was certain that they would get along just swell.

"Say, you hungry?" Amy asked. She plotted the rest of their evening in her head. They could find a pub selling fish-and-chips and make a proper welcome-to-London meal out of it, followed by some exploring. London might've been a city at war, but there was still so much to see, from the Houses of Parliament to Tower Bridge to Hyde Park. After all that excitement was over, she would sit herself down and finally catch up on her letters. She'd been meaning to write to Father, who was serving in the Pacific theater as a chaplain, and she owed a note to Fred Vaughn as well. She supposed she could write to Laurie, too, but what was the point? She had faithfully penned him a letter once a month ever since he joined the Army Air Forces, but he hadn't responded in ages. And she couldn't forget to send an update to her cousin Florence, considering the fact that Flo was the only soul who knew about Amy's ruse with the Red Cross.

Amy flopped onto her bed, feeling tired all of a sudden. It had taken weeks of convincing to get Flo on board with this whole shenanigan, since it involved so much cover-up, but in the end her cousin had agreed. The two of them concocted a story to tell their families, which detailed how Amy had been offered a scholarship at an art academy in Montreal, only a few streets over from Flo's new boarding school. Amy had even fabricated an acceptance letter to l'École des Beaux-Arts to make everything look official, but Marmee had been hesitant to give her blessing. After all, Jo had just recently left for Connecticut and it hadn't even been a year since Beth died, but after repeated wheedling on Amy's part, Marmee had relented.

Ever since then, Flo had acted as Amy's postmaster in miniature. Upon her arrival at boarding school, Flo had told their families to route Amy's mail to her dorm address to save money on stamps. Then she had collected Amy's correspondence and passed it on to Amy's address in a big envelope at the end of each month. In turn, Amy would send her mail to Montreal, where Flo would redirect it to Concord. It was all a bit dizzying to keep up with, and Amy was almost sure that Meg or Marmee or another March would've sniffed out her secret by now. And yet no one had. Between the war and Beth's passing, they were too busy to notice that she had trotted off to a foreign country.

Amy chewed at her lip. She was running out of made-up stories about the classes she was taking and the memories she was making in Montreal. She didn't feel so bad about fibbing to Meg and Jo, whom she still hadn't forgiven after their fight, but Marmee? It split her heart in half when she remembered what her mother told her when they parted ways at the train station.

I'm so glad that you're painting again, Marmee had said before pulling in Amy close. *I know Beth would be happy too to see you doing what you love.*

Amy winced. All this deception was giving her a headache.

"Hope you two don't mind that I took the single," a voice said from the doorway.

Amy's head turned toward the young woman striding into the room, who was wearing the winter Clubmobile uniform, hose and heels included. She looked to be in her midtwenties, with the smoothest skin that Amy had ever seen and whose dark hair had been carefully curled to hang above the collar, as per Red Cross guidelines.

"I'm Marion Greeley. Your roommate," the girl said by way of introduction. She shook both their hands, firm and businesslike. "You two ought to get dressed. Didn't you hear Supervisor Owens downstairs? We're leaving in twenty for the shipyards."

"Shipyards?" Amy swore that she must've misheard. "For what?"

"For our shift," Marion said plainly. She glanced at herself in the window's reflection and frowned at a loose strand of hair that had fallen out of its pin, which she remedied within seconds. "I know you've just arrived, but some of our soldiers are leaving port tonight, so we're giving them a proper send-off."

"We haven't had time to even open our bags!" Edie protested.

"And what about orientation?" Amy asked. That was when they were supposed to receive their ration cards and go over what to do in case of an air raid. Then they'd have a whole class on how to make the Clubmobile's signature coffee and doughnuts.

"Orientation will have to wait. I've been here since Tuesday, so I'll give you a primer on the fryer." Marion looked at the little clock on her nightstand. "Time's a-ticking, ladies. You need a hand unpacking?"

"I suppose I'll manage," Edie said, sounding frazzled. "What time do we have to be downstairs, again? Six o'clock?"

"Eighteen hundred hours." Marion corrected her with a twitch of her lips. "Remember to put your hair up, too. We want to look our best for the boys before they head off to the front."

After Marion departed, Edie sighed. "*Eighteen hundred hours!* Gosh, she sure rolled out the welcome wagon for us."

Amy had to admit that her first impression of Marion wasn't precisely warm and fuzzy, either, but she'd worry about that later. They were already down to nineteen minutes and counting.

Tearing off her traveling clothes, Amy hopped around on one leg as she rolled on her stockings. There wasn't time for a bath, but she did manage to hoist on her girdle, slip into her uniform, and even spray a puff of perfume onto her neck before she heard Supervisor Owens hollering. With seconds to spare, she gave herself a once-over in the mirror to make sure she hadn't missed anything. The Red Cross uniform manual was ten single-spaced pages long, with an endless list of rules—no earrings, no "brilliant" shades of nail polish—but she thought she looked downright jaunty in her wool blazer and crisp white gloves.

Amy gave herself a little salute. She would make Rosie Pace proud—she was sure of it.

Down in the lobby, they barely had time to locate Marion before they were ushered outside to meet their Clubmobile.

The vehicle didn't look too different from a school bus back home, except for the rounded corners and AMERICAN RED CROSS CLUBMOBILE emblazoned on the sides. Their driver— a fiftyish Englishman by the name of Davey, no last name given—grunted at them to climb aboard.

The Clubmobile chugged along London's streets, and they made decent time considering there were only a few cars on the road due to the petrol rationing across Britain. Amy wished that she could stare out the window to glimpse more of the city, but Marion insisted that they get acclimated fast.

"We won't have long before the soldiers are lined up at our doors," she said, like a schoolteacher clucking her tongue at her students. It reminded Amy a bit of Meg, which made her sigh a little. "I've started up the water heater. Barnett, why don't you measure out the coffee for the urns. Pace, I'll show you how to mix the dough."

Amy and Edie exchanged a look. All of the Clubmobile girls held the unofficial rank of captain, but it wasn't a formal title. The Red Cross wasn't the military, after all, but Marion had seemingly given herself the position of a general.

"Let's move quickly, ladies," Marion added, her voice urgent. "We've got troops to serve. That's why we're here, isn't it?"

Amy pursed her lips, but she couldn't quarrel with that. Now that the Clubmobile was pulling into the port, their prep time was ticking away.

Despite the nippy temperature outside, Amy's face was soon covered in sweat. The fryer gave off heat like a miniature sun, radiating its warmth inside the cramped Clubmobile. There was hardly any elbow room to work, either, since most of the narrow space was taken up by the coffee urns, the water heater, and the giant doughnut-making machine itself. But Amy had to make do. Under Marion's detailed instruction, she carefully weighed the ingredients before mixing everything up. Soon, her pretty new gloves became spotted with oil stains, which made her whimper.

"How's that coffee coming along?" Marion called to Edie, who'd been tasked with heating up the water. She turned her attention back to Amy, who was still stirring the doughnut batter. "Can you put some more muscle into that?"

Amy ground her teeth together. It sure felt like she was back in old Mr. Davis's classroom, where she could never do anything right, but she bit back any complaint. It was her first day on the job—her first hour, really—and she didn't want to get pinned as a whiner.

"That's more like it. You're almost to the right consistency," Marion said approvingly as she looked over Amy's shoulder. Then she flashed an apologetic smile. "I don't mean to sound like a drill sergeant. I guess it's a force of habit—I'm the oldest of five girls, and I was usually the one in charge at home."

Hearing that, Amy softened. The two of them probably had more in common than she'd thought, considering they'd grown up in houses full of little women. Maybe Marion wasn't such a crumb after all.

"You got any sisters?" Marion asked.

Amy was about to say "three of them" before she caught herself. "You know, I haven't had the chance to ask you where you're from," she said, dodging the question.

"Honolulu," Marion replied as she tested the heat of the oil.

"Hawaii!" Amy exclaimed. She'd never met anyone from the

territory before. "That sounds like a ball. Did you hear that, Edie?"

Edie looked up from the heavy coffee urn that she was lugging into place. "You must be missing all that sunshine. I bet you went to the beach all the time."

"Only the tourists really get to do that," Marion was quick to point out. "In any case, there are lots of rules and curfews to follow now. The National Guard took over everything after Pearl Harbor."

Edie paled a shade, and Amy had a hunch that she was thinking about her cousin Bobby who'd been a sailor on board the USS *Oklahoma*. The ship had been docked at Pearl Harbor when the Japanese launched their attack. Over four hundred souls had gone down with that ship, Bobby among them.

Amy sought to change the subject—fast. She nodded at the little ruby ring on Marion's left hand. "You've got a fiancé back home? What's his name?" she asked, figuring Marion would relish the opportunity to gush about her special someone.

Except, oddly enough, Marion didn't. "His name is James, but we aren't engaged," she said, her face flushing pink.

"Is he in the service?"

"No. He wanted to but . . ." Marion looked flustered. "Well, it's complicated."

"Was he a Class Four or something?" Amy asked softly. She knew a couple boys at school who'd gotten designated as Class IVs during the draft process, usually due to a physical ailment, and thus were turned away from military service.

Marion clapped her hands together. "We're wasting time with this squawking. I bet those GIs will be hungry."

Which was an understatement.

When the men arrived half an hour later, they gave a whoop at the sight of the Clubmobile, then an even louder one when they spotted the girls. Within minutes, they had formed a neat line to wait for their free coffee and doughnuts, as if Judy Garland herself were serving them.

"What's cookin', fellas?" Edie said as she propped up a little ledge by the vehicle windows to hold a tray of coffee cups.

Amy squeezed next to her with a dozen doughnuts looped onto a long metal stick. The hot oil dripped onto her fingers, but she didn't care too much, because soldiers were whistling and telling her that she was the prettiest dish they'd seen in months. She rather liked this part of her new job. She had just passed out her last doughnut when she felt a sharp tap on the shoulder.

"Keep an eye on that fryer," Marion whispered while pointing at the rapidly browning dough in the oil. "That batch is starting to burn."

Amy yelped. It had been her job to mind the fryer, but she'd gotten carried away with greeting the soldiers. She lurched for the tongs, but accidentally knocked them into the oil instead.

"I'm sorry!" Amy said, not knowing what to do aside from gesturing helplessly at the oil.

Marion pinched her lips together before grabbing the spare tongs from under a cabinet and fishing out the others. "Let's chalk it up to first-day jitters."

Amy smiled in relief. "Thank you—"

"Word of advice, though? Remember why we're here. It isn't to flirt with handsome privates and sergeants." Marion handed her another twelve doughnuts on a metal stick and jutted her chin toward the soldiers. "I'll take over the fryer."

Amy swallowed at the dryness in her throat, feeling chastened. Had she been flirting too much? She'd only meant to be friendly! It wasn't like she had been given a primer on all this—Marion was the only one in their Clubmobile who had completed orientation.

Tomorrow will be better, Amy told herself. Clubmobile-ing was probably a lot like painting. Soon enough she would get a handle on it.

But the next day came and went, followed by a few more, and Amy kept mucking things up. She might've had a natural knack for art, but doughnut making? Either she burned the damned things or undercooked them—never in between—and she was only marginally better with the coffee. At least she hadn't scalded that yet, but the urns were tall and heavy, and she had toppled more than a couple of them.

Am I the fathead of the bunch? Amy thought miserably whenever she sank into her bed at night. Edie had gotten the hang of the kitchen while Marion never seemed to make a mistake—the girl even popped awake at five-thirty every morning without an alarm. Meanwhile, Amy had to admit that she was no good at the job and, well, she didn't like it much, either. Her hands had gotten chapped, and she smelled like fry oil all the time (a scent that Edie had coined *eau de doughnut*), but she couldn't even scrub off the stink, because she was allowed only five inches of bathwater per week. She was also tired all the time, between these late-night shifts and the fourteen-hour workdays. There wasn't enough concealer in all of Britain to hide the dark circles under her eyes.

"Don't forget to smile, Captain Pace," Supervisor Owens said as the girls left for yet another shift on a dreary November morning. Amy replied with a tired wave.

"At least we'll have a change in scenery today," Edie said, peeking out the Clubmobile's window toward a sheet of gray clouds overhead. "Although here's hoping that we won't get rained on."

Amy yawned. Instead of the shipyards, they were heading to a local hospital, where some American soldiers were convalescing due to the severity of their injuries. Marion manned the fryer while Edie poured the coffee, leaving Amy to welcome the soldiers, some who had gotten wounded by enemy gunfire while others had been hit by flak. Despite everything they'd been through, the men seemed in good spirits and it should've been an easy shift for Amy, but her eyelids drooped anyway and she struggled to follow along with the conversation.

"You're looking a little beat there, doll," one of the soldiers teased her.

"You'll have to excuse my colleague," Marion said to the men before elbowing Amy in the ribs as a wake-up. "She didn't get enough beauty sleep last night."

Amy felt her cheeks warm at the dig, and they warmed even more when one of the boys heckled, "I'm sure we can find you a cozy spot to take a nap, Sleeping Beauty! How about my shoulder to start?"

"That's nothing a little coffee can't fix. Right, Captain Pace?" Marion said, handing Amy a mug right before taking a sip from her own.

Amy smiled wanly. Usually she didn't mind the banter with the enlisted soldiers, but today all she could think about was changing out of her uniform and diving into bed as soon as they got home.

Thirty more minutes, she thought. She had to get through only another half hour before the Clubmobile would head back. Of course, she still had to wash out the cups and coffee urns before their shift formally ended, but at least she could sneak in a nap during the return trip. Even ten minutes of sleep sounded downright luxurious.

"I got another fresh batch ready for you," Edie called out, nodding at a metal tray where twenty cups of hot coffee sat steaming. With a wink, she added, "Feeling all right there, *Sleeping Beauty?*"

"Very funny," Amy mumbled. She picked up the tray and went to move it onto the wooden ledge by the truck's open window, where more soldiers awaited. Rounding her shoulders, she said, "Hello there, boys! Who'd like some—"

Her throat closed up as soon as she laid eyes on the next man in line.

It couldn't be him. It wasn't possible.

But he was staring at her, too, his mouth sliding open in shock.

Oh no. Oh *God,* no.

"Laurie, I can explain—" she said, right before she lost her grip on the tray and the whole thing hit the ground with a *splat.*

Laurie

Theodore Laurence,
those twinkling eyes
and hair forever
blocking them from view,
his perpetually rumpled state
overshadowed by his charm.

Behind the hair and twinkle,
the boy who we thought
lacked for nothing
desperately longed
for what we had to give.

We took his offered heart,
caring for it as though he were ours,
for he was, though that meant
sometimes his heart got taken
for granted, just like our own hearts
in each other's hands.

For Granted

If you think I didn't
take you all for granted,
if you think me some sort of angel
incapable of rage or envy or deceit
    (and I know you do,
      especially now)
you're wrong.

There were no deathbed revelations, either.
No shedding of earthly grievances
as I glided toward the light.
I struggled for sleep as always,
expecting another day of pain,
but that one time I didn't wake.

What I wouldn't give
to take you for granted again.
To assume Laurie and his twinkling eyes
would always be there, just across the way.

You've crossed an ocean
and still he's there.

CHAPTER 7

MEG

Meg was kneeling in the Victory Garden out by the baseball field, harvesting carrots and winter squash with the Junior Red Cross, when one of the girls shrieked. Meg scrambled to her feet. A couple of senior boys had been out playing catch, and Mae Chalfont kept wandering away to flirt. Had one of the boys gotten fresh and earned a slap for it?

Meg found Albert Woodhouse laid out on the grass, blood trickling from the corner of his mouth. Doro stood over him, legs splayed, shaking out her right hand.

"Dorothy Scott!" Meg gasped. "What on earth?"

Doro's heart-shaped face was flushed. "That fathead said navy boys are a bunch of—"

"It's not fit for polite company, what Woody said, miss," Ginny insisted.

"You punched him in the mouth for insulting the navy?" Meg asked, disbelieving. Doro must have hit him quite hard to knock him down. Probably he hadn't been expecting a girl who looked like Rita Hayworth to pack a punch.

Doro propped her hands on her hips. "I'd do it again, too."

The sass! Meg's jaw tightened. There was always good-natured teasing about which branch of the armed forces was the roughest, toughest fighting machine. Loyalties tended to run in the family. Woody had taken summer classes in order to graduate at the end of January and enlist in the marines, like his brother Paulie, whereas Doro's brother was in the navy. But that was no excuse to haul off and hit a boy!

Woody was scrambling up now, one hand to his split lip. The rest of the Junior Red Cross had stopped gardening to gawk. Boy-crazy Mae Chalfont offered Woody her pink handkerchief and whispered in his ear.

"Woody, are you all right?" Meg asked. "You ought to go see the nurse and get your mouth looked at."

"I'm okay, miss." He shifted, red-faced. "Doro, look, I'm sorry. I was just kidding around. I didn't know."

"Know what?" Meg demanded. What on earth had Woody *said*?

"Nothing!" Doro crossed her arms over her chest. "And I don't accept your apology, you dumb—"

"Mae, could you please walk Woody to the nurse's office?" Meg asked. Mae was happy to oblige. Meanwhile, Doro still looked ready to fight, and Ginny was hovering like a mother hen. The other girls stood by silent and solemn.

"Doro, I'm awfully disappointed," Meg said. "Losing your temper like this—it's very unbecoming of a girl your age. I'm sure Mr. Hamilton will have more to say about that. If you won't tell me what happened, I have no choice but to send you to the principal's office for brawling. You might want to work on looking sorry."

"I'm *not* sorry!" Doro burst out. The girls looked between her and Meg, wide-eyed at her impudence.

"Well, you ought to be," Meg said grimly. "I daresay if Mr. Hamilton gives you a suspension, you will be, and your mother will be, too, when she hears about it."

"My mother?" Doro's bravado deserted her like the air squealing from a pricked balloon. "He's going to telephone my mother?"

"But, Miss March—" Ginny began.

"You punched a boy, Doro! I'm quite sure Mr. Hamilton will be phoning your mother." Even as the words came out of her mouth, Meg felt like she was playacting the strict teacher. What she really wanted to do was take Doro aside and ask what had gotten into her. The girl talked too much in class and she could be impertinent, but it wasn't like her to strike someone.

But Meg could hardly back down in front of a dozen other students. She felt her inexperience right then.

"Miss March." Ginny eyed the set of Meg's shoulders. "May I go with her?"

"No, you may not," Meg snapped. She watched as Doro trudged away, head down. "Get back to work, girls."

The girls were quiet as they pulled carrots from the ground and severed squash from the vine. All their high spirits seemed to have deserted them.

"Miss March." Ginny plucked at Meg's coat sleeve, whispering. "It's Richie. Mrs. Scott got the telegram day before yesterday. He was at Guadalcanal, and he . . . he didn't make it."

Meg's hand flew to her mouth.

She hadn't taught Richie, but she had seen him in the halls: tall and lean and grinning in his baseball letterman's jacket. Was he even nineteen yet? He'd been in Beth's class.

"No one told me," she said, horrified.

Doro had been out sick the previous day, but Meg hadn't thought anything of it. She'd attributed the girl's puffy eyes and red nose to a November cold. Now that she thought about it, Doro *had* been awfully quiet in class that morning, and Ginny had stuck to her like glue.

"She didn't want anyone to make a fuss. I don't think she ought to be back at school yet." Ginny's dark eyes were full of sympathetic tears. "But she said she couldn't bear to be at home."

Meg knew how that was, didn't she? Poor Doro. Punching Woody was unacceptable, no matter the circumstances. But she couldn't let Mr. Hamilton suspend Doro while she was mourning her brother. No wonder the girl had looked appalled at the thought of the principal phoning home! That was the last thing her grieving mother needed.

"Ginny, can you keep an eye on the other girls? I've got to speak to Mr. Hamilton." Meg smacked soil from her palms and pulled off her gardening gloves. Ginny bit her lip, looking anxious. She often kept to herself when Doro wasn't around, but she was easily the most responsible of the bunch.

"Girls, I need to go see Principal Hamilton. Ginny will be in charge till I get back." Meg noticed Alma Gilbert and Sarah Byers rolling their eyes at each other, and she frowned. "I expect you to show her the same respect you would show me. Is that understood?"

Meg fluffed her hair, then squared her shoulders and marched toward the principal's office. She knew what it was to be a whirlwind of grief and anger, especially in those first days after Beth had died. If someone had given her the smallest excuse—well, she still wouldn't have punched anyone. But Jo might have.

Meg imagined the naval officers knocking, caps in hand, at the Scotts' door. Handing Mrs. Scott the telegram with the dreaded words *We regret to inform you . . .* It made Meg's stomach sink, thinking of it.

Father's ship had been at Guadalcanal, too. She and Marmee had been anxiously awaiting news that he had come through all right. *Dear God, please let him be all right.*

Doro was sitting on the hard wooden bench in the front office, cradling her fist in her lap. She turned away, but not before Meg glimpsed tears on her round apple cheeks.

The school secretary, Miss Beecham, looked up from her filing. "Principal Hamilton is in a meeting, but he'll be with you in a moment."

"Actually, we no longer need Principal Hamilton. Miss Scott is free to go," Meg said, in her most authoritative voice.

Doro went wide-eyed. "I am?"

Miss Beecham's thin mouth was as straight as a pin. "She said she punched Albert Woodhouse in the mouth."

"It was all a misunderstanding," Meg explained. "Woody's taken responsibility for the incident. He's apologized. If the Woodhouses have any complaints, I'd be happy to tell them what happened."

"Well, no matter what the boy said, she can't go around punching people," Miss Beecham huffed.

Meg frowned. She didn't care for being second-guessed in front of a student. "Dorothy, please wait in the hall."

"You have a good heart, Meg, but if you give those girls an inch, they'll take a mile," Miss Beecham chided as the door clicked shut behind Doro. "Better to make an example of her."

Meg approached Miss Beecham's desk and lowered her voice. "Richie Scott was killed in action at Guadalcanal. The family got word Wednesday. Doro doesn't want anyone making a fuss, but—"

"Oh," Miss Beecham said softly. She pulled out a starched white handkerchief and dabbed at her eyes. "I'm sorry to hear that. Richie was a fine boy. And a good first baseman, too. Mrs. Scott ought to have phoned us."

Honestly, Meg was surprised word hadn't already spread throughout the school. After Beth had passed, the Marches had received a steady stream of casseroles and condolences. She didn't blame Doro for wanting to forestall that, but it was inevitable. People would want to offer some small comfort, however they could.

"Ginny Tanaka told me privately after I sent Dorothy to the office. This outburst—I'm of a mind to overlook it, just this once." Meg kept her voice firm, though her hands trembled. "Losing a sibling—well. It's awfully hard."

"Yes, I imagine it is." Miss Beecham patted Meg's hand and then went back to her filing. "I suppose there's no need to mention the altercation to Principal Hamilton. I doubt you'll hear from the Woodhouses. Woody won't be in any hurry to tell his folks he got that split lip from a girl."

The Cocoanut Grove nightclub was the most glamorous place Meg had ever been. She tried to make note of everything so she could describe it to Amy later: the columns that looked like palm trees, the lights that looked like coconuts, the bamboo wall coverings, the blue satin canopies, the handsome tuxedoed waiters. Before the war, Meg would have been charmed by the South Seas tropical paradise theme. But so soon after the naval battle at Guadalcanal, drinking champagne and dancing in a place like this felt wrong. Their soldiers were off fighting in the real South Seas. Some of them, like Richie Scott, were making the ultimate sacrifice. Meg couldn't stop worrying about Father—they still hadn't heard from him—and Doro. By the time she'd finished talking with Miss Beecham yesterday, the girl had disappeared.

Meg's date was handsome; he was tall and broad-shouldered, with pomaded black hair that fell over his forehead and long-lashed gray eyes. But he wasn't John. She missed John's unruly brown hair that glinted red in the sun and his warm brown eyes that crinkled at the corners when he smiled. She missed the way he listened to her—really listened, like what she had to say was important. Andy had ordered for her at dinner and interrupted her half a dozen times. Now, as they listened to a big band play, he scooted his seat closer to hers and rested an arm on the back of her chair. Meg sat up ramrod straight. Had she given him the impression that she wanted to canoodle?

"Sal says you're a teacher at your old high school," Jack said. Further acquaintance with him had not improved Meg's first opinion. He was a real blowhard.

"I am. Junior-year English," Meg said. "American literature. We've finished *The Scarlet Letter,* and now—"

Andy groaned. "Shakespeare was always Greek to me. Never made a lick of sense."

The Scarlet Letter *isn't Shakespeare,* Meg wanted to say, but she bit her tongue. No one liked a know-it-all. "Shakespeare is wonderful. And very funny. The jokes can be quite bawdy," she said instead.

Sallie elbowed Jack. "Oh. Right," Jack said. "Meg, my aunt is headmistress at a private girls' school north of Boston. Plumley. A few of her teachers left to join the war effort. . . . Damned unbecoming, if you ask me. Women have no place in the army, or in factories, either. That's men's work." Sallie cleared her throat, and Meg tried not to roll her eyes at Jack's old-fashioned attitude. Goodness, Jo would *loathe* him. "Anyhow, I could put in a good word for you, if you want."

"Oh, that would be *perfect,* wouldn't it?" Sallie stared at Meg expectantly. Sallie looked like a dream. Her evening gown had a black Basque bodice with a daring off-the-shoulder neckline and a green flared four-gore skirt that fell to the floor. Meg had made her dress herself from a McCall's pattern. It was a royal-blue rayon crepe shirtwaist that fell just below her knees and twirled around her calves beautifully when she danced. Before tonight, it had been her favorite. Now it felt girlish and home-spun compared to Sallie's.

"I'm not looking for a new position," Meg hedged. She was only in her second year of teaching. And John was right down the hall. Not right now, of course. But he would be back. *He would be,* she assured herself with sudden anxiety. "It's awfully kind of you to offer, Mr. Moffatt—"

"Jack," he said with a grin.

"One of my girlfriends went to Plumley," Sallie said. "You boys know Norma. She's at Mount Holyoke now. Plumley girls can get into any college they want. It's awfully prestigious. I think it'd be just the place for our clever Meg." Sallie gazed at her as though she were a trick pony.

"Only the best class of girls attend Plumley. You wouldn't have to put up with any smart alecks," Jack said, sipping his Scotch. Clearly, Doro had made a lasting impression on him. "No Japanese, either."

Meg bristled, but Sallie plowed on. "I bet the girls there are heaps more interested in Shakespeare. And I bet it pays loads better, too."

Meg let herself think about what it might be like to teach girls who actually did the reading, who were genuinely interested in the classics, who would raise their hands and have a lively discussion without Meg's desperate prompting. She pictured herself walking down marble hallways with no pea-soup walls or leaking stairwells in sight. She imagined the *library* there. She imagined having the money to buy a dress like Sallie's.

No. She couldn't. Even if she wanted to apply to Plumley—which she didn't; she loved her students, even if they were a handful sometimes—she couldn't possibly leave Marmee all alone. Not with Jo and Amy gone.

"Another glass of champagne for the lady, please," Andy said as the tuxedoed waiter swung past their table.

The waiter winked. "On it, pal."

"No, thank you," Meg said. "I—" But he was already gone.

Sallie stood up. "I've got to powder my nose. Meg, come with me?"

Meg practically leapt out of her chair. "Of course. Excuse us."

She followed Sallie to the powder room, where Sallie set her hands on her hips. "Why are you sitting out there like a bump on a log? You've hardly danced all night. Andy's going to think you aren't having any fun."

Meg opened her mouth to protest that she was having a swell time, but what came out was a plaintive "I miss John."

"Don't be silly. I never thought of you as the lovelorn type." Sallie pursed her lips and reapplied her Victory Red lipstick. "You have to rate pretty high to get a second look from Andy, and trust me, he's looking."

Meg thought Andy liked her well enough—as long as she kept her mouth shut. "We don't have anything in common. All he wanted to talk about was Boston College football. He didn't ask me anything about myself or my work. And he doesn't like Shakespeare!"

"Meg, no one likes Shakespeare." Sallie was fixing her blond curls in the mirror. "And no man wants a wife who works. Plumley would only be a lark till you get married."

Meg frowned. Her work was hardly a *lark*. And John *respected* her. When she'd gone to him last year for advice, he'd urged her to trust her instincts. *You're a fine teacher, Meg. All you need is a little experience. It's obvious how much you care about your students.* They had never talked about whether Meg would keep her job when they got married; that had felt premature. When they had children, of course she would quit teaching to raise them—though when she'd mentioned as much, Jo had been furious that there was any "of course" about it. Somehow, Meg was too traditional for her little sisters but too modern for Sallie's crowd.

"I like my work," she said stubbornly. "I'm sorry, Sallie, but I don't think Andy's the guy for me."

Sallie sighed. "I really thought you'd hit it off."

Why? Meg wondered. "I'm sorry," she said again, then wondered why she was apologizing. She had told Sallie she didn't want to be fixed up in the first place!

"Well, you might as well make the best of it. When are you ever going to get back to the Cocoanut Grove? I doubt Mr. Brooke could afford it on a teacher's salary," Sallie needled. "Although, if you took the job at Plumley, you could come into the city *every* Saturday night. And just think—you wouldn't have Miss Pennington breathing down your neck! Don't all our old teachers treat you as though you're still a kid? At Plumley, you'd get the respect you deserve. Promise me you'll apply. It couldn't hurt, could it? You might not even get an interview."

"You don't think I'd get an interview?" Meg asked, stung. She'd had very good reviews last year, despite Miss Pennington's remarks about her leniency.

Sallie shrugged. "I'm sure it's very competitive." She caught Meg's scowl in the mirror and gave a *haw*-haw. "See, you *do* want to apply. I knew it! Now come on. Let's get back to our boys. Try and smile, would you?"

Meg didn't want to be a spoilsport. "All right," she sighed. She followed Sallie to the ballroom.

Andy grinned when he saw her. "Wanna dance?"

Meg grabbed her champagne flute and took a few sips, then pasted on a smile. "I'd love to."

Andy insisted on walking Meg to her front door. She was half asleep after hours of dancing, three glasses of champagne, and the late-night drive from Boston back to Concord. The lamp was still burning in the parlor—Marmee had waited up. The thought pleased her somehow.

Andy put out a hand. "I had a swell time tonight, Meg."

"Thank you for dinner," Meg murmured, shaking his hand. "It was lovely."

Andy smiled. "Can I call you next week?"

Meg didn't know how to say no without being rude. She'd thought their lack of chemistry was obvious and mutual. Maybe he was only asking to be polite, because she was Sallie's friend; maybe he had no intention of actually phoning her. "Sure," she agreed sleepily. "Thanks again, Andy. Good night."

"Good night, Meg."

She came blinking into the bright parlor. Marmee was sitting in her wingback chair with some mending, but she'd nodded off. She startled awake as the front door closed behind Meg. "Did you have a good time?"

Meg shrugged. "It was all right."

She waited for a barrage of follow-up questions, but there were none. Marmee simply nodded. "I think I'll go up to bed, now that you're home."

Meg frowned. When she'd announced that she was going out with Sallie and her fiancé and their friend Andy, Marmee hadn't batted an eyelash. Meg had expected disapproval. Marmee valued loyalty. *Meg* valued loyalty. She had been a little glad to avoid a lecture, but now she wondered at it. Marmee was usually brimming with advice. Had things gone so wrong between them that she didn't care *what* Meg did anymore?

Marmee paused in the doorway. "Thanksgiving is coming up, and . . ."

Meg's mind whirred awake. Had Jo phoned? Was she going

to take the train home from Connecticut? She mustn't be too angry if she was coming home. They could iron things out in person, Meg knew it.

"It seems a waste to make a big meal for the two of us," Marmee finished, and Meg's heart sank like a lead balloon. "Since you'll be helping with the Thanksgiving celebration at school, why don't I volunteer, too. We can spend the whole day there. It'll cheer us both up, doing good for those who aren't as fortunate as we are."

Fortunate? Last year they had all crowded around the groaning table in the dining room: Marmee, Father, Meg, Jo, Beth, Amy, Mr. Laurence, and Laurie. There had been so much laughter. Beth had only managed a few bites, but they had all been together. They had been *happy*.

Meg knew that if she complained, Marmee would remind her of everything they still had to be grateful for.

Right now, looking around the empty parlor, she didn't think she could stomach a speech like that. But she looked at Marmee's lined face and tired eyes and swallowed her unhappiness.

That was Meg's role, wasn't it? To paste on a smile and pretend she was fine? To sail on uncomplainingly, no matter how much she might want to scream? To make things easier for everyone else?

"Of course," Meg said slowly. "That sounds perfect, Marmee."

Sailing

When Jo took me to the seashore
we watched the boats float by.
Motorboats and trawlers,
yachts and freighters. Sailboats.
I loved the sailboats most of all.

So graceful,
enormous birds
with billowing wings
catching the wind
and slicing through the sea like air.

Jo wanted to know more.
Perhaps a sailing story
buzzed about her brain,
or perhaps she thought
to haul me aboard
to be healed by the sea.

She accosted a sailor
as he tied up his boat,
knots tighter than a sister's bond,
and asked him all the questions.
You know how she is.

Trimming sails, turning winches,
pulling ropes that bear a heavy load,
always balancing, moving quickly
in response to winds and seas
more powerful than any sailor;
I tired just from listening
to the tasks required.

Of course, we could join him
on his sailboat, sitting pretty,
moving side to side as needed,
nothing more than ballast
while he did all the work.
Jo declined the offer.

She's never been one for sitting pretty.
She wants to sail the ship.
Not just sail, but captain.
So do you. You have more in common
than you'll admit. Both sailing alone
when you could be sharing the work.

Work that looks elegant, effortless,
to the sickly girl on the shore but really
takes every ounce of muscle, heart, and grit.

CHAPTER 8

JO

The warehouse that held the riveting lines lay long and low on the riverbank. Windows and a winding set of vents and fans above circulated air, but the smell was hard to escape: heated metal, the chemicals that treated it, engine oil, sweat and grime, and just the barest hint of a mixed concoction of perfumes underneath it all. If Jo was seated next to Molly on the line, she'd get a whiff of the fresh Chantilly perfume that came out just last year, but if she and Anna were paired up, it was all jasmine-drenched Shocking by Schiaparelli, an older scent, but one that Jo thought suited Anna's wilder spirit.

Jo never wore a scent to work, but she certainly brought one home: stale sweat, exhaustion, and the harsh industrial soap they kept in the locker room to scrub the grease off their arms and hands—and sometimes faces, in a pinch. Though if Peg proved true to her word, Jo could look forward to a soak in the boardinghouse tub with more than a trickle of hot water sometime this week (though a not-so-luxurious one, in a house of so many women). The thought was considerably cheering as they began to take their places. The warehouse was divided into three lines: two standing stations, and one large sitting station in the back corner. The work done sitting tended to be more detailed, while the standing lines meant more movement—and sometimes required more muscle. Today, like most days, Jo was on the right standing line. She grabbed the goggles at her station and fixed them over her eyes.

Because this factory mainly produced engines, other parts of the planes came from different factories across the country. The job of Jo and her friends was to help assemble everything from engine parts produced on-site to plane wings that were shipped in, so that the men could do the final assembly of the planes in the two hangars on the airfield. So much of their work was minute in detail. There were days Jo did nothing but clamp engine parts together she couldn't even name, but could likely sketch in her sleep. Other days, she did nothing but fix hundreds of rivets into wings that had to be brought into the warehouse through the big doors.

"Landing gear again," Dorothy groaned when she saw the circular pieces of metal set out on the line. "I hate wheels."

"You just don't like the way the goggles mark under your eyes," Molly scoffed. "At least it's not the throttles. I *despise* the throttles. So many little parts."

Jo grabbed her drill—the landing-gear wheel plates required precise holes so that everything lined up—and her punch guide, which showed her the pattern of the holes if she fitted it over the plate. She arranged the punch guide and began to drill the first circular plate as Dorothy and Molly continued to list jobs by their least favorite.

The bustle of the factory burst around her in fits and starts, as the women on the morning shift fell to their tasks for the day. Noise reigned: clanging from the assemblage warehouse next to them, the soft hiss of the soldering irons from the seated line, the chatter of everyone's voices, and occasional laughter.

"Isn't that right?"

Jo looked up from the neat hole she was drilling. "What?"

"Jo, your head is in the clouds today," Molly scolded. "The dance next Thursday, it'll be fun, won't it?"

"Dance?"

"At the hall. After Thanksgiving supper." Dorothy laughed. "I told you about this last week!" She finished her final hole in the wheel plate, lining it up with the punch guide to be sure, before adding the plate to the growing pile she was building and reaching for another.

"I must've forgotten," Jo said.

"You don't look too enthused about it," Molly commented.

"Of course I am." Jo pasted on a smile. She had promised herself she would find a way through the grief, and she would. That meant smiling and going where her friends wanted and dancing, and hoping someday she'd find a way back to feeling . . . something other than this grasping pain, always on the edge of pulling her in for good. "I'll even let you do my hair if you want."

Molly's eyes lit at the thought. "I've been dying to get my hands on that mop of yours!"

"Well, dreams do come true," Jo said.

With Molly appeased, Jo's attention turned back to her work. She was grateful for the monotony of it; here on the factory floor is where she lost herself the most—in a good way. She needed to concentrate on her tasks, even if it was something as simple as making sure the punch guide's smooth, round edges matched up perfectly with the wheel plate. That was the beauty of this work: She could do it without feeling like a failure. She wasn't letting anyone down. She wasn't getting her hopes up. There was no rejection. No gentle hints that she really should write something less daring.

It was just her and the weight of the goggles pressing against her skin and the little shavings of metal curling around the drill as she pressed.

Down, down, punch through.

Perhaps this was all she needed.

Perhaps.

By the time Thanksgiving dawned, Jo had almost forgotten the dance all over again. She woke to the smell of roasting turkey and the sound of excited girls debating what to wear that evening—like it would take all day to decide with their limited wardrobes.

She busied herself with helping chop wood outside—hopeful that Mrs. Wilson wouldn't ask her to help in the kitchen if she was otherwise occupied—and so lost herself in the task that by the time she was called inside to clean up for supper, she had a towering pile ready for Mrs. Wilson's stove. When she went up to her room, she found Peg stationed near the phone, watching it like a hawk. She was almost in the same position as she had been hours earlier, when Jo had tugged on her gloves and woolen cap to go outside.

"Are you all right, Peg?"

"Just waiting for my sister to call," Peg said. "She was supposed to phone from the train station before she left, but I suppose she forgot. Which means I don't know what time she's arriving."

"Is she coming for a visit?"

"Well, she was," Peg said dryly. "She's certainly not going to make it for supper."

"I hope nothing's happened."

"Oh, no, she probably got distracted chasing a story or interviewing someone and had to catch a later train. She'll call me from the station when she arrives. You could buy my sister a watch for each wrist, and she'd still find a way to be late."

"What are you two doing gabbing in the hall when there's a whole spread downstairs?" Anna demanded, bursting out of her room as soon as the dinner bell that Mrs. Wilson was so fond of ringing clanged through the boardinghouse.

"We're going to need the energy for all the dancing we'll do tonight!" Molly added, hurrying after her.

Jo groaned at the mention.

"Not a fan of dancing?" Peg asked, following as Jo went to the bathroom at the end of the hall and washed her hands and then splashed water on her face hastily. Peg took her own turn at the sink, taking the proffered towel Jo held out to her.

"Parties at the hall are good for the airmen's morale," Jo said, almost like she was reciting a rule from a manual.

"They're good for all of us," Peg said, with a good-natured nudge at Jo as they made their way downstairs. "Good music, good company, a night of good dancing . . . what more could a girl want?"

"Quiet and a good book," Jo said, and Peg laughed.

"I didn't take you for the nunnery type."

"I'm not suited for a nunnery!" Jo was insulted at the thought, and it made Peg guffaw harder, which made Jo roll her eyes and smile reluctantly as they walked through the narrow halls of the lower levels of the boardinghouse.

The dining room was a narrow affair as well, but the long table they all sat around was always cheerful . . . sometimes downright raucous. Mrs. Wilson believed in flowers on the table whenever she could grow them and winter greenery when she could not, good, hearty food—none of that fancy French stuff; that was too rich for her blood—and conversation that never dulled.

With the crowd that lived at the boardinghouse, Mrs. Wilson always got her wish for lively conversation. Jo had once witnessed Ruth and Anna almost come to blows over the last of Mrs. Wilson's biscuits. Though she could hardly blame either of them. Mrs. Wilson's biscuits were worth fighting for.

This afternoon, the table was set with Mrs. Wilson's best china, and she had outdone herself, with not just a turkey, but baby potatoes and carrots that Evelyn had pulled from the sparse winter Victory Garden she and Mrs. Wilson had nursed through the snow. Plus, the famous biscuits and plenty of honey and butter. Jo's stomach rumbled as she sat down next to Anna.

"What's the topic du jour tonight?" Peg asked as she took a seat near the head of the table—and closest to the biscuits. Jo wished she'd have done that!

"The *Casablanca* premiere is tonight," Molly said, never one to be without some Hollywood gossip. "I can't wait to read about it in the magazines."

"Why do they have the premieres so early? It's not out for ages. Next year," Ruth complained.

"The coming attractions makes it look too violent for me," Evelyn said, shaking her head. "So many guns!"

"But it's *Bogie*," Anna countered. "And there's got to be a love story. That's why Ingrid Bergman is there and weeping so."

"And they talk about her strange fascination with him," Mrs. Wilson added, much to the girls' delight. "If that doesn't hook you, I don't know what will."

"You should come with us to see it, Mrs. Wilson!" Ruth said.

"I'll go to anything with Paul Henreid in it," Mrs. Wilson said. "I may not like French food, but I do love a French man."

"Ooh," Anna teased.

"I'm still not sure," Evelyn said. "Ingrid's holding a gun on Bogie in one of the scenes!"

"Now *I'm* sold," Jo joked, and the table laughed before quieting so Mrs. Wilson could say grace. Once that was over, the girls fell on their food with appreciative noises and the careful clink of silver against good china.

"This is delicious, Mrs. Wilson," Peg said.

"We owe our thanks to Evelyn and her green thumb. And Ruth helped me with the cooking."

"To our Hestias," Jo said, raising her glass, and the women laughed and cheered at the reference, glasses tinkling together in the chorus of camaraderie and thanks.

"It's strange and sad, to think of all the men overseas right now," Ruth said, pouring gravy on a slice of turkey breast with an elegant little flourish. "What must *they* be eating for to-night's meal? Are they even celebrating?"

"Of course," Anna said encouragingly. Everyone knew

Ruth's fiancé was serving overseas, though she rarely spoke of it, or him. But twice now, Jo had found her staring out the boardinghouse window at the end of the hall, holding on to the locket she wore around her neck like it was the only thing keeping her there. It was a lonely sight, one that Jo had no business intruding on, though she wished she could find the right words to comfort Ruth.

"Christmas will be lonely," Ruth said.

"They'll find a way to make the best of it," Mrs. Wilson said. "Just like we will."

"We must put on a good front for the boys tonight," Anna said. "Their training will be coming to an end after New Year's."

"They'll be leaving," Molly added. "A pity. There were a few of this bunch I liked."

"There's *always* a few of *each* bunch you like," Ruth said.

"Ruth!" Molly tossed a biscuit at her, which Ruth dodged with admirable reflexes.

Mrs. Wilson tutted. "Don't you be getting into any trouble, now, Molly."

"I'm a good girl, Mrs. Wilson. I'm just the best dancer *and* the prettiest of this lot, so the airmen will miss me the most."

The other girls crowed in protest, and Jo just laughed as Ruth rolled her eyes and the table descended into chaotic, good-natured debate over Molly's claim.

Once dinner wound down and they all pitched in to clean so Mrs. Wilson could rest her feet, Jo was starting to feel the effects of spending her morning chopping wood. A soak in the tub for her sore muscles while all the girls were at the dance sounded like heaven. More than ever, she wanted to beg off, but when she got upstairs with that plan in mind, she found Molly standing in front of her door with a pack of bobby pins, a hairbrush, and several tortoiseshell combs that would for sure pop out of her unruly mane at some point in the night.

"You promised," Molly said before Jo could protest, and there went any idea of begging off the dance.

"I did," Jo said.

"You mustn't look so skeptical. I'm very good with hair! Doesn't mine always look fantastic?"

"It does," Jo said, and Molly pushed her into her room and made her sit at the vanity. Molly began to unbraid Jo's two plaits, and Jo caught Molly's frown in the mirror.

"What?"

"You're going to give Veronica Lake a run for her money, with all this length," Molly said, combing her fingers through Jo's hair.

Jo rolled her eyes at the absurdity at being compared to the glamorous, long-haired star. "Her hair is practically *platinum*," she said.

"She's so beautiful," Molly sighed wistfully. "I wish I were that stunning." She began to brush Jo's hair out, taking care not to yank it, which Jo appreciated. "But you would be able to style your hair easier if you cut it. It's very long for the modern styles."

"I don't need a pageboy or a poodle," Jo protested. "Where did you learn all this anyway?"

"Oh, here and there." Molly shrugged. "My mother was a pianist before she married my father. Very elegant, you know. She used to do my hair. I guess I got it from her."

"You also got her musical talent," Jo pointed out. Molly made the slightly out-of-tune piano in Mrs. Wilson's parlor sing like no other.

"That's sweet of you to say, but I won't be distracted! If your hair were shorter, it'd be more fashionable."

"And if it's long, it's easier to plait and tuck into my kerchief."

"But, Jo, you won't be tucking it into a kerchief *forever*, will you?" Molly frowned. "Don't you want to find a fella? Get married? Beauty is pain."

"That's bosh," Jo scoffed. "Or if it's true, I don't want any part of it. I think I look better when I feel comfortable."

Molly frowned at the idea. "If you say so . . . ," she said. Taking a deep breath, she stepped back to survey Jo's hair. And then she got to work. Jo let her do whatever she wanted, succumbing to the combing and the pulling, and when Molly was done, Jo had to admit the girl did have a flair for hair. And she had seemed to take Jo's comment to heart, because she had arranged Jo's hair into simple braids pinned around her head, a tortoise-shell comb tucked into the braids giving it a little prettiness.

"Well, don't I look fine," Jo said. "Watch out, Veronica."

Molly giggled. "What are you going to wear?"

"I hadn't thought much about it," Jo confessed, and Molly sighed in an entirely annoyed way that made Jo's heart ache, because it reminded her so much of Amy.

"Honestly, Jo." Molly hurried over to the tiny closet, which was more of a cabinet than an actual closet. She began to rummage inside before letting out a triumphant squeal and handing Jo a dress with a flourish. It was her black rayon one, with the taffeta plaid ribbon threaded across the chest.

"Wear this one," Molly ordered.

"Are you sure?" Jo asked. "My little sister always told me it was plain."

"The way the rayon's cut will make the skirt spin up when you dance," Molly said with a smirk.

"Molly!" Jo clutched the dress to her chest, and Molly's mischievous smile grew.

"You deserve to have some fun, Jo," Molly said seriously.

Jo felt a stab of alarm in her stomach. Had her maudlin mood been that obvious?

"You should go get ready," Jo said. "I've wasted enough of your time."

"It's not a waste. You look beautiful," Molly said. "But I should do my hair, and all my other pins are in my room. I don't want to be late! I'm dreadfully excited about tonight's band. See you in about twenty minutes?"

"I'll be ready," Jo said.

She managed to keep her smile on her face, even after Molly left the room.

Dear Jo

You're the bravest
of us all, but are you
brave enough to fail?

Over and over
in your wild life,
will you be brave enough
to run aground?

Flounder, fall flat on your face
when you venture onto a dance floor.

Write terrible stories.
Char the roast.
Disappoint your loved ones.

I hope you muster the courage
to speak to someone
who's caught your eye
only to be disappointed.

Be late.
Be wrong.
Be loathed.

Rip your best coat.
Get a traffic ticket.
An overdue notice.
An angry letter
from someone you've offended.

And maybe, if you're truly lucky,
drop a tray full of coffee
all over someone
you love.

CHAPTER 9

AMY

A s luck would have it, Laurie leapt out of the way before the coffee tray dropped onto the street with a crash. His boots missed most of the deluge, but a puddle soon pooled in front of the Clubmobile, giving off tendrils of steam.

"You all right there?" Edie called out.

"That's twenty cups of coffee!" Marion exclaimed at the same time.

"I'm fine!" Amy blurted. Everyone was staring at her now—not only Laurie, who still looked shell-shocked at finding her in London. "I'll get that cleaned up straightaway."

Ripping off her apron, she grabbed the broom and hopped out of the truck to sweep up the broken cups, feeling Laurie's eyes following her the whole way. What in the world was he doing in England—and at this hospital of all places?

She hadn't seen him in months. After he and Jo graduated from high school, he had attended a music conservatory for a term, but dropped out to enlist following the attack on Pearl Harbor. Amy had written him faithfully while he was in training with the Army Air Forces, where he'd put in over two hundred hours in the cockpit and finished near the top of his class. He was awaiting his first piloting assignment when his grandfather had called in a few favors with an old military friend to keep his only grandchild safe, effectively grounding Laurie stateside. The last that Amy heard, he was stuck at an airstrip out in Utah, slapped with desk duty.

Laurie stooped down to help her gather up the broken cups. "What are you doing here?" he asked, bewildered. "I hardly recognized you."

She could've said the same thing about him. His hair had been cropped short, and his body had grown lean and muscular from all those military drills. And his uniform? *Dear Lord.* Amy had always thought Laurie handsome, but seeing him in that jacket and with his cap sitting atop his head at a slanted angle, he looked as debonair as Cary Grant.

He pointed at her lapel, looking even more confused than before. "Captain *Pace*?"

"I said that I can explain," Amy whispered before straightening up fast and shining a nervous grin at Edie and Marion, who were peering at them curiously. "This is a friend of mine from home! Small world, isn't it?" She tried to sound breezy but couldn't hide the shakiness in her voice. She knew she'd better make her escape before Laurie said anything suspicious, like calling her Amy. "We're going to do some catching up!"

"'Catching up,' hmm?" Edie said with a hand on her hip before she looked Laurie up and down. "Say, what's your name, soldier?"

Amy stepped in front of him before he could get a word out. "Can you cover the rest of the shift for me, Edie? I'll catch a cab home later," she said before dumping the cups into the bin and dragging Laurie through the rest of the soldiers who were hooting at them.

"Looks like Laurence nabbed himself a Doughnut Dolly!" one of them snickered.

Amy ignored that and hurried up the block, determined to put plenty of space between them and the Clubmobile.

"Will you slow down for a sec?" Laurie said, trying to wriggle his arm free.

But she had to keep moving, full steam ahead. If he breathed a word about her true identity to anyone here, Supervisor Owens would send her packing on the next ocean liner home.

"Amy, wait! You're going to make me pull a stitch."

That finally made her stop. Glancing back, she saw his face twisted in pain. "Stitches? Are you hurt?"

"I had a burst appendix last week." He winced, and his hand dropped toward his abdomen, where his shirt must've been hiding his bandages. "I'm actually stationed north of London, but since there's no military hospital there, I had to come here for the operation."

"Burst appendix?" she said, blinking. "That's major surgery! What are you doing out of bed?"

"The nurses said that I could get some fresh air, and I heard that there were free doughnuts and coffee downstairs," he said wryly. He eyed her lapel again. "So are you going to tell me why your name tag says "'Pace'?"

Amy scrambled for an explanation. Any explanation. "One of the other girls and I switched our tags for the fun of it," she said, attempting a lighthearted laugh.

Laurie didn't look convinced, though. "I thought you had to be twenty-two to join the Red Cross."

Shoot. "They make exceptions from time to time."

"Aren't you sixteen, though?"

"Seventeen, actually." She'd had her birthday back in Washington, but there'd been no candles or cake since the real Rosemary Pace was born in February. It had been Amy's dullest birthday yet.

Laurie went quiet, his gaze toggling back and forth between her face and her name tag until his eyes went wide. "Did you use a false name to get in?"

Amy squirmed. That wasn't entirely true. It was more like a *stolen* name, but she doubted that sounded much better.

"You did, didn't you?" He swore under his breath. "If anyone finds out, you'll be in a heap of trouble."

She shushed him. "No one's going to find out."

"I don't know what you were thinking but—"

"I'm serving our country, just like you are! Who cares if I'm a March or a Pace?" she said fiercely. "And what good would I be doing stuck at home and telling the neighbors to go buy war bonds?"

Laurie yanked off his cap to jam his fingers through his hair. He muttered to himself, "I go halfway across the world, but I can't seem to shake the March girls."

"What's that supposed to mean?"

"Never mind," he said, pacing along the pavement. "Does your family have any clue where you are?"

"No, and you better not say a word to them." Not to her parents. Not to Meg. And certainly not to Jo, who would chide Amy endlessly for this, calling her impulsive and irresponsible. "Promise me, Laurie."

He stopped walking. "Or what?"

"Or . . . or . . ." Her heart was a wild drumbeat. How could she convince him? Goodness, to hell with it. "I'll never speak to you again, Theodore Laurence!"

Almost immediately, Amy winced at how petulant she sounded, like she was five years old and Jo had taken her favorite doll. She snapped her eyes away from him, embarrassed by her outburst, but then he did something that made her angry all over again.

He let out an incredulous laugh.

Was he *laughing* at her?

She went to punch him in the arm, appendectomy be damned, but at that exact moment a bolt of lightning zigzagged across the sky and a spray of raindrops fell over her skin. With a groan, she searched for a place to keep dry, like a tree or a shop overhang, but soon the damp English rain had soaked through her blouse and she realized she'd forgotten her coat back on the Clubmobile. She stared up at the traitorous sky, tempted to raise her fist at it.

"I know where we can wait out the storm," Laurie said as another crack of lightning fanned out overhead. He shrugged off his jacket and held it over Amy's head as he led her down one side street and then another, the buildings growing narrower and dingier as they went. Amy couldn't help but notice that the shop signs around them were written both in English and in another language that she didn't recognize.

Laurie stopped in front of a little restaurant. "We can wait here until the rain lets up. I know the owner."

"What is this place?" Amy whispered, motioning at the sign overhead, which said THE GOLDEN LOTUS on one side and had three Asiatic characters on the other.

"A restaurant. I figured we could grab a bite to eat since I didn't get a chance to try your doughnuts," he said, the corners of his mouth kicking upward.

"What sort of restaurant?" Amy asked warily.

"Chinese. I think you'll like it."

Amy cast a long glance over her shoulder. She'd never ventured to this part of the city, which appeared to be a small Chinatown. Many of the buildings lay crumbled from the Blitz, but a handful of businesses had stubbornly remained open—a tobacconist and a grocer, a couple of lodging houses, and a few restaurants like this one.

Laurie opened the door for her. "Come on, we're both drenched, and you can tell me how you got yourself into this 'Captain Pace' mess."

Amy pushed her wet hair out of her eyes. She didn't think she owed him any explanation, but the restaurant did look warm and dry, and her teeth were chattering. "Fine," she mumbled. "Lead the way."

Inside the Golden Lotus, the room smelled like tea, but not the kind that the Marches drank back at home in the summer months, which Marmee would prepare in a pitcher with plenty of ice cubes. This tea smelled heartier. Earthier. *Different.* A kid approached them, perhaps ten or eleven years old, with a friendly grin and a mop of thick black hair.

"Back already, Lieutenant Laurence?" the boy said in a London accent that caught Amy off guard. She'd thought that he would have a Chinese accent, for some reason, but perhaps she shouldn't have assumed that. After all, one of her schoolmates at home, Ginny Tanaka, spoke with an American accent just like everyone else in Concord. Even their choir teacher,

Mrs. Folger, had commented how Ginny spoke English so well, which had made Ginny blush furiously and murmur that she'd been born in California.

"I couldn't resist your steamed fish, Jimmy," Laurie replied.

The boy glanced over at Amy, a shine in his eye. "And you brought a date!"

Laurie was quick to clear his throat. "This is a pal of mine from home. You got a table for us?"

The restaurant was only a quarter full, so Jimmy showed them to a spot by the window, where he set down a pot of red tea and handed them menus before trotting off to the kitchen.

Amy poured herself a cup and warmed her hands around it. "How in the world did you find this place?"

"One of my buddies brought me here when we were on leave, and he got me hooked," Laurie explained. "It's too bad we don't have a place like this back home."

Amy wasn't sure what to say to that. Chinese cuisine seemed like quite a stretch for the residents of Concord, where Italian food was considered exotic.

"Let me know what looks good to you," he said.

Her eyes grew wide as she read the menu. About half of the items had been crossed out due to rationing, and what remained befuddled her. Abalone soup? Chicken liver chow mein? She felt entirely out of place—and it wasn't only because of the food. Aside from her and Laurie, everyone else in the restaurant was Chinese, or seemed to be. She knew that England was a different country from America, but this was the first time since her arrival that she really felt like a foreigner.

"You know, I think we passed a nice-looking pub on the way over," she hinted at Laurie.

He glanced up from his menu. "Where's your sense of adventure? You used to chew pickled limes by the jarful," he said as Jimmy returned with a small plate of fried . . . *something.*

"Spring rolls on the house," Jimmy proclaimed. "My mom told me to say hello to you and your *pal.*" The boy smiled mischievously, and Laurie got a little color on his cheeks.

"I'll have the wonton soup with the steamed fish and fried rice," Laurie said with a cough.

"Powdered eggs okay with the rice?"

"No problem, kiddo," Laurie said before glancing at Amy. "Anything catch your eye?"

She grew a little rattled. "Um, I'll have what you're having," she said before snapping the menu shut. Her gaze flicked across the restaurant again, and she saw a couple of patrons staring back at her, probably because she and Laurie were the only Caucasians in the establishment. She busied herself by spreading her napkin over her lap, and she wondered if Ginny ever felt this way, except flipped around since she was the only Japanese girl at their school. Heck, in most of Massachusetts. It must've been awfully lonesome, which was something Amy had never really considered until now.

Laurie leaned in toward the table. "So let me see if I've got this straight. You used false papers to get yourself into the Red Cross, and you gave your family some cover story so they wouldn't worry about you. Does that sound right?" He watched her shift uncomfortably before continuing. "Where exactly do they think you are right now?"

"Why don't you write to Marmee and ask her yourself?" Amy said smartly as she reached up to remove the pins from her cap to wring the thing out.

"I could write her a letter as soon as we're done here," Laurie said, a quiet challenge in his tone.

She rolled her eyes while she tugged at a stubborn hair pin. "They all think that I'm attending an art school in Montreal, all right? With Flo."

"Flo knows how much danger you're in, and she hasn't told anyone?" he said, nearly choking on his tea.

"Don't go blowing your stack! I bet you're in far more danger than I am day in and day out. How long have you been in England anyway?"

"You can't compare the two," he replied with a shake of his head. "What you're doing is reckless."

"You're one to talk. Tell me, how many times have you flown over the Channel?" At last, she freed the cap from her hair and tossed it onto the table. "Your poor grandfather. He pulled all those strings to keep you safe."

Laurie made a face. "I'm no coward. As soon as an opening came up here in England, I volunteered. I couldn't stomach sitting at a typewriter while the Axis conquered half the world."

"Then you should understand why I joined the Red Cross! This is a woman's fight, too, you know."

"I never said otherwise, but you went about this all wrong. Your family already lost one daughter last year." All of a sudden his voice went soft, like it had done at Beth's funeral. "Don't make them mourn you as well."

Amy gripped the sides of her teacup, hating the truth in his words and forcing them away. "Need I remind you that you're the only family your grandpa has left?"

Laurie's jaw worked as he tried to come up with a response to that, but before he could say anything, Jimmy arrived with their food. The boy set the soup down first, followed by the rice and a platter of fish.

Amy nearly yelped at the sight of it. The fish had been cooked whole, with its head, tail, and eyes still intact. She could swear it was staring at her.

"Still want to go to that pub down the street?" Laurie asked, a single brow raised.

In reply, Amy filled her plate with food, the fish included. As she lifted the first spoonful toward her mouth, she could feel Laurie's gaze on her and she was determined not to chicken out. She was ready to drown each bite with a long sip of tea, but she needn't have worried—the food was delicious. The rice was fragrant, and the wonton soup wasn't too different from Marmee's chicken noodle. Even the fish, which she'd taken only a tiny bite of, was as soft as silk.

"Not too bad, eh?" said Laurie.

Amy kept a poker face, not wanting to give him the satisfaction that he'd been right. "As long as you're paying."

He let out a laugh, and as Amy joined in with him she realized that this was the first meal that they'd ever shared alone. Back in Concord, there was always somebody else with them, either her sisters or his grandfather or a mutual friend like Fred. Maybe it should've felt awkward with only the two of them, but it felt—oddly—like home.

Which made his silence over the last year all the more painful.

"Why didn't you write me back?" Amy said, setting down her spoon. "Did you even get my letters?"

Laurie froze midbite. "Of course I did. And I was glad for every one."

"So glad that you never returned the favor?"

"I just . . ." He frowned, then sighed, and then frowned again. "I guess I wanted to forget about home for a while."

You mean you wanted to forget about Jo, Amy thought. Something had happened between him and her sister right before he'd shipped out. Jo had gone to the train station to see Laurie off, but after she returned home she had gone straight up to the attic, with her face white and her hands shaking. Meg had knocked on the door to talk things out, but Jo told her to leave her alone already. And that had been that.

"I'm sorry I didn't write," Laurie said quietly. "Water under the bridge?"

That was quite a lot of water to forget about, but in some ways Amy could understand why he had never replied. She avoided writing home, too, not only due to the lies she had to spin but because it forced her to think about Concord, and why she'd left in the first place: the awful row she'd had with Meg and Jo, the raw grief of losing Beth, and the too-quiet house that reminded her of everything she'd lost.

She couldn't let Laurie send her back there.

"I'm doing good work here with the Red Cross," she began. "I'm helping our soldiers. I'm doing my part in the war. Please don't tell my family."

Laurie looked hesitant as he counted out the coins to pay their bill. "Your parents are the best people I know, and I'm not sure if I can keep this from them."

"I'll be as safe as I can be! I'll never break curfew, and I'll stick to the other girls like glue. The Blitz is over anyway."

"That hasn't stopped the Nazi bombers from sneaking over

the Channel. London is still at war." He looked at his watch. "I better be heading back."

She started to protest, but he was waving goodbye to Jimmy and ushering her outside to hail a cab. When a car pulled up, he slipped the driver a bill from his wallet, but Amy refused to climb into the passenger's seat just yet.

"Promise me you won't say a word," she said, looking up to meet his eyes. Lord, he was tall.

"Or else you won't ever speak to me again?" he replied with his mouth quirked on one side.

Perhaps she'd deserved that, but she wanted to pummel him anyway. "Please, Laurie."

But he wouldn't give her a straight answer. Instead, he opened the door to the car and said, "Someone has to look out for you."

"Do I have to remind you that I'm not twelve years old anymore."

His gaze was hard to read as he gave her a tip of his cap. "You'll always be a kid to me, Amy."

Frail

I'd rather
Laurie saw me
as a kid than
how he truly did:
   frail, pale,
      eternally old.

You each had
something
that caught the eye.
Meg's elegance.
Amy's confidence.
Jo's quick wit.

It would have taken
quite the light
to outshine you;
I never had the wick.

The spotlight's not
what I wanted, anyway.
But I did daydream

   nightdream
   all I did was dream

of a boy one day
looking at me the way
Laurie looked at Jo
John looked at Meg
all the boys looked at Amy.

A boy who saw me
as something more than frail.
As a girl whose fingers danced
up and down piano keys
because music was the way
she spoke her mind.

As a girl who would risk her life
to care for those less fortunate—
     yes, I also longed for acclaim.
Does that shock you?

You say you want to be great or nothing,
but I don't think you realize, Amy,
what it truly is to be nothing.

Nothing

A smitten boy
can't take Nothing's hand,
can't whisper secrets in her ear.
He can't pen a letter to Nothing
describing his dreams for their life together.

Nothing can't tear open the letter,
convinced at least for a moment
it holds the key to her happiness.

Even before she became Nothing,
when she was Something, for a time,
she never tore open a letter like that.
Of course she didn't, because she was
      something frail
      something fleeting
      something finite.

If some foolish boy
had offered his heart,
he'd only have had it broken
when she'd inevitably
turned to Nothing.

CHAPTER 10

JO

The dance hall was already a smoky haze by the time Jo and her friends arrived. The old Masons' hall downtown had become the meeting place on weekends and holidays for the young working set of East Hartford to entertain themselves. Dancing, music, sometimes a nasty brawl if some of the boys were feeling wild . . . there was always a good time to be had at the hall.

A small band had been hired for the night, and things were in full swing as the girls crowded into the mass of people. The singer, a tall redhead in a studded mustard gown, was crooning about the fanciful ingredients in moonlight cocktails, as couples swayed on the dance floor and even more people milled around the tables.

Jo let herself get lost in the music, in her friends' laughter and the dark-haired airman who smiled and flirted at her like she was beautiful. She danced with him for four dances, until her cheeks were red and his eyes were shining with more than exertion. When he went to get them drinks, she felt no guilt for slipping out the back door before anyone could miss her, away from it all. Her friends would be more sore about it than the airman. He'd find someone else to spin around the floor.

Jo pulled her brown-checked swing coat tighter around herself as she breathed in the fresh night air. The back of the hall opened up to a narrow alley, but all that was in it was a stack of crates that Jo promptly fashioned into a seat for herself. She could still hear the music—but faded, in a pleasant, muted sort of way, like it was coming from another world, but she could still enjoy it.

Her relief at her quick respite from the bustle inside faded when she realized what she had done after she had sat down. Almost automatically, she had opened her corded handbag, pulled her ever-present notebook out, and flipped it open, like she had done countless times. Like she always did when she had a moment alone with her thoughts.

Why was this so instinctual—muscle memory, practically— but writing was not? Had she used all her imagination? Had it just been shriveled with grief, never to grow again?

In the cracked alleyway light, Jo stared down at the notebook. Fingers tracing over the spirals that bound the pages, she thought of the countless books she had filled before this one. There were stacks in her closet at home. She'd read of the Brontë sisters, writing on tiny tears of paper, on the backs of letters, on any scraps they could find, their need to get the words down so great that nothing could stand in their way.

She had felt that need, once. Maybe she'd taken it for granted. No. There was no *maybe* about it. She'd been cocksure and flying, until that dark storm settled in her breast and never left.

It wasn't only the magazine editors who had rejected her stories of grand women on even grander adventures with polite wording that amounted to *You should maybe think about writing stories about the affairs and concerns of home.* Jo could've weathered that, built a thicker skin, but then . . .

Beth. War. Teddy.

A terrible trio of loss and change she could not outrun.

Desperate to distract herself, she flipped to the middle of the notebook, her stomach seizing as she saw it. The first draft, tear-smudged and barely readable now.

The last thing she had written.

Beth's obituary.

It flared, sharp and angry in her chest, a wounded animal of a thing, and before she could even think it through, she'd chucked the notebook across the alley. For a moment—a glorious moment of reprieve—she actually felt better.

And then, to her utter humiliation, a low whistle filled the air. Someone had witnessed her fit. Her cheeks burned as she hopped off her perch on the stack of crates, peering into the darkness, as a shadow strolled from the mouth of the alley into the light.

A young woman in wide trousers, which moved with her long strides like water, bent down and picked up the notebook.

"You've got quite the arm," she said, holding it out to Jo.

Jo smiled, trying for ease and failing miserably. "Sorry," she said, hoping it was enough to get her out of such an awkward moment with a stranger. "My sisters say I'm all artistic drama."

But the blonde didn't let go of the notebook when Jo grabbed it. "I know a case of writer's block when I see it," she said.

Jo's cheeks were hotter than they got in the factory.

"I've thrown my share of notebooks across the room," the woman continued. She had a smile that made it feel like Jo's ears had just popped and she could hear the music buzzing from the hall again.

"You're a writer?" Jo asked.

"When my pitches get selected." She let go of the notebook to hold out her hand. "Charlotte Yates. Everyone calls me Charlie."

Jo didn't know why, but she suddenly felt the need to wipe her hand on her coat before shaking Charlie's hand. She never liked gloves, but she wished she'd brought some. Maybe the barrier would've dulled the electric shock she felt when their fingers touched.

"Josephine March," said Jo. "Everyone calls me Jo."

Charlie grinned, dimples on each side of her mouth flashing. "You're not serious."

"Call me Josephine on pain of death," Jo said deadpan before cracking her own grin.

Charlie laughed. "It'd be a shame to die before I found out more than your name."

"Yates," Jo said, thinking. "You're Peg's sister?"

Charlie nodded, sticking her hands in her pockets. "She around? I stopped by the boardinghouse, but Mrs. Wilson said all the girls were here."

"She's inside, dancing with everyone else."

"And you, Jo March, are out here," Charlie said. "With your notebook, instead of dancing."

"I've always been the one on the sidelines at parties," Jo said, trying not to think thoughts of dances and radiator-scorched dresses and Teddy's flourish of a smile, sweet memories turned bitter.

"An alleyway is quite the sideline." There was a glint in her eye. Was it just the light? Or was it something else?

Jo didn't know. She didn't know if she wanted to.

"If I went out front," Jo said, "the fellas there would just bother me."

"I shudder at the thought."

"And how," Jo said sincerely, and Charlie's laughter was almost drowned out by the music rising from the hall.

"Peg mentioned in her last call the new girl was a card," she said. "Is that what you write? Comedy?"

"I don't write much of anything these days," Jo said. "When I do, it's fiction. Sometimes funny. But not always. But I'm not like you. Not published or important or anything."

"Oh dear, has Peg been gassing me up?" Charlie let out a nervous chuckle. "My sister likes to brag, but I'm really not all that much. It's more struggle and strife than glamour. It's not like *Life* or any other of the fine periodicals are slavering for women war correspondents."

"Is that your goal?" Jo marveled at the idea of Charlie in a foxhole somewhere, reporting behind enemy lines. "Sounds dangerous."

"Which is why I'm unlikely to get such a gig." Charlie sighed.

"You're a good writer. When the girls mentioned you, I realized I'd read your article about the early widows of the war," Jo said. "The one in *Life*, that came out in early February, I think? I was still home. It was back when our lives still felt like . . . I don't know. Like we'd all fallen into a surrealist paint-ing as everything changed so quickly. What was down was up. I clipped it out to save. Those women . . . their bravery . . . it made me feel like up was up."

A long silence followed her words, and Jo's skin crawled as it grew. As the little divot between Charlie's brows deepened. She shouldn't have said anything. She should've just offered to find Charlie's sister for her and—

"That—thank you," Charlie said. "I'm glad their bravery came through. That was my aim."

"You hit your target," Jo assured her.

A burst of sound—the little band inside playing—filled the alleyway as the back door opened and a group of girls came spilling out. A shriek split the air, making Jo wince and Charlie laugh as Peg broke off from the group and came pelting down the alley to hug her sister.

"You're here!"

"I promised you I wouldn't let you spend Thanksgiving without me!" The Yates sisters rocked back and forth in their embrace, beaming at each other. "How's tricks?"

"You should see what they had me training the new girls on in Texas. You'd die." Peg turned to Jo, her arm slung around Charlie's neck. "Did you meet my sister, Jo?" she asked as the rest of their friends came hurrying over to greet Charlie.

"I did," Jo said as Charlie ducked out from underneath her sister's arm and the two of them disappeared into the excited gaggle of women who were asking questions a million miles a minute.

"Let's go to Harvey's!" Anna suggested, naming the late-night coffee shop that had sticky cherry pie and stickier seats.

But it was cheap and open late, so it had quickly become a factory-girl mainstay.

"I'd kill for some pie," Molly groaned.

"It's decided," Peg declared.

"You girls go without me," Jo said. "My head's pounding. I'm going to walk back."

"Are you sure, Jo?" Ruth asked. "Do you want me to come with you?"

"I'm fine," Jo insisted. "The walk will probably make my headache go away."

They parted, the rest of her friends setting off for the diner, and Jo heading back east, toward the boardinghouse. While the walk didn't make the pounding in her head and heart go away, it was bracing and brisk, and the movement of her body reminded her: *You're still here.*

But no matter how fast she walked through the streets of East Hartford, she couldn't walk away from the image in her head of Peg running toward Charlie, the way they'd slung their arms around each other's necks, the easy camaraderie of sisters, of knowing someone so well, so deeply.

It made her ache in an entirely new way, one that she had no name for. Missing her sisters was not new. But she had never felt so separate from understanding them or being understood by them than now.

Sometimes she feared that the only person who did understand her, she had lost forever.

Why couldn't it have been Jo, instead of Beth? Why was the world so cruel? Her little sister had been worth twenty of her, yet here Jo stood, in the November chill, her body moving capably and surely, still hardy, still alive, still so undeserving.

She had slung her arm around Beth's neck countless times. She had cuddled her close, their temples pressing, hair tangling, until you couldn't tell where her locks began and Beth's started. When was the last time?

She could not remember.

Did she deserve to? She should've been memorizing every moment. Committing every gesture and nose wrinkle and idiosyncrasy to paper, in case . . . in case . . .

Jo shoved her cold hands deeper into the pockets of her coat and picked up the pace.

The tip of her nose and fingers were bright red by the time she got back to the boardinghouse, but after shedding her black dress and toeing off the heels that made her feet pinch, she had thawed out some. A quiet cup of tea before everyone else came back sounded perfect, so she wrapped herself in her robe and made her way out to the hall.

As she passed by the phone at the end of it, she paused, her tea and the cold momentarily forgotten, as temptation beckoned.

It was late. If she called home now, she'd almost for sure get Marmee. She might avoid Meg and all the questions that had been flung out before.

A deep, steeling breath, and her hand was on the black receiver, then heavy in her palm as she lifted it free. She hooked her finger on the rotary, spinning it back as she dialed home. Her heart pounded as she lifted the phone to her ear, desperate to hear Marmee's gentle *Hello, sweetheart* as soon as she heard Jo's voice.

A few rings, and then her pounding heart stuttered, because the voice that answered wasn't Marmee's.

"Hello?" Meg echoed on the line.

What are you so scared of, Jo? She could hear it like Meg had spoken it right into the phone after her greeting.

Jo slammed the phone on the receiver and spun on her heel, hurrying back to her room, all thoughts of comfort swamped by cowardice.

Hello

If I had the chance
to pick up a phone
dial a number
reach from where I am
to where you are,
much less mere miles,
do you think I would squander it?

Do you think I would ever
pass up the opportunity
to tell you how much
I miss you I love you
I'm not at a peace
and how could I be
when the March sisters
are scattered to the winds
because apparently
the only thing
holding us together
was my brittle bones?

You are a coward, Jo.

Striving

I never had
your ambition,
or Amy's.

I never had
Meg's either—
not for the stage
but neither for the home,
those dreams of hers
you do not see
as grand, but they are.

They are, Jo.

I did not strive
beyond daydreams
because I knew
my world would never
grow beyond the one
Marmee stitched together
for us from love and will,
and it was enough for me.

It truly was.

Don't let it
be enough
for you.

CHAPTER 11

MEG

M eg surveyed their Thanksgiving feast: roast turkey,
Virginia baked ham, giblet gravy, oyster dressing,
cranberry sauce, celery soup, mashed potatoes, candied sweet
potatoes, baked squash, cooked carrots, creamed corn, and hot
Parker House rolls. Everything was being kept warm in chaf-
ing dishes. A neatly dressed girl stood behind each dish with a
serving spoon and a smile.

A dozen members of the Junior Red Cross had reported
for duty, a few of them dragging beaus or siblings in tow. Meg
had posted a faculty sign-up, but most of the teachers had plans
with their families. Her friend Frankie had been full of apolo-
gies; she and her mother were eating with her soon-to-be in-
laws; she'd been nervous as a cat all week. Helen Gagnon, the
music teacher, had come, declaring that she wasn't much of a
cook, but she was happy to wash dishes. Mrs. Pratt, the home
economics teacher, had arrived with some beautifully sewn
tablecloths and an absolute vat of candied sweet potatoes. Her
husband was with the Allied forces in North Africa.

Marmee was stationed behind the dessert table with its two dozen pies. A few of the teachers had been kind enough to donate their sugar rations, and Meg had been baking all week; a dozen of the pies were hers.

Marmee had taken Mrs. Scott under her wing. The woman was still grieving her son, but she had shown up with a smile on her face and two pecan pies in hand. Doro was there, too. She had sulked at being asked to set the tables. Ginny had done all the work while Doro trailed after her, slumping, scowling, and muttering under her breath. If she'd thought being a grump would get her out of work, she was mistaken. Meg was used to recalcitrant little sisters. She paused in her inspection, wondering if Amy was even celebrating Thanksgiving today. Was she terribly homesick in Canada? Meg couldn't tell from her letters; they were brief and jaunty and contained nothing of any real substance.

It made her sad. Amy used to tell her everything.

The scarred cafeteria tables were covered with Mrs. Pratt's beautifully embroidered tablecloths, set with borrowed china and silver. The girls had lit votive candles and made Tom Turkey centerpieces out of felt, and while one couldn't quite forget that they *were* in the school cafeteria (those pea-green walls!), the overall effect was homey. Theo Harkness had brought his record player, and the Andrews Sisters' "Boogie Woogie Bugle Boy" was livening things up.

"All right, girls! It's four o'clock. Time to let in our guests!" Meg grabbed Doro by the arm. "You're on creamed corn, right next to me."

The first hour flew by while she scooped mashed potatoes

and made chitchat with a steady stream of neighbors. Folks made a point of saying "please" and "thank you" and waited patiently in line, even when the girls spilled soup or got a smear of sweet potatoes on a jacket sleeve. Honestly, it gladdened Meg's heart. Marmee had been right. It did feel good to help—and to be reminded that they weren't the only ones struggling through this Thanksgiving.

Several young families had been at the front of the line, and now that they'd finished eating, the children chased each other across the cafeteria. Two blond-braided girls with identical noses shoved each other and shouted till their mother intervened. Meg felt a pang of homesickness. Was it possible to be homesick when she was the one left behind at home?

Marmee had tried to telephone Jo that morning. Jo wasn't there, the girl who'd answered the boardinghouse phone had said. Had she gone home for the holiday with one of the other girls? Or had she dodged Marmee's call?

Meg's smile warped and wavered.

Next to her, Doro wasn't even *trying*. She scooped creamed corn onto an elderly woman's plate without so much as a hello. "Miss Scott, how are you holding up?" the old woman asked in a quavering voice, peering at Doro through thick Coke-bottle glasses. "I'm very sorry about your brother."

"*You* didn't kill him," Doro muttered.

The old woman sputtered.

"Mae, could you cover for me, please? Ginny! Could you take over for Doro?" Meg grabbed Doro by the elbow and hauled her toward the kitchen. Ginny stopped filling cups with coffee, tied on a spare apron, and straightened her shoulders like she was going into battle.

"Doro, that poor woman is about a hundred years old, and she was trying to express her condolences!" Meg hissed. "I know this is difficult, but—"

"I'm tired of people saying they're sorry for my loss. Like I mislaid a book or a hair ribbon. He was my brother!" Doro snapped.

"I know. I *know*," Meg said. "But there are no good things to say. Would you rather people pretend that nothing's happened?"

"Yes! No. Oh, I don't know." Doro slumped back against the pea-green wall.

"Do you want to work in the kitchen instead? You and Ginny could wash dishes with Miss Gagnon." Meg had taken Ginny aside earlier after noticing that three women in a row had put their noses in the air and declined the gravy Ginny was ladling out. Imagine being so hateful you'd pass up *gravy*! Meg had asked if Ginny would prefer to work in the kitchen, but Ginny had refused. She didn't want to be hidden away. They'd agreed on a compromise: Ginny would switch stations with Lizzie Talbot, filling cups of coffee and setting them on the pie table.

Doro stomped her loafers like a child. "I don't want to be here at all."

"Do you want to go home?" Meg asked. "I'm sure your mother would understand."

"No!" It burst out of Doro. "I don't want to be there, either. I can't bear it."

"If you're going to stay, you have to *try*, Doro. People are here because they haven't the money for their own dinner. Or because they can't bear to have Thanksgiving at home without fathers or sons or brothers or—or sisters who ought to be there.

So they're here, trying to make the best of it. Our job is to give those people a hot meal and a little cheer."

"Well, I'm not feeling very cheery," Doro muttered.

Meg was out of patience. "Do you suppose I am? Do you know what I'd give to be at home with my family right now? With my sisters, *all* of them, crowded around the table laughing and bickering, and Marmee's mashed potatoes with a whole heap of butter on top, and Father saying the blessing?" Meg's voice broke. "*Anything.* I'd give anything on this earth. But stomping around being rude to everyone won't bring Beth back. And it won't bring Richie back, either. Why don't you go on home? You're not doing anyone any good here."

The girl's shoulders slumped. "I'm trying, miss. I am. It's hard for me."

"It's not always easy for me, either," Meg admitted.

"You make it look easy." Doro bowed her head, her soft brown curls falling into her face. "Prim and proper Miss March. You're like an—an automaton."

Meg frowned. "I'm young for a teacher, and I need to earn my students' respect," she said stiffly. "But it's not easy. I get flustered and frustrated, and sometimes I want to yell. Instead, I put on a smile, and I pretend. Like today. I had a good little cry this morning. But it wouldn't do for me to come in with red eyes and scowl at everyone."

"Why not? Why pretend?" Doro asked.

Meg thought for a moment. It was an awful lot of work sometimes, hiding her grief and her anger. Why did she bother? There was a sense of decorum, she supposed: young women were expected to be pretty and pleasant, to smile and make everyone comfortable. But it was more than that.

"I don't know if you remember my sister Beth, but she was the sweetest, most generous girl," Meg said finally. "She didn't have much, but she was always happy to lend Amy a hair ribbon or money to buy a *Photoplay* magazine. Beth was terribly shy, but she always wanted to make her little corner of the world better and brighter. When I have to make a decision, big or small, I think: What would make Beth proud of me?"

It was true. This week—after an observation by Miss Pennington in which she had corrected three of Meg's students, utterly undermining her!—Meg had nearly written a letter expressing interest in the position at Plumley. She and Marmee could use the money. She could come home on weekends. If she got an offer, she wouldn't have to accept, but it would prove that she had what it took. . . .

But no matter how many rationalizations she made, she kept coming back to one point: she couldn't leave Marmee with an empty nest. Not so soon after losing Beth.

Not when Meg felt responsible for driving Jo away.

"I think Beth would be proud of the work we're doing here," Meg said.

Doro stood up straighter. "That's a pretty thought, Miss March. But why do some folks have to give more than others? We already lost Dad, and now Richie—it's not fair. I wish I could be good like you, but I'm not. I'm just so mad all the time I could scream!"

Meg bit her lip. She remembered standing in the parlor after coming home from the Cocoanut Grove, learning that Jo wouldn't be back for Thanksgiving, looking at Beth's dusty piano, and thinking that if Marmee told her to count her blessings right then, she would scream. She glanced toward the bustle of the serving line. The girls seemed to have the situation well in hand. Ginny was laughing with a grandmotherly woman.

"I've got an idea. Follow me."

Meg led Doro into the kitchen, where Miss Gagnon was singing "For Me and My Gal" while she washed dishes. Meg found a stack of clean white school plates. She selected a few that were already chipped or had cracks spidering through them. She grabbed two thick towels that had been set aside for drying dishes. Then she slipped out onto the blustery-cold loading dock. Doro followed her, mystified.

"Miss March, it's freezing out here! What are you doing?"

Meg laid the towels side by side on the concrete. "Hold these," she said to Doro, and handed her four plates. She took the fifth and raised it over her head with both hands. Then she threw it at the ground, as hard as she could. It splintered into dozens of pieces that scattered across the towels.

"Your turn," she told a wide-eyed Doro.

"But . . . this is *wasteful*," Doro said.

Meg shrugged. "They were chipped anyway. It's better than punching people in the face."

Doro laughed. Then she sobbed. She smashed two plates on the ground in quick succession. Shivering, she handed another to Meg. "Your turn. Miss March, if anyone saw us, they'd think—"

"Oh, who cares." Meg let out a wild yell as she dashed the plate to bits. "I have to admit, that's quite satisfying!"

She couldn't remember the last time she'd *yelled* like that, formless and free.

Doro was staring. Meg tucked a flyaway hair behind her ear and blushed. "What? Have I got mashed potatoes on my face?"

"No, you—you're pretty. When you smile for real, you're pretty," Doro said.

"Why, thank you, Doro." Goodness, was she in the habit of giving such phony smiles that a real one was remarkable? Meg brushed off the worry. "What do you think? Can you manage a smile for one of those little old ladies?"

"Well, when you put it like that . . ." Doro rolled her eyes in that way that reminded Meg of Amy. "But . . . Miss March?"

"Yes?"

Doro smiled. "Can I smash one more?"

Meg handed her the last plate and smiled back. Genuinely. "Absolutely."

Fine China

This serving platter
has a lovely border
of English roses
and in the center a family
with tattered clothes
and barely enough to eat.

This soup bowl
with holly leaves
and cheerful berries
that twine around
depicts a man
with grand ideas
and intentions.

This salad dish
with scalloped edge
shows a woman
(at the margins, not the center)
following through
on every promise.

This butter plate
has a saintly girl
too pure for this world.

This soup tureen
a girl so scared of who she is
she hides from herself.

This gravy boat
a girl too busy comparing
to see the good in what she has.

This saucer
a girl who'd be great or nothing
but there's no greatness in deceit.

This dinner plate
edged in gold
depicts a funeral,
grief building walls
around each family member
until they're all alone
in their own graves.

Smash them all.

CHAPTER 12

AMY

The days passed, but Laurie's parting words pricked at Amy like a shard of glass that she couldn't root out.

You'll always be a kid to me.

Was that all she was to him? Forever the twelve-year-old girl who'd fallen through the ice and needed saving? Laurie was such a gorilla sometimes.

"I think you've just about murdered that dough," Edie said as she sidled up next to Amy inside their Clubmobile.

Amy blew the hair out of her eyes and realized that she had beaten the doughnut dough stiff. She cursed under her breath.

"My word, where did a Red Cross employee learn to swear like such a sailor?" Edie bumped shoulders with her, and then she got a little smile on her face. "Looks like something's on your mind. Or, rather, *somebody*."

"I'm just tired," Amy said, which did have some truth to it. Work was busier than ever, and even her limited hours off duty were dominated by laundry and chores—and, well, *Laurie*. He had taken it upon himself to check on her as often as he could sneak out of the hospital. Like last week when he'd stopped by

146

Amy's billet after an air raid to make sure she was okay. Edie had found it terribly romantic.

"You know what I think? That boy is keen on you," Edie said.

Amy flushed, and it wasn't from the oil warming up in the doughnut fryer. "Laurie thinks of me as a little sister, that's all."

"And you've never felt anything toward him except for brotherly affection?" Edie asked with a smirk.

"Something like that," Amy murmured. She'd told herself over and over again that her feelings for Laurie had been a childhood crush, something she had outgrown, like dolls and hair ribbons. She was a different person now since she saw him last—older and wiser, especially when it came to love.

Well, sort of.

Amy had gone on over a dozen dates with Fred Vaughn before he left for his naval training and they'd even kissed a few times in his sleek Studebaker coupe. She wouldn't say that she was head over heels for him, but he had the makings of a devoted boyfriend. After he'd taken her to see the Boston Symphony on their sixth date, Meg had demanded all the details and had nodded approvingly when Amy assured her that he had been a gentleman through and through. Jo, however, had remarked that Fred might've been rich but he was as boring as a Sunday sermon.

Amy had tossed a pillow at Jo's head for saying that—although she had to admit that she'd said something similar about John Brooke—but deep down she wondered if her sister was right. Fred *was* a little dull. He talked about the Red Sox quite a lot, and he was a dead hoofer on the dance floor, but Amy was quick to remind herself that he was sweet and doting.

Plus, he had taken her on some very fancy dates, like that one Saturday when they drove up to ski on Mount Wachusett. Amy had always wanted to go, but the entry tickets were too pricey on the Marches' budget.

"You've honestly never thought about kissing him?" Edie said.

Amy blinked. "Kiss who?"

"Lieutenant Laurence, you dolt!"

"Of course not," Amy said swiftly, but she chewed on her lip as she watched the oil sizzle. Edie's question started to grow roots in her mind, and she considered all the times when she'd kissed Fred, which had been rather pleasant. Her heart never did a loop de loop when he leaned in toward her after a date, although couldn't those feelings grow with time?

But then she started thinking about Laurie standing in front of her instead, with his head dipping down to meet hers, licking his lips as his fingertips brushed her hip, and all of a sudden she was feeling much too warm.

It must be that uniform of his, she thought. Even a toad would look like a million bucks in an air force getup.

"You two need a hand? The boys will be lining up soon," Marion said. She squeezed next to Amy and Edie as she checked her hair in her compact. Then her eyes fell on the mixing bowl. "Goodness, that dough looks . . . overdone."

"I'm sure they'll taste all right." Amy went to scoop the dough into the frying canister, but Marion was shaking her head.

"We better mix up a fresh batch."

Amy fought the temptation to roll her eyes. Wasn't Marion the one always urging her to work faster? "It looks fine to me. The men won't mind."

"This'll be their last taste of home before heading off to war," and it's our duty to make it a good one," Marion said, motioning at Amy to hand over the bowl. "I'll mix it up myself."

"Be my guest, then," Amy said with a shrug. It was a Friday night, and they'd already put in fourteen-hour shifts every day of the week. If Marion wanted an extra turn at that devil's machine, then Amy would be glad to oblige.

While Marion wrangled with the fryer, Amy bustled to set out the coffee cups. Edie soon sidled up next to her with the napkins and with an elbow in the side. "Say, do you think Laurie is feeling well enough to go dancing with us this week? Maybe he could invite that friend of his from the hospital, the one with the dreamy Southern accent."

"You mean Private Hathaway? I'll see what I can do." Amy grinned. Edie had already been on four dates this week! "Could you hand me a dishrag? Some of these cups need another wiping down. Hold on, I see one."

Amy turned around to reach for the rag, not realizing that Marion was behind her until it was too late. The two of them collided, and Marion's mixing bowl went tumbling down, with the dough splattering over her legs.

Amy's hands flew to her mouth. "Are you all right?"

"My nylons are ruined!" Marion exclaimed.

"Don't worry. I've got an extra pair to replace them back in our room," Edie offered.

"But I'll have to go bare-legged this shift. It's incredibly unprofessional," said Marion, grabbing the rag out of Amy's hand to clean up the mess.

Amy felt awful, but she didn't know why they were arguing about *hosiery*, of all things. "We won't say a word to Supervisor

Owens. Anyway, I bet the GIs wouldn't mind getting a glimpse of your cheesecake. You could give Betty Grable a run for her money!" she said, hoping to lighten the mood.

Marion's cheeks heated up like a griddle. "This isn't a joke. You need to treat our job with more care."

Amy's mouth slipped open. "It was an accident."

"I saw the whole thing, and Rosie's right," Edie said, swooping in to defend Amy. "Stop busting her chops, Marion. She's working as hard as the rest of us."

Marion yanked off her nylons and tossed them into the bin before straightening to meet their eyes. Her voice cracked a little as she said, "We didn't come to England to go dancing with the privates and making doe eyes with pilots from home."

Edie was so taken aback that she laughed. "Now you're dragging me into this?"

"Doe eyes?" Amy said at the same time. It wasn't like she had asked Laurie to pop in and check on her. "That's completely unfair!"

"What's unfair is how you're treating your fella from home, the one who keeps writing to you," Marion said. "Fred, isn't it?"

Amy sucked in a sharp breath. She wished that she could spit out a clever retort—something with a real zing—but her tongue wasn't cooperating. And . . . and was Marion right? Was she leading Fred on? She shoved the thought away. No, Marion didn't know what she was talking about. There was nothing going on between her and Laurie. Nothing at all.

As soon as the troops started to queue up outside the Clubmobile, the trio made sure to put on a good show for the soldiers. They smiled and chatted and cracked jokes with the men, but tension hung in the air like summer humidity. Amy and

Edie gave Marion the cold shoulder, while Marion refused to ask for their help, even when a few doughnuts started to crisp in the fryer.

"Captain Sanctimonious over there really needs to take things down a notch," Edie whispered to Amy while they were washing out cups at the end of the shift and Marion had stepped out for a bathroom break. "You want me to give her an ol' Baltimore talking-to?"

Amy cracked a laugh. "I'm sure Supervisor Owens would get wind of it somehow, and then we'd both be in big trouble. Thank you, though."

"Of course. I'm protective of my pals," Edie said with a wink.

Amy warmed from the inside out. Edie was a real friend, through and through. More than Meg and Jo ever were.

After they returned to the Hotel Royale, Amy was about to head upstairs for a nap, but Supervisor Owens called them over to gather up their mail, which had just arrived. Amy hurried to look through her bundle, where she found a few letters each from Marmee, Meg, and Flo. Nothing from Jo yet again. Amy wasn't surprised, but it stung nevertheless. Her older sister sure knew how to hold a grudge.

Marion tore through her stack like she was starved, flipping through the envelopes until she reached the last one. "You're sure there's nothing else?" she asked Supervisor Owens.

"Are you waiting on something in particular? A parcel?" the older woman said.

"Just a letter," Marion said, trying not to sound too disappointed.

"From your beau back home?" Edie said, her tone a touch too sweet.

"As a matter of fact, yes," Marion replied tightly.

"Must be nice for him to enjoy all that Hawaiian sunshine, safe and sound. I guess it was a blessing in disguise that he couldn't enlist."

Marion's cheeks flushed so red that they were practically glowing. She'd always been tight-lipped about her relationship, and today was no different. Frowning, she gripped her mail and ducked out the door to read the letters out on the stoop.

Amy watched her go before turning to Edie. "She does look upset."

"I was only teasing," Edie said. "If you ask me, she deserved it after her tirade today in the Clubmobile."

Amy chewed the inside of her cheek. As much as she appreciated Edie's protectiveness, her remark about Marion's beau did seem too mean-spirited. "It isn't her boyfriend's fault that he couldn't join the military."

"Fine. Maybe I crossed a line." Edie sighed before she giggled to herself. "But if I were the one dating Marion Greeley, I sure would hope to get deployed somewhere far, far away from her!"

"Edie, you're terrible!" Amy said, but she couldn't help giggling, too, and she stopped only when she thought about how disappointed Marmee would be with her. Her mother would never laugh at someone else's expense, and she expected the same out of her girls. Guilt chewed at Amy's heart, but she told herself that this wasn't so bad. It wasn't like Marion had overheard them, and besides, Edie was only letting off some steam. No harm done.

Once inside their room, Edie scrambled onto her top bunk

while Amy flopped onto the bottom one and went through her mail again. She started with one of Marmee's letters to make sure Father was safe before she tore into an envelope from her cousin:

> My mother visited Montreal last weekend and kept asking to see you. I came up with an excuse that you were off in Ottawa with one of your classmates. I figured I'd tell you, to keep our stories straight, but you owe me a shopping trip in Monte Carlo when this is all over. Before I forget, what am I supposed to tell your family about the holidays?

Amy rubbed her temples. She had already written to Marmee that she would have to miss Thanksgiving and Christmas this year because she'd be joining a friend in Quebec City. She knew her mother would be upset by the news, but Amy was secretly relieved that she would be an ocean away for the holidays.

Would Christmas even be Christmas without her family? Without her sisters?

It would have to be, Amy thought, even as her heart sank. She was already thinking about Marmee's mashed potatoes and Meg's homemade gingersnaps, along with the scent of Father's pipe while Beth played a carol on the piano and Jo hollered at everyone to sit down already or else she'd start eating without them.

But with Beth gone, they'd never have another Christmas

like that again, especially after everything had gone south between her, Meg, and Jo over the summer.

Another memory invaded Amy's mind—of the terrible row that had split the three of them apart. Amy remembered it clearly, how she'd been sitting in her bedroom and going through Beth's old clothes to donate to Marmee's charity group. It was just about the last thing she wanted to do on a Saturday afternoon, but she had done it as a favor to her mother, who was laid up in bed with a terrible cold. Just as she'd reached for a drawer of sweaters, she heard a commotion coming from the attic.

There were voices: Meg's and Jo's. Amy couldn't make out their words exactly, but the two of them were getting louder. And flustered. Heaving a sigh, she trudged up the stairs to ask them to pipe down, since Marmee needed her rest, doctor's orders, but her voice dried right up when she saw her sisters' faces. Meg's cheeks had gone red while Jo was swiping at her eyes.

Has Jo been crying? Amy wondered. Jo never, ever cried. Even at Beth's funeral, she had stood by the coffin stoically, her face like a marble statue.

But now Jo looked far from placid, with her eyes narrowing at Amy. "Were you eavesdropping on us?"

Amy blinked at the accusation. "No. Marmee's sleeping, remember? So keep your voices down."

"Don't lie. You were listening, weren't you?" Jo said, a flush of color rising up her throat.

"Jo, don't," Meg had murmured, but Jo wouldn't let it drop.

"How much did you hear?" Jo pressed Amy.

"Nothing, all right?" Amy scowled. When it came to Meg

154

and Jo, she knew she'd always be the outsider, but it still hurt to be excluded, especially now that it was only the three of them. What had they been discussing before and why was Jo so upset? She'd been in a real mood ever since a certain neighbor of theirs had shipped out. "Is this about Laurie?"

Jo went white at the mention of him. "You *were* eavesdropping!"

"I told you I wasn't!" Amy shot back. There went Jo again, assuming the worst about her. "Why won't you tell me what's going on?"

"It's none of your business," Jo barked out of nowhere. "Now leave!"

Amy was breathing heavily now. "Stop shutting me out! I'm only worried about you." Her eyes shifted from Jo to Meg, pleading. Hoping Meg would let her in.

Meg, however, gave a drawn-out sigh. "Please give Jo and me a moment."

Amy felt the words like a punch. How many times had she tried to tag along with them, only to inevitably get left behind? *You're not old enough,* Meg would say. *Go home already,* Jo would add. And Amy would return to the house in tears, where Beth would give her a glass of warm milk and they'd spend the rest of the afternoon together, doing whatever Amy wanted. Beth had never let her feel second-rate. But now Beth was dead and Amy was alone.

"Go away," Jo said, her chest rising and falling fast. She reached for Amy's arm to escort her to the stairs, but Amy twisted away.

And then she got angry.

Amy pushed Jo on the shoulders, making her stumble back. In return, Jo roared and made a grab at Amy's hair, as if they were squabbling little girls again.

"Stop. Please stop!" Meg begged, wedging herself between them. "Beth wouldn't want you to fight."

"Tell that to Jo since she started it!" Amy said. "You think this is what Beth would want, Jo?"

"Don't you dare, you selfish brat!" Jo shouted, her eyes wild. "Where were you when she got sick, huh? Off in Montreal with your paints!"

Amy pulled back, going pale. That was plain mean, and Jo knew it. As soon as Amy had returned home from Canada, she'd never left Beth's bedside, not until the very end.

Jo was blinking fast, like she was coming out of a daze, but when she glanced back at Amy, she didn't say a word. Not a whiff of an apology.

"That's enough, both of you," Meg said, her hands visibly shaking.

"*Me?* Did you even hear what Jo said?" Amy said incredulously.

"Both of you need to take a breath," Meg went on. "Amy, go cool off downstairs. I'll speak to you later."

"You always take her side!" Amy said, throwing her arms up. Meg ought to have been defending her and chewing out Jo.

Meg's lips pinched together. "Let me finish up with Jo, and then I have to meet with John in forty minutes, but—"

"That boring old fuddy-duddy?" Amy said, furious. She liked John well enough, but it sure hurt that Meg would prioritize him over her own sister.

"Oh, grow up," Meg snapped, finally losing her cool. "Romance isn't like the movies, Amy! You'll understand when you fall in love with someone besides yourself."

By then, no one was listening. Jo raced down the stairs and out of the house, off to who knows where, while Amy stormed back into her room and slammed the door shut, positively stewing in her fury.

A scant week later, Jo had left home. She'd packed a single suitcase and taken a train up to Connecticut, telling their parents that she'd gotten a job at a factory and she'd give them a call when she arrived. Meanwhile, Meg stayed later and later at school in the evenings, with some thin excuse about attending faculty meetings, but Amy knew that Meg was avoiding her. It seemed that she'd lost all of her sisters in one fell swoop—and that was when she decided to walk herself down to the Red Cross.

"Look what my aunt sent me!" Edie said, hanging a bottle-green velvet dress over the side of her bed for Amy to see.

Amy sat up in bed, an idea whizzing through her head. She was determined not to cry the night away over Meg and Jo, who probably didn't even miss her.

"We should take that dress out for a spin tonight at the Savoy!" Amy said, dropping the rest of her letters and shooting to her feet. A few of the officers had invited the Clubmobile girls out for a night on the town since they hadn't had the chance to properly celebrate Thanksgiving earlier that week. The perfect distraction.

"You don't have to ask me twice," Edie said, scooting off her bunk to start changing. She jutted a chin toward Marion's bed. "I wonder if that sourpuss will join us. She did get an invite, too."

"Sourpuss?" Amy chuckled. "If we're lucky, maybe she'll get an early start on the doughnut batter for tomorrow, since we'll be occupied making doe eyes tonight."

Edie started laughing, but Amy felt a flash of guilt. She couldn't help but think about Marmee and how disappointed she would be if she'd overheard what Amy had said. But didn't hoity-toity Marion deserve it a little?

Amy tucked her letters away and launched herself into getting ready. She'd packed an evening dress from home just for an occasion like this, a knee-length number in a brilliant sapphire hue that played off the color of her eyes. She loved the details, too, from the ruched shoulders to the matching belt. The V-neck collar didn't reveal any cleavage—because Red Cross gals weren't supposed to be sexy—but it certainly kept things flirty. And Amy was in the mood for flirty. Anything to take her mind off her old family memories.

The two girls treated themselves to a cab, which zigged and zagged through the dark London streets, and Amy's jaw went slack when they pulled up to the hotel's curb.

"Wow-ee," she breathed.

The Savoy stood proudly in front of them, a grande dame on the Thames. It had been London's first luxury hotel back in 1889, and it still looked the part, although many of its windows had been blacked out due to the Blitz, and hundreds of sandbags lined the front of the building in case of another attack. But that hadn't deterred the wealthy Londoners from flocking to the place. Apparently, Churchill himself liked to frequent the Savoy for lunch.

"I don't know if I brought enough shillings for this," Amy whispered.

Edie winked. "I doubt we'll have to pay for a single drink tonight."

Her words proved prophetic. As soon as they entered the glitzy cabaret, they joined a group of American military officers, who bought them flutes of champagne with an easy snap of their fingers. Amy sipped at hers carefully—she'd never had champagne before, and this was the good stuff from France— and glanced around. A big band played on the stage, covering songs like "Moonlight Cocktail" and "Serenade in Blue." Amy had barely finished her glass when she got asked to dance, and she didn't sit down for the next full hour. Every time one song ended and another began, a new companion would ask her for a spin. She jived with an army captain from Texas. She jitterbugged with an older British gentleman, who may have been an earl. After that, she and Edie attempted a quickstep for the fun of it, and they were soon laughing and stepping on each other's toes.

"Looks like Marion came after all," Edie said, catching her breath after the song had wrapped. "Over there by the punch table."

"I don't think she approved of our performance," Amy replied, noting the tightness around Marion's mouth at the sight of her roommates cutting a rug like fools. But why should Marion care what Amy and Edie were doing? They were off the clock and having fun—a lesson that Marion ought to learn.

A Lindy Hop started up, and Amy found herself dancing with a handsome Belgian named Marcel, whose diplomat family had taken refuge in London after Hitler steamrolled across his country. Not only was he a fine dancer, but he spoke with a French accent and called her *chérie,* which sounded quite debonair to her ears. It helped too that he offered to get her more champagne.

"I'd love some. Shall we head to the bar?" Amy said.

They moved through the throng, and Marcel placed his hand on the small of her back to steer her through the crowd of politicians and diplomats and socialites, all of them swaying to the drumbeat of an Artie Shaw melody.

Amy was starting to feel the effects of her last glass of champagne, when her eyes landed upon the newest arrival at the cabaret and she froze at the edge of the ballroom. There he was in that uniform again, the one who made her heart go *thud-thud-thud* to the brassy rhythm of "Chattanooga Choo Choo."

She stared at him, and he stared right back.

"I've been looking for you, Captain Pace," said Laurie.

Tether

The tale we've always told
was Jo and Laurie, Laurie and Jo,
the tether fixed between them.

But there's always a moment
in Jo's rollicking stories
when something happens
completely unexpected.

A tether snaps and its frayed ends
remake themselves into something new,
connecting two souls who aren't bound
by the rope, but simply given the chance to grab on.
Not inevitable, but possible.

Looking back at Jo's stories
told over tea around the table
you could always see
how she laid a trail of clues
you might have noticed
if you hadn't been so absorbed
in the telling of the tale.

Perhaps these clues were always there.

CHAPTER 13

MEG

"Marmee?" Meg asked tentatively. It was a rare night when her mother was sitting across the kitchen table from her, wearing a flowered blue housedress, her face freshly washed and slathered in Pond's cream. She'd missed a spot by her left ear; it needed rubbing in. Meg would have leaned over and done it herself, but lately . . . lately, she and Marmee circled each other like strangers.

The Voice of America crackled from the radio, and twin cups of chamomile tea cooled beside it. Marmee had given Meg the cup that Jo usually used, the blue one with a little chip in the handle. Had she forgotten that Meg always used the pink one with the gilt edge?

It didn't matter; it was silly to mind.

Marmee looked up from her letter. "Yes, dear?"

"What do you write to Father?" Meg asked.

Her own letter had sputtered out after *My dearest John.*

She wanted to tell him how she and Doro had snuck outside and smashed plates on Thanksgiving. How she felt she'd been able to genuinely help Doro with her grief. But that would mean admitting she'd recognized something of herself in Doro: that she was so angry and sad she wanted to scream sometimes, too. That, already grieving Beth, she resented the way this blasted war had scattered the rest of her family. Sometimes she wanted to wail and stomp her feet and complain that it wasn't fair.

But what kind of woman felt that way? Meg wasn't sixteen anymore. It wouldn't be very becoming to admit all her ugly feelings to a man who had left his comfortable teaching job to enlist. Who was willing to give his life for freedom, if it came to that. *Please, God, let it not come to that.*

Doro's assertion that Meg was an automaton had gotten under her skin. *I wish I could be good like you, but I'm not,* Doro had said. The more Meg thought about it, the more it troubled her. She wasn't sure that stuffing away all her feelings was the virtue Doro thought it was. Lately, her jaw ached from clenching it, and her teeth hurt from grinding in her sleep.

"If it's been a . . . a trying day, for instance," Meg explained to Marmee. Or a trying month, or a wholly infuriating year. "If you're feeling a little blue . . . do you tell him about it?"

Marmee took a sip of her tea. "No, I don't," she said.

Meg's heart sank.

"Your father's got enough on his plate comforting soldiers who are ill or dying, and those who have shell shock, and contending with the awful things he sees in battle himself," Marmee said.

They'd had a letter from Father: He had made it through the naval battle at Guadalcanal, he was well, he missed them, and the Pacific was beautiful. They weren't to worry about him. But that was easier said than done.

"I have to dig deep sometimes," Marmee admitted, "to be cheerful. But the last thing I want is him fretting about me. His sacrifices are much greater."

Meg glanced down at the latest issue of *Mademoiselle*, which had a feature on war wives. Beautifully serene, courageous, uncomplaining—that was the ideal. Maybe at school Meg pulled it off, but in her heart of hearts, she didn't feel serene, and she certainly didn't feel courageous, and she wished she had someone to complain to.

Meg hoped that if John ever felt worried or afraid, he would confide in her. By all accounts, army training was no picnic. War would be worse. She wanted to be a comfort to him. Wouldn't he feel the same way? Wouldn't he want to know about her worries and frustrations, as trivial as they might seem?

But Marmee and Father had been married for nearly twenty-five years. If Marmee said it was best for Meg to keep her troubles to herself, she must be right.

Meg wished more than anything that she could talk to Jo. What she wouldn't give to stroll up to the attic and find her sister sitting there at her scarred wooden desk, typing away at her old Remington, a stack of pages and a half-eaten apple beside her. Meg would wrap herself in Jo's counterpane—the attic was always drafty—and flop onto the floor and confess all her sins. Jo wouldn't judge.

Or would she? The ghosts of their arguments rose up around Meg. Jo had been awfully disappointed when Meg said she'd leave her job to raise her children someday. *But you worked so hard to get your degree!* When Meg's name had been announced at her graduation, Jo had whooped louder than anybody. *I love teaching,* Meg had told her, *but I want to be a mother, too.*

Anybody can be a mother, Jo had said. Which wasn't true, and it wasn't kind. Meg thought of Mrs. Pratt, the home ec teacher, who'd been married for ten years and hadn't been able to have children. Meg had found her crying in the ladies' room after Esther Grotowski had announced that she was having twins.

Don't you want more than that? Jo had pressed.

Meg thought she could be happy as a wife and mother. Maybe when her children were older, she'd go back to teaching. But the way Jo had asked—as though that wasn't enough—had made her feel ashamed. Jo had her writing; Amy had her painting. Beth had been a wonderful pianist. What was Meg's gift? She'd starred in the amateur theatricals Jo wrote back when they were kids, and in high school she'd performed in a few plays. She'd enjoyed it. But acting had never driven her the way writing drove Jo. Meg could be complete without it.

Jo hadn't understood that. Perhaps she wouldn't understand Meg's current predicament, either. It would seem straightforward to her: Of course Meg should say how she felt, and damn the consequences. If John didn't accept her as she was, warts and all, then by God, he wasn't good enough for her!

But what if it were the other way around: What if Meg wasn't good enough for *him*?

John made her want to be better. She loved that about him.

But lately . . . lately, Meg felt terribly inadequate.

Marmee finished writing her letter and set it aside. She hummed along to the radio as she washed her empty cup. Meg stared down at the blank page in front of her. She felt restless, like she could burst right out of her skin.

The telephone rang, and her breath came fast. *Jo?* It felt like she'd summoned her.

"Hello. March residence," Marmee said. Then she listened. "Certainly, just a moment. Meg, dear, it's for you."

Meg took the phone, fumbling it in her haste. Could it be John, calling from New Jersey? Was he shipping out? Her heart hammered. Marmee switched off the radio and went into the parlor to give her some privacy. Meg took a deep, calming breath. "Hello. This is Meg."

"Hello there, Meg. This is Andy. Andy Fitzhugh."

Meg's heart sank. Not John.

"Hello, Andy." She tried to keep the disappointment from her voice. "How—how are you?"

"I'm doing well, thanks." Without asking how she was in return, he launched right into his reason for telephoning. "Look, I was wondering, would you like to go with me to Sallie's Christmas party next Saturday?"

"Oh, I . . . Thank you for asking, but—"

"I had a swell time at the Grove," Andy plowed on. "You're a great dancer."

"Thank you." Meg laughed, uncomfortable, twirling the black telephone cord around her finger. "I'm a little rusty, I'm afraid."

"No, not at all. But I bet we could get some practice at Sallie's. Her parties are always a real gas. Now, she said you might put up a fuss but I should ignore that. She said to tell you she'll be awfully disappointed if you aren't there, and after the year you've had, you deserve to cut loose a little."

"You sound just like her!" Sallie was a terrible snob, but she did want Meg to be happy. They just had different ideas of what that looked like.

There was a lot of that going around these days.

"You know how Sallie is—she's liable to give you a real earful if you don't show up." Andy chuckled. "Jack's got his hands full with that one."

"Andy, I'm flattered, but—"

"She told me about your sister," Andy said, interrupting again.

Meg was stunned into silence.

"I'm real sorry for your loss, Meg. My kid sister, Mattie—she died a couple years back. It was a boating accident. It was . . . Well, it was rough. Especially at the holidays."

"Yes," Meg said softly. "I'm sorry to hear that. About Mattie, I mean."

"I hope you don't mind that I was asking about you," Andy continued. "You just . . . You seemed a little blue at the Grove. I know you said you had a good time and all, but I wasn't sure if I should call you again. Sallie said not to take it personal. She said you're still grieving. She knows I know what that's like, losing a sister myself and all. I came home a lot that semester to be with my folks. Ma especially—I knew she liked having me around. But then my dad sat me down and told me to go back to school. He said Mattie would want me to live my life. And I bet your sister would feel the same way. I understand if you're not up for a party, but I hope you'll at least think about it."

Meg hadn't expected *any* of this. Her mind was spinning. Beth hadn't gone to many parties herself, but she had waited up to hear about them when her sisters got home, eyes shining, hugging her doll to her chest.

"I—I guess so," Meg said uncertainly.

"Is that a yes?" Andy was persistent; Meg had to give him that. And he'd been surprisingly candid. Maybe there was more to him than she'd thought. Maybe Andy was someone she could talk to. As a friend. She didn't have very many of those these days.

"Sure," Meg said. "Yes."

"Great. I'll pick you up at seven. And . . . Meg?"

"Hmm?" Meg was already lost in her thoughts. What would she wear? She had a closet full of skirt-and-sweater sets from her college days and shirtwaist dresses perfect for teaching, but nothing fine enough for a party like this.

"I'm looking forward to it. See you."

"See you," Meg echoed, hanging up the receiver.

What had she gotten herself into?

She took a sip of her tea and was reading a short story by P. L. Travers in *Mademoiselle* when the telephone shrilled again. This time she didn't get her hopes up. It was late; Jo was probably already in bed if she had an early-morning shift.

"Good evening. March residence, Meg speaking."

There was a loud squeal at the other end of the line. "Meg! I heard you're coming to my party with Andy. I'm ever so glad! Let me loan you a dress. I have just the thing, and you deserve to wear something nice for once. You'll be an absolute vision!"

Meg hardly knew what to take offense at first. She had loads of nice dresses, just not evening gowns; it wasn't as though she had many occasions to wear one. Had Andy telephoned her from Sallie's? Had she talked him into it? Was this a *pity date*? "That's sweet of you, Sal—"

"I'm happy to do it. I'll drop it off on Friday afternoon after

168

school. But that's not why I called. Meg . . . guess who's going to be in Concord next week?" Sallie barely paused. Meg did not guess. "Jack's aunt Viola!"

She squealed again. Loudly. Meg held the receiver a few inches from her ear. "That's lovely. Are they close?"

"No, you dummy!" Sallie *haw*-hawed. "Jack could care less about his spinster aunt. But she's the headmistress at Plumley! I've invited her for tea, and I want you to come. Then when you apply for the position, she'll remember how lovely you are."

Meg sighed. "Sallie, I can't apply to Plumley. I can't leave my students midyear like that. And even if I wanted to"—she lowered her voice, glancing at the closed kitchen door—"I couldn't leave home. It wouldn't be right."

"That's hogwash. Why is it all right for your sisters to go off and live their lives, but not you?" Sallie demanded.

"It's *because* they've gone off that I can't. I couldn't leave Marmee here all alone." *Couldn't you?* the voice in the back of her head nagged. *Would Marmee really mind? Maybe she would prefer it.*

Sallie gave an unladylike snort. "What would she have to say about you turning down a marvelous opportunity like this to stay home with her? You said she was fine, on a thousand different volunteer committees!"

Meg eyed the door to the parlor. Sallie had a point. Tonight was the first time in ages that she and Marmee had eaten dinner together. Even over the Thanksgiving holiday, Marmee had kept plenty busy with various church committees, calling on friends who were ill or bereaved, volunteering at the Red Cross . . . Meg had barely seen her. When she did, Marmee was quiet. She answered Meg's questions but seldom asked any of her own. Meg had chalked it up to grief—this first holiday with only the two of them—but maybe it was more than that.

Maybe Marmee would prefer being on her own to being stuck with Meg.

"Meg? Are you still there?" Sallie asked.

"Yes," Meg said, choking back tears. "And, yes, I'll come to tea. Thank you, Sallie. Plumley—it sounds wonderful. Maybe getting away from home is just what I need."

Impulse

Impulsive Jo, passionate Amy
stumbling into lives of adventure
while you and I, Meg,
we stayed at home.

By choice or circumstance
it hardly mattered.
They couldn't be blamed
for their natures any more
than a cat can be blamed
for toying with a mouse.

Except sometimes
those natures led them
to sink a claw in,
drawing blood.
Burning manuscripts,
leaving a sister
to plunge through ice.

Saying,
    Anyone can be a mother.

Practice

I spoke to my dolls,
dressed them, brushed their hair,
sat them up for stories
and laid them down for bed,
long after my sisters
had given up their dolls.

I took in stray creatures,
stayed up nursing kittens,
fed them with bottles
like I'd never feed
an infant.

Not my own.

It wasn't practice
since I'd never play the role.
Not everyone can be a mother.

CHAPTER 14

JO

The week after Thanksgiving brought a dusting of snow. Anna ferried the shivering girls to the factory in her truck at half the speed she normally did, since some roads the plow had yet to reach.

"I never thought I'd see the day Anna would slow down," Molly said as they unloaded in the parking lot. Overhead, a plane was making its descent toward the airfield. Jo shaded her eyes with her hand, trying to identify it, but she still wasn't skilled enough at picking the different kinds out to recognize it from this far away. She should study more—maybe that'd impress Mr. Bates.

Before joining her friends, Jo stamped her scuffed fur-lined boots free of snow and wood chips. Jo and Anna had helped Mrs. Wilson haul a few truckloads of firewood from her brother's farm over to the house that weekend.

"Mr. Bates was asking me about you the other day, Jo," Ruth told her in the locker room.

"He was?"

"Well, he was asking about girls on the riveting line that I thought would be good for more complicated work," Ruth said. "I mentioned you."

"Ruth, thank you," Jo said. "Not that I'm not glad to be where I'm at," she added hastily. But Ruth smiled.

"I understand."

"Oh, Ruth?" Anna said. "If Mr. Bates asks again, do you think you could mention me? I know he values your opinion."

"You're interested?" Ruth asked Anna in surprise.

Anna shrugged into her coveralls, slipping the wide buttons into their places. "It's more money, right?"

Ruth nodded.

"Then I'm interested. I need to find a way to send more home. I'm up for anything."

"I bet we'd make a great corrugating team," Jo said, shooting a smile at Anna.

"Anna might be too petite for the machines that press the sheet metal," Ruth said tactfully. "But a small size means you can fit into places that the men typically can't. The men don't want to admit it, but smaller hands"—she held up her own—"can make some of the engine jobs quicker. I'll recommend you as well, Anna."

"You're a doll, Ruth." Anna placed a smacking kiss on Ruth's cheek, leaving behind a smear of pearly-pink lipstick. "My mother will be grateful."

"Work still hard to find for your father?"

Anna nodded. "He's a farmer at heart, but that land isn't what it used to be."

"Isn't that the case in so many places," Ruth said, with a regretful shake of her head.

Jo finished tying up her hair, feeling a frisson of excitement at the thought of moving from the buzz and monotony of riveting to the concentration of cutting and shaping metal. If anything could take her mind off things, it would be that.

The bell to signify the shift change clanged and the girls made their way down for the morning inspection before heading out onto the floor. The sound hit them at full blast, the pounding, erratic beat of the factory that rose and fell like a wave.

Taking her place on the riveting line next to Molly, Jo grabbed her buffer—they were clamping parts today, which required the pincerlike tool—and tried to ignore the twinge in her back from stacking the firewood that weekend. Turning her focus on her work and the long line of machine parts set in front of her, she found that the smooth handle of the buffer in her hand was almost a comfort.

"Do you really want to work with those big machines?" Molly asked as they began the repetitive task of clamping each piece together.

Press. Clamp. Hold. Push to the right. Press. Clamp. Hold. Push to the right.

"I heard the men talk about workers who've lost fingers or hands if the timing isn't perfect," one of Molly's friends added, a row down from them. Jo wondered if the girl had some wolf in her, her hearing was so good.

"Then I'll just have to be perfect," Jo tossed back.

She laughed, but Molly looked concerned. "You don't want to lose a finger, Jo!"

Jo shrugged. "It'd make for interesting dinner conversation."

There was a whistle, sharp and piercing, that made the girls' heads whip to the left, where Mrs. Harris, formidable in her kerchief and sensible oxfords, stood.

"Tuck in, girls. Transports coming through!" she called.

Almost as one, the girls crowded against the line they were working when men with heavy-duty carts full of supplies and engine parts began to wheel them down the center of the aisle.

"You would think they could do that *before* we came in, without disrupting our work," Molly muttered.

"That would require them to think our work is important," Jo pointed out.

"We only keep the planes and engine parts fixed together," Molly added sarcastically. "That's nothing at all."

The other girls on the line tittered as the carts rattled behind them.

Jo saw it coming a split second before the shout came. The strap holding one end of the metal rods snapped free, and the rods swung wide, making the cart wheels spin forward out of a man's grip. Molly was half turned toward Jo, the cart in her blind spot. Jo grabbed her hand and hauled her out of the way, and the cart crashed into Jo's side. The rods swung downward, and that was the last thing Jo saw for quite a few minutes.

She came to in pieces, as one does when delivered a hard knock on the head. Voices tuned in and out at first, making her temples pound. Her eyelids felt impossibly heavy, and she didn't even bother to try to open them after the first attempt.

"Give her some air!"

"That's *blood*, Anna! She doesn't need air; she needs an ambulance!"

"Get those carts out of here! Scram!"

"Mrs. Harris!"

"Where's Mr. Bates?"

"Where's Mrs. Harris? Oh, she'll be so angry!"

"Molly, calm down. This wasn't our fault!"

"Evelyn's right. This was the men's fault! They didn't secure the rods properly for transport, and now they've killed Jo!"

"They haven't killed anyone. My goodness, Molly, stop with the dramatics. Everyone step back. I need to check her. Josephine?"

Something strong and sharp filled her senses, and Jo's eyes flew open as she coughed away from the open bottle of iodine that Mrs. Harris had thrust under her nose as makeshift smelling salts.

Her head pounded something awful, and the gash on her forehead ached, but Mrs. Harris was right: she wasn't dead.

"There you are." Mrs. Harris smiled reassuringly, pressing a handkerchief against Jo's forehead. "Do you think you can get up?"

"I'm fine," Jo mumbled, trying to struggle to her elbows and failing when her head spun rather sickeningly.

"She needs a doctor, Mrs. Harris," Molly said.

"Of course she does," Mrs. Harris said. "Girls, no need to worry. I'll take care of Josephine. All of you need to get back to work." Gentle pressure under Jo's arms helped lift her to her feet. "Come with me."

Mrs. Harris took her to the locker room, where she kept pressing the handkerchief to Jo's head. "Can you hold this for me while I call the hospital?"

As off-kilter as she felt, the mention of the hospital sent a cold enough spear through Jo's heart to jolt her from her daze. "No hospital," she croaked out. "I'm fine, Mrs. Harris."

"My dear, you were unconscious, and that's quite the nasty cut on your forehead. You need—"

"A doctor. But no hospital. Please, Mrs. Harris."

The older woman's mouth twisted in thought. "Very well. I'll call a doctor to check you on-site. But I won't have you driving in this condition. Do you hear me?"

"Anna drives us to work," Jo said. "I don't."

"Well, I'll be driving you home after the doctor sees you, I suspect," Mrs. Harris said, making it sound like some sort of indictment. "Stay right here. I'll make the call. And I'll have to report this to Mr. Bates, you know."

There went any chance that Ruth's good word about Jo would get her on a corrugating team.

Jo leaned back against the lockers, the discomfort of the ridges against her sore back nothing compared to the aching in her head. Careful to keep the handkerchief against her throbbing forehead, she didn't dare pull it back to see the damage. Instead, she closed her eyes. She mustn't fall asleep, but couldn't resist resting her eyes. Just for a minute.

The blow and the pain that had followed seemed to have stripped her not just of her senses, but of her defenses. The inner ones that kept thoughts better buried. She drifted as she waited, skipping from the pained pauses during Marmee's calls to the grip of Laurie's hands in hers, his pleading eyes . . . of Beth, in that bed, so pale, so still.

No. She could not think of that. Anything but that.

But refusing to think of one sister . . . it led to thinking of another.

"What are you doing up here?" Meg's voice was light, and Jo's face had been turned from her, looking out the window, so Meg

hadn't seen it yet. But when she turned toward her sister, her eyes so red-rimmed, Meg's gentle expression changed.

"What happened?" Meg asked. "Why do you look like that?"

"Teddy loves me."

A curious smile played across her sister's face. "Of course he does. It's Teddy."

"He proposed."

Meg's eyes widened. "Jo! Oh my goodness. What did you say?"

Jo couldn't bear it; she had to look away, from her sister's wide eyes and the flair of happiness in them.

"I don't love him like that," she said, and it wasn't just to Meg. It was to the world outside this window. It was to herself.

A truth she had always known.

One she had never run from. That had to mean something, didn't it? It had to.

"No, you must. You two are thick as thieves," Meg said in protest.

"No. Not like that," Jo said firmly, a contradiction in four words, the shutting of a door on a hope that everyone but her seemed to hold.

Did everyone see their own version of her, instead of the girl she was and always had been?

"Jo?"

It wasn't Meg's voice in her ear. It was Mrs. Harris, gently prodding her shoulder. "The doctor's here."

Wincing and shaky, Jo succumbed to the doctor's ministrations with an uncharacteristic meekness. By the time her forehead was stitched up (just three stitches, the doctor said; nothing to worry about too much), she'd been ordered to stay home for the rest of the week, with instructions for someone to monitor her for the next few days.

"Do I really have to rest for the whole week?" Jo protested

as Mrs. Harris helped her to her car, which seemed like a Rolls-Royce compared to Anna's beat-up truck, even though it was just a simple Ford.

"I don't know many girls who would complain about getting to miss work," Mrs. Harris observed as she pulled out of the parking lot and checked the slip of paper Jo had written the boardinghouse address on.

"I probably don't even have a concussion. Mr. Bates will think I'm a weakling."

"Mr. Bates has been informed that you pushed your friend out of the way and blocked the cart with your own body, preventing further injuries. He is the one who told me to make sure you rest up, so that when you come back, you can start training on the more complicated machinery."

Jo's heart twisted with hope. "You're not pulling my leg?"

"My dear, I don't do that," Mrs. Harris said, and it must've been the blow to the head, because it made Jo laugh like it was a real joke. "Mr. Bates likes tenacity and quick thinking. You showed both today. You didn't lose your head when you saw the cart coming at you, and you prioritized the weakest link— Molly is very sweet, but she talks so fast I fear she doesn't hear half of the things that go on around her. She could've been speared by those rods. You very likely saved her life."

Jo flushed, which made her head throb further. "I don't know about that."

"I've seen my share of accidents on the floor," Mrs. Harris said. "You have not."

"Point taken," Jo said, properly cowed. "Can I ask how you got into this line of work?" She shifted in the seat of the Ford, trying to find a position that didn't make her whole body ache.

Whatever excitement and thrill the danger had caused to pulse through her had started to fade, her aches and pains becoming more apparent with each breath.

"I was Mr. Bates's secretary before we started increasing production," Mrs. Harris said. "Once it was realized they'd need to start hiring women, I was asked to be in charge of the girls. Mr. Bates hasn't stopped complaining about losing me to the floor since."

Jo grinned. "Do you like the floor better than the office?"

"It's a lot more walking," Mrs. Harris allowed. "But I'm good at managing. I was the oldest of twelve."

"I'd let out a whistle, but I'm afraid my head will hurt," Jo said, which made Mrs. Harris smile as she took the turn onto Peach Street, where the boardinghouse stood. She pulled into the driveway and got out, opening the door for Jo and helping her inside.

"Why don't you go upstairs, and I'll have a quick chat with the head of the house," Mrs. Harris said.

Jo inched up the creaky boardinghouse stairs as she heard the murmur of Mrs. Harris greeting Mrs. Wilson. By the time she got to her door, her head was aching even more fiercely than before. Maybe a day or two of rest *would* be good. But the rest of the week was still absurd.

"Jo?"

Jo winced at the sound. She turned slowly to see Charlie standing in the doorway of Peg's room.

"You're home early."

"Little accident," Jo said, gesturing to her forehead.

"My God." In seconds, Charlie had closed the space between them, her hand cupping Jo's face gently. "What happened?"

"Some rods got too close to my forehead," Jo said. "I just need to rest."

"What you *need*," said a warm but scolding voice at the end of the hall, "is to be monitored closely for signs of a concussion."

Mrs. Wilson had arrived, having been briefed by Mrs. Harris. Jo flushed guiltily at the thought of causing so much fuss.

"I'm really fine," she insisted. "I'm not concussed. I'm just tired."

Mrs. Wilson tutted. "I'm going to bring you a tray with tea, straightaway," she said. "Do you want me to call your family, or do you want to tell them yourself?"

"I'll phone when my head doesn't hurt so much," Jo said. "The sound . . . it hurts." She attempted to look pitiful then, hoping it would lead to less fussing, but Mrs. Wilson wouldn't be dissuaded from caretaking.

"I'll be right back with that tea," she said. "The factories are so dangerous. I worry about you girls."

She bustled away, muttering to herself, and Jo leaned against the fading rose-papered wall, feeling more than a little faded herself.

"Why don't I sit with you?" Charlie suggested. "I won't make a peep."

"I just said noise hurt so she wouldn't push me about calling home," Jo said, the stress of the day loosening her tongue horribly. But Charlie had the grace not to ask any questions as Jo opened the door to her room and beckoned her inside.

"You've got Peg's old room," Charlie observed as she strolled in.

"So I've heard."

Jo collapsed as gently as she could on her bed, wanting desperately to curl up in her blankets and sleep for a year. She toed off her heavy boots, two clunks on the worn rug, and stretched out with a sigh.

"Can I?" Charlie gestured to the chipped vanity, and Jo nodded, flushing when she realized her stockings were still tossed over the mirror. She'd left her clothes at work. Hopefully, one of the girls would bring them home.

Jo closed her eyes, grateful for the silence, until she heard the rustle of paper and she realized what else was on the vanity. Eyes snapping open, alarm filled her when she saw that Charlie's elbow was inches away from a stack of paper that was one of the last stories she wrote before . . .

"This your work?" Charlie asked, glancing down at it, but then fixing her gaze back on Jo.

Jo nodded again.

"Don't worry, I won't snoop," Charlie said. "It would seem like taking terrible advantage, even if I am curious. I always hated it when my sisters tried to read my work before it was finished."

"One of mine burned an entire manuscript once," Jo said.

"On purpose?"

"She was very mad at me."

"And you two still talk?" Charlie asked, eyes wide.

Jo shrugged. "I suppose I got back at her, even if I didn't mean to. The first boy she ever had a crush on proposed to me, though I don't think she knows of it."

Charlie's thin brows rose, her mouth pursing. "Jo March, you seem to be unable to escape adventure, be it romantic or catastrophic."

"This is one adventure I wish I could've dodged," Jo said, touching the stitches on her forehead.

"I didn't realize you were engaged," Charlie said.

"I'm not," Jo replied.

"If he broke your heart, I hate him," Charlie offered, and it made Jo smile.

"He didn't, so no need."

"Well, now I *really* want to hear the story. Were *you* the heartbreaker?"

"I suppose I was," Jo said, with a twinge of realization. The memory of Teddy's crumpled expression, the defeat and hurt in his face, hit her like it was fresh again. "I didn't mean to be. I didn't even know he . . ." Her eyes burned, and then so did her throat; it was like a weight being pressed on her chest.

"I've touched a nerve," Charlie said hastily. "I'm sorry for ribbing you. I shouldn't have. You've been through an ordeal."

"I guess it's just complicated," Jo confessed. "And confusing."

"Why?"

"Because he's the boy I grew up with. He's as good as family. But I didn't realize he wanted to make *us* a family. And when he proposed, I felt . . ." She trailed off, trying to find the right word for that horrified lurch in her stomach when he'd pressed his lips against her hands and then said, *Marry me, Jo.* She couldn't quite settle on one. "It was just not what I expected," she said slowly. "Not what I wanted."

"What *do* you want?" Charlie asked, like it was a question that had a simple or easy answer.

But before Jo could scoff or dodge or lie in answer, there was a knock at her door and Mrs. Wilson saved her the trouble by arriving with the tea.

Later, when Jo found herself alone in her room, between Mrs. Wilson's routine checks to make sure she hadn't fallen into some sort of coma or seizure, she found she could not escape the thoughts she had worked so hard to avoid. Still aching and wishing more than ever that she could lay her head in her mother's lap and sob, she had to fight back the urge to cry every few minutes. Finally unable to bear it any longer, she dragged herself out of bed, still wrapped in her blanket to ward off the chill. Tucking her feet underneath herself in the rickety chair, the end of her pen in her mouth, she stared at the notebook on her vanity, the empty page beckoning.

There *was* a word for it. That lurch she'd felt, when Teddy had begged her to see things his way. To just trust him. To love him. To marry him.

What was it? Not sadness. Not anger or frustration.

Her hand was writing the word before she was fully thinking it. And then there it was, in ink and paper.

Betrayal.

His confession had been a lifted burden and then a heartbreak for him.

His proposal had led to a realization that shook the marrow of her.

She had thought he had seen her. As sure as her name was March and the sky was blue, she'd always thought Theodore Laurence didn't just *see* her but valued her. For who she was—as difficult and strange and ornery as that girl was—and for how she thought.

But then she found herself in that train station, seeing him off for training. The hustle of the crowd and goodbyes were all around them as he promised to be a saint to her. He talked of love and other people's expectations in the same breath, like the latter had ever mattered to her, let alone him.

Had he ever seen her? Or had he seen his vision of her, some version where she didn't say what she meant and played games she *never* would if she loved someone?

Because she *did* love him.

She just didn't want him. Not like he wanted and loved the Jo he thought she was.

Jo could not pretend. It's why she left home. Meg was the one with the flair for the stage, not her, and eventually, her family would've realized just how broken she'd found herself. Meg already suspected.

What are you so scared of, Jo?

She traced her finger over the word she'd scribbled in the notebook, drawing out each letter, lingering on the *l*.

What do *you want?* Charlie had asked her earlier.

Was it that she didn't know?

Or that she didn't want to admit it to herself?

With a trembling hand, she flipped to a new page in the notebook.

Dear Teddy,

I don't know if this letter will be welcome. I cannot blame you if it isn't, though I cannot help but blame you for other things, maybe unfairly. But when have *I* been some great torchbearer of what is fair? My life is a study of the world not being so.

I have cursed you and that day and that <u>damnable</u> question you cornered me into answering, so many times. I hurt you, I know it, and maybe you hate me for turning down your proposal, even now.

Or perhaps, with this time and an ocean and war between us, you have seen my side of it a little in this secret battle we've found ourselves in. Is that too much to hope? Too selfish? Desperate, even?

I am all those things. Hopeful and selfish and desperate. Because you are my _dearest_ friend and I THOUGHT I was yours, and now I worry that we are nothing. And if we are nothing, not family, not even friends, then did my friendship mean so little?

I don't want to think so. But life has been so terribly unfair to both of us in different ways that I fear that it is so.

—Jo

Betrayal

Believing what he wanted
Even though your
True self had been there
Right in front of him
All along.
You're so close,
Almost ready for
Love.

Blame

It's easier for me now
to see you as you are
from this place where I find myself
outside a world of expectations.

But I promise,
if you let them,
the ones who matter
will see you too.

Is it quite fair
to blame them
for failing to see
what you haven't
been willing to show?

CHAPTER 15

AMY

"You're out past curfew, you know," Laurie said, loudly enough so that Amy could hear him above the Savoy's band.

Amy almost laughed. Didn't he realize how ridiculous he sounded? She didn't need a chaperone like some character out of an 1800s novel. Laurie ought to remember what century they lived in. A young woman like her could stay out late and dance with whomever she pleased.

"Heaven forbid!" she said dramatically, pressing a hand against her cheek in feigned shock. "Will you have me court-martialed, Lieutenant?"

Laurie drew a step closer. "Amy," he said with a frown, "you said you wouldn't break curfew."

"I don't believe I signed a contract and, as you can see, I'm perfectly fine." She threaded her hand around Marcel's elbow and couldn't help but notice how it made Laurie's jaw twitch. "I'm simply enjoying a drink with a new friend."

"Is this fellow giving you trouble, *chérie*?" Marcel asked as he curled a hand around her waist possessively. In response, Amy sighed and tried to angle her body away from his, but his grip was as firm as a viper's.

A fire lit in Laurie's eyes. "There's going to be trouble if you keep manhandling her like that," he warned Marcel.

This time, Amy's eyes widened with genuine shock. The Laurie that she knew was almost always genial, the type of person who played pranks on his tutor and tugged on Amy's hair to make her laugh. She'd never seen this side of him before.

"I have this under control, Laurie," she told him under her breath. She'd gotten plenty of practice dealing with soldiers who got a little too touchy. Most of the enlisted men were very gentlemanly when they interacted with the Red Cross workers, but a few of the officers had gotten aggressive at the get-togethers that Amy and the other Clubmobile girls were expected to attend.

Marcel released her suddenly so that he could stand nose to nose with Laurie. "Do you know who my father is?"

"Let me guess. Is he a handsy drunk like his son?" Laurie said right back.

Amy watched, speechless, as everything unfurled from there.

Marcel grabbed Laurie by the collar while Laurie launched a fist into the Belgian's side. The hit had little effect, though. Marcel might've been halfway soused, but he also had at least twenty pounds on Laurie and soon wrestled him to the floor.

"Stop it, you dolts!" Amy cried. But the boys kept tussling and slinging punches, and she knew she would have to do something.

As Marcel pulled his arm back to clock Laurie in the nose, she entered the fray, shoving her weight against Marcel to throw him off balance. She figured that would be enough to knock some sense into him, but he had the audacity to try to push her away. Out of instinct alone, she slapped him across the cheek.

Now, *that* certainly got their attention. Marcel cradled his face with a whimper while Laurie just stared at her, stunned. At that exact moment, Amy looked around and realized that they had an audience. The whole room had fallen silent—even the band had stopped playing. Everyone had taken notice of them, including a pair of beefy bouncers who were elbowing their way through the crowd. One of them laid a thick hand on Amy's shoulder while the other jerked Laurie to his feet.

"You two better come with us," the bouncer said.

"Hold on, what about him?" Amy said, pointing at Marcel.

"He's a guest of the hotel," the bouncer said curtly before he escorted her and Laurie out of the room and across the lobby floor.

"Wait a second! Are you tossing us out?" Amy said, right before the guards did just that, shoving them both into the cold.

She let out an exasperated huff—the nerve of those men!—before she started pounding on the door, but Laurie stopped her.

"It's no use," he said.

"No thanks to you, Theodore Laurence!" She whirled around, ready to let him have it, until she saw how his left eye was bruising and how he was clutching at his side, right where he'd had his appendectomy. Her fury quickly shifted into worry. "Did you pop a stitch?"

"Feels like it." He unbuttoned his blazer to reveal his white dress shirt underneath. "How does it look?"

"You're bleeding!" she said, noting a few droplets of blood on the fabric.

Laurie lifted up his shirt to survey the damage, and Amy

balked at the wound there. It was four inches long and, sure enough, he had pulled a couple of stitches.

"Will I live, Doctor?" he quipped. A chilly wind blew in, breathing goose bumps over his skin, and Amy snapped her eyes away when she realized that she'd been staring. She wasn't sure why her mouth had gone so dry. She'd seen Laurie without a shirt dozens of times before, thanks to all the days that she'd gone swimming with him and her sisters at the Concord city pool. This situation wasn't that different, aside from the weather. And the fact that they were thousands of miles from home. And that they were alone.

Amy cleared her throat. "Chances are fifty-fifty, soldier."

"My superiors are going to kill me," he murmured as he tucked his shirt back into his trousers. "They want me back at the airfield as soon as possible."

She planted a hand on her hip, reminding herself that she was still mad at him. "You should've thought about that before you got into an unnecessary fistfight tonight."

"Unnecessary? That knucklehead was trying to maul you!"

"Hardly, and I could've handled it," she retorted. "Do you know why I came to the Savoy? Because I wanted just one night to dance and laugh and forget about the war." *And my sisters,* she said to herself. "But then you had to follow me here and get me tossed out."

"I—I didn't do it on purpose!" he stammered.

"How did you even find me here?"

He dragged his fingers through his hair and admitted, "I stopped by your billet, all right? One of the girls mentioned that you went to the Savoy."

"I was managing just fine before you arrived." She motioned

at herself. "Take a good look, Laurie. Do I seem like a kid to you?"

He went quiet and followed her orders, his eyes taking her in slowly, and something seemed to shift on his face. Amy blinked, feeling shy all of a sudden, and crossed her arms.

"I'm going home," she announced. "Good night."

She'd made it only half a block, though, when she heard his footsteps behind her, which made her feel simultaneously irritated and pleased. Without turning around, she said, "You ought to get to the hospital and have those stitches of yours looked at."

"It's only a scratch. Doesn't even hurt." He caught up to her and sucked in a long breath. "Look, I'm sorry."

Amy felt a tug at her heart, that traitorous thing, but she wouldn't let him off that easily. "For?"

"For ruining your night."

"That's all you're sorry for?"

He jammed his hands into his pockets. "And for treating you like a kid, okay? Although in my defense, we're living in a war zone. London isn't Concord. I was worried about you."

She glanced up to search his face. He had sounded sincere, not patronizing, but she wasn't ready to call a truce yet. "It's funny you should say that when you're the one flying across the Channel on nighttime air raids."

"True, but the risk comes with the job. I knew that when I signed on the line."

"I could say the same about mine," Amy replied smartly.

That made Laurie go quiet again, but it didn't stop him from following her. She made a turn when they reached the next road, with the River Thames flowing to their left and a city garden growing wild on their right. The park had been redesigned into a little farm to raise fruits and vegetables to supplement the war rations. Even the iron fence surrounding the grounds had been plucked out like teeth to melt down for parts. No corner of London had escaped the shadow of battle, including the streetlights.

"Oof, sorry," Amy said. Her toe had caught on the pavement and she bumped into Laurie. They had only moonlight to guide their way, thanks to the citywide blackout, and it wasn't long before he nearly tripped over himself. If Amy hadn't caught his elbow in time, he would've planted his nose right there on the road.

"We'd better link arms," Amy said. "That's how the other girls and I manage to get around after dark without falling onto our faces."

"Before curfew, you mean?" he said, a smile in his voice.

"Oh, go jump in the river, Laurie," she replied, but there was a smile in her voice, too.

So that was how they carried on, arm in arm and side by side. And even though Amy hadn't quite forgiven him yet about the Savoy, she had to admit that a moonlight stroll with him wasn't a terrible way to cap her night.

Suddenly, she heard him laugh.

"What's so funny?" she asked.

"I was thinking about the look on that French fella's face when you left your fingerprints on his cheek. I swear I'll remember that until the day I die."

Amy smirked. "He was Belgian, actually."

"Belgian or French, he deserved it. Say, where'd you learn to hit like that?"

"I must be a natural, although I did ask Fred to teach me

how to punch someone once." She had gotten the idea after they'd watched *The Maltese Falcon* together, in particular the scene where Humphrey Bogart's character had knocked the daylights out of Wilmer. Amy figured that a girl ought to know how to defend herself like that, but Fred had chuckled and said that she'd probably break a nail and that, anyway, he'd be happy to protect her. She supposed that was the chivalrous thing to say, but it had chafed at her.

"You mean Fred Vaughn?" asked Laurie. His head whipped toward hers. "How's he doing, by the way?"

"Still in naval training, but he'll be shipping out to the Pacific in a few weeks."

"Are the two of you . . . ?"

"Nothing official." *For now.* Amy had gotten the impression that Fred desired more out of their relationship, but she wasn't sure how she felt about that, which confused her. Fred was everything she should want, wasn't he? He was easygoing, not to mention easy on the eyes, and his family's money sure didn't hurt, either. So why wasn't she wishing that Fred were here in London instead of Laurie? Amy had to wonder if there was something wrong with her heart.

"Meg told me once that Fred was a real catch," Laurie said.

"That sounds like something she would say," Amy admitted. Meg had mentioned more than once how respectable and polite Fred was. Jo, on the other hand . . . Without thinking, Amy blurted out, "Jo thinks that Fred is far too dull."

Laurie bit back a laugh. "Can't say that I agree, but that does sound like something Jo would say." He slowed to a stop to look out at the Thames, watching the moonlight over the water. "How's she doing these days?"

"Haven't you heard? She's working at a factory in Connecticut and making airplanes," Amy said, recalling the update from one of Marmee's letters.

"Jo March with a wrench and a drill bit?" He sounded a bit bewildered. "I guess I shouldn't be surprised. I can't see her staying in Concord and tending to the home fires."

Amy flicked a glance his way and wondered all over again what exactly had happened between him and her sister. The two of them used to be practically inseparable, but then Jo refused to talk about him after she saw his train off. Had Laurie asked Jo to be his girl and she had turned him down? Or was it the other way around? Amy didn't feel brave or brash enough to ask him.

Up ahead, they spotted Piccadilly Circus. Despite the late hour, the place was abuzz with young Londoners and American GIs looking for a good time. Many of them had flocked to the Red Cross's Rainbow Corner club, which was open twenty-four hours a day and always bustling with its rec rooms and snack bar. Amy and Edie had spent a few evenings there already, dancing and playing pinball and chatting with the troops over burgers and waffles, a real taste of home.

Come to think of it, Amy was parched after all this walking. "You thirsty?" she asked. "I could use a Coke."

"It's getting pretty late," Laurie said with a shake of his head.

Amy tried to ignore the disappointment she felt. Would he have turned Jo down?

But then he said, "When's your next day off?"

"Monday, actually. Why do you ask?"

"If you don't have plans, I'd like to make up for the fact that I got you thrown out of the fanciest hotel in London. How about I stop by around five? We could make an evening out of it."

Something zipped through Amy's belly, something that felt a lot like excitement, but she tried to sound nonchalant. "Well, I suppose that's only fair."

He grinned at her ribbing. "We could visit the National Gallery if you'd like. They've been holding concerts there with Myra Hess at the piano, and after that, we could see the picture of the month."

Amy bit her tongue to keep herself from blurting *Sign me up, soldier!* The Gallery had all but closed when the war broke out, but following the end of the Blitz, the staff had deemed it safe enough to take a prized painting out of storage every few weeks and put it out on public display, dubbing it the "picture of the month" exhibit. Amy had narrowly missed the chance to view Rembrandt's self-portrait, and she was itching to find out which painting had replaced it.

But it didn't matter. She hadn't visited the museum and had no plans to do so. She was a Clubmobile girl now; she'd put her art long behind her.

"Why don't we go to Claridge's for tea instead?" she offered, looking at the pavement.

This took him by surprise. "You're turning down the chance to visit a world-renowned art institution?"

"It's lady's choice, isn't that right? And I'm in the mood for tea and biscuits."

Laurie chuckled. "Tea and biscuits, it is." Then he offered his arm to her again so that they could make their way through the crowd. "See you soon," he said as he escorted her to the Hotel Royale. "And why don't you wear something nice? We'll make a night out of it, if that sounds good to you."

It sounded more than good—it sounded absolutely splendid, as the Brits might say—but Amy reined in her enthusiasm. "You keep yourself out of trouble until then," she replied. "Don't get thrown out of any more classy establishments, do you hear?"

"As long as you stay away from the Belgians," he said with a grin.

After she watched him disappear into the shadows, Amy turned around, and it felt like she was floating up the steps to the front door. All things considered, her evening hadn't turned out so badly after all.

Over the next day and a half, Amy had plenty to keep her busy, from making doughnuts to catching up on laundry to writing letters home about her grand life in Montreal. Meg's letters kept pestering her to send more details about the city and asking if Amy had been on any dates or if she was holding out for Fred. Interestingly, Meg had mentioned very little about John. Amy couldn't exactly blame Meg for that, since she *had* called him a boring old fuddy-duddy, which made her groan looking back on it. But she'd been so angry! Meg always took Jo's side. Amy would bet money that the two of them were swapping letters twice a week, sharing their secrets and all the gossip per usual.

Thank goodness she had Edie.

And Laurie.

Amy's face flushed whenever she thought about him. She told herself that he hadn't asked her on a real date and she'd be silly to think that was the case, but she couldn't help but plan her outfit anyway. He *did* say to wear something nice. And so she asked Edie to curl her hair like Hedy Lamarr's in *Ziegfeld*

Girl, and she begged Gloria up on the third floor to borrow her aubergine dress with the sweetheart neckline.

She'd show Laurie that she definitely wasn't a kid anymore.

But on the morning of her day off, Amy awoke to a sharp knock on the door. Scrambling out of bed, she opened it to find another Red Cross girl standing with a package in hand.

"This was left for you on the steps," the girl said before hurrying off to start her shift.

Amy's heart thumped at the sight when she realized that the package was from Laurie. Had he gotten her a gift? She ripped open the envelope taped to the box, giving the note inside a skim, and her stomach promptly plummeted toward the floor.

"Who was at the door?" Edie said with a yawn. When she saw the look on Amy's face, she sat up straight. "Everything all right?"

Amy walked numbly toward Edie's bunk. "Laurie got called up to the airfield. He received word about it last night and had to leave this morning," she said, a swell of emotions overtaking her—surprise, shock, unease. Laurie was heading back into the cockpit. Back into danger.

"He'll be all right. Our boys are the bravest in the world, and our planes are top-notch," Edie assured her, although Amy couldn't help but think about Edie's cousin Bobby, who'd died at age nineteen. The US Navy, despite all its might, hadn't been able to protect him.

"Would you two mind keeping it down a bit?" Marion said sleepily from her bed.

"Yes, Your Majesty," Edie muttered, although Marion didn't hear her since she had already rolled over. To Amy, she said,

"Look on the bright side—he got you a present! What do you think it could be? Not flowers. And that parcel is much too big for a ring."

"Edith Barnett!" Amy said with a startled laugh. "He's not even my beau."

"You better open that box before I do it myself. I'm dying of curiosity over here."

Amy tore open the package to find a bundle of charcoal drawing sticks and a leather sketchbook that must've cost a mint on an airman's salary. There was a short note accompanying them, too.

I'm kindly commissioning a few drawings from Captain Pace to hang on the blank wall next to my bunk. I can provide payment in the form of high tea, biscuits, and excellent conversation during my next R&R.

Edie's nose wrinkled at the sight of the supplies. "I was hoping for something more romantic, like chocolates or perfume. Do you even draw?"

"A little," Amy murmured as she dragged a finger down the soft leather cover of the sketchbook. Laurie must've traveled all around London to find these gifts, since so many items had been rationed, but he had put in the effort—for her.

For the first time in a long time, Amy wanted to draw. To make something with her hands.

But that was an itch she couldn't scratch—not even for Laurie. She'd sworn off art, and she'd better swear him off too while she was at it. For all she knew, he still saw her as a kid. As Jo's little sister.

Launching onto her feet, Amy shoved Laurie's gift into her drawer and whipped around to face Edie. "Why don't we go take pictures by Marble Arch today? We've been meaning to do that for weeks."

"Sure thing," Edie said. "But not until we've had breakfast. I'm starved."

The two of them got dressed and were making their way down the stairs toward the scent of toast and jam when they ran straight into Supervisor Owens.

"Just the girls I've been looking for," said Owens, who was holding a mop in one hand and a bucket in the other. She urged Amy and Edie to take them.

"Good morning," Amy said, baffled. "It's our day off—"

"I'm well aware of that, but I've also been alerted to the fact that the two of you made quite the spectacle of yourselves at the Savoy last week."

Amy had to grip the banister. "How did you hear about that?"

"Never mind how I know. The point is that you've sullied the good reputation of the American Red Cross and that can't be ignored."

"B-but let me explain!" Amy couldn't believe this. Who had ratted her out? "And you can't blame Edie for what happened. She didn't do a thing."

But Supervisor Owens held firm. She pressed the mop into Amy's hand and the bucket into Edie's. "Get to work in the kitchen. After you're done with that, you can tackle the windows."

Penance

Marmee once made Amy clean windows
as penance for stealing streusel muffins
cooling on the windowsill and pilfering them
to share with the girls at school.

Amy maintained she'd taken them
out of a generous, benevolent spirit
and therefore should not be punished.
Marmee stood firm, as we all knew she would.

What even Marmee couldn't know
was how Amy's righteous indignation
would cause her hand with dirty rag
to smack against the glass so hard

the window would crack
and we would all shiver through
a drafty winter until the funds
could be gathered to repair it.

Luck

We make our own luck, Marmee would say
while Father gazed out the window,
seeing not the crack but the clouds outside
arranging themselves into visions
of his next grand plan.

A utopian farm on unfertile ground.
A school so revolutionary no one would enroll.
Discussions of philosophy with the great thinkers of
    the day.

Marmee loved him for those plans—we all did.
But I saw from my perch on the couch
how while he dreamed
she took the steps to keep our family afloat.
His visions didn't repair the crack. Ideas didn't feed us.

Marmee did that, and even Jo,
who spun tales out of nothing
like Father,
but different, for Jo honed her talent
into a skill that would fix the broken glass.

CHAPTER 16

MEG

Andy picked Meg up at seven on the dot for Sallie's Christmas party.

"We got lucky, huh, kid?" he said as he slid behind the wheel of his jazzy blue Ford Super Deluxe convertible coupe.

Meg nodded. She didn't care for being called "kid"—Andy was only a few years older than she was—but it felt petty to object in the face of real calamity. The war had taken a temporary back seat; the local papers were full of the tragedy at the Cocoanut Grove. Last Saturday, a terrible fire had started in the basement lounge in an artificial palm tree, and it had spread quickly. The crowd had been trapped inside after the revolving door onto the street got jammed. Over four hundred people were dead, and hundreds more badly injured.

"It's awful." To think they'd danced there only a few weeks ago!

"You know, there was supposed to be a party at the Grove that night to celebrate Boston College going to the Sugar Bowl. Jack and I talked about going. But BC lost to Holy Cross—it was a real upset—and nobody was in a party mood. Jack and

I went to a pub to drink away our sorrows with some of our Alpha Sigma Nu brothers. We heard the fire alarms, and saw the smoke when we left, but we had no idea it was the Grove."

"Well, thank God the Eagles lost," Meg said.

"I wouldn't go that far," Andy joked, his eyes darting to Meg, then back to the road. "I heard they're still identifying the victims. The gals are harder, because lots of 'em got separated from their handbags."

What a gruesome thought. Meg shivered and squeezed her beaded black clutch. "This is a lovely car. I bet it's fun with the top down!"

"Yeah, she's a real beaut." Silence fell between them, and Meg smoothed her red skirt over her knees. Sallie had dropped the dress off yesterday after school, getting in half a dozen little digs in the process. But it had a black camisole bodice with a long torso that flowed into a full skirt, and Meg felt as glamorous as Ingrid Bergman. She was wearing her best heels, black suede peep-toe pumps. Her caramel curls were arranged in painstaking Victory rolls, and her lips were painted rosy red with Crimson Glory.

"So, you're the only one left at home, huh?" Andy asked.

Meg nodded. "Do you have any brothers or sisters? Besides Mattie."

"Two older brothers. They'd already left home when Mattie passed. It was easier on them, I think, being out of the house."

"I know just what you mean! I'm envious of my sisters sometimes." It was a relief to say it out loud. "I don't particularly want to leave Concord. This is my home. Only . . . it doesn't feel like home anymore, without Beth. Without Jo and Amy and Father."

"What about that job Sallie keeps flapping her gums about?"

"I've been thinking about it. Sallie invited me to tea next week with Jack's aunt, the headmistress. But I'm not sure I should leave home. Even if I came back on weekends . . . I worry about my mother. My sisters are in Canada and Connecticut now." Meg hesitated. "Everyone's always saying how marvelous it is that Jo's doing her part, how *modern* of her, and it is—I really think it is!—but I suppose sometimes I feel the tiniest bit . . . trapped. And unappreciated."

But was it a trap of her own making? Would Marmee *prefer* an empty nest? Meg still didn't know, and there was no one to ask, to fret over the change in Marmee with her. Sometimes she resented her sisters for running off and leaving her at home—to face their absence every single day, in addition to Beth's. To face the sadness in Marmee's eyes and the dust on the piano and the constant reminders.

"*I* appreciate you, doll," Andy flirted, and annoyance crept over Meg. He must have seen it on her face, because he backtracked. "Nah, I hear you. I got a two-A deferment, because of working at the light plant. Civilian occupation in support of national health, safety, or interest. But I could still get called up in a couple months, and I know it'd be rough on Ma. The last thing she needs is all three of us overseas. I'm no coward, but maybe it's better I stay here in Concord, huh?"

Was he fishing for Meg to say she'd miss him if he went away?

"Well, we can do our part right here in the meantime, can't we?" she said brightly. She and Andy were not kindred spirits, but she felt better for having confessed her selfish thoughts. Maybe he did, too.

"I've bought a lot of war bonds, that's for sure." Andy

laughed. "Every time I get to feeling guilty for not fighting the Ratzis like my brothers, I go out and buy another one."

Meg couldn't help comparing his outlook with John's. As a teacher, John could have deferred service, too. But he'd reasoned that enlisting in June—and being able to choose his branch of service—was better than potentially getting called up in the middle of the term. Of course he hadn't wanted to leave Meg, or his mother (he was her only son), but he felt it was the honorable thing to do, and the practical thing. Meg admired that.

"Wow-ee," Andy said as they pulled up to the Gardiners' white-columned mansion on the outskirts of Concord. Meg was surprised to find music and laughter and light spilling out from every room in the house. There was no need for a blackout this far inland, although Concord had held its share of drills: air-raid sirens wailing and wardens patrolling the neighborhood as streetlights were extinguished, citizens snapped down the blinds, and motorists pulled over and took cover. But there was still a war on, and they were all meant to conserve where they could.

Andy helped Meg out of the car and tossed his keys to a valet. There was a steady stream of young people coming and going, women in fur stoles and long evening dresses, men in smart black dinner jackets with wide silk lapels and nipped-in waists, starched white shirts, and snowy pocket squares. Meg was grateful that Sallie had loaned her the dress, even if she'd offered in her usual tactless way.

Inside, tuxedoed waiters carried trays of champagne and hors d'oeuvres. An orchestra played on a bandstand laden with hothouse flowers while couples twirled to a Glenn Miller tune. Chandeliers threw glittering pools of light across the dancers. In one corner, an enormous fir—why, it had to be ten feet high!—was festooned with silver and gold ornaments and sprinkled with tinsel. Fairy lights wound up the banisters of the grand staircase.

Meg was breathless with the beauty of it, and discomfited by the excess.

"Meg, darling!" Sallie came to greet them and handed her a glass of champagne. "You look marvelous. My dress really suits you. Isn't she stunning, Andy?"

"She's a real beaut," Andy agreed.

Meg frowned. Hadn't he said the exact same thing about his car? She took a long sip of champagne.

"The two of you make such a lovely couple. I *knew* it!" Sallie clapped her hands in self-congratulation. A diamond tennis bracelet sparkled on her gloved wrist. "Meg, let me introduce you to my friend Kate. She's very influential in the Daughters of the American Revolution. Andy, go and get yourself a drink! Jack's over at the bar."

As Andy headed across the room, Sallie leaned in close, her sugared breath cool against Meg's cheek. "He fancies you. I can tell. I'm glad you decided to give him another chance."

Sallie seemed awfully invested in her matchmaking; Meg hated to tell her Andy had no chance at all. "It's not like that, Sallie. I—"

"Oh! There's someone here I think you know." Sallie looped her arm through Meg's and hauled her toward a familiar figure. "Helen! Look, it's Meg. The two of you work together, don't you?"

Meg stared at Helen Gagnon in mute mortification. It had never occurred to her that she might run into anyone from school. Sallie ran with such a different crowd; her friends were more likely to get their Mrs. degrees than teaching certificates!

"Hello, Meg. What a surprise!" Helen was wearing a slinky black dress that hugged her curves. With her long blond hair in a peekaboo style, she looked straight out of a Hollywood noir.

"Meg's here with our friend Andy Fitzhugh. And Helen came with Jack's friend Lloyd Bartlett," Sallie prattled on.

"Hi, Helen." Meg was sure her colleague must be wondering what she was doing here with a man who wasn't John Brooke. She wanted to sink right through the parquet floor.

"I thought you two must know each other; the high school isn't that big," Sallie said. "But hopefully, Meg won't be in that dreadful place much longer, if everything goes according to our little plan."

Helen raised her thin, arched eyebrows. "Oh? What little plan is that?"

Meg flushed. "It's nothing, really."

"Meg's being modest, as usual. She's applying to a position at Plumley," Sallie explained. "Jack's aunt is the headmistress, and if he puts in a good word, Meg's a shoo-in!"

Only if Jack put in a good word, huh? That needled Meg. Why couldn't Sallie keep her big mouth shut? The last thing Meg wanted was word getting around school that she'd applied for another position *and* she was stepping out on John. "That—that dress is a real stunner, Helen. Excuse me, I've got to powder my nose!"

Meg rushed away, draining her champagne and dropping off the glass on a passing waiter's tray. What should she do? Should she corner Helen and explain? Ask her not to say anything about the Plumley job *or* seeing her with Andy? Or would that be making a mountain out of a molehill—and insulting Helen at the same time? Oh, what a mess.

Meg was passing the bar when she overheard her name. She snagged another glass of champagne and ducked behind an enormous parlor palm. *Eavesdroppers never hear anything good about themselves,* Marmee was wont to say—mostly to Amy, who had a habit of lurking around corners and beneath open windows. But Meg couldn't resist.

"She's easy on the eyes, that's for sure," Andy was saying. Meg flushed.

"She's got nice legs," Jack allowed. "But do you really want a gal you have to drag onto the dance floor?"

Meg cringed. Had she been that much of a spoilsport at the Grove?

"Aw, give her a break, Jack," Andy said. "Her sister just died."

Thank you! Meg thought.

"I bet she's full of sob stories about it, too," Jack retorted.

"Sorta." Andy sounded uncomfortable, but Meg didn't care. What a crummy thing to say. He was the one who had brought up Mattie, several times, and Meg had hardly gotten a word in edgewise!

"She seems like a real cold fish," Jack said. Meg gasped. The front seat of John's Buick would beg to disagree! She wasn't fast, but with the right man, she was hardly *cold.*

Meg peeked between the fronds and saw Andy nod, the big jerk! "To tell you the truth, I don't think Meg's the gal for me."

She *wasn't.* Especially if he was spineless enough to be swayed by what that donkey Jack Moffatt thought.

"I don't know why Sal's so keen on her. Feels sorry for her, I think," Jack said. "The father's got no head for business. Lost everything in '29. If it weren't for his rich aunt, they'd've been in a tent city."

Sallie and her big blabbermouth! Meg's face burned, but Jack wasn't finished.

"You know that dress Meg's wearing is one of Sal's. Meg's a sort of charity case for her. She's been nagging me nonstop to put in a good word for her with my aunt Viola."

Meg wanted to throw her glass of champagne right in Jack Moffatt's stupid, smug face. What a meatball! Then she would use her nice legs—she *did* have nice, shapely legs; he was right about that—to kick her date in the shins.

No. She'd show them both that she was *nobody's* charity case.

Meg gulped her champagne, set it on the corner of the bar, raised her chin, and strolled out to the dance floor. "Hiya, Joe," she said, to a young man whose name she did not know, hips swinging and eyes inviting. He promptly asked her to dance. When she caught Andy's gaze, she smiled up at the young man—whose name, it turned out, was Carl—as though he'd set the sun and moon and the stars in the sky. They had so much fun he introduced her to a few of his friends, who all wanted a turn around the floor with the enchanting Meg.

Andy managed to cut in half a dozen dances later. "Excuse me, that's my date."

"Too bad," a young man from Boston University snarled.

"Aw, don't be sore, Eddie. I'll dance the next one with you," Meg promised.

"Aren't you popular tonight," Andy said. It didn't sound like a compliment.

"Who, me?" Meg ducked out of his arms as the song ended and the band struck up the opening notes of "Boogie Woogie

Bugle Boy." "Oh, I love this song!" she said. "But I promised Eddie!"

"Hey," Andy started, but Meg was gone.

The evening should have felt like a triumph. Meg was an unqualified hit with Sallie's crowd. She had only stopped dancing long enough to sip another glass of champagne. The fellas called her "baby" and "doll" and "sweetheart" and, when she dodged their good-natured advances, "a real little spitfire."

While she drank, she chatted with Sallie's friends Kate and Norma and Hazel. It turned out that several of them were college girls—Hazel was up for the weekend from Wellesley, and Norma had graduated from Mount Holyoke last spring—and Meg picked up pretty quickly that they weren't actually very fond of Sallie.

"You know how Sallie is," Norma divulged, voice low. "She's always making those awful little jabs of hers. Every time we meet for lunch, I end up going home in tears!"

"Oh, yes," Meg said. "She let me borrow this gown. She said I deserved to have something *nice* to wear for once, and she was sure that was difficult on a schoolteacher's salary. Do you know I actually thanked her?" Meg laughed bitterly. "She's a real saint, our Sal."

"You're a hoot, Meg," Hazel said. "You should come for lunch at the club with us sometime."

"I'd like that," Meg said, though she wasn't sure she would.

Eventually, Andy found her and said he was leaving, if she still wanted a ride home. He was clearly miffed. Meg tucked her arm through his and suggested they say their goodbyes to Sallie.

"Thanks for inviting me. I'll make sure you get your dress back," she told Sallie, her smile sharp and toothy. Sallie looked a touch bewildered, as though her favorite kitten had grown claws. She drew Meg aside.

"Why don't you keep the dress? It's lovely on you, and I have so many others."

Meg's temper—enhanced by one too many glasses of champagne—flared. "I don't want your dress! I'm not your charity case."

Sallie raised her eyebrows. "Watch your tone, Meg. You should be grateful. Don't forget about tea with Aunt Viola next week."

Meg saw Helen Gagnon out of the corner of her eye and felt suddenly ashamed of herself. What would John think of the way she'd acted tonight? Good God, what would *Beth* think? Or Jo, even?

She considered the empty parlor at home and Marmee's silences. The promise of rows of neatly uniformed girls, diligently taking notes, their hands shooting into the air, eager to participate in discussions. She thought of marble halls and bigger paychecks. None of that was worth her self-respect.

"I don't think I can make it to tea," she said slowly.

"I haven't even told you when it is!" Sallie burst out. She looked at Meg, realization dawning. Her mouth set in a thin line. "Andy only asked you out because I told him to, you know. Out of *pity*. You were such a drag at the Grove."

Meg shrugged. "I don't care. I can find my own dates."

"The math teacher?" Sallie wrinkled her nose.

Meg rolled her eyes. "Have a good night, Sallie."

Andy was silent on the ride home. When he walked her to the front door, though, he leaned in for a kiss. Meg turned her head and stepped back so that his lips brushed the empty air where her cheek had been.

"I don't know why you'd want to kiss a girl who's full of sob stories, or such a cold fish," she snapped.

"Wh-what?" Andy stammered. "How did you hear . . . ? Don't blow your stack, Meg, I—"

"*Don't* call me!" Meg slammed the door behind her.

Marmee was waiting up in the parlor. She slipped her needle into its little strawberry pincushion. "Is everything all right, Meg?"

"It's fine." Meg was shaking with shame and anger. She'd had the silent drive home to think about her behavior, and she wasn't very proud of it. Maybe it had been satisfying to show Sallie that she was nobody's charity case, to be catty behind her back, to ignore Andy and flirt with a bunch of men who thought she was pretty. But it had been petty. It had been unkind. It had been disloyal to John. That wasn't how Marmee had raised her.

Andy was no real loss, and Sallie hadn't been much of a friend anyway. It was obvious to Meg that Sallie had only been keeping her around to make herself feel better. But now it was time to face the music; if Marmee asked about her evening, she wouldn't lie. She swiped a hand over her hot eyes and turned to face her mother.

Marmee looked at her splotchy face but didn't ask questions. Why didn't she ask? Why didn't she care anymore? "All right. I'll go up to bed, then. It's been a long day."

Meg waited until Marmee's footsteps had disappeared upstairs, then flopped into the wingback chair. It was still warm from the heat of her mother's body; it smelled like rose water and freshly baked bread. Like Marmee. Meg inhaled deeply and wished she were still small enough to ask for a hug, to crawl into her mother's lap and be rocked and petted till everything felt all right again.

Unburden

You could ask, you know.
You could ask to be held.

I understand why you don't.
Sometimes I waited for Marmee's return, longing
to unburden myself of the day's injustice
but when she arrived, her shoulders already heavy
I couldn't bear to add another weight.

But do you know what I think?
Marmee didn't bear children because
    anyone could be a mother or
    it was her duty or
    she had no other options.

Marmee bore children, bore us
because she is a mother
in her core.
A caretaker, nurturer.
Had her body not been able
she would have mothered
other ways, other people.
She did. She does.
She always will.

CHAPTER 17

JO

During Jo's forced break from work, a letter from Marmee arrived. Mrs. Wilson brought it up to her with a tea tray, still acting like Jo was an invalid even though the lump on her forehead was at least half the size it was yesterday. She was a little sore, sure, but other than that she was *fine*.

"I'll leave you to it, but you call if you need me," Mrs. Wilson said. "I think Charlotte's across the hall today as well. Though that girl's always running off to places when she visits."

"I'm fine. I promise," Jo said for what felt like the millionth time. She'd never been a good patient, and she seemed to be less of one now, as well meaning as everyone was.

But when Mrs. Wilson left her alone with the tray and the letter, Jo could not bring herself to open it. Enough days had passed since Thanksgiving for Marmee to have written it and sent it after the holiday.

Was she angry that Jo had been dodging all the calls her mother had made to the boardinghouse? That for every four or five letters Marmee sent, Jo would send back just a few hasty lines?

Had her mother figured out that she was the only person Jo spoke or wrote to apart from Papa's rare but beloved letters? Had Marmee and Meg talked of it? Of their fight? Of all the terrible things Jo said?

The thought of Meg sobbing her heart out in Marmee's arms made Jo feel both absurdly grateful that Meg had Marmee and horribly jealous that Meg had Marmee. A terrible twist of things that propelled her to her feet, to get dressed for the day. Trousers and sweater, her chore coat over it, and she was ready to brave the outdoors.

Mrs. Wilson was sure to object if Jo went for a long walk, but she thought she could stroll around the garden without rustling up the woman's ire and worry. Yet she found herself sneaking out, all the same. Just in case.

As her feet crunched across the quickly hardening snow, she tried not to think of the cold at home. The ponds and lakes icing over, the skating in the park that Amy loved so.

The yard behind the boardinghouse was not large, but there was a towering oak tree in one corner that Jo liked to sit with her back to, and she found herself pressed against its trunk, hoping the ancient wisdom in its bark and branches would somehow seep into her. Or at least she'd summon up the bravery to open the darn letter.

It took a good twenty minutes of sitting against that tree before she got the nerve. In that time, the snow had soaked through the cuffs of her pants, but she paid no mind to it as she slid her finger underneath the envelope flap and pulled out Marmee's letter. It was dated Thanksgiving and sent the next day.

My dearest Jo,

It troubles me, how far away you feel. I tell myself that it is a daughter finding her footing, something that would've happened no matter what. I remind myself that if the war hadn't come, you would have left our home anyway to seek out adventure and fortune, as is your wont and journey in life.

Out of all my girls, I always knew for sure that you would leave my nest and likely fly the farthest. But I can feel your grief, Jo, between the lines of your letters and in the spaces between your words when you do call. I have wished you would speak of it with me and I have understood why you have not.

I do not have pretty words for you, my stubborn, precious girl. I am not the writer you are. But I do have years and a mother's heart and all the love in the world for you and your sisters.

It is not an easy thing, losing someone. And I know your anger, because it is mine as well. I would rage at the world if I thought it would help. And you should, if you think it will give you even one moment of relief.

But this is what I have learned, in this terrible new world without her: that I must fill it, not just with mundane, distracting tasks of life, but with good. With purpose and passion and focus.

It is what she would've wanted, Jo. For all of us.

I am thankful for you, my sweet daughter, on this day that is about giving thanks. I am thinking of you and I am here, always.

I love you,
Marmee

Jo's tears splashed on the paper, smearing the ink when she hastily tried to wipe them away. With a shuddery breath, she folded up the letter so she wouldn't ruin it further.

What was wrong with her, that she was so unable to wrench herself from the grip of this? But before she could even contemplate an answer, a door slammed and a voice called, "Josephine! Are you out here?"

Mrs. Wilson had found her. Jo scrubbed at her face with the sleeve of her jacket and shoved the letter into her pocket before getting up. "I'm right here, Mrs. Wilson," she called. "Just getting some fresh air. The doctor said I should, once I was feeling steady."

"You'll catch cold," Mrs. Wilson scolded as she ushered Jo inside. "Go straight upstairs and get into bed."

Jo was halfway up the stairs when another slamming door startled her short. Before she could decide what to do, the loud, angry voices of Peg and Charlie made up her mind. She knew the difference between a sisterly spat and a fight, and this was definitely the latter. The Yates sisters sounded spitting mad at each other.

"I'm not discussing this with you, Charlotte."

"When you use my full name, it tells me I'm on the right track, you know."

"Drop this. I mean it. Do not go chasing after this. Have some respect."

"Respect?" Charlie's tone sharpened and then turned almost vicious. "What do you *think* I'm doing? If the rumors are true, that woman died a hero's death, and you're just going to hide it?"

"It's not hiding. It's war. And you are not part of this."

"I'm a journalist," Charlie said. "Not a war propagandist."

"It's cute that you think it's not the same thing," Peg said. "You were sent here for a reason. To write fluff for the folks at home who buy war bonds. Not to do some tacky investigative reporting."

"Don't condescend to me!"

"Then don't talk about matters you don't understand. I mean it, Charlotte: do not go digging into Mary Nielsen's death."

"Too late."

"If you think the military won't go over your head to your editors—"

"Do you think I haven't considered those consequences?"

"You have no idea what you are messing with!" A thump. A fist against the wall perhaps? Jo couldn't know for sure. But Peg's angry voice that followed was unmistakable. "It is a damned good thing you never had any true talent in the air. You would've never made it through WASP training. You don't have the sacrificial spirit. You *never* see the bigger picture."

"That's rich, coming from you," Charlie said. "When a woman is dead and it was covered up."

"There is no cover-up!"

"You're fodder to them," Charlie hissed. "*That's* the bigger picture. You are a means to an end, and once the end is here, they will have no more need of you. You talk of sacrificial spirit, like she was taken down by Nazis. She wasn't. Mary Nielsen was killed by *our* boys and their poor aim in a training exercise! The military says women aren't suited for war, that we could never handle true combat, and then that same military trains men so careless at their jobs that they kill the woman towing targets."

"You must leave this alone. Your self-righteousness has no

place here. Mary knew what she signed up for. All of us do. And you know the dangers of merely going up in a plane, so acting like this is absurd."

"You do not get to bring the past into this," Charlie said. "Engine malfunctions are not the same thing as being shot down!"

"This is the cost of war. Of progress. There is no cost too great to defeat the enemy. Mary understood that. Every girl who signs up understands that."

"And if, next time, it's you, Peg?" Charlie's voice cracked, and Jo's heart squeezed at the sound.

"Oh, Charlie." Peg's voice was ripe with the kind of sympathy only a big sister could possess. "I'm sorry—"

"I've lost one sister," Charlie said. "Don't make me lose another."

There were footsteps now, coming toward the stairwell. Jo looked around frantically—almost comically—as Charlie came into sight, and their eyes met.

A flush was already on Charlie's delicate cheeks, and it grew when she was confronted with Jo's presence. But she said nothing to alert her sister as she continued down the stairs; she simply beckoned Jo to follow her.

Out on the back porch, the December air was bracing as the day crept into the afternoon hours and Jo shoved her hands into the pockets of her jacket, not knowing what to say.

"How are you feeling?" Charlie asked as she fumbled for a cigarette, offering one to Jo, who shook her head.

"Better than before," Jo said.

"I'm glad to hear it." Charlie lit her cigarette, taking a drag. "My sister says smoking's a nasty habit."

"Your sister says a lot of things," Jo observed, leaning against the porch railing, her hands still in her pockets. "I didn't mean to eavesdrop," she added.

"We were squabbling so loud that if you'd been resting in your room like I assumed you were, you would've heard us all the same." Charlie shrugged, blowing out blue smoke.

"You're here for a story, not a visit," Jo said.

Charlie nodded.

"I'd be a little sore at you, too," Jo admitted.

Charlie laughed. "You are not good for my vanity, Jo March."

"You could've told her."

"No, I really couldn't." Charlie sighed. "We don't see eye to eye on this. I'm not part of the club, after all."

"What exactly is 'this'?" Jo asked tentatively.

"I get a lot of letters," Charlie said. "Especially after my first big article in *Life*. The one you mentioned when we met? There are lots of letters from women, wanting me to tell *their* stories. Much of it is the war-wife stuff that's so popular in the news-reels, but sometimes . . . sometimes there's a story that hooks you. That haunts you."

"And you have to go searching for answers," Jo said. She knew that feeling, when inspiration came and the pull was irresistible.

Charlie nodded. "A woman wrote to me about her sister. A pilot who worked at Camp Davis who was shot down during anti-artillery training. She was heroic, serving her country, sacrificing herself to train others, but they didn't treat her like a hero."

"What do you mean?"

"Her family had to pay for her body to be brought home," Charlie said. "Her fellow WASPs were the ones who pooled together money for the funeral. People don't know her name. Her sacrifice. She doesn't get a parade or a folded flag. She won't be buried in Arlington."

"I don't understand. . . ."

"They're not militarized," Charlie explained. "It's a military program, but even though they're freeing up male pilots all over the country to go overseas, the women are considered civilians. Therefore: not important enough to pay for when they're killed."

"That's . . ." Jo was so mad at the thought she wanted to spit.

"Vile? Wait until you hear the rumors I've dug up about Camp Davis. The general in charge over there is a real piece of work. He doesn't like female pilots, and his men act accordingly. There's talk of sabotage."

"That's horrific. I see why you want to break the story."

"That's why I was here," Charlie said. "To talk with Mary's sister, because I couldn't get anywhere in North Carolina at Camp Davis. But now that Peg's on to me, it'll all be for naught. Mary's sister is the only one who wants this to get out. Everyone else in her family keeps telling her it wouldn't be patriotic." She shook her head bitterly. "I'm in a spot, here. I went behind my editor's back with this one. If they get in his ear"— she sighed—"I'm toast."

"Do you have a backup pitch? A different reason you told your editor you're here?"

"I told him I was working on something to do with flying," Charlie said. "Nothing else. I wanted to have more proof."

Jo drummed her fingers against the porch railing. "So you could give him a different story? Would that get you out of the hot water?"

"Possibly," Charlie admitted.

"Well, then it can't hurt to try," Jo said. "As unfair as it is, to walk away from the other story, the only way you *ever* get to tell it is if you stay in your editor's good graces."

"So you think I should waltz into my editor's office with an entirely new pitch?"

"To mitigate any trouble your investigation caused? Absolutely."

"I don't have anything else."

"You can come up with something," Jo said. "If you can't write about the WASPs, write about other working girls. The parachute factory girls in Manchester maybe."

"Or your factory," Charlie said, straightening like she'd been struck with a pin.

"Oh, I didn't mean—"

"No, that's perfect," Charlie said. "You're making the planes the boys'll fly. It has an angle for everyone. Plus, they actually treated you well after your accident. That means the foreman must understand how important you all are."

"Forewoman," Jo corrected. "Mrs. Harris supervises all the girls at the factory."

"Do you think she'd let me and a photographer inside?"

"I don't think it'd be up to her," Jo said. "But she has sway with Mr. Bates."

"I'd have to get approval from my editor," Charlie said. "Write a formal pitch. But, my God, Jo, you might have just saved my hide if someone does get in his ear about my snooping about Mary."

"It is the kind of story that makes everyone look good," Jo

said, trying not to think of the sister's search for truth in Mary's tragic sacrifice.

"That's very practical of you," Charlie said.

"My sister Amy would be proud."

"My sister is anything but right now." Charlie angrily stubbed out her cigarette, her mouth twisting. "Dammit," she muttered. "As glad as I am to have an escape route handily plotted by you, investigating Mary's story felt important."

"That's because it is," Jo said swiftly. "The men need us right now—the world needs us, in ways they normally don't. They don't want to; they're afraid it'll give us ideas. And they *should* be afraid. A woman with ideas is terrifying to a certain kind of person."

Jo couldn't quite identify the expression on Charlie's face as the last haze of cigarette smoke faded into the afternoon light. All she knew was that it made her stomach twist and her heart thud when the blonde asked, "Are you a woman with ideas, Jo?"

It should've been a simple yes or no answer. But Jo found it wasn't. She found, like with each conversation she had with Charlie, it went much deeper.

"I am a woman who wants to be free to *always* have ideas," Jo said. "Outside of excuses of eccentricity or the demands of war. I am a woman who wants to be free to . . . *be*." Jo didn't know why (or perhaps she did), but she found tears pricking her eyes. When she looked away, Charlie had the grace not to mention it.

But the pressure of her hand on Jo's shoulder was suddenly there.

And it was not unwelcome.

Ideas

When we were small
your wild dreams
went beyond mere ideas
to foundation shaking
paradigm shifting
universe imploding
revolution.

You dressed us as boys
because it was the only way
we could imagine
having the power
to fulfill your vision.

You wrote your rebellion,
revolting girl, wrote pirates and bandits,
insurgents, for what other way
to get what you wanted
than seize it by force?

You planned to change the world.
You still can.

Soft

I donned the top hat,
the moth-eaten blazer,
fastened the bow tie
about my neck.

But I didn't care
to be a boy.
I didn't see
what they had
that I could want.

All hard edges,
feelings blunted
by a world that said
they had to bear
injustice, disappointment
with dry eyes.

You find a balance, though.
For all your hard edges, Jo,
you also sob and feel things deeply
and love so hard I fear
your heart will break.

Perhaps I shouldn't fear it,
your heart breaking open, spilling
out all its secrets, wrapping them around
you, not as a shield but a love-worn quilt.

CHAPTER 18

AMY

Amy was one hundred percent convinced that Marion had blabbed her big mouth to Supervisor Owens.

"Who else would've tattled on us? None of the other Clubmobile girls went to the Savoy that night," Amy said as she pushed her mop over the sticky kitchen floor. She and Edie had been cleaning for hours already, starting with the ovens before moving on to the countertops, and yet there was so much more to be done, like the windows in the front room. She dared a glance at Edie. "I'm really sorry that you got dragged into this."

"You don't have to keep apologizing. This is all on Greeley." Edie was scrubbing out a soup pot that was almost as big as she was. Her voice soured as she added, "I bet she's lapping up her day off while we're stuck inside like Cinderella."

"With no sign of Prince Charming coming to save us," Amy mumbled.

Three more hours later, the girls had finally finished their duties. By then, the windows were spotless and the kitchen was spick-and-span, not a mote of dust to be seen, but Amy felt wrung out like an old rag. She couldn't remember ever cleaning her own house so diligently. How did Marmee do this sort of thing every day?

As soon as they returned to their room, Amy collapsed into bed without bothering to change or unlace her boots; she merely let her feet dangle off the edge of her mattress while she tried to nap. But sleep didn't come easily, and her most recent bundle of letters kept calling her name. Giving up on the shut-eye, Amy opened Meg's missive first, which was written in her neat cursive script. Meg had bumped into Sallie Gardiner at a blood drive at school, and Marmee was staying busy with her numerous charity committees. Mrs. Mahoney at church was expecting her first, and the furnace was acting up again.

Amy set the letter down on her bed. How had she and Meg come to this, writing to each other like strangers?

I miss her, Amy thought as she hugged her pillow to her chest.

She even missed Jo.

But Beth most of all.

Amy felt her grief starting to rise from that locked place where she kept it banished, so she stuck Meg's letter back into its envelope, with the last third of it left unread. She couldn't start crying now—how would she ever explain it to Edie? Rosemary Pace didn't have any sisters.

She moved on to Fred's letter next. He told her that he would have a few days of leave before shipping out to the Guadalcanal campaign. Would she be able to sneak away from Montreal and meet him in Boston? He'd treat her to a lobster dinner and a night out at the theater, where his father had season tickets.

I'll make it worth your while, I promise, he had written.

Amy had a hunch that he wanted to ask her to be his girl,

and a tingle shot down her spine at the thought. Except it didn't feel like an excited sort of tingle. More of a nervous one.

Jeez, what was wrong with her? She should've been jumping up and down as she imagined catapulting into Fred's arms and covering his face with kisses.

Except the thought of kissing Fred didn't make her heart thump at all.

Laurie, on the other hand . . .

She shook her head. Fred Vaughn was giving his heart to her on a platinum platter, and yet all she could do was dream about Laurie?

Laurie, who treated her like a kid.

Laurie, who belonged to Jo.

Laurie, who could never be hers.

Amy forced herself up and searched her drawers for the notebook and charcoal that Laurie had given her. She gathered them into her arms before stuffing them under her bed, far, far into the corner.

There, she thought, dusting off her hands. That was that.

"What in the world are you doing?" Edie said, swinging her head over the side of her bunk.

"A little housecleaning," Amy replied. Or, rather, a sweeping of the heart.

The door swung open, and Marion entered the room with her cheeks still red from the wind outside. She gave her snow-dusted hair a good shake.

"Enjoy your time off work?" Amy said, her tone as frosty as the windowpane.

"It was fine, aside from the weather," Marion replied, running her fingers through her tangled hair. "What were you two up to?"

"We haven't even left the building, since we were stuck inside cleaning," Amy huffed. "I wonder whom we have to thank for that."

Marion's hands went still. "Excuse me?"

"You ratted us out to Owens!" Edie yelled from the top bunk.

"Exactly!" Amy added. "You told her that I got thrown out of the Savoy, and she lumped poor Edie with me on cleaning duty."

A flush fanned over Marion's face. "It wasn't like that at all. The Savoy staff themselves called Owens about your exploits, and she only asked me to confirm them."

"You couldn't have fibbed a little?" Amy said.

"She put me on the spot!" Marion replied, flustered. "I thought she'd give you a slap on the wrist, not send you to the kitchen."

"Is that supposed to make us feel better?" Edie said.

Marion kept her chin up, refusing to be cowed. "I'm no blabbermouth, but don't expect me to lie for you—that's what I've always told my sisters. Anyway, I worked my tail off to get into the Red Cross, and I won't jeopardize that."

"We *all* worked hard to get here," Edie said, fuming.

"I'm sure you both did," Marion started, "but if I'm being honest, I have to wonder sometimes if you two took this job to serve the troops or to go all khaki-wacky over them."

Amy sucked in a breath. "That's unfair, and you know it!"

"You need to get off your high horse, Greeley," Edie said,

climbing down from her bunk to face Marion herself. But Marion was buttoning up her coat again. She mumbled that she needed some air and ducked out of the room.

"The *nerve* of her." Edie made a grab for her own coat and started to shove her feet into her shoes. "You know why I joined the Red Cross? To honor Bobby."

"Where are you going?" Amy asked, alarmed.

"Giving Marion a piece of my mind!"

"Wait, don't." Amy grabbed Edie's hand to anchor her in place. "Let her go. Hasn't she ruined our day enough?"

Edie dug her nails into her palms. "Didn't you hear what she said?"

"Loud and clear," Amy said. "Believe me when I say that Marion should eat a big fat slice of humble pie."

Edie paused and tapped a finger against her lips, a slow smile forming. "That isn't a bad idea. We just have to figure out the recipe."

"Recipe?" said Amy, confused.

"You know, for humble pie."

Amy tilted her head to the side, feeling uneasy. All she knew was that Edie Barnett wasn't a girl you wanted to cross. "What are you cooking up in that head of yours?"

Edie only gave a little shrug, but there was a sparkle in her eye. "Maybe a slice of just deserts for dear old Captain Sanctimonious."

The month of December grew chillier by the day, but the girls were busier than ever. More and more soldiers streamed through

London each day on their way to North Africa, where the war was ratcheting up. Thus far, the Allies had overtaken the cities of Casablanca, Algiers, and Oran, which had sent Hitler scrambling to defend Vichy Tunisia, his last stronghold in the area. The string of victories had put all of London in good spirits, and the troops kept asking the Clubmobile girls to sing songs for them, Christmas carols in particular since the holiday was around the corner. Amy had to put in a special request to the Red Cross to provide a record player for their truck, since her voice was growing hoarse from all this impromptu warbling.

"All ready to go?" Edie said, popping her head into the bathroom after another long shift at work.

"Do we really have to?" Amy said with a groan as she applied her mascara. "I'm beat."

"Put on that lipstick, Captain," Edie said with a clap on the back. "We've got morale to boost."

"More like egos to stroke," Amy mumbled. She dabbed another layer of concealer under her eyes, but the bags sitting there refused to stay hidden. What she really needed was a decent night of sleep, but that wouldn't be happening anytime soon. She bit back another groan. A year ago, she would've relished the idea of getting dolled up and going dancing with dashing GIs, but now all she dreamed about was a night in alone. She'd come to dread these events with the officers, who invited the Clubmobile gals out for jiving and drinking at least twice a week. Amy begged off whenever she could, but she had to make an appearance once in a while. It was all part of the job.

The girls headed to Piccadilly Circus, with Amy wearing a borrowed number from Edie—a pink shirtdress with a keyhole neckline and puffed sleeves that gave it pizazz. She had been too tired to do anything with her hair, so she'd tied a ribbon around it and called it decent—the soldiers would simply have to accept her ponytail. Once inside Rainbow Corner, she sipped on a glass of club soda while trying to laugh at the officers' jokes, but it was a real effort, since she didn't find any of them particularly funny. She kept a close eye on the clock, figuring she would stay an hour before feigning a headache and making a beeline for the exit.

I shouldn't have called John Brooke such a boring fuddy-duddy. Now I've turned into one myself, she thought glumly.

The officers headed to the bar to grab themselves another round of drinks, leaving Amy and Edie on the sidelines of the dance floor. Marion stood a few steps away, but the three of them didn't chat. Weeks might have passed since Marion had tattled to Supervisor Owens, but Amy hadn't forgotten about that yet and neither had Edie.

"Let's go find a place to sit. My feet are killing me," Edie said.

"You don't have to ask me twice," Amy replied.

As they tried to maneuver through the crowd, however, Amy accidentally bumped shoulders with a passing soldier.

"Sorry about that," she said quickly.

"Not a problem, miss." The soldier offered up a polite smile while Amy blinked up at him. She had seen a few Black soldiers out and about in London, but she had yet to interact with any of them. Just as the US military was segregated, the Red Cross had followed suit, assigning their white workers to serve the white troops while their Black workers served the Black GIs, with limited crossover in between.

"Maybe I'm hearing things," this soldier said, "but you sound American."

"I'm with the Clubmobile, actually," Amy said. She understood his confusion, though, because there weren't many American gals in the UK, aside from her fellow Red Cross volunteers and the Women's Army Auxiliary Corps recruits. Most of the women who frequented Rainbow Corner were local Brits who came to the club for the food and drinks and who chatted up the Yankee troops with little regard to the color of their skin.

"You're a long way from home," he remarked. "Whereabouts are you from?"

"Massachusetts. Concord, if you know the area. How about yourself?"

"Sunny California. I've never been so cold in my life until I came over to jolly old England." He pretended that he was out in the snow, chattering his teeth together. Amy laughed. She got the sense that he was a bit of a jokester.

The band struck up a jitterbug and he gestured at the dance floor. "I can never sit out a Benny Goodman number. Care to take a spin?"

Amy stared at his hand. She had never danced with a Black GI before. Or any Black fella, period. That sort of thing didn't happen at her school dances, where there weren't any Black students to start with. She blinked around and wondered if people were staring at them, but everyone else was moving to the music, too busy to notice. Except for Edie.

"I'm awfully thirsty," Edie said rather loudly and tugged on Amy's hand. "Let's get some sodas from the bar."

The soldier's smile tightened. "How about I grab them for the three of us? My treat."

"You can save your money, *Private*," Edie told him, emphasis on his rank.

Something shifted in his eyes, like a memory rising, and he gave a single nod. "You ladies have a nice evening," he said, ever polite, but his cheery tone was now subdued.

Amy almost called him back. What was the harm in a single dance? But when she saw the hard look on Edie's face, her courage faltered.

But the soldier from sunny California didn't stay unattached for long. Out of nowhere, Marion popped up next to him and offered him her hand. "Don't mind my friends," she said, casting a brief glance at Amy and Edie. "Wanna dance?"

The soldier smiled cautiously in reply, and the two of them headed off, with Edie staring after them the whole way.

"Can you believe her?" Edie whispered.

"It's only a dance," Amy said, not sure what else to say.

"My mother would disown me if I pulled something like that. Wouldn't yours?"

Amy went quiet. She thought of Marmee, who'd taught her girls from a young age that all people were created equal, no matter their race, creed, or station. Father liked to tell stories, too, of one of their ancestors who was an abolitionist in Boston, which Amy had always taken pride in. The Marches came from a lineage of acceptance and tolerance; they were the good guys, weren't they? So why wasn't she out on the dance floor right now, jitterbugging with that soldier?

Edie elbowed Amy's side when she noticed the officers who'd invited them to the club making their way back toward them. "Here they come. *Smile*."

Amy couldn't muster much of a grin. She was once again

looking at the Black soldier, who was swinging Marion around the dance floor. Why had she hesitated when he'd asked her to dance? He seemed funny and friendly, and she loved Benny Goodman.

Would she had hesitated if he'd been white?

Amy's stomach shrank into a pretzel-sized knot, because she thought she knew the answer to that.

"I feel a migraine coming on. I think I'm going to call it a night," Amy blurted to Edie. The officers made their protests—*Just one more round, sweetheart,* they pleaded—but Amy was already heading to the exit, eager to take the bobby pins out of her hair, slip under the covers, and forget about this night altogether.

But before she could reach the door, a tipsy sergeant caught her by the elbow. "Hey, you look familiar."

Amy's patience thinned and she pulled her arm free. "I'm afraid I'm all danced out, soldier."

He was persistent, though. "Wait a sec. You're Laurence's Doughnut Dolly, aren't you? Did you hear the news about him yet?"

Amy felt the world shift beneath her and found herself grabbing his shoulders. "What news?" she forced out.

"Aw, you don't know?" He rubbed his jaw and shook his head, and for a second Amy thought her knees might give out, because he was pausing for a beat too long. But then he said, "Laurence got into a prang on his last rodeo. His kite took heavy fire, but he made it back over the Channel before bailing."

Amy tried to make sense of all this. What in the world was a prang or a kite? Only one thing mattered to her this instant. "Is he alive?"

"The Brits fished him out of the water, but he was banged up real good. They brought him to the same hospital where he was laid up last month. He might be in surgery now."

Amy was on the move before he'd finished talking. She heard Edie calling after her to slow down, but she couldn't turn around, not when her whole body was singularly focused on one mission, and one mission alone.

Mission

Laurie with his mission to take down Nazis,
Jo building planes to get him there.

Amy serving with a smile and reminder
of the home Meg keeps warm for his return.

Even Father, Mother have their roles
while all I do is watch this new world turning.

I fought my war already,
from a battlefield of tear-stained sheets.
Quiet combat between a fleeting body
and the will to stay in a world
where I could have a mission too.

My mission now:
watch you live your lives
intent on saving a world
as it bombs itself to oblivion,
never realizing you do the same
to the only world I ever knew.

CHAPTER 19

JO

The next morning, Jo woke early to the sound of honking outside. She climbed out of her brass bed and got to the window just in time to see Charlie's blond head ducking into a cab. As she watched the taxi drive away, she felt a bereft sort of twist in her chest. Jo hadn't realized Charlie was leaving so soon. She would've liked to say goodbye.

Footsteps on the creaky boards drew Jo's attention, and she peeked into the hall, finding Peg going back to her room after seeing off her sister.

"You're up early, Jo," Peg said, catching sight of her. "Are you feeling better?"

"Barely a headache," Jo said. "I'll be right as rain for work on Monday. I see your sister's gone."

"Yes, she got what she wanted," Peg said, and Jo couldn't help but hear the note of bitterness in her voice as she folded her arms and leaned against the wall. Her red hair blazed compared to the faded roses on the wallpaper. Mrs. Wilson was a brilliant cook and kept a cozy home, but on the cutting edge of home furnishings and fashion she was not. "She'll be back by New Year's," Peg muttered, almost to herself.

Jo bit her lip, thinking of Charlie's anger over her sister's interference in her pursuit of the story of how Mary Nielsen died. "You two are close," she said, because how could they not be, when this contention between them caused so much strife? Isn't that why Meg's words and questions haunted her just as much as Laurie's upturning of everything she'd thought (told herself) was true?

Peg let out a noise that could've been a laugh or a snort. "Do you have younger sisters, Jo?"

"I had two younger sisters. Now I have one." She wasn't sure why she'd felt compelled to volunteer this information. Maybe it was because she felt for both the Yates sisters. She could see both their perspectives. Peg had sworn herself to a cause much bigger than just one individual, and she would not be swayed from it, for she was loyal and a fighter. Charlie had dedicated herself to the pursuit of truth at any cost, even her sister's ire, because she hungered for justice and fought as well. Two different women, weighing the exposure of the loss of one life against a terrible world, but neither devaluing Mary's sacrifice, Jo felt. She had heard the pain in Peg's voice when she had talked to her sister about the fallen pilot.

It felt wrong, though, that Mary's fellow sisters in flight were the ones fronting the costs of funeral expenses so her family would not be burdened, in a country that they were giving so much to. Jo understood why Charlie was outraged—and why she wanted others to be outraged. Sometimes outrage was the only way to change things.

"I'm so sorry about your little sister," Peg said. "I've lost one as well. I understand how hard it can be."

Jo gave a short nod of acknowledgment.

"You understand, then," Peg continued. "You feel protective of your younger sisters, watching them make mistakes. Sometimes the same mistakes you made. And losing a sister . . ." She pressed her lips together, like she was holding back a memory by the skin of her teeth. "It makes you guard the ones you have left, doesn't it?"

"Yes, it does," Jo said, even though it was a lie on her part. Beth's death didn't turn her into some stalwart guardian, armed with swords that she never dropped, no matter the weight.

She had tossed whatever she owed her family to the side to bolt. She could've stayed, like Meg. Been the good daughter her father thought she was. But she wasn't that girl, deep down. She was nothing like they thought. Would they love her if they saw her as she was, this mess of a girl who didn't know which way was up?

"Charlie will be back," Peg said again, and this time, it was almost like a wish uttered.

"Of course," Jo said.

Peg smiled at the reassurance, before ducking into her room with a grateful wave. Jo turned to do the same and, to her surprise, found an envelope with her name scrawled on it taped to her door. She plucked it free and went inside before opening the letter.

Dear Jo-not-Josephine,

    I had to scram before my sister started doing an impression of a teakettle and steam came out of her ears.

But I wanted to thank you for talking me down the other day. Without you, I probably would've gone back inside and Peg and I would've descended into hair pulling like we were kids again (oh, who am I kidding, she pulled my hair when she was twenty, too).

Thank you for giving me an out in this tangle I've found myself in. Your idea to pitch an article about the factory girls who build our planes was sublime. I have a favor to ask—perhaps it is too much, considering you're toiling away every day—but I wonder if you'd like to help me with this story? Give me feedback? Maybe suggest angles? It always helps when a writer has an expert—and to have one who is a writer as well is a boon indeed.

I appreciated our talks. I'm not sure if it came through, but visiting my sister is a welcome but trying experience. You made it a little easier. And it's not often I find a friend with just as many Virginia Woolf books and lectures stacked on her dresser as I have.

If you'd like to collaborate as I suggested, my address is on the back of this letter. And even if you don't, we could always just write. We could discuss Virginia's core premise: that room of one's own, away from it all, a metaphorical and actual space to explore words the way men are free to do, financed and supported and valued. I think about it often: a life free of feminine expectation and full of the kind of creative pursuit that should not fall to just men but seems to.

It's the dream, isn't it? To have that room, that time, that pursuit? It is certainly mine.

Your friend,

Charlie-not-Charlotte

PS: I know I said I wouldn't, but I couldn't help but glance at the first page of that story on your vanity when you were recovering. I promise: I didn't read any more. And I told myself I wouldn't ask, but I can't stop thinking about how you introduced the character, almost like a film shot closing in. I must betray myself to ask: What is the bloody woman in the woods doing there?

Jo felt a true smile curl across her face. Her cheeks almost ached from it, like those muscles were sensitive to such use after so long.

She sat down at the chipped vanity, her eyes sliding to the stack of pages that she hadn't touched in weeks. She'd unpacked it and set it there as a sort of reminder—perhaps a way to make herself feel guilty, to spur herself into action.

It had done nothing but make her feel terrible.

But Charlie . . .

Charlie had liked the way she'd introduced the woman in the woods. She'd called it cinematic. The glow of the praise lit Jo up like an ember.

For the first time in a long time, she reached for her box of stationery and a pen.

Dear Charlie-not-Charlotte . . .

Glow

An ember
sparks a fire
but also

glows
long after
a fire has gone out,
hot as the flames themselves.

Always with the potential
to destroy, refine.
To spread, consume.

Unless it's starved
of what it needs
and then it turns
to ash.

The Fireplace

The mantel
above our fireplace
was always crowded
as a train platform
just as the train arrives.

Photos and trinkets,
books and flowers,
an entire family history
on one narrow shelf of brick.

Such a stark contrast,
the mantel at Aunt March's.
A showy vase, some candlesticks.
I never saw them lit.

I sometimes wonder, had I lived,
would I have ended up alone?
Perhaps she'd leave me the house,
for you all would have had other lives to live.

But if she had, I would have filled
that barren mantel with my own platform
of travelers with their joys and sorrows, busy lives.
Photos, trinkets, mementos from my sisters
and their families, my family too.

CHAPTER 20

MEG

Meg was having a rotten day.

Her fourth-period class had been full of sass; she'd had to send Bradley Braithwaite to see Principal Hamilton. Fifth period hadn't done their reading, and their discussion of *Walden* felt like pulling teeth. Then the seventh-grade boys had started a food fight while she was serving as lunch monitor. Meg still had spaghetti sauce on her sleeve. And she was supposed to visit her father's aunt after school! She looked in the mirror of the ladies' washroom, dabbing at the stain with her wet handkerchief. It was clearly visible against the pink wool, and Aunt March was sure to comment on it.

Helen Gagnon came in, and Meg wished she could disappear. Yesterday she'd seen Helen down the hall, turned tail, and practically *run* in the other direction. She wasn't proud of it. She flushed and scrubbed at her elbow.

"Oh no!" Helen gave Meg a sympathetic smile. "Did you get caught in the food fight?"

"I did." Meg didn't know what else to say. Helen must think so badly of her after the way she'd acted at Sallie's.

Helen peered down at her. "Meg, are you all right?"

"I'm fine. Nothing a little Lux can't fix," Meg said brightly.

Helen propped her hip against the sink. She wore a kelly-green shirtwaist dress with white polka dots. "I don't mean the spaghetti. You didn't seem like yourself on Saturday."

Meg met Helen's kind brown eyes in the mirror. Her hands fell to her sides. "Gosh," she said. "I've made such a muddle of things."

"Do you want to talk about it?" Helen asked, as Meg glanced toward the washroom door. "It won't leave this room. I haven't breathed a word about anything that happened at Sallie's, either. I'm an absolute vault."

Meg bit her lip to ward off tears. She had been dreading what Helen might say to the other teachers, and here she was, offering a shoulder to cry on. "You shouldn't be nice to me."

"Of course I should." Helen handed her a clean white handkerchief embroidered with HLG in the corner. "Here. Just in case."

"Sallie and I were friends in school," Meg explained, sniffling. "I ran into her again a few weeks ago—her fiancé came to the blood drive—and she talked me into going out dancing with her and Jack and Andy. I shouldn't have. I don't want to date anybody but John. But . . . how well do you know Sallie?"

Helen grinned. There was a gap between her two front teeth; it made her smile a little mischievous. "I don't. My date went to BC with her fiancé, but to tell you the truth, he was a real dud. And, I have to say, Sallie seems like a piece of work."

"She has this way of making me feel so *small*. I didn't want to go to the party, but when Andy called and asked me, I was feeling awfully lonely. Nothing's been right at home since we lost

Beth." Meg glanced at Helen. Beth had loved her music classes. "My sister Amy's in Montreal in art school, and Jo is working in a factory in Connecticut, and my mother is on a thousand different committees. It sounds silly now, but I couldn't bear spending another Saturday night home alone. So I said yes, I'd go. And then I overheard Andy and Jack talking. Saying I was a sort of *charity project* for Sallie. It turns out Andy only asked me out because she talked him into it."

Helen winced in sympathy. "I don't know if I quite believe that. He was pretty green-eyed when you were dancing with all those other fellas."

"It doesn't matter. But I had too much champagne, and Sallie's always brought out the worst in me." Meg gave a rueful laugh. "It hurt my pride, so I decided to show them I didn't need their charity, and I danced and flirted."

"Then no real harm was done." Helen patted her arm. "Don't be so hard on yourself. You're a good egg. I'll miss you if you take that position at Plumley."

Meg sighed. "I've ruined any chance I had by mouthing off to Sallie."

Helen ran a hand over her sleek blond hair. "You don't need Jack Moffatt to put in a good word. Half a dozen teachers here would write you a letter of recommendation. You're a good teacher, Meg. Your students adore you. Especially the Junior Red Cross girls. We'd be awfully sorry to lose you, though."

"That means a lot, coming from you. You were Beth's favorite teacher, you know." Meg sniffled again, and Helen gave her hand a quick squeeze. "I don't want to leave. I love my students. I love being right down the hall from John. I want to be here when he comes back. It's only . . . I went to high school here, and I still feel like a kid sometimes. Miss Pennington certainly sees me that way."

"Agatha called Principal Hamilton a 'young man' the other day," Helen said.

Meg giggled. Principal Hamilton had to be at least sixty!

"*Everyone* is a kid to her," Helen added. "Don't let her treat you with anything less than respect."

Meg looked pointedly at the leaky faucet of Helen's sink. "It would be nice to work in a school that wasn't falling apart. With students who *want* to talk about Shakespeare."

Helen gripped the faucet handle and gave it a good hard twist. The trickle of water stopped. "Do you think those rich private school girls need you as much as our students do? You're doing a lot of good here, Meg. And it's partly because you're you, but it's also because you're part of this community. The kids know you. Their brothers and sisters went to school with you and your sisters. They know what you've lost, and—especially now, when we're all losing so much—it helps them to see you soldier on with grace and good humor."

Meg shrugged. "I don't know about that."

"I do." The bell rang for the next period, and they both straightened.

"Thank you." Meg stuffed Helen's handkerchief into her pocket. "I'll launder this and get it back to you."

Helen smiled. "If you want my advice—write and tell John the truth. He'll understand. He's a good egg, too."

After school that day, Meg gave three sharp raps on her great-aunt's front door. *Perhaps Aunt March isn't home,* she thought hopefully. The old woman was persnickety; she tried Meg's patience on the best of days.

Aunt March's maid, Brigid, opened the door. "Hello, Miss March. Your aunt is in the parlor."

Just Meg's luck. She ran a hand over her shoulder-length curls. "Thank you."

The parlor was exactly as it had been when Meg was a child—probably exactly as it had been when Father was a child, too—airless, and crowded with heavy antique furniture. A few silver candlesticks and an ugly vase sat on the mantel. Aunt March sat in her armchair in front of a blazing fire. Her dreadful little terrier yapped at Meg's heels.

Meg pasted on a smile, resolute, and prayed she didn't have lipstick on her teeth. "Good afternoon, Aunt March."

"Is it?" the peppery old woman asked, casting a critical eye at Meg's elbow. Meg cringed. "You've got a loose thread in your hem. Didn't your mother teach you to sew?"

Meg gritted her teeth. "I made this dress myself, actually, from a pattern in *McCall's*."

"Pink doesn't suit your coloring," the old woman grumped.

"Thank you for bringing that to my attention," Meg said sweetly.

"Are you going to stand there all day? Sit down."

Meg dutifully perched on the uncomfortable horsehair settee.

"Has there been any news from my nephew?"

Aunt March was actually very fond of Father, despite taking

every possible opportunity to criticize his financial acumen and remind him of her substantial loan. Meg recounted Father's latest letter from the Pacific.

"I daresay he could write more often and let me know he hasn't been killed by one of those Japanese destroyers. *Yet.* Imagine going back to sea at his age," the old lady grumbled. "I haven't heard a peep from those sisters of yours, either. Off gadding about when they should be at home! At least one of you has some sense. I was glad to hear you've thrown over that schoolteacher!"

"I . . . Pardon me?" Meg said, flabbergasted.

"Well, a husband like that would hardly help rescue your family from penury, would he?"

"Penury?" Meg echoed, attempting to keep things light-hearted. "I don't think we're in such dire straits as all that!"

"Not at the moment, perhaps. Thanks to my money. But you never know." Aunt March fussed with the amethyst brooch on her ample bosom. It was a family heirloom: Victorian mourning jewelry. Inside was a lock of her long-dead husband's hair. Meg found it rather creepy, but she supposed people grieved in all sorts of strange ways.

"Well, I'm sorry to disappoint," Meg said, not an ounce of apology in her voice, "but I haven't thrown over Mr. Brooke at all, if that's who you mean."

"I heard you were quite the belle at Sarah Gardiner's ball." Meg winced. How had Aunt March heard about Sallie's party? "And that you were escorted by Andy Fitzhugh."

Oh no. Meg trusted that Helen hadn't been gossiping behind her back, but there had been close to a hundred people at the party. What if word got back to John? Maybe Helen was right; maybe she should write and tell him what had happened, how foolish she had been. Surely he would understand.

But what if he didn't?

"I won't be seeing Andy again. I'm committed to Mr. Brooke," Meg said.

"Oh, Meg, do be sensible!" Aunt March entreated. "If he tried to take liberties . . . Well, all men are—"

"It was nothing like that!" Meg said hurriedly, horrified and a little bit fascinated by the direction the conversation had gone.

Aunt March peered at her over her half-moon spectacles. "Did he *not* take liberties that you wished him to take?"

"No! Oh, for heaven's sake." She could have been kissed by half a dozen different men at Sallie's party if she'd had a mind to be. Not that she would have! But she *could have.*

Aunt March waved one plump, ring-laden hand in outrage. "Andy Fitzhugh is from a good family. A graduate of Boston College. Those Jesuits don't put up with any nonsense, you know. And now he's an executive at the electric plant. He's a younger son, but his older brothers are both in the army, so who knows what the future holds?"

"Aunt March, that's awful! He's already lost a sister," Meg gasped.

"So have you. You're the eldest, Meg, and you aren't getting any younger, you know. It's your duty to make a good match. We certainly can't rely on Josephine. She's entirely too headstrong. Who would want to marry a girl like that, working in a factory like a man?"

Laurie would. And Laurie was plenty rich.

Jo might be—*was*—headstrong, obstinate, and entirely pigheaded sometimes; Meg didn't always understand her. But she loved her. She would never, ever betray her by throwing Laurie's proposal in Aunt March's face.

"I think it's wonderful, what Jo's doing," Meg said loyally. No matter if she and Jo weren't speaking, she would defend her to the death from Aunt March. "Loads of women are working in factories these days. We all have to do our part."

Aunt March sniffed. "And look at Amy! She's the pretty one, you know." Meg bit her tongue. Amy *was* pretty. "But she's off painting in Montreal like some sort of *bohemian*. Next we know, she'll be living in a garret in Paris. How long does she expect Fred Vaughn to wait for her?"

Meg didn't think her baby sister's heart was really in that romance. She wondered, though, what gossip Aunt March might have heard. Amy always used to confide in Meg, but lately her letters were nothing but fluff: breezy, superficial accounts of the artists she was studying, the friends she was making, and descriptions of Montreal that half sounded like she'd cribbed them from a guidebook. Meg was glad her sister was happy— one of them should be!—but Amy could have been writing a complete stranger.

At least she wrote. Unlike Jo.

"Amy's always wanted to travel," Meg said, stalwart. "I hope she does get to Paris after the war."

"And what about you? What do you have to say for yourself?" Aunt March skewered Meg with her fierce blue-gray eyes. "Why isn't Andy Fitzhugh good enough for you?"

"Because I don't love him," Meg snapped. "I love John!"

She fell silent. It struck her that she hadn't said those words out loud before. How funny that Aunt March, of all people, should be the first to hear them. But they struck Meg as true; they felt right. She *was* in love with John Brooke.

"I see. Well then." Aunt March leaned forward in her chair. "Mr. Brooke doesn't have any rich relations, does he? You'll have to scrimp and save all your life if you marry him."

Meg thought of John: his steady brown eyes, his thatch of reddish-brown hair, his slightly chipped right incisor, his collection of tweed jackets. He smelled like Barbasol shaving cream and chalk dust, and somehow that had become appealing. He got excited about the elegance of algebraic equations, and that had become adorable.

"Then it's a good thing I sew most of my own clothes, isn't it?" Meg smiled.

"You say that now! Everything seems romantic when you're writing to a soldier. But once you're married—once you're keeping his house and bringing up his children—will you still be happy to make sacrifices? Or will you be envious of your old friend Sarah, who can afford a nursemaid and a fine house?"

"I daresay I'll have my envious moments." Meg knew her own nature, and she didn't expect it to change overnight. "But I couldn't regret marrying John. If he asks me, I mean."

"Of course he'll ask you! He'd be a fool not to," Aunt March harrumphed, and Meg bit back another smile. "What if I told you that if you marry him, I'll cut you out of my will? I'll leave everything to your sisters. You won't get a penny."

Meg stiffened her spine and looked Aunt March right in the eye. "I suppose I'd say that it's your money, and you can do with it what you like."

Aunt March scowled. "Easy to say that now."

"I have my own money from teaching. It might not seem like very much to you, but it affords me the independence to do as I like." Meg got to her feet. "John may not be rich, but he's clever and he's kind and he's *good*. He works hard, and everyone at school likes and respects him. He listens to me, really listens, and he doesn't treat me like a child. He hasn't said it yet, but I think he loves me, and, more than that, Aunt March, he *respects* me. I won't settle for any less. And I won't stand here and let you tear him down, any more than I'd let Amy and Jo do it."

Meg thought about storming out, but she worried the old lady would see it as childish dramatics. So she stood there, her breath coming fast, feeling rather awkward.

"Are you quite finished?" Aunt March asked.

"Yes, ma'am," Meg said.

"You have more moxie than I thought. Good for you. I daresay you'll need it." Aunt March offered her a thin smile. "Now, why don't you sit down and read me a chapter of that Agatha Christie novel. My old eyes aren't what they used to be. I'll ring for some tea."

Meg sat primly on the settee, mollified, and reached for the latest Miss Marple mystery. She suspected Aunt March's eyes were just fine. A smile crept slowly over her face. If she had managed to say all that to Aunt March, what was to stop her from saying it to Amy? Or Jo? She felt more certain than ever: she loved John, and if he asked, she would marry him.

But would he ask, when he knew how silly she'd been?

Moxie

On that seaside holiday
Jo and I shared a bottle
of ice-cold Moxie.

Fizzy, dancing on my tongue,
a tickle from my nose
all the way down my throat.

Made from gentian root,
which the bottle claimed
could banish nerves, insomnia,
fevers, rheumatism, gout.

I think Jo believed
for one blissful second
it could be that easy.
Fresh sea air,
fizzy sugar water,
a sister's love,
and I would be whole.

Like the time Amy broke
the porcelain doll
Aunt March had given me

and Jo and Meg helped
glue the pieces back together,
the lines so fine, the work so dear
almost no one could find the damage.

But I could. I saw the crack
from her temple to the lips
that would never speak.
I felt it under my fingers,
faint as my own pulse.

Breath

Once upon a time
in the darkest hour of the night
when she felt sure I was sleeping,
her breath sweet in my face

Jo told me she'd do anything
to make me well.
She'd pay any price,
travel the world for a cure,
become a doctor.
And she would have.

I'm glad she never had time.
For Jo and I both
would have lived out our days
under harsh white light,
running tests, chasing a cure
that didn't exist

when all I needed
was her head on the pillow
next to mine.

CHAPTER 21

AMY

A s Amy awaited news on Laurie's condition, she channeled the name on her lapel—she paced and paced over the cold hospital floor. Visiting hours had long passed, but the nurses had taken pity on her when she explained why she was there. They slipped her cups of water and gave her updates whenever they could, and ever so slowly Amy pieced together what had happened to him.

Laurie had volunteered for a mission forty-eight hours ago. Over on the Continent, his kite (which was pilot-speak for plane) had taken fire during a rodeo (a mission), which had forced him to bail out (eject) over the English Channel. He'd managed to bob along in the cold water for hours before he was rescued, so he had hypothermia on top of a fractured ankle and a reopened appendectomy wound.

Amy had nodded off on a bench when an old nurse shook her shoulder and told her that she could see Laurie now. Jolting awake, Amy followed the nurse down the hallway and entered the third door on the right. The room itself was narrow and chilly, with multiple beds lined up one after the other. A sheer curtain provided privacy in between each mattress, and Amy found Laurie's bed by the window.

She rushed forward, both relieved and alarmed at what she saw, the aftermath of the crash all over his body: His foot in a cast. Burns and bruises. Bandages covering his midsection, and more on one side of his head, hiding what looked to be a nasty gash.

Amy grazed his hand with her fingertips. He'd always been so strong, so steady—she still remembered the pull of his arms when he'd saved her from drowning—and yet he had been breakable all along.

"Damned Nazis," she whispered. They did this to him. They'd nearly killed him.

She shuddered to consider how close he had been to dying.

Without thinking, Amy gripped his hand, sliding her fingers against his, but she startled when his eyelids twitched. "Laurie? Can you hear me? You're back at the hospital in London."

He blinked slowly, and when he saw her standing over him, a drowsy smile kicked up on his lips. "You sure are a sight for sore eyes."

Amy laughed in surprise; the anesthesia must've made him loopy. "How're you feeling?"

"Like I've spun around the merry-go-round a few too many times."

"I should get the doctor." She went to leave, but his grip tightened, keeping her close.

"They'll only poke and prod at me. Hey, is it me, or is it freezing in here?"

"I bet there's an extra blanket somewhere," she said, taking her hand back reluctantly before searching around the bed. She found a scratchy-looking throw stowed underneath and spread it over him, careful to tuck it under his feet to keep his toes warm. She had done the very same for Beth during her sister's final days.

But Laurie wasn't going to die.

She had to remind herself of that.

"You really gave me a scare today," she blurted, cringing at how much her voice was trembling. She wanted to sound un-flappable in front of him, not like some whimpering girl.

"But I'm fine, aren't I?" he said with a wink.

"Hardly. Look at where you are, Laurie!"

"Aw, give me a week and I'll be fit enough to jive you all over Rainbow Corner. And I still owe you tea and crumpets. I haven't forgotten, you know."

Amy's mind filled with an image of him spinning her on the dance floor, followed by him escorting her to Claridge's for their long-awaited date.

Not a date, she had to remind herself. It wasn't that long ago when Laurie was calling her a kid and a pal so she had to temper her expectations, but the way he was talking to her right now . . . she dared to wonder if he was starting to look at her differently.

"How are my commissions coming along?" he said hoarsely.

"Oh. That." She blinked hard, falling back into the moment. How could she begin to tell him why she didn't draw anymore? "Things have gotten awfully busy at work—"

"It's all right. I've been a terrible pen pal so I guess I deserve it," he said, cracking another grin. Despite the bandages on his head and the scratches on his face, that smile of his still managed to tug at Amy's heart. "I did keep all the letters you sent to me, though."

She looked at him with a skeptical brow.

"I really did save them," he went on. "Other than my grandfather, you are the only one from home who's written to me regularly."

"That can't be true," Amy said. Laurie had always had plenty of friends at church and at school, especially in his music classes. She figured he would've gotten a bag of mail per week.

He shrugged. "There are a lot of soldiers to write to these days. Guess I've got a lot of competition. So your letters meant a whole lot. More than you know," he said, taking her hand and lifting it to his lips, where he kissed it softly.

Amy's skin tingled all over, especially when he kept his hand on hers. She dared not to breathe or move, only staring at where they touched.

But the nurse soon returned, smiling to herself when she spotted the two of them together, and she sounded reluctant to announce that Amy would have to return later.

"Looks like I'm getting the boot," Amy said to Laurie. She turned to go, but he didn't let her leave just yet.

"You'll be back, though?"

"Soon as I can," she assured him, squeezing his hand while her stomach went all fluttery. "Get some rest before then. That's an order."

"Aye, aye, Captain." He tried to give a salute, but it looked like the drugs were pulling him under.

On her way out of the hospital, Amy couldn't stop looking down at her hand. The old nurse caught up with her and chuckled.

"Did you and your beau have a nice chat?" she asked.

Heat shot up Amy's neck. "He isn't my beau. Only an old friend."

"Old friends make the very best beaus, if you ask me," the nurse said slyly before carrying on in the opposite direction.

Amy felt her face turn as red as Marmee's strawberry pie before she ducked toward the nearest door. That was when the guilt kicked in. Why didn't she ever feel warm and flushed on her dates with Fred? Besides, Laurie hadn't professed his undying love to her or anything of the sort. But whenever she glanced at the spot on her hand that he'd kissed, she got a giddy feeling in her stomach all over again.

And she wasn't sure what to do with it.

Back at the hotel, Amy crept up the stairs, careful not to wake anyone. Despite her best efforts, though, as she slipped into her room, the door let out a creak and Edie popped up.

"You're back!" Edie said, climbing off the bunk and striding over to Amy. "Look at you. You're glowing."

"Am I?" Amy touched her cheek and wondered if her feelings were that transparent. She was quick to clear her throat. "It must be from the cold. Anyway, Laurie made it through surgery just fine."

"That's wonderful! How long will he stay at the hospital this time around?"

"I'm not sure. A few weeks, I imagine."

"Plenty of time to play nursemaid." Edie waggled her brows.

Amy didn't think her face could grow any redder, which was why she breathed a sigh of relief when Marion stirred and propped herself onto her elbows.

"What time is it?" Marion asked groggily.

"Early," Amy said, girding herself for Marion to start clucking about her being out so late.

Instead, Marion tossed her blanket from her legs. "How's Lieutenant Laurence doing? Edie filled me in."

"He got lucky. He should make a full recovery."

"That's wonderful news," Marion said, and she sounded genuine about it. "I'm sure that you're very relieved."

"Now, let's all keep mum about Rosie slipping in late. Nobody go tattling to Owens, hmm?" Edie said suddenly. Her tone was light, but Amy noticed Edie eyeing Marion, a not-so-subtle reminder about that night at the Savoy. "Well then, ladies, we should get some shut-eye before our alarms go off."

"It's nearly time to get up anyway," Marion said coolly, "and I've been meaning to finish a couple letters."

Marion moved past Edie and took a seat at her desk, where she grabbed her stationery and twisted the knobs on the Murphy wireless that she'd recently bought secondhand. She dialed it to the BBC to hear the news reports, which detailed the latest war developments. The Battle of Stalingrad waged on, and the RAF had bombed the city of Eindhoven in Nazi-controlled Netherlands. Amy was only half listening, though, her mind still floating somewhere between here and the hospital.

"And now we bring a story from across the Atlantic," the newscaster said in a crisp English accent. "The US Army has announced that it will create a new regiment to debut next year, consisting of American citizens of Japanese descent. The War Office has called for fifteen hundred volunteers from the territory of Hawaii."

Marion sat up straight and turned up the volume.

Edie snorted from her bunk. "Will you turn off that drivel?"

"I hardly think the BBC counts as drivel," Marion said, not even turning around.

"Roosevelt is full of malarkey. Did he conveniently forget what the Japanese did to us at Pearl Harbor?" Edie's eyes found Amy, silently asking for support.

"It was terrible," Amy said, wanting to be a good friend. "We'll never forget the men who died there."

"You don't have to remind me. I saw the aftermath first-hand," Marion said, shutting her eyes like she was trying to ward off the memory. When she opened them again, there was a hardness in her gaze. "But I think you're mixing up Hirohito with regular Japanese Americans."

"Tell that to Bobby," Edie said, a tremor in her voice.

The whole room went quiet. Amy's eyes shifted between her roommates, and she wished she could say something to smooth things over.

In the end, it was Marion who broke the silence. "I'm sorry about your cousin, Edie. Really, I am. But . . ." She looked like she wanted to say something more, and yet nothing came out.

"But what?" Edie said fiercely.

"We're never going to see eye to eye on this. That's all," Marion murmured. She grabbed her shower caddy. "I'd better get ready."

After the hasty departure, Amy snuck a glance at Edie, who

was sitting up in her bunk, her face pale. She reached up to pat Edie's hand. "How about I make you some toast and tea?"

Edie didn't answer the question. "Did Marion even hear herself? She goes around calling us khaki-wacky while she's the one sticking up for the enemy."

"I don't know if she was doing exactly that," Amy said, choosing her words carefully.

Edie jerked her hand from Amy's. "Japanese, *Japanese Americans.* Honestly, what's the difference?"

Amy looked down at her nails as her pulse thumped. She had heard these types of comments right after Pearl Harbor, too. Her classmates had said them; her neighbors as well. Even Brother Randall from church had commented during their annual Easter brunch that he was mighty glad that Roosevelt had signed Executive Order 9066, which had led to the incarceration of Japanese Americans out west. Amy had listened to all of that while stewing in her seat. She couldn't help but think about Ginny Tanaka's father, who'd been interrogated by the FBI and had gotten sent to the East Boston Detention Facility even though he had done nothing wrong. The authorities only released him after his college provost had gotten involved.

She had been sorely tempted to cup her hands around her mouth and call Brother Randall a know-nothing dipstick in front of the entire congregation. Except Amy had stayed quiet. She'd lost her nerve.

Amy blinked up, feeling tongue-tied all over again. Edie wasn't a dipstick, though, like Brother Randall had been. Edie was her friend. A very dear friend, to boot.

"Please don't be mad at me," Amy found herself saying. "I'm on your side."

Edie glanced at her skeptically. "Truly?"

"Truly."

"Then you'll help me play a little prank on Marion?"

Amy got a squirmy feeling in her gut, but she ignored it. "What sort of a prank?"

"I have to work out the details, but I think it's about time to make up a batch of that humble pie. You in?" She stuck out a hand for Amy to shake.

Amy regarded Edie's palm for a moment before swallowing at the swell in her throat. A prank was all in good fun, right? She reached up and grasped Edie's hand.

"Sure thing. Count me in."

An hour and a half later, the girls headed to work again, yet another day at the docks to give the GIs a proper send-off. Amy found herself back at the fryer. With every bowl of dough that she mixed, she wondered about Laurie and what he might be thinking. With every doughnut she served, she would glance at her hand, right at the spot where his lips had touched her skin. More than once, Marion had to remind her to refill the doughnut trays, but Amy let the criticism slide for once—her mind was already elsewhere.

As soon as she finished rinsing the very last coffee cup, Amy was off to see him again, only pausing to change her clothes and make another pit stop before beelining for the hospital. She was a little out of breath by the time she arrived.

She found Laurie in bed with his broken ankle propped up while he picked at his dinner tray, which consisted of various brown lumps of food. Amy stepped in front of his cot, with her arms spread wide.

"Surprise!" she said, grinning.

"Amy?" he said, his tone a little unsure. His cloud of anesthesia had obviously cleared by then. "One of the nurses mentioned that you dropped by yesterday."

Her smile started to fade. "You don't remember?"

"Bits and pieces mostly. I hope I didn't say anything too odd. The doctors mentioned that anesthesia can have that effect on some people."

Something withered inside Amy. Something like hope.

When Laurie had told her that she was a sight for sore eyes and when he'd kissed her hand . . . was it all because of the drugs?

"God, what did I say?" Laurie said, mortified, as he watched her face.

"Not a whole lot," Amy blurted out. She realized that she must've looked like a fool, standing there openmouthed while holding on to a bag of Golden Lotus takeout. She'd thought it would be a wonderful surprise, and she'd hoped that he would be thrilled to see her. Now she was tempted to drop the bag on his lap and run the other way. But she had just enough pride intact to pretend that she wasn't bothered at all.

"Jimmy sends his regards," she said breezily. "As soon as I mentioned that you were at the hospital, his mom made you some steamed fish on the house."

Laurie peeked into the bag, and his face brightened like it was his birthday. He set his hospital tray aside and opened the containers of fish and rice before thanking her profusely. "Care to join me?"

She eyed the exit. "I should get going, actually."

"The Clubmobile comes a-calling?" he said. He was trying to make a joke of it, but he sounded disappointed. "Aw, pull out a chair and stay a little while."

Amy hesitated. Why was it so hard to say no to him?

"Do it for a sad, injured sack like me?" he added.

Her mouth twitched upward. "However will you survive? Oh, very well, but I can't stay long. I didn't get much sleep last night."

"I can't thank you enough for this. Christmas sure came early for me this year," he said, digging into the steamed fish with gusto and giving her a wink.

It was a small gesture—a single blink of his right eye, nothing more—but Amy's pulse did a little waltz anyway, and she wanted to strangle the damned thing.

"Speaking of Christmas, I had an idea I wanted to run past you," he continued. "How about you come and spend a little time at the hospital that day? I could play a few carols on the piano, and maybe you could sketch some of the soldiers. I bet that would really lift their spirits."

Amy froze at the request, which would have sounded absolutely lovely . . . if she hadn't set aside her pencils and brushes over a year ago.

Laurie noticed her reaction and backpedaled. "Sorry, I shouldn't have volunteered you like that. If you already had plans—"

"It isn't that." She took a long breath and decided to tell the same lie that she'd told her family. "I realized not too long ago that I'll never be a Waterhouse or a Turner when it comes to art. I don't have the genius for it like they did. So I gave it up."

"You . . . gave it up?"

"Painting. Sketching. All of it." She shrugged. "I either want to be great or nothing. Not something in between."

It took Laurie a minute to take this all in, and even after he had thought it over he still looked confused. "Ever since I've known you, you've either been painting or drawing or making a plaster mold of something. I got the sense that art made you happy and that was enough. Like it was for Beth and the piano."

Amy smoothed the creases in her skirt, wishing she hadn't said anything at all, because she didn't want to cry in front of him. "Beth's gone, Laurie."

He went quiet again, but she refused to meet his eye. Instead, she looked out the window and watched the military trucks pass by, until she felt his hand over hers.

"I miss her, too," he said softly.

Her heart split in half. He'd had to go and say that, hadn't he?

The tears came unbidden, flowing down Amy's cheeks like small rivers. She wasn't sure how it had happened, but the next thing she knew Laurie was holding her in his arms and she was crying into his shoulder while he stroked her hair and told her that she should let it all out and that he was right here.

By the time her tears finally dried, Amy was more miserable than before, because now she knew one thing with absolute certainty.

It was useless to fight it.

She was falling for him.

Falling

It's a little like falling in love, dying.
At least, I think so.
I've only done one of those things.

The more you fight it, the harder it is.
Some parts are bound to be painful.
It's messier than you expect.

You have to give up control.
But you end up somewhere
you never could have imagined.

CHAPTER 22

MEG

Meg was leaving the teachers' lunchroom when she turned a corner in the corridor and ran smack into Doro Scott.

"Pardon me." Meg knelt to pick up the textbooks Doro had dropped. Then she realized the girl's books were covered in something pink and sticky. She handed them back to Doro, brought her palm to her nose, and sniffed. Peppermint frosting? Meg looked more closely at Doro. Her red sweater, white Peter Pan collar, plaid skirt, black Mary Janes, even her *hair*—the poor girl was splattered from head to toe.

Meg pulled a handkerchief from her pocket and handed it to Doro. "Home ec mishap?"

"That stupid Sunbeam Mixmaster!" Doro wailed. "Mrs. Pratt thinks I did it on purpose!"

"*Did* you?" It was not beyond Doro, if she thought it would get a laugh.

Doro looked indignant—or as indignant as one could while covered in sugar-cookie icing. "No! Those cookies are for

Santa's workshop at the fire station. I know sugar's in short supply. I just got distracted and lifted up the beater, and frosting went everywhere. Mrs. Pratt was *hopping* mad."

"That's been happening a lot, hasn't it? Getting distracted?" Meg said, sympathetic. "I noticed you woolgathering in class today."

Doro's shoulders drooped. "It's almost Christmas, is all."

"It'll be a hard one this year," Meg said. For her, too.

She had been trying to keep herself busy. The Junior Red Cross had sewn dozens of khaki twill comfort kits to be filled with shaving, sewing, and writing materials for soldiers. They were also organizing a donation drive for the Victory Book Campaign—a national Red Cross collaboration with the USO and the American Library Association—to collect books, magazines, and newspapers to send to the men fighting overseas.

Personally, Meg had already checked everything off her Christmas list. She and Marmee had sent Father a package of coffee, candy, cigars, socks, and other treats ages ago, because it took so long for parcels to reach the Pacific. She had mailed Christmas cards illustrated with adorable frolicking kittens to all her old school friends. John's gifts had been mailed, too: a folding checkers set and a khaki ditty bag. She had made Marmee a smart new apron and had splurged on a bottle of her mother's favorite scent, Je Reviens. She had sent Jo a Parker Vacumatic fountain pen—maybe she would get the hint and write!—and Amy a red Bakelite bracelet.

Still, Meg couldn't help feeling that something was missing. What would she have given Beth this year? Maybe she would have crocheted a new collar and cuffs onto Beth's tattered pink sweater, her favorite, so that it looked brand-new. Or she could have bought her sheet music for that Bing Crosby song that was all over the radio, "White Christmas."

Meg started back to her classroom, Doro walking alongside her. "It's going to be awful, Miss March. Just me and Ma, staring at each other and crying."

"I'm dreading it myself," Meg admitted.

As they passed her classroom, Miss Pennington poked her head out the door. "What's this? Miss Scott, why aren't you in class?"

Meg frowned. "Agatha, I have this well in hand."

Miss Pennington looked from her to the frosting-splattered, downcast Doro. Meg wasn't sure what she saw, but the older woman gave a brisk nod. "Carry on, then."

As they reached Meg's classroom, an idea hit her. Miss Pennington would never. But Marmee wouldn't mind a whit. It was, in fact, a very Marmee idea. "Doro. What if you and your mother spent Christmas at my house? I can't promise there won't be any crying, but I'll try to keep it to a minimum. We'll have a tree, and I'll make gingersnaps, and we can listen to carols on the radio."

"Really?" A smile crept over Doro's face. "Your mother wouldn't mind? We wouldn't come empty-handed. Ma makes a good pecan pie. And her chestnut stuffing is swell. It was Richie's favorite."

"I think she would love it, actually. The more the merrier!" Meg and Marmee would both like having someone to fuss over and take their minds off their own sadness, and dinner for five (Laurie's grandfather was already invited) wasn't much more work than dinner for three. "I'll have her ring your mother this evening."

"That would be *wizard*, Miss March. Thanks. Hey, want me to erase this?" Doro pointed at the chalkboard. She really ought to go get cleaned up—she had managed to smear the frosting all over her face with the handkerchief—but she seemed to want to linger, and Meg had a few minutes before her next class.

"That would be very nice, thank you, Dorothy."

Doro attacked the chalkboard with an eraser in each hand. "You're so *good*, Miss March. I wish I could be more like you."

Meg was touched, but also a little concerned. "I'm not perfect, Doro. I can be awfully vain, and when I get my feelings hurt, I can be mean. I worry too much about what other people think, and I'm proud. And I have an awful singing voice! It's terrible, truly."

Doro laughed. "Nobody's perfect, miss. But you really care about people. Like inviting me for Christmas so I won't be stuck at home with Ma, crying my eyes out. And letting me smash those plates."

"You inspire me, too, you know," Meg said, and Doro turned to face her, surprised. "You're fiercely loyal, and you are the most honest person I've ever met. You face things head-on, and you tell people what you think . . . even when you might be better off holding your tongue. There's courage in that. It makes me want to be brave, too, and tell certain people how I feel."

Doro got a sly look. "Like Mr. Brooke?"

"Hush, you!" Meg flushed. "*And* you've got a great right hook. You laid Woody out flat." She winked. "Not that I approve of violence, mind you!"

Doro laughed so hard she cried. Or maybe she was just crying now. "Richie taught me," she sniffled.

Meg patted her on the shoulder. "He was a pretty great big brother, wasn't he?"

"The best." Doro used Meg's frosting-covered handkerchief to mop up her tears.

The bell rang. "You'd better go wash up or you'll be late for your next class. But ask your mother about Christmas, all right?"

"All right, on one condition." Doro grinned. "You have to promise not to sing!"

When Meg came through the front door that afternoon, she found Mr. Laurence slumped on the brown leather chesterfield. The old gentleman was holding a Western Union telegram in his liver-spotted hands. Marmee sat beside him.

"We've had some news," he said when he saw Meg. His voice shook.

Meg's heart stuttered. "Father?" She barely managed to get the word out.

"No! No, Meg, it's not Father." Marmee rushed to Meg and wrapped a comforting arm around her waist. "Father's all right."

John? A training accident? Meg swayed and caught herself on the back of Marmee's wingback chair. Fear swamped her. She couldn't bring herself to say his name. She looked at her mother wordlessly.

"It's Laurie," Marmee explained. "He's been wounded. His plane took fire over the English Channel, and he had to bail out. He's in the hospital in London."

Mr. Laurence handed Meg the telegram:

```
REGRET TO INFORM YOU THAT YOUR
GRANDSON LIEUTENANT THEODORE LAURENCE
WOUNDED IN ACTION OVER ENGLISH
CHANNEL STOP YOU WILL BE ADVISED AS
REPORTS OF CONDITION RECEIVED
```

Meg handed the telegram back, then sank onto the old rose-colored davenport.

"Was he badly injured? Do you know anything else?" Meg pictured Beth, so still and pale in her bed.

"Mr. Laurence made some calls. He's pretty banged up. A broken ankle. But he'll be all right," Marmee said.

"Thank God." Meg peeled off her heavy wool trench coat.

"He could have been killed!" Mr. Laurence said. "I had a word with an old friend in the War Office, you know. He was supposed to stay in Utah for the duration, but he was too damned stubborn."

Marmee sat next to Mr. Laurence and patted his arm. "We would keep all our little chicks in the nest if we could. He only wants to do his part. Prove himself."

Prove himself to Jo? Meg wondered. Had Laurie signed up for some foolish, dangerous mission to try to win her heart?

Jo! She didn't know about Laurie yet. Would Marmee phone her? Would Jo come to the phone if she did? Meg could picture her sister, a whirlwind of fear and fury and admiration. Even if Jo wasn't *in love* with Laurie, Meg knew she cared for him very much, and she would be devastated to think of him lying in a hospital in London.

Meg's mind went to John, as it did so often these days. He had graduated from officer training; he was now Second Lieutenant Brooke. His unit would be shipping out soon after the New Year, and he didn't know if he'd be granted a leave beforehand. Meg imagined the worst: a German U-boat sneaking along and torpedoing the ship as it ferried John across the Atlantic. Dread flooded through her.

She had to make sure he knew how she felt. Who cared about the rules of decorum? There was a war on, and anything could happen.

John deserved to know exactly who she was, warts and all. If that changed his feelings for her . . .

She hoped it wouldn't.

Meg made polite chitchat with Mr. Laurence, but the moment Marmee had seen him to the door, she flew into the kitchen and pulled her stationery from the shelf.

My dearest John, she wrote. She broke the news of Laurie's injury. Then she paused, fiddling with the pearl necklace at her throat.

> *When I saw Mr. Laurence with that telegram in his hands and such a grim look on his face, for a moment, I thought it was Father. Then I thought of you, and I could scarcely breathe. I can't let another moment go by without telling you, John. I wish I could say it in person, but here it is: I love you.*

Meg went back and underlined the last three words for emphasis.

> *I hope you won't think me too forward for saying it, but who knows what could happen while you cross the*

Atlantic, and I couldn't live with myself if I didn't tell you the true depth of my feelings.

I haven't been entirely honest with you, John. I haven't wanted to complain, I suppose, when you are working so hard and sacrificing so much. Marmee says it's our duty to be cheerful and keep our soldiers' spirits up. But the truth is that it's been very lonesome here since Jo and Amy went away. Sometimes I'm furious with them for leaving. Beth had no choice in it, but they did. They've left me alone with Marmee and a house full of happy memories turned bittersweet. Marmee's not herself, and neither am I. I've been awfully mixed-up, John. Sometimes I think you'd be ashamed of me. I've been angry and petty, and even a little bit mean. I'm embarrassed to say it, but I went out with another fellow. It was a mistake, and nothing happened between us. I wished he were you the whole time. And I swear my feelings for you have never wavered. I'll tell you everything when you come home, safe and sound. I pray that you will come home to me. I'll wait for you.

Yours,
Meg

The Words

How much we loved each other
was never a question
but now that I no longer have a voice
I wonder if I said the words enough.

They almost seemed ridiculous.
We wouldn't say the sky is blue,
the ice is cold, so why would we bother
with something even more apparent?

I wish I'd said the words more often
and not because I think you doubt my love.
I never doubted any one of yours.
I wish I'd said it because it was the truth.

It is, and saying it
reminds me of nights
before the fire, kittens
under blankets, stories
from Jo's pen, and sisters.

I love you.

CHAPTER 23

AMY

Amy tried to wean herself off Laurie. Really, she did.

She even made a list of rules to follow. Number one: She would not think about him in excess. Number two: She would restrict her hospital visits to every other day and for half an hour each. Forty-five minutes tops. That was plenty of time to check on his recovery, and besides, she had Fred to consider. Fred, who was attentive and attractive. Fred, who could provide a life without stresses and worries. If she married him, she would never have to wring her hands over how to pay for the leaky roof or the broken oven, like Marmee often did. She'd have a husband who doted on her to excess and who thought she was prettier than Joan Fontaine. So who cared if he talked about the Red Sox too much? She'd have comfort all her days.

But would she have love?

Love can come with time, Amy thought.

In any case, it wasn't like Laurie was offering her an alternative. He thought of her only as an old friend. A chum. A pal. For all Amy knew, he still had eyes for Jo.

So that was that. She needed to put an end to her feelings

once and for all, and she really needed to respond to Fred. She'd tell him that she couldn't meet him in Boston on account of school, but that she was thinking about him (which was very much true) and that she cared for him (which was true, too . . . in a friendly sort of way).

"Amy, dear, you've got a visitor downstairs. A gentleman caller!" Edie declared in a put-on Southern drawl while her socked feet drummed up the stairs to the hotel's third floor. Both Amy and Marion were standing in the hallway, mops in hand, since it was their turn to clean the shared washroom and corridor.

Amy wiped the sweat from her forehead. "What? Who?"

"I'll venture a guess as to whom it might be," Marion said dryly.

Amy's pulse tapped out a quick beat. "It can't be. What's he doing out of bed?" she thought aloud as she propped her mop against the wall. She hurried down the stairs, where she found Laurie in the foyer.

"Laurie!" she exclaimed when she caught a glimpse of his crutch. "You shouldn't be up and about!"

He took off his hat as soon as he spotted her, which made her traitorous heart do a flip. "Don't worry. The doc gave me the go-ahead to start moving around."

"I doubt he meant for you to hobble across the city! You should be resting."

One side of his mouth kicked up. "You sounded like Marmee when you said that."

"I'll take that as a compliment. Let's get you back to the hospital."

"I'm not going to keel over, if that's what you think. Besides,

I've got an errand to run, and I was hoping you'd come with me. I could use your advice."

Her brow furrowed. "What sort of advice?"

"I need to pick out a Christmas gift for my grandfather. I know, I know, I should've sent it over a month ago considering how slow the mail can be, but what do you say? Ever been to Selfridges?"

The offer was tempting indeed. Amy had heard about London's premier department store, of course, but hadn't yet had the chance to visit. She rather liked the thought of spending the day trying on fancy hats and suede gloves, but a trip like that would mean breaking her own rules—she'd be spending much longer than forty-five minutes with Laurie.

He poked her in the side. "If you don't come, I'll probably end up buying my grandfather a scratchy wool sweater or a tin of haggis."

Amy knew that she should say no. She needed to finish cleaning upstairs, lest she get an earful from Marion or Supervisor Owens, but her heart had other ideas. Didn't she want to help out old Mr. Laurence, celebrating Christmas on his own in that big mansion of his? And after everything he had done for Beth, didn't the Marches owe him a nice holiday present?

"Let me get my coat," Amy said before she could stop herself. She ran back up to the third-floor landing where Edie and Marion awaited. "Would I be an awful fathead if I finished up my chores later?"

Marion's mouth pursed. "Supervisor Owens likes to keep to a schedule."

"I'll finish up Rosie's tasks," Edie chimed in. "I'm almost

done anyway, and Owens won't mind as long as the work gets done."

"Thanks, doll, I owe you one," Amy said to Edie, blowing her a kiss before grabbing her coat from their room and sweeping on a little pink blush to put some color on her cheeks.

After hailing a cab, Amy and Laurie took a short drive over to Oxford Circus, the heart of the city's shopping district. The area had been badly damaged during the Blitz, and Amy's mouth dropped open at the sights. A German oil bomb had exploded in the neighborhood back in 1940 and had completely ravaged some of the buildings there. She stared up at the charred skeleton of the John Lewis department store, still standing on the bare legs of its foundation, with all the windows blown out.

But London had plowed onward. The cab pulled up to their destination, which took up the entire city block. The Selfridges building had been damaged, too, during the blast, but not badly enough to have shut down. The Beaux-Arts masterpiece was still stunning, with its towering pillars, and business was booming. The store was packed with Londoners eager to get their holiday shopping finished, considering Christmas was only two days away.

"Careful there," Amy said on the way inside. Laurie's crutch had caught on a slick piece of pavement and he'd almost tumbled into a middle-aged woman carrying an armful of holiday boxes.

"This damned crutch," Laurie mumbled.

"Here, take my arm," Amy offered, and they walked into the store linked together. Amy figured that this was merely the practical thing to do—she couldn't have him tripping again, after all—but when she glimpsed the two of them in a mirror together she thought that they rather suited each other.

Don't think like that, she cautioned herself.

But it was too late. She'd broken another one of her rules.

Amy removed her arm from Laurie's to create a little distance and refocused on why she had agreed to come with him in the first place. They had a mission to carry out.

They spent the next half hour picking out gifts for Mr. Laurence—a wool scarf in a tartan pattern, a fine ballpoint pen with accompanying monogrammed stationery, and a beautiful silver picture frame that was fine enough to become a family heirloom.

"You should put a picture of yourself in that frame before you send it to your grandfather," Amy said. "I bet it would look lovely on the mantel in the parlor."

"The frame actually isn't for him," Laurie said vaguely.

"Oh, I shouldn't have assumed," Amy replied, trying to sound casual but furiously wondering whom the frame would be for. His superior? A pretty English girl he'd met? *Jo?* She was tallying up all the possibilities when they wandered into the ladies' section of the store.

"How do you like me in this?" Laurie said as he tried on a red beret from a nearby display and pretended that he was Fred Astaire in *You'll Never Get Rich.*

Amy swatted him in the arm and tried to tell him that the saleswomen were frowning at him, but she was giggling too much to get a word out, because now he was moving and shaking like Ginger Rogers.

After Amy's giggling fit subsided, Laurie returned the hat

and nodded around the store. "Do you want to pick up anything for your sisters? We might as well, since we're here already."

They'd wandered into the dress section of the store, filled with evening gowns and party dresses that Amy could never dream of affording. She trailed a single finger along a floor-length dress made from lilac silk and sighed a little, wishing that Meg were here, because she would ooh and aah over everything in sight, especially the delicate silver beading. Beth would've loved this excursion, too. She'd been shy, yes, but even she would've appreciated the pretty pairs of ankle-strap pumps.

Jo, however, would've rolled her eyes and sulked in a store corner, groaning about how bored she was. At which point Meg would've planted a hand on her hip and said, *Then go find a bookstore.* And they all would've had a good laugh.

Amy's heart ached as she wondered how they were doing. Were Meg and John close to getting engaged? How was Jo doing at her new job? Did they ever regret how they had parted ways?

Did they miss her like she missed them?

"Everything all right? You look sad," Laurie said, his face dipping toward hers and his eyes filled with concern. They were standing so close.

Too close.

Amy drew back a step, swallowing hard. "I better head home before Marion kills me."

"I can tell something's bothering you," he said gently.

"Me? I'm swell," she replied, her voice strained, and she made herself smile. "I really should get going. Duty calls and all that. Walk me outside?"

"But—"

Amy was already in motion, threading through the shoppers, until she exited onto Duke Street. Eventually Laurie caught up and they waited in line for a cab with their breath fogging in the cold and their ears turning pink from the nippy air. Amy cursed herself for forgetting her mittens, and she rubbed her hands together to keep them from going numb.

"Here, take my gloves. I think I have some extra on me," Laurie said. He gave her his still-warm pair while he searched for another in his coat, but in the process of rummaging, an old letter slipped out of one of the inner pockets and landed by Amy's shoe. She stooped down to retrieve it and couldn't help but notice that it was addressed to Marmee.

"Trading state secrets with my mother?" Amy said, teasing him, and pretended to open the envelope.

But Laurie didn't chuckle in return. Instead, he grew flustered and made a grab for it. "I meant to throw that away."

She pivoted away from him. "You're really turning red!"

"Will you give that here?" His face was looking truly scalded now, and he plucked the letter out of her hands before ripping it clean in half.

Amy's laughter shriveled up in her throat. "Goodness, Laurie." She'd thought they were only having a little bit of fun. "What did you write in there that has you so bothered?"

"It doesn't matter," he said before he shook his head and stared at the two halves in his hands. He looked a bit shocked at what he'd done. "I'm sorry. I was embarrassed."

"Embarrassed about what?" She saw his jaw tense, and now her curiosity was well and truly piqued, but she didn't want to pry too much. "You don't have to tell me if you don't want to."

"No, no, I should explain." He drew in a long breath and held it for a moment. "You know that day when we first saw each other in London? When we ate at the Golden Lotus?" He waited for her to nod before he continued. "After I returned to the hospital that night, I wrote a letter to your mother. This one right here. And I . . . I told her that you'd used a false name to join the Red Cross and that you were in England, not in Montreal."

Amy's eyes went rounder and rounder as he spoke. "You were ratting me out?"

"No! Well, yes, at the time. But I didn't mail it, obviously," he said, waving the ripped envelope at her. "I changed my mind about the whole thing, but then I couldn't find the letter for the life of me. Until now."

Amy blinked at the letter, then back at his face, letting his revelation settle in her mind. The sting of his confession had begun to cool, but she still had some questions.

She studied his gaze. "So what made you change your mind?"

"Honestly?" A ghost of a smile played at his lips. "When you slapped that Frenchman at the Savoy."

Amy let out a startled laugh. "He was *Belgian*."

"I'm pretty sure your handprint is still on his cheek," Laurie said, and both of them shared a wicked grin.

"You can tell me the truth, though," Amy said. "Why didn't you mail that letter?"

"I *was* telling you the truth." He rubbed the back of his neck, looking like he was searching for the right words. "I think something clicked together in my mind at that moment. I realized that you didn't need my protection. Or your parents'. Or anyone's, really. And that I was being an ass for assuming otherwise."

Impulsively, Amy stood on her tiptoes and kissed him right on the cheek. He *had* been a bit of an ass, but at least he saw that now. "Thank you for saying that," she said before scuttling back, feeling shy at what she'd done.

Another smile spread across his face. "Remind me to fess up my mistakes more often."

Was he . . . ? No, he couldn't be. . . . But was he flirting with her a little?

As the cab pulled up, Laurie pressed the tattered letter into her hands. "Here, take this. Shred it. Burn it. Do what you want with it." He seemed eager to be rid of the thing. "I'll see you at the hospital in a couple days? For our little recital?"

"You know I wouldn't miss it," she said. She had already agreed to go to the hospital on Christmas Day to sing carols for the soldiers and listen to Laurie play the piano. She'd come with a couple of pies, freshly baked by the other Clubmobile girls, as well as pencil and paper to sketch the troops. Amy still wasn't sure how she felt about that last part, but she figured she would do this as a favor to Uncle Sam. And to Laurie, of course. Her holiday this year would surely look different from the ones she was used to back in Concord, but Amy was looking forward to it. She might've been a whole ocean away from Massachusetts, but she'd have a little piece of home with her here—in fact, he was standing right in front of her.

"Glad to hear that, because Christmas isn't Christmas without the Marches," Laurie said. And then, much to Amy's surprise, Laurie gave her a squeeze, his arms lingering around her just long enough for her to smell his aftershave. She drank it in, trying to memorize the scent, before he reached for the car door.

After settling in the cab, Amy had a hard time sitting still. She couldn't stop thinking about Laurie's hug and puzzling over it. It had felt like more than a friendly gesture, hadn't it? A giddy thrill zipped through her, and she couldn't wait to see him again. Edie could help put up her hair in Victory rolls, but Amy still had to figure out Laurie's present. She'd already bought him a new calendar and a tin of hard candy, but those seemed too dull now—like something she'd buy for a teacher or a neighbor whose name she couldn't keep straight. She ought to give him something special. Something from the heart.

An idea struck her then, making her blush from cheek to cheek.

It might just be perfect.

The question was—would she be brave enough to give it to him?

The next forty-eight hours passed in a blur. Between frying up doughnuts in the Clubmobile and doing chores around the hotel, Amy had to find snatches of time whenever she could to work on Laurie's gift, usually when she should've been sleeping. With a charcoal stick in one hand and the leather notebook splayed on her lap, she sketched for the first time in nearly a year. She drew far into the night, curled up in one of the comfy armchairs in the common room so that she would have more space to spread out. It felt strange at first. Her fingers, rusty after disuse, had started to cramp a mere hour into the session but her old muscle memory came back eventually.

Her hands remembered what to do, so she let them fly. She sketched Laurie's form first, how she remembered him from that night at the Savoy, with his cap askew and his shoulders broad. Then she tossed that draft aside and started again, drawing him in profile this time. Yes, that felt more right.

In the flickering candlelight, Amy stretched her fingers and looked over the drawing, feeling exhilarated and scared at the same time. The sketch was really taking shape, but what if Laurie sighed and shook his head at her present? What if he gave the drawing back to her with a shrug and, with it, her heart?

She went to rip the sketch out of the notebook and dip it into the candle's flame, but something made her stop. A memory of Beth wriggled free from a corner of Amy's mind, from one of the last days that she was lucid. It had been a cold and gray morning, matching Amy's mood, as she held on to Beth's hand and tried not to cry.

Don't worry for me. I'm not afraid, Beth had said, her voice thin and reedy by that point.

I wish I could be as brave as you, Amy had whispered.

You are. Beth had pushed the hair back from Amy's eyes. *You already are.*

Amy blinked at her drawing, her eyes filling with tears. Beth had been so strong at the end. If she could muster only a quarter of that courage, she could certainly go through with this.

And so she lifted her charcoal stick once again.

By the time Christmas arrived, Amy was ready for it. More or less. She arose a few minutes after sunrise and, while Edie and Marion dozed in bed, she opened the notebook and gave the finished drawing one last look.

Amy had never been great with words—that was Jo's domain—but she had another way to pour her feelings onto the page. That was why she had sketched her and Laurie walking together along the Thames, just the two of them, a half-moon hanging over their heads. They each stood in profile, Laurie in his uniform and Amy in the same dress that she'd worn to the Savoy the night that he'd gotten them kicked out.

But here was where she strayed from memory.

In the drawing, she and Laurie were holding hands. They were staring at each other, too, and if only you could flip ahead a few pages, you'd be sure that they'd be kissing.

A shiver traveled up Amy's arm.

There was just one thing left to do.

Feeling breathless already, she snipped the paper from her notebook, rolled it up like a map, and tied it with a pretty ribbon. She hoped he wouldn't mind the simplicity of the wrapping, but it was the inside that counted, right? Her pulse did a fluttery flip. Oh, she was on pins and needles to see him.

As Amy hurried to curl her hair, the rest of the hotel stirred awake. Soon the hallways filled with the sounds of the girls getting dressed and saying "Merry Christmas" to each other. Even Supervisor Owens was in a giving mood, and she spread some holiday cheer by disbursing a new batch of mail, like a stern-looking Mrs. Claus. Amy went to fetch the parcels for Edie, Marion, and herself; and by the time she'd climbed back up to the third-floor landing, her arms were positively aching.

"Here, let me help you with that," Edie said as she stepped out of the washroom and bumped into Amy in the corridor.

"Your mail should be in my left hand," Amy grunted out, "and here's a box for you, too."

Edie took her things with a thank-you, but her eyes lingered on the remaining letters held in Amy's right fist. "How about those?"

"Those are Marion's."

"Mind if I take a peek?" Edie asked. When Amy wavered, her tone sharpened. "Come on. You said you'd help with my prank."

"Oh, right." Amy fidgeted, realizing she'd forgotten about that since she had been a little busy making Laurie's present. "You never told me what you had planned."

"Don't you worry. It'll be a real gas." Edie proceeded to grab and thumb through Marion's stack of mail until her eyes popped wide. "Jackpot! This one has to be from Marion's beau. Look at the return address!"

Amy peered at the envelope over Edie's shoulder. There had been some rain damage on the paper, so she couldn't make out the sender's last name, but the first name was still readable. *James.* Suddenly Amy felt unsettled. She'd assumed that Edie would try to dye Marion's hair blue or let a mouse loose under her covers. Something they could eventually laugh about. This, however, seemed more personal.

"What're you going to do with that?" Amy asked slowly. Marion had been waiting for a certain letter for weeks, and this had to be the one.

Edie only grinned. "I better get to work before Captain Sanctimonious wakes up. Aren't you supposed to be on your way to the hospital already?"

Amy looked at her watch and gave a little squeak when she

saw how late she was running. "Look, how about we chat about this little prank after I get back? I've got to go for now—and merry Christmas!"

Throwing on her coat, Amy made a mad dash for the hospital, with her drawing in one hand and with what felt like her heart in the other. Soon, she'd give both to Laurie to see what he thought of them.

Her pulse was humming by the time she reached the entrance, and her fingers were trembling when she neared Laurie's room. Goodness, she was nervous. She took a moment at the door to breathe in and out, then glanced at the ceiling.

I could use your help today, Beth, she thought as she gathered up all her courage.

"Knock, knock," she said softly before peeking through his curtain.

Laurie was asleep, and she smiled softly at the sight. His hair was combed and he was already dressed in his uniform, so he must've awoken earlier, then drifted off again. She tiptoed forward to shake him awake, until her gaze landed on the letter in his hand. She figured that it must've been a Christmas card from his grandfather, but she frowned when she recognized the script.

Amy knew her sisters' handwriting as well as she knew her own. Meg's, always neat and orderly. Beth's, with her loops and little flourishes. And Jo's, the easiest to spot of them all, with some words underlined and others completely capitalized, because she tended to think and write at the same time.

This letter was definitely from the latter.

Amy knew that she should look away. She ought to leave the thing be, but the damned letter seemed to have a magnetic pull on her, tugging her toward it inch by inch. Without thinking, she pulled the paper out of Laurie's fingertips and started to skim. And it didn't take long for her eyes to snag on a particular paragraph that sent a thorn straight into the softest spot of her heart.

I have cursed you and that day and that damnable question you cornered me into answering, so many times. I hurt you, I know it, and maybe you hate me for turning down your proposal, even now.

The letter continued, but Amy had already put it down. With her hopes severed, she turned on her heels and ran.

Brave

So brave, so strong,
noble little martyr.

Courage is when you have the choice
to do the thing that terrifies you
and you step toward the terror.

It's not courage if you're shoved
into the only option laid before you,
without a chance to retreat.

If I was brave
for playing out
the hand that I was dealt,
that erases the courage of

Laurie, shedding privilege
in order to fight Nazis;

Amy, crossing an ocean
to do her part;

Meg, holding steady
in the eye of the storm.

It erases Jo.

Light

I know you need
to remember me
as heroic and otherworldly
because otherwise
I was nothing more than
tragic.

But you don't have to die
to be brave. You don't
have to suffer to deserve
what the world has for you.
You don't undo my death
by hiding from your life.

Step into the light.
Be seen.
Be loved.

CHAPTER 24

JO

Dear Jo-not-Josephine,

I was pleased as punch to get your letter . . . and the enclosed story. I'd send you what I'm working on in return, but I'm not sure you'd find my current assignment interesting—it's about silk shortages and how it's affecting the stocking industry. Nothing terribly groundbreaking, I'm afraid.

While I'm still working hard on the factory-girl outline for my editor, I fear Peg's higher-ups did say something to him . . . thus the stocking story, as punishment. Please don't judge my sister too harshly, I beg of you. She was doing what she thought was best, and I'll bounce back. Sometimes I forget that Peg has more sisters than me—the bonds and kinship she shares with those in the air is something I've observed my whole life but never really got to be a part of. And big sisters have a way of knocking us back to earth, don't they?

Your friend,
Charlie

PS: I've written up a few notes on "The Woman in the Woods," mostly a few questions and then an idea for the scene right after the climax, but I feared sending them without asking first would be pushy. Feel free to tell me to shove off with my opinions. It's a riveting tale, even without any of my bits of advice.

Dear Charlie-not-Charlotte,

I suppose I cannot judge Peg, when I forgave my _own_ sister for destruction of another kind. But it hurts me to think of such a story being suppressed. There's comfort, though, in the idea of it someday coming to light, isn't there? Today will not always be TODAY. We will not always be at war. Someday, there _will_ be a new world. Perhaps a better one.

I so hope it's a better one. For all of us.

This week marks my first back after my "drastic collision," as Molly has taken to calling it. Mr. Bates, the factory manager, has asked to speak with me on Friday, and I'm worried I'll be kept on the riveting line forever if he agrees with Molly about the collision being so drastic. Our forewoman, Mrs. Harris, insists that I'll be fine, but who wants a girl who gets injured in her first few months on the factory floor?

Like I promised, I'll try to feel Mrs. Harris out about journalists and photographers. But I have a feeling Mr. Bates will go for it, especially if someone from LIFE actually calls him. Publicity is publicity, after all.

Please do send the notes you made on my short story. You could not be harsher than any of the editors who encouraged me to write about hearth and home rather than woods and bloody violence.

—Jo

302

Dear Jo,

I hope your meeting with the manager went well and none of your fears were realized. I wait with bated breath to hear what Mrs. Harris said, if you had a chance to ask her about letting LIFE inside the factory.

I've enclosed my notes, as well as the outline for the factory-girl story. It's finally finished! Huzzah!

I'd appreciate your thoughts and expertise on it, if you have the time. I want to turn it in to my editor for approval after the holiday so we can get the gears moving for next year.

What are your plans for Christmas? Are you going home, or staying in East Hartford?

Your friend,
Charlie

Dear Charlie,

Christmas was spent at the boardinghouse, and the arrival of your notes and your story were a welcome present. I haven't had the chance to give your outline the proper attention it deserves; forgive me for not having any notes of my own yet. Christmas was RATHER busy—Anna and some of the other girls couldn't afford to travel home. Though I don't think Mrs. Wilson was disappointed to have us, since her son lives so far away. She likes a full house.

We played games, and Molly played the piano until her fingers were aching, and we all sang until we were hoarse. Anna got the idea of fashioning holly crowns for all of us to wear, which is a better idea in theory than in practice. My scalp STILL hurts from those prickly leaves! And now there's a picture of us all dressed like we're Santa's helpers somewhere on Ruth's camera. Let us hope she NEVER gets that film developed!

I spoke with Mrs. Harris about the possibility of letting the press inside the factory. She seemed <u>quite</u> intrigued and told me she'd pass it along to Mr. Bates if I had something official in writing. So that's where we are with getting access for you and a photographer. Do you think your editor could provide something for Mr. Bates?

I hope your own Christmas was cheery. Peg's absence was felt here, but I'm sure your parents were happy to see her. Did you go home as well? Or are you still in New York? I imagine it's beautiful there at Christmas.

—Jo

PS: My meeting with Mr. Bates was not about firing me! You were right; it did go well! I've been selected as a swing worker between the riveting line and the warehouse where they cut and press the metal. My training on the new machinery will start this spring!

Dear Jo,

Congratulations on the new gig! See, I told you there was no need to worry.

Christmas was quiet this year. I was supposed to go home, but I changed my mind at the last minute and stayed in New York. If my sister arrives back in Connecticut in a foul mood, blame me. She was not pleased when I called to tell my parents.

Deadlines, you know.

That's a lie. There were no deadlines. I just was still too

damned mad about lost opportunities that wouldn't have been lost if it weren't for my damned sister.

The idea of you, reluctant in a holly crown, makes me smile. It makes me wish I were back there and things were easier than they are now.

It's strange how one choice—one fight—can change things, isn't it?

Forgive me, Jo, for being so maudlin. Perhaps I shouldn't send this.

Happy New Year, Jo.

—Charlie

Dear Charlie,

I'm glad you did send your letter. I know what you mean, far too well. I find it strange, with every conversation, we find such commonality. I'm used to being the odd duck, but perhaps I am not, when I keep finding you in the same pond.

Before I left home, I had a fight with my sisters. _The_ fight, though I didn't realize it at the time. We had all pushed so much aside when our little sister Beth passed. And all those things we didn't say before came spilling out, so terribly and viciously— viciously because of me, <u>only me</u>, because my sisters are many things, but I am the wolf where they are lambs.

Things have not been the same, partly because I haven't been able to let them, and partly because they can never be the same, because I am not.

It is strange how one choice can change things. Can change you. So very strange.

—Jo

Dear Jo,

I'm sorry that you find yourself at odds with your sisters as well. Grief is a beast, I've found. One that is truly hard to conquer. When we lost our sister Harriet, it was all I could do not to scream out my anger. There's a pond by the house we grew up in, and sometimes I'd go to throw myself under and scream and scream until my lungs felt like they'd been shredded. One day, when I popped back up to the surface, I found Peg standing at the edge, waiting for me. I felt ashamed—weak and caught and so many other things—but all she said to me was "Do you feel better?"

I did, Jo. As feral as it may sound, grief is vicious, and expelling it is blood sport.

My sister was not one to join me under the water to scream. It was hard not to resent her for it—not to assume that because she'd gone still instead of screaming, she didn't care as much as I did. It took me a while to understand that my way was not every way. I think that Peg expected me to fall back to that thinking with the story I was chasing, but that, I find, is more difficult. Especially when I feel so stuck here, churning out pitch after pitch, and having my contacts ignore each one.

Every day, I ask myself if I'm doing enough. I rarely have an answer that pleases me.

–Charlie

P.S. Your thoughts of commonality made me think of this:

I'm Nobody! Who are you?
Are you—Nobody—too?
Then there's a pair of us!
Don't tell! they'd advertise—you know!

It was always my favorite.

Dear Charlie,

Sometimes I want to scream. No. That's not right.
I want to scream all the time.

There were SO many things I was supposed to do and supposed to be. Even as wild and stubborn as I proved, I was expected to be tamed. Shackled by love. Stripped of my ambition for someone else's. But there is little room for anything but truth in the fresh gnaw of becoming.

I ran from it, once. But maybe I don't have to.

More than Nobody, I have felt like an outsider. Once, I was safe in my cozy enclave of sisters, where I was loved—sometimes despite myself, but still steadily. Where hurts were forgivable even when they were hard to bear. But cracks grew as losses did, and I found myself falling through the frozen pond that was my life, the ice suddenly paper-thin. And the water beneath washed away every denial and secret I'd kept, even from myself.

What makes me an outsider is what made me never contemplate for a moment accepting that proposal from a boy who loved me the way I could not love him. It's what's made me always feel so different from even my sisters.

~~It's what's made me want to take your hand that night on the porch.~~

—Jo

307

Dear Charlie,

    *I hope that I haven't offended you with the copious notes
I sent you on your outline. It's occurred to me, over the last week,
that I might have been overeager?*

—Jo

Dear Charlie,

    Have I done something?

Creak. Creak. Creak.

Jo looked up from the letter, a drop of ink bleeding into the
paper at her distraction from the worry eating at her. Had she
not scratched out that last part of her letter? Had she been too
open? (Had she driven her away?)

It was late—nearly midnight. Who in the world . . . ?

She got up, crossed her small room in a few steps, and opened
the door. In the light pouring from her room, she caught sight
of Molly's hair. Her back was to the stairs, so Molly couldn't see
the shadows shift behind her—someone had flipped the light
on downstairs at the sound of the footsteps. Mrs. Wilson was
awake.

"Molly," she hissed, beckoning her over. "Someone's coming.
Hurry." Molly ducked inside Jo's room, and Jo shut the door
quickly as Molly threw her jacket over Jo's lamp to dim the
glow of the light.

They stood in frozen silence as Mrs. Wilson's footsteps
sounded across the wooden floor in the hall and then paused.

Jo's heart thumped, her mind seized with the idea of Mrs. Wilson finding Molly in her room and kicking them both out for breaking the rules. But then, to Jo's great relief, the footsteps continued on, fading down the hall and then coming back again and fading for good as Mrs. Wilson did her circuit and returned down the stairs.

"Phew," Molly sighed, leaning against Jo's vanity turned makeshift desk. "That was close."

"Molly, what are you up to?" Jo hated how much she sounded like Ruth or Evelyn, but she couldn't be like Anna, turning her back on Molly's strange behavior. Not anymore, when she was hiding her in her room from Mrs. Wilson! She didn't want to admit what a welcome distraction it was from the fact that Charlie hadn't answered any of her letters as of late. But it was that, too.

"I'm not up to anything," Molly said, like she always did.

"Is it a fella?" Jo pressed, trying to sound understanding. "One of the airmen?"

Molly rolled her eyes. "I may like to dance and flirt, but I have grander plans, thank you very much."

Jo gestured for her to take a seat at the vanity, taking the edge of her bed in turn. "Do those grand plans have to do with all these late nights? All the girls have noticed. I think all of us have covered for you at some point."

"And I appreciate it," Molly said. "I'm happy to do it in return. Though you never seem to get farther than the garden in your late-night excursions."

Jo flushed. "I just like to look at the sky, is all. I have a feeling you're doing more than that."

Molly stared at her hands. The silence that followed wasn't

unpleasant, but there was a heaviness that made Jo wonder what was to come.

"Do you ever think about it, Jo?" Molly asked. "What you're going to do after all this?"

"Sometimes."

"My father, he talks about me coming home after the war is over like it's a given," Molly said.

"It doesn't have to be." Jo knew those were brave words from a girl who felt anything but. Was she a hypocrite for offering them?

"No, it doesn't," Molly said, her mouth flattening with determination. "My mother taught piano lessons after she married my father. But she went to a conservatory. She was a wonderful musician. One of her old teachers retired in Hartford. I looked him up when I moved here. He offered to give me lessons. So that's where I go on Thursdays."

"So late?" Jo asked skeptically.

"Sometimes I stay for dinner with him and his wife," Molly explained. "I usually miss the first bus and have to walk a ways to the next stop. Goodness, Jo, what did you think—that I was doing something salacious? What an imagination you have."

Jo shrugged. "I don't know! You have been sneaking in awfully late for months now. Ruth and Evelyn both have been worried."

"Monsieur Dubois may be a musical genius, but he is nearly seventy!" Molly giggled.

"So is your plan to become a musician someday?" Jo asked.

"I don't know," Molly said. "I just . . . My mother said she never regretted giving it up. Because she got me. And that's sweet, isn't it?"

"It's lovely," Jo said.

"But I don't know if I'd feel the same way. I think I would regret it. Not trying. I want to see if I'm made of the right stuff. Otherwise I'll wonder forever."

Jo understood Molly perfectly. She'd thought she'd lost her spark for writing. It was reignited when Charlie came into her life, but she feared it wasn't enough to become the full flame it had been.

"Some eternal wonders are good ones, while others haunt," Jo said.

"That's exactly it," Molly said. "My father doesn't understand. He wanted me to give up music after my mother died. But it's in me, just as it was in her. I think he was relieved when I fibbed about wanting to work in the parachute factory. At least it wasn't music."

"You shouldn't give it up," Jo said. "Not if it's what you want."

Molly smiled. "You're a good friend, Jo."

"I won't tell anyone about where you go," Jo promised. "Though I'm sure the other girls would understand, too."

Molly got up from the vanity stool. "I should sneak into my room before I get caught during Mrs. Wilson's final pass of the house."

She hesitated at the door. "But, Jo, why were *you* up so late?"

Jo pasted on a smile, that horrible twinge in her stomach back. "I was just writing letters," she said. "Nothing important."

The lie felt like chalk in her mouth.

Thread

Sometimes
I wish
I'd left something behind
besides grief.
Something important.

Words on a page,
paint on a canvas,
students molded by my faith in them.

But instead I danced
fingers upon ivory,
music a thread entwining us,
but the notes only hung in the air
for a moment before fading away.

The thread broke.
The Marches scattered.

CHAPTER 25

AMY

Amy trudged back to the hotel in a daze, hardly noticing the wind that chapped at her cheeks. It all made sense to her now, the giant chasm that had split Jo and Laurie apart. He had proposed.

And she had turned him down.

Amy started to piece it together in her head. No wonder Laurie hadn't written to her after he joined the military. He'd probably wanted to put everything in Concord out of his mind, the Marches in particular. He really must've loved Jo.

Did he love her still? Those kinds of emotions didn't simply go away. Would he marry Jo now if she changed her mind?

Amy pulled her coat tight around her, wanting to vanish into it. Would she always be second best to Jo in absolutely everything?

She returned to the Hotel Royale, feeling the loneliest kind of blue. Inside the building, the air smelled of cinnamon and spice and the wood-burning fire. A dozen girls had gathered in the common room to exchange little trinkets and open up packages that they'd gotten from home, while Bing Crosby's

"White Christmas" played over the record player. It reminded Amy of her sisters all heaped on top of each other during the holidays, but those memories felt so far away. So distant.

One of the other Clubmobilers beckoned for Amy to join in and patted the seat beside her, but Amy declined and said she wasn't feeling well. She just wanted to wipe the lipstick off her mouth and curl up in bed.

What a merry Christmas it would be.

She slogged upstairs, shedding her outer winter layer as she climbed, unwinding her scarf and pushing her hat off her head. Hopefully, Edie and Marion had other plans for the next few hours, because Amy wanted to cry in private. But as she drew closer to their room, she heard their voices.

Heated voices.

Amy opened the door to find the two of them facing off for battle. Edie was holding a white envelope in her hand, keeping it just out of Marion's reach.

"You give that back! You had no right!" Marion cried, reaching for the letter again. Her eyes flew to meet Amy's. "Edie has gone mad. She stole my mail and read it!"

Amy dropped her scarf to the floor. *Oh no.* Didn't she tell Edie to put off their prank until they had talked things over?

Edie fended off Marion and hurried toward Amy. "Do you know why Marion has been so cagey about her boyfriend?"

"Edie, stop!" Marion said, finally snatching the letter out of Edie's fingertips. Her eyes looked wild, but there was something else in her gaze, too. Not only anger, but fear. "Don't do this."

But Edie barreled on. "Because he's Japanese! The letter was signed 'James Kinoshita,' and it gets worse from there. He's incarcerated."

Marion was on the verge of tears by then. "You should bother reading the paper sometime! Our own government has been rounding up people like James and tossing them behind barbed-wire fences."

"What would you expect after Pearl Harbor?" Edie countered. "Sailors like Bobby never came home because of people like your little beau."

"Stop it!" Amy tried to wedge herself between the two of them, like Meg used to do when she and Jo had one of their spats, but it was useless. Edie and Marion just talked around her.

"James had nothing to do with Pearl Harbor!" Marion shouted. "He's an American through and through, like you and me. Like Bobby."

Edie shouted right back. "Bobby was a hero! Don't you dare make comparisons. No wonder you've been keeping James a secret this whole time. Didn't want us knowing you were dating a traitor, huh?"

Marion flinched, like she had been slapped, but a scant second later, she rounded her shoulders and said, "I've been in love with that 'traitor' since we were seventeen years old." Her gaze roamed to Amy, iron in her eyes. "You've got anything to add?"

"Rosie agrees with me," Edie insisted. She turned toward Amy, awaiting her assent.

But Amy faltered, her thoughts all jumbled. She wanted to say that Marion's boyfriend wasn't a traitor. She wanted to say that Edie was in the wrong. The words sat on the tip of her tongue—all she had to do was release them—and yet she couldn't seem to muster the courage.

"I think we should all take a breather," Amy said weakly, echoing what Meg had said to her and Jo during their big fight.

"Don't mind if I do," Marion muttered. She made a beeline for the door and was sure to slam it behind her.

"Good riddance!" Edie said, still fuming. "Can you believe that we've been sharing a room with someone like that?"

Amy whirled around to look Edie in the eye. "What were you thinking by opening her mail?"

"I was trading out the real letter for a fake one! It was supposed to give Marion a scare that her beloved James was breaking things off with her." Edie's eyes went narrow. "Might I remind you that you were in on the prank."

"I didn't know what you had planned! In any case, I thought we were going to talk this through first."

"You were busy," Edie said defensively. "And Marion needed to eat some humble pie—you said that yourself."

"I didn't mean for all *this* to happen!"

Heat crept up Edie's face. "Are you taking her side? I thought we were friends!"

"We *are* friends," Amy said automatically. Weren't they? She wasn't so sure anymore.

"You sure have a funny way of showing it." Edie's face flushed pink and she yanked on her coat. "I'm leaving."

Amy slumped against the dresser, feeling numb and hollowed out, but that didn't last long. Her eyes soon landed on the drawing that she had made for Laurie, which was still rolled up with a pretty ribbon, and suddenly she snapped. Before she knew it, she had lurched onto her feet, grabbed ahold of the thing, and torn it down the middle. Then she did it again. And again.

By the time she was finished, her breaths had grown labored

and her drawing lay in front of her in pieces, but she didn't feel much better at all.

Amy slung the coat over her shoulders anyway and bolted down the stairs and onto the street. She wasn't sure how long she'd be out or how far she'd go. She knew only that she had to head away from the Thames, because it would remind her too much of her walk with Laurie. So north she went, cutting through Marylebone, until she reached Regent's Park. She wandered around the grounds for a long while, a lone figure against the leafless trees and the brown grass. The war had left its mark here as well. German bombs had pockmarked the ground, flattening the rolling lawns that the Victorians had favored and making the park smell like dirt and dead leaves.

Amy kept hoping that the cold wind would clear her head, but her thoughts refused to leave her be. She had started the day feeling so brave, but all that bravery had left her when she needed it most—fleeing from Laurie's room when she saw Jo's letter and biting her tongue when Edie had said those terrible things.

Her courage had failed her.

No, Amy thought miserably. *I failed myself.*

She kept going, taking step after step, telling herself that the pain in her heart would surely ebb at some point; it had to lessen, even if only a smidge.

But it didn't. Indeed, now her feet were aching and her fingers had grown numb, and only then did she release a little whimper and turn back.

What she would give to trade this Christmas for one from her past. More than anything, she wanted to be home in

Concord, with the house smelling of cookies and plum pudding. Marmee would be salting the potatoes in the kitchen while Father would try to pour himself another eggnog without anyone noticing. Beth, as always, would be sitting at the piano, playing a jazzed-up version of "Joy to the World" while Jo would make up some bawdy lyrics to replace the original ones. Meanwhile, Meg and Amy would whirl around to the music, spinning and spinning until they got too dizzy and fell onto the living room rug, laughing the whole time.

As a kid, she'd always thought that their Christmases were humdrum. Far too dull and a little too ordinary. She'd daydream about growing up and spending her holidays in some far-off place. Hollywood or New York. Maybe even Rome or London.

What a fool she'd been.

Forcing herself back to the hotel, Amy tried to ignore the blisters on her heels, but her dread only multiplied when she turned down the last block and spotted Laurie immediately. He was standing in front of the building, huddled in his flight jacket, his crutch under one arm and a wrapped box under the other.

Warring emotions tore through Amy's chest. A part of her wanted to throw her arms around his neck and sob into his shoulder while the other part told her to spin around and sprint in the opposite direction.

It was too late for that, though. He had already seen her.

"Everything all right? When you didn't show up at the hospital, I figured something must've happened," he said, making his way toward her and holding out his gift. "This is for you."

She murmured a thanks, her heartbeat a flutter. Here was her chance to be brave. She ought to seize the opportunity and ask him about Jo. But Amy felt her resolve slipping away again—she didn't want to admit to him how she had found out about the proposal in the first place. "I'm sorry. I guess I woke up this morning and decided I'd rather be alone."

"On Christmas?" Hurt flashed over his face, and for a moment he looked ready to leave, but something held him back. His eyes had zeroed in on her hands, so very cold and red, and he took them into his. "How long have you been outside? You're freezing."

"I needed the fresh air," Amy said through chattering teeth. She told herself to pull away and flee inside already, but her feet remained planted on the pavement. It felt wonderful to be this close to him, and it took everything she had not to bury her face against his collarbone and ask him to hold her tight.

"Does this have to do with Beth?" he said as he massaged the warmth back into her fingers. "Christmas can't be easy without her. I should've realized that before."

Amy almost laughed. For once, this wasn't about Beth—it was about him.

Because Laurie was so perfect in every way. He even smelled like peppermint.

It was too much for her to take.

"I should get going," she said, wrenching away.

"Wait!" He caught her by the elbow. "What is it? What's wrong?"

Everything is wrong, you foolish, wonderful boy, she thought as she fought off tears. She wouldn't let them spill.

"Please," she whispered. "Let me go, Laurie."

He released her, but had one more thing to say. "Whatever I did, I'm sorry," he whispered.

She raced away and burst into the hotel, taking the steps two at a time until she reached her room. Thankfully, it was empty—Marion and Edie were nowhere in sight—so Amy threw herself onto the bed and let everything out. Her shoulders shook, and her eyes pooled with tears, and she didn't know how to stop them.

She yearned for her sisters.

How she needed Jo's strength.

And Meg's comfort.

And Beth . . .

She just wanted Beth returned to them, alive and whole, because everything had fallen apart without her.

Amy wanted to lie low for the rest of the week. As soon as she got off a shift, she dove under her covers and emerged only to use the washroom or steal a knob of cheese from the kitchen. Edie did ask her once if she was coming down with the flu, but aside from that they barely spoke. Marion, on the other hand, had said nothing at all to either of them. After their bitter fight on Christmas Day, she had moved up to the fifth floor, and apparently she had put in a transfer to a Clubmobile in Leicester.

New Year's Eve soon arrived, but Amy was in no mood to count down the seconds to '43. A few of the other girls had made a bet to see how many dance halls they could visit in one night, and they'd invited Amy to tag along, but she said that she had letters to write.

"What ever happened to that nice pilot who kept calling

on you?" one of them asked with a wide grin. "Does he have anyone to smooch at midnight?"

Amy gave a shrug. She hadn't seen or heard from Laurie since Christmas, and she told herself that it was for the best. It would be too painful otherwise. Laurie was welcome to kiss whomever he wanted to tonight—but it wouldn't be her. She refused to be second best to Jo.

And Amy had her own plans for the evening, didn't she? There were plenty of books to choose from in the common room and she could curl up with a great big mug of tea. It would be downright cozy.

"Who am I kidding?" Amy whispered to herself. Her night would be absolute dullsville if she stayed in. She'd been sulking for days already, and she was tired of crying and moping. For all she knew, Laurie could've had three dates lined up that night, all of them with pretty nurses he'd met at the hospital, so why should she sit at home with her nose in a book? There was still time for her to get dolled up and head out with the others. She might've been lonely, but she didn't have to be alone.

With newfound energy—and a dash of desperation—Amy was about to head upstairs to get changed and do something with her hair, but then Supervisor Owens popped her head out of her office and asked Amy if she could have a word.

"Of course, ma'am," Amy said, surprised. She wanted to ask why, but she figured she'd find out real soon.

"I hope you had a nice trip," Amy said as they entered the little office that was barely wide enough to fit a desk and a couple chairs. Supervisor Owens had taken a few days off to spend time with an elderly cousin near the Scottish border. Amy couldn't say that she was glad to have Owens back, though, considering the woman always had a pinched look on her face and tonight was no different.

"It was pleasant enough," Supervisor Owens said. She took a seat behind her ancient oak desk and rummaged through a filing drawer while Amy lingered by the door.

What could this be about?

"I've heard that Marion put in a transfer request," Amy said, hating the awkward silence.

"*I* put in that request," Owens corrected her. "It was for the best, considering that Captain Greeley has chosen to date an 'enemy alien.'"

Amy grimaced at that phrasing. "May I ask who told you that?" she said, almost certain that Edie had been up to no good.

"Greeley told me herself," said Owens, which made Amy's eyes go wide. "She wanted me to hear it from the horse's mouth, and she said that she wasn't ashamed of it."

It took Amy a moment to let that sink in. Marion had revealed her big secret—and to their boss, no less. That must've taken a lot of fortitude. "And you're punishing her for that?"

"Leicester is no punishment. It is, however, much quieter than the rumor mills here in London," Owens said, not even looking up from her file drawer. "I can't say that I'm pleased about Greeley's choice in men, but she's young and I can only hope that she'll come to her senses."

Amy felt a fire in her belly. Owens had never met Marion's beau! Neither had Edie. And yet both of them saw fit to judge him, based on nothing other than his race.

Say something, a voice inside her urged.

But the moment passed, and Owens had finally located the file she'd been searching for. She splayed it open on her desk.

"Would you care to explain this?" Owens asked. She lifted up a handwritten letter that had been ripped in half, but taped back together. Amy had to squint at it before she realized what it was.

Her mouth went dry as ash. It was the letter that Laurie had written to Marmee, where he'd confessed that he had bumped into Amy right here in London and how she certainly wasn't in Montreal.

"There are serious charges laid out here. Lying to the Red Cross? Falsifying records?" Owens continued. "What do you have to say for yourself?"

Amy gripped onto the side of the desk because her knees had gone wobbly. How did Owens get ahold of that letter? She hadn't showed it to anyone. After Laurie had given her the ripped-up pieces outside of Selfridges, she'd thought that she had tossed them away. Could she have left them in her overcoat?

Wait.

Back on Christmas Day, Edie had accidentally taken Amy's coat instead of her own when she'd gone out. If Amy had forgotten to clear out her pockets . . .

"Did Edie give you that letter?" Amy said hoarsely.

Owens ignored the question. "Now, I've reached out to a few contacts to seek more information, but we all know how slow the mail can be. That's why I called you in here." She sat forward, her fingers forming a steeple. "Did you or did you not use a false identity to join the Red Cross?"

Amy's pulse took off like a rabbit at the racetrack, but she told herself to breathe and think. It could take months before Owens heard anything. By then, perhaps Amy could've proven that she deserved her spot here—didn't the Red Cross need all the experienced Clubmobile girls that they could find?

All she had to do was toss a few more lies onto the pile.

But as soon as Amy opened her mouth, she shut it once again. She couldn't help but think about Marion, standing in this very same spot, fessing up her secret when she didn't have to. Maybe she had been tired of hiding a part of herself.

And Amy realized that she was tired, too.

Of the lies and deception. Of her own cowardice.

Of pretending to be a Pace when she was a March girl, through and through.

"It's true. All of it," she said, not much louder than a whisper. "My name isn't Rosemary. It's Amy."

To-Do List

Back when we dreamed
of a sister trip to London,
I thought practically.
How would we travel?
Where would we stay?

The only way for me to play along
with what I knew to be impossible
was to ground it in some reality.

But you, Amy,
you had other dreams.
You always did.
You'd meet the Queen,
kiss an English boy,

Steal the crown jewels
for a night on the town,
then put them back
before the sun came up.

You can't help but fall short
of dreams like those,
but even in falling short
you surpass us all.

CHAPTER 26

MEG

"Doro! Happy Christmas!" Meg said, ushering her inside. Doro looked smart in a snow-white sweater and a gray pleated skirt, her brown hair neatly curled, but she had that set to her jaw that meant she felt like smashing things. "Come in, Mrs. Scott. We're so happy to have you. Is that your pecan pie? I had some at Thanksgiving, and it was delicious! This is our neighbor, Mr. Laurence. Mr. Laurence, this is my student Dorothy and her mother, Mrs. Scott."

They exchanged handshakes and pleasantries and juggled dishes while shrugging out of their coats. Mrs. Scott took off her mauve pillbox hat. Beneath it, her brown hair was short and waved. She wore a mauve sweater with a calf-length houndstooth skirt.

"Here, let me hang these up," Meg said, "and we'll go put the pie in the dining room."

"I brought my chestnut stuffing, too." Mrs. Scott smiled, but Meg spotted the signs of a crying jag in the not-so-distant past; beneath her powder, her eyes and nose were both as red as Rudolph's.

"Let's give that to Marmee. Maybe you can convince her to let *you* help with dinner. I haven't had much luck." Marmee had been acting oddly all afternoon. She'd assured Meg nothing was the matter, but it seemed like she could hardly stand to look at her. She'd shooed her out of the kitchen so often Meg felt like a cat who kept getting underfoot.

Meg got Mrs. Scott situated, heating up peas on the range while Marmee mashed potatoes. Then she led Doro back to the parlor, where Mr. Laurence sat in Father's armchair, reading the newspaper and smoking his pipe.

Doro looked at the tinsel-covered tree. "That looks real nice," she said wistfully. "Ma and I didn't do much decorating this year."

"Oh, it's not finished yet. You can help. Here." Meg handed Doro a Pyrex bowl full of popcorn and a piece of string; she'd already tied a kernel around one end.

"All right." Doro plopped down on the nearest seat: the sunken left cushion of the old rose-colored davenport.

"Wait, that's—" *That's Beth's seat,* she'd almost said. Meg took a deep breath. "Never mind."

Now the memories swamped her. Beth had spent most of her time there, in the seat nearest the fire. On days when the pain was bad, she'd lain with a hot-water bottle and her head in Jo's lap. They all had their places: When Jo wasn't cozied up with Beth on the davenport, she was sprawled across the floor or pacing the room with a pencil stuck between her teeth. Father had his old armchair; Marmee had her wingback with her basket of sewing in the corner. Meg always ended up on the battered leather chesterfield, usually with Amy's icy little feet pressed against her leg as she curled up on the opposite end.

Amy's side was all scratched up from the time she'd brought a stray kitten inside and tried to hide it under a quilt, much to Marmee's dismay—and the kitten's.

Lord, Meg missed Amy. She missed all of them. The parlor felt full of the ghosts of Christmases past.

"You all right, Miss March?" Doro asked, as keen-eyed as ever.

Meg nodded. She put her hands on her hips and surveyed the room. Yesterday, she and Marmee had gone out and bought a tree. Marmee had considered getting the artificial kind, but Meg had insisted on a real balsam fir, despite the shortage. They'd hauled Jo's runner sled down from the attic and used it to drag the tree home. It was only five feet tall, and scraggly to boot, but Meg had turned the bare side to the wall and now you could hardly tell.

Last December, after the United States had entered the war, in a fit of patriotism the Marches had thrown out all their old glass ornaments, which had been made in Germany. Marmee had gone to Woolworth's and come home with Shiny Brite ornaments, made in New York. There were three dozen bells and lanterns and balls in bright jewel colors. Meg and her sisters had taken turns hanging them just so on the tree.

This year, Meg had hung them all herself. She'd scattered the tinsel without Amy stepping back every two minutes and adjusting it to better fit her artistic vision. Instead of Beth playing the piano, Meg had listened to carols on the radio she'd carried out from the kitchen. Last weekend, she had found a pattern in a magazine for a wreath made of pine cones, and she thought the result looked pretty swell on the front door. Marmee had placed electric candles in the windows, and Meg had hung all six of their stockings from the mantel. She hadn't been able to leave Beth's alone in the box. It was a good thing Doro hadn't been there yet, because Meg and Marmee had both cried.

"I heard you can combine Lux soap powder with two cups of water and brush it on the branches to make 'em look snow-covered," Doro said now. "Want to try it?"

Good Lord, no, Meg thought.

"I'm afraid we don't have any Lux. And that sounds like an awful mess."

"Fine." Doro sighed. "Here, I'm all finished with this."

She handed Meg her popcorn garland—half the popcorn had ended up in her mouth—and helped her wind it around the tree. When she finished, she stood staring up at the golden-haired angel. "We have one like that. Richie always put it on top, because Ma and I are so short."

Meg eyed their newest ornament: a brass piano hung right beneath the angel. It had been a gift from Mr. Laurence, in remembrance of Beth, and they had all gotten misty-eyed when Marmee opened it. Even the old gentleman had needed to clear his throat a few times.

Meg snatched up her latest project from the side table: an elaborate snowflake, painstakingly cut out of folded white paper. She handed Doro a pair of scissors. "Your work isn't finished yet."

"You're trying to keep me busy so I don't cry," Doro accused.

"Is it working?" Meg grinned at her. "You can cry if you like, but I betcha you can't make a snowflake better than mine."

"Can too!" Doro grabbed a stack of paper from the table. Mr. Laurence looked up from his newspaper long enough to wink at Meg. On the radio, Guy Lombardo sang "Winter

Wonderland." Meg threw another log on the fire, and by the time Marmee and Mrs. Scott had finished their dinner preparations, Meg and Doro had created a whole army of snowflakes.

They had quite the spread: roast turkey with giblet gravy and Mrs. Scott's chestnut stuffing, mashed potatoes, peas, cranberry relish, rolls, Marmee's plum pudding, Mrs. Scott's pecan pie, and Meg's gingersnaps. Mr. Laurence had brought mulled wine, and Doro was thrilled to be allowed a glass with dinner. Mr. Laurence carved the turkey. It was strange not having Father there to do it, or to say the blessing while Jo squirmed in her chair and Amy kicked her beneath the table.

"Heavenly Father," Marmee began as they all bowed their heads. "We are thankful for this bounty and the friends we share it with. Help us to keep a joyful heart and a spirit of service to others. Be with us in our sorrow, and give us strength. Watch over those far from home, and keep them safe. Amen."

"Amen," Meg murmured, but her heart was not joyful, nor was it particularly thankful. There were too many empty chairs at this table. She only picked at her food. It took all her strength not to weep into her mashed potatoes—and not just because butter was so scarce that Marmee had had to make do with that awful oleo.

They'd just finished eating when there was a knock at the door. Meg looked askance at her mother. They weren't expecting anyone else.

"Could you get that, Meg, dear?" Marmee said. "I'll clear the dishes."

Could it be Jo? Maybe she had taken the train up as a surprise. It seemed a Jo thing to do, buying a ticket at the last minute when she realized how much she missed them. She *must* miss them, Meg thought, a trifle desperately. It was *Christmas.*

Meg opened the front door and let out a little scream.

"Happy Christmas, Meg," John said.

For a moment, she could only look at him: his lovely reddish-brown hair, now cut army-short; his shoulders broader and his arms more muscular than when he'd left; and his cheeks red from the blustery cold. He was terribly dashing in his uniform, with the brass buttons marching down the front. He gave her that sunrise-slow smile of his, and Meg launched herself at him, her arms flying round his neck, her mouth colliding with his. He staggered back a step, and then his hands went to her hips, holding her close.

Doro let out a whistle, and Meg came back to herself. Marmee, Doro, Mrs. Scott, and Mr. Laurence were all crowded in the dining room doorway.

She didn't care. She would kiss him right there on the front step in front of God and everybody.

"Happy Christmas, John." She smiled up at him, then straightened the velveteen collar on her cherry-red sweater, grateful that she'd worn something pretty even though she hadn't much felt like it. She grabbed John's hand and pulled him inside.

"Marmee, Marmee, look!" she said, lacing her fingers through John's. She couldn't seem to let him go. He was *here.* He was right here, and as much as she'd wanted to see her sister, she was thankful he'd been the one on the other side of that door.

"Hello, John," Marmee said.

Meg squinted at her lack of surprise. "Wait—did you know he was coming?"

"He phoned this morning," Marmee admitted. "Did you suspect anything? I was nervous I'd given it away!"

"You said that it was Mrs. Lowell, wishing you a happy Christmas!" Meg said, astonished. That was why Marmee had been acting so strangely all day!

"I asked her to keep it a surprise," John explained. "You don't mind, do you?"

"Mind? It's the best surprise in the world!" Meg couldn't stop smiling.

"Why don't we go have some pie, and let these two have a few minutes to themselves?" Marmee suggested, bless her.

As soon as they were gone, John laced his arms around Meg's waist and lowered his mouth to hers. She ran eager hands over his arms, his back, the shorn nape of his neck, refamiliarizing herself.

Eventually, she pulled away. "John . . . did you get my letter?"

"I did." John's smile crinkled his eyes.

"And you're not angry?" she asked.

"Do I seem angry?" He brushed another kiss over her lips. "I don't expect you to be perfect, Meg. I can't say I like the thought of you going out with another man, but—"

"It will never happen ever again." She clutched his hand. "I don't want anybody but you."

"And I love you just as you are."

Meg bloomed. She felt like a flower unfurling toward the sun. "Say it again."

"I love you," John said, and he kissed the tip of her nose. "I love that you invited Dorothy Scott here even though she's spent two terms driving you half-mad with her wisecracks. I love that you let me ramble about algebraic equations. I love this sweater on you, and—" He whispered something a little bit naughty in her ear, his breath hot and ticklish.

Meg giggled and kissed him again.

They sat side by side on the chesterfield. "How long can you stay?"

"Not very. I came straight from the train. I've got to get home and see my mother," he said. "But I can spend the whole day with you tomorrow. We can go ice-skating, or see a movie. Whatever you like. It's a three-day pass, then I've got to get back. My company will ship out in January."

Only three days. Meg squeezed his hand. Hers was shaking. "I know," John said softly. "But I will come home to you, Meg."

He couldn't promise that. They both knew it. Meg didn't bother putting on a brave smile. "I'll wait for you, however long it takes."

His thumb traced lazy circles over her palm. "When I get back, I mean to ask you to marry me," he said quietly.

"If you asked me now, I'd say yes." Meg didn't care to play games. "I'd marry you tomorrow."

"I want to do better by you than that. I want to be able to give you a ring." Meg opened her mouth to protest that she didn't need a ring, but John forestalled her with a quick kiss. "I know. But if we got married tomorrow, it'd be without your sisters, without your father."

He was right. As much as Meg wanted to be his wife, she couldn't imagine taking such a big step without Jo and Amy by her side. Without Father there to officiate.

The sound of laughter drifted in from the dining room, along with "Santa Claus Is Comin' to Town."

"Oh, but I don't have any presents for you," Meg said. "I mailed them already!"

"I bet they'll be waiting for me when I get back. The only present I really needed was your letter. That was a very romantic letter, Miss March."

"Just wait and see what I write when you're overseas," Meg teased. She hopped up. "Come on. Let's go have some pie. I'm starving now."

Salt

The first time
you baked a pie, Meg,
the crust was saltier
than the sea.

But we each took our piece
to the parlor and mustered
the cheer we knew you needed,
focused on the filling, which tasted of nothing.

Jo's eyes danced, dying to spill
the honest truth of your terrible cooking.
Laurie sat beside her on the floor,
elbowing her when she threatened to burst.

I shared the davenport with Mr. Laurence,
who did not seem to mind the taste.
Serene, he polished off his piece
and when you'd turned your back
he switched his plate with mine
and ate it too. He winked.

One's taste buds dull with age.

CHAPTER 27

JO

J o tried to put it out of her mind—Charlie's lack of response. But she found it ate away at her more than she could bear as the New Year became less new and the snows of January continued to whip around the boardinghouse, causing the girls to stay inside on their days off, even the most social too wary to venture out.

Jo was starting to think that she didn't just run—she drove everyone away. That Saturday, Jo tucked herself into the parlor that served more as a library and storage room and tried to ignore the terrible ache in her stomach. She had a stack of poetry—not Dickinson; purposefully, not Dickinson—and she had planned to while away her entire afternoon immersed in the neat pile.

She was absolutely not going to think about Charlie's article and how it had sparked something inside her, like a match being dragged across a surface too lightly to catch until the very last second, then spitting fire.

Jo knew now, from Charlie's silence, she had crossed a line—she shouldn't have been open with her feelings like that.

She should've rewritten the letter, removed that last sentence completely instead of scratching it out. And now . . .

She couldn't think about it. She wouldn't. Charlie would just be added to the long list in her head of things to run from. It was hard not to fall back into old habits.

She let out a sigh, her fingers tightening around the tome of Shakespeare's sonnets she'd picked up off the top of her pile. She needed to stop hurting and take advantage of her cozy day off. Soon, she'd be so exhausted from her new training that she'd probably be snoozing through her Saturdays.

A thrill filled her at the thought of early spring and her soon-to-be part-time home in the cutting and shaping ware-house. Mrs. Harris hadn't been pulling her leg when she'd said Mr. Bates had been impressed with her quick action on the floor. The manager had praised her during their meeting before Christmas and had spoken to her twice since then during his visits to the riveting floor. Luckily, there had been no more drastic collisions or accidents of any kind, and the stitches in Jo's forehead had been taken out. The little pucker of a scar was easy to hide with her hair, but she privately thought it made her look rather roguish, like she was a pirate on the high seas.

A fanciful thought, for sure, and one that she didn't think she would've had last year. But now . . .

It wasn't as if things had changed. She was still dodging many of Marmee's calls and rarely answering letters, especially after Charlie stopped answering hers. She still had no way back to her sisters, though she at least could admit she wanted one. She still woke sometimes reveling in those moments where she forgot, just for a second, that Beth was lost.

She felt a little less stuck; like she was an anchor that had been sunk in the depths, the tide and moon and movement of the waves—time and care—the only things that could fully free her from the sand. But it was as if she could see herself again, the rusted and battered bits that had been buried, each nick and scar with a story, sometimes still untold even to her.

Jo opened the book of sonnets, losing herself in the words, as muted footsteps creaked above her and the faded music from a Tommy Dorsey record floated through the boardinghouse from somewhere upstairs. Snug in her spot in the parlor, Jo didn't look up again until the sound of the front door slamming startled her from the page. Pressing her hand against her racing heart, she turned back to her book.

"Who's that?" she heard Molly's voice call from the dining room. "Oh! I didn't know you were coming! Why didn't Peg tell us?"

Jo's eyes snapped up from the sonnets, and if she thought her heart had been beating fast before, it was nothing compared to now. Getting to her feet, she cracked the parlor door open, feeling something like hope and dread mixed together as she caught sight of blond hair and long legs.

As if she sensed her, Charlie looked over her shoulder, her eyes meeting Jo's. Her face split into a grin.

"Jo! I'll talk to you later, Molly," she said, hurrying toward the parlor door. "I came as soon as I could."

Jo frowned. "As soon as . . . ?"

"I have so many ideas," Charlie continued, pushing into the parlor and upending the leather satchel she was carrying on the pink fainting couch that was Mrs. Wilson's pride and joy. Several notebooks spilled out, along with a bunch of pencils looped together with a piece of string.

"Ideas?" Jo asked, feeling a little like an echo.

"For the article," Charlie said. "The outline I sent you, re-member? Your notes were just what I needed. Your idea to ex-plore the duality of work and home life, without glamorizing it like the newsreels do, was a smash hit with my editor. I think I'm finally back in his good graces."

"You're not mad?" Jo asked. Had she not seen the words that Jo had scratched out? She must not have.

Jo knew she should be relieved, but there was an odd stab-bing in her heart at the thought.

Charlie, who had been a whirl of excited movement until this moment, abruptly stilled. "Mad?"

Now she was the echo.

She laughed, almost nervously. "Why would I be mad?"

Because . . . because . . .

Jo found she couldn't bring herself to think it. Not if it would be dashed against rocks like her silly hopes.

"You never wrote back," Jo said, unable to keep the hurt out of her voice. "And I marked your article up something awful. . . ." She wouldn't speak of the letter. The first one that was left unanswered.

"Oh, Jo." Charlie closed the space between them, and Jo suddenly found her fingers held between Charlie's gloved hands. The wool was damp from the snow falling outside; flakes were still caught in her hair. Jo could see them, this close. "I'm sorry. I did get a little sidetracked in revising the pitch with your notes. I get lost in my work, but I promise: I wrote back."

"I never got a letter."

"My response must've gotten delayed or misplaced or some-thing."

"Oh," Jo said, not knowing what else to say, and not wanting to pull her fingers away. "I thought . . ."

"That I was ignoring you?"

Jo nodded, her cheeks burning.

"I didn't ask for your notes because I was being nice, or because I thought you'd be nice. I asked because you're a good writer, on top of having direct experience on the subject at hand. And I thought someone who wrote fiction would have a different angle into the factory-girl story . . . and you did. You saw the life in it that I didn't. I was too focused on the work. You brought the heart."

Even if she had prepared for the onslaught, Jo could not have stopped the tears that came. Between one breath and the next, they welled in her eyes, and hot salt poured down her cheeks, and it was as if that anchor that was her had torn free of the seafloor, finally and for good.

Charlie didn't even hesitate, and Jo found herself in the kind of embrace that was as comforting as it was thrilling. There was a heart-thumping sort of a swirl in her head as every emotion she'd held back for so long rose to the surface.

"It's all right," Charlie murmured as Jo cried in her arms like she hadn't done since that morning that she came downstairs to find that Beth had gone before the sun had come.

"It's not," Jo managed to garble out, after long moments—minutes, hours? She did not know.

"It is," Charlie insisted.

Tear-drenched and pink, Jo pulled away and hurried over to the fainting couch, where she at least had the sense to have a handkerchief tucked in her sweater. She slumped on the couch, wiping her face, because some gentle dabbing wasn't going to cut it.

"I'm a mess," Jo said.

"You're brilliant," Charlie insisted. "You're just in the thick of it, Jo."

"In the thick of what?" she asked.

"Of grieving," Charlie said. "If there was a pond somewhere, I'd take you to it, show you how to scream underwater."

Jo sniffed. "I'd like that."

"I guess I can offer you some sort of distraction," Charlie said.

"What's that?"

She smiled then, and it was like sun across Jo's skin after months of cold. "When my editor approved my pitch, I told him I had a cowriter. You won't prove me a liar, will you?"

She felt as if she was on a cliff, wanting more than anything to jump off into clear blue water. She could sink beneath the surface. Scream her lungs out. And when she broke to the top, burning for air, she would be free.

Jo smiled, dawning and bright. "No," she said. "I won't prove you a liar."

Scream

Scream the rusted, battered bits,
the seafloor daring to restrain you.
Scream every grain of sand
convincing you your place is darkness,
hidden away from the light of the surface.

The nicks and scars
from every time we failed you
with words and expectations
of a girl you weren't meant to be.

Wounds from a world
that would tell you
your heart is somehow wrong,
that what you feel cannot be trusted.

Scream everyone
(yourself included)
who saw your obstinance
as something to be overcome
instead of proof that who you are
is fixed, immovable, innate.

CHAPTER 28

AMY

Supervisor Owens wasn't the gossiping sort, and yet news traveled fast about Amy getting the boot from the Red Cross. Whispers chased her throughout the hotel—*How old are you really? Did someone put you up to this?*—but there wasn't much Amy could do except count down the days until she boarded a ship home and pretend to look unbothered while she was at it.

On the inside, though, Amy was feeling the worst kind of awful.

No, *awful* wasn't quite the word for it.

She felt *humiliated.* Not only for using Rosemary's identity and opening her heart to the only boy she'd ever really loved, but for her last interaction with Marion. Amy had flagged her down before Marion left for Leicester, the words spilling out of her mouth in a tumble. She had apologized for siding with Edie during their last night and not speaking up sooner. She'd relayed too how sorry she was that James had been imprisoned and how she would be sure to start a petition for his release as soon as she got home. And before Marion could get in a word edgewise, Amy had added that maybe they could write to each other, start over fresh. They both had grown up in a house full of sisters—they had more in common than they realized.

"I know we haven't always seen eye to eye, but you're a damned good Clubmobiler," Amy had said, daring to hope.

But Marion's mouth had tightened and she'd given Amy a polite handshake in return. "I wish you well, Miss March," she said before heading off to the train station.

Amy couldn't wait to put London and all these memories behind her. She wasn't looking forward exactly to facing everyone in Concord, but at least there'd be a few thousand miles between her and the Red Cross girls. Not to mention Laurie.

But first, she had to finish packing and cleaning up.

Amy swept her gaze across her near-empty bedroom. Marion was long gone, while Edie had moved upstairs to bunk with Gloria. Both of their beds had been stripped, leaving only Amy to clear out before Supervisor Owens could install a new crop of girls. Soon enough, it would be like she had never been here.

Amy closed her suitcase and rubbed her tired eyes. By this time next week, she would be nearly home. The Red Cross had already sent a notice to her parents that revealed her whereabouts along with the date of her ship's arrival, but she was dreading the reunion with her family. She didn't want to face Meg's disapproval or Marmee's disappointment. Her one consolation was that Jo wouldn't be there to berate her.

How could you do this to Marmee? Jo would say. *To Father?*

Amy wondered what sort of punishment awaited her. Would she be grounded for months? Years even?

Maybe she deserved it. She had lied and deceived people, after all.

She'd hurt herself in the process, too.

If she had never joined the Clubmobile, then she never would've bumped into Laurie again—and she never would've fallen so foolishly in love with him. She supposed she only had herself to blame for this mess.

The door swung open suddenly, and Amy gave a little jump in surprise. Edie stood at the threshold.

"I thought you'd taken the train already," said Edie.

"Sorry to disappoint," Amy said coolly. "Did you forget something?"

"My black wool socks. Mind if I take a look in the drawer?"

Amy made a sweeping motion with her arm, as if to say, *Go right on ahead,* before she grabbed the broom to clean the floor and wait for Edie to leave.

Except Edie was dawdling. "When do you clock out?"

"Tomorrow." Amy didn't even bother masking the hurt in her voice. How did they go from close pals to this? "All thanks to you for ratting me out."

Edie cringed, but quickly composed herself. "You lied to me for months. You were my friend. My *best* friend."

"A best friend would've talked to me first before going straight to Owens with that letter! I could have explained why I did it." Amy stormed forward so that she could move Edie out of the way and search the drawer herself. "There you go. Your wool socks."

Edie still didn't leave, though. "Look, I wasn't thinking straight after we had that fight with Marion. When I found that letter in your coat, well . . . I let my temper get the best of me."

Amy had been ready to rage at Edie, to really let her have

it, but she'd never expected this sort of admission. And yet, she was wary. "Did you apologize to Marion, too?"

"Why would I?" Edie asked, eyes narrowing.

"For stealing her mail. For calling her boyfriend a traitor."

"He's a felon."

Amy's chest rose and fell. Not even a month ago, she would've kept her lips zipped together, but she couldn't allow that any longer.

"No, he's not," she began slowly. "He's not a traitor either, and neither is Marion for loving him." She swallowed as she thought about the Black soldier who'd asked her to dance at Rainbow Corner and how she had merely stood there. She thought too of all the times she saw Ginny Tanaka rushing through the halls at school, clutching her books to her chest while the senior boys taunted her. Amy had always wanted to say something, but had she? No, not once. But she would do better from now on. She had to. "Actually, I think Marion Greeley could teach us a thing or two."

Edie was shaking her head. "You know, I don't think I ever knew you at all. Have a nice trip home."

After Edie left in a huff, Amy blinked at their shared bunk, remembering how close the two of them had gotten after they'd met at training back in Washington. Amy had thought that she had found a true sister in the Clubmobile program, but looking back now, she realized that she had been too quick to overlook Edie's faults. Maybe she had been a little desperate, too, to replace Meg, Jo, and Beth. She'd been so angry at them when she left Concord. At Meg for treating her like a baby. At Jo for calling her a brat. And at Beth for leaving them forever.

But there were no replacements for her sisters. Yes, they may have shouted at each other and said some terrible things, but old wounds could be patched—and Amy finally felt ready to swallow her pride and admit that she was sorry. Through thick and thin, they were bonded. They were blood.

Amy dragged her gaze around the room, ready to be done with this place. There was little left to do aside from throwing her bed linens in the wash and sweeping under her bunk, so she'd better get to that. Crouching down, she stuck the broom into the gap and it bumped against something hard.

A box.

It was Laurie's Christmas present to her. Amy had been so upset that day that she'd tossed the thing under her bed and had forgotten all about it. She wondered what to do with the thing. Toss it unopened? But curiosity got the best of her in the end.

She cut through the tape and drew in a sharp breath at what she found. Laurie had given her the silver picture frame that he had picked up at Selfridges—the same frame that she thought he might've gotten for Jo. And that wasn't all. He had included a picture inside it, too, a photograph of him and Amy and her sisters.

Amy remembered exactly when it was taken, right before she'd left for Montreal and not long before Beth had started to deteriorate. They were all crowded into the back garden, with Marmee's dahlias in full bloom behind them. Beth and Meg were grinning at something that Jo must've said while Amy and Laurie stood a little to the side, not even looking at the camera. Amy was laughing, because Laurie had just told her teasingly that she'd better watch out for Quebecois boys who wore berets. It hadn't made much sense, but she'd found it hilarious anyway, and that was when Marmee must've clicked the shutter.

Amy's lips lifted at the corners.

Because there was more. At the bottom of the frame, she noticed an engraving, which read:

THE UNSTOPPABLE MARCH GIRLS.
MERRY CHRISTMAS, AMY—ALWAYS, TL

She touched her fingertips to the *Always*.

Laurie had given her the loveliest moment, frozen in time.

It was perfect.

He was perfect.

Oh, how she wished she could dive inside the photo and turn the clock back to before Pearl Harbor was attacked and before Beth had passed away, when Amy's whole world was left lonely and cold. But ever since Laurie had crashed back into her orbit a few months before, she'd felt like she had stepped back into the sunlight.

Which was why she had pushed him away. She'd had to protect her heart. Beth's death had shattered it already, and she couldn't risk Laurie doing it again. . . .

But hadn't that happened anyway? Look at her now, moping by herself in an empty room, willing the hours to tick by until she left London and Laurie behind.

Amy's head jerked toward the window. Judging by the position of the sun, it must've been a little past noon. She had less than twenty-four hours before her ship left port—so how did she want to spend them?

Before she knew it, she was on her feet and hopping along the creaky floorboards as she tugged on her shoes. She searched through her toiletries for her lipstick before remembering that she'd tossed it out earlier that day, since it was almost used up. But Amy wasn't too proud to go rummaging through her own trash, because she needed to look as stunning as Gene Tierney in *Sundown*. She thrust her hands into the bin, sifting through the dust and old mothballs to find the tube, but she discovered something else instead.

The tatters of her drawing. Her present for Laurie.

Most of it was torn beyond repair, but she stared at the largest intact piece, not much bigger than her palm. It depicted her and Laurie's faces, his head dipped toward hers.

She pressed the paper against her chest, and it was abruptly clear to her what she needed to do.

Swinging her coat across her shoulders, Amy hurried across the city, a March girl on a mission, but when she arrived at the hospital, she couldn't find Laurie in his usual bed. Alarmed, she tracked down a nurse to ask about his whereabouts.

"Looks like he was discharged this morning," the nurse replied as she looked over the patient roster.

Amy's breathing skidded to a stop. Relief hit her first—Laurie was all right, thank goodness—but that didn't calm her confusion. "How could he have gotten discharged? His ankle couldn't have healed that fast."

The nurse held up the paperwork for Amy to see. "Says right there: 'Laurence—Discharged.' The doctors must've thought he was fit for duty."

Amy felt a little dizzy. "Does that mean he returned to the airfield?"

"He's likely en route. You may want to check at the train station."

Panic rose in Amy's throat, but she forced it back down. She couldn't give up now.

Running outside, she called for a cab and practically threw her shillings at the driver, adding that she'd give him more if he floored it fast. They whizzed through the streets in record time and, keeping to her word, Amy handed the man a few more coins before she took off at a sprint.

The station was cavernous, and crowded with holiday passengers, but her gaze caught on a man in an Army Air Forces uniform, threading through the throng ahead. He didn't have Laurie's height or build, but since Amy had nothing else to go on she decided to give chase. She followed him toward platform 3, where the train at the track was readying for departure. The cars were already half-full, with more soldiers queuing at the doors to get in, and Amy raced toward the nearest batch.

"Laurie!" she called out, her eyes darting across the men's faces. "Laurie!"

"You lost, doll?" one of the soldiers said, winking.

She gave him a shake of the head and kept moving. "Laurie!"

Her pulse was skipping fast, and she wondered if she was even at the correct platform. Had he left an hour or two before? Her shoulders drooped, and she felt like a fool. What was she even doing here, with her hair barely brushed and with a ripped drawing in her hand that she'd fished out of the trash?

"Amy?"

She whirled around, and there he was, standing in front of her like a dream. He was leaning on his crutch and wearing that damned uniform of his, which made her go all tongue-tied.

She blurted out the first thing that came to her mind. "You can't go back to duty with a broken ankle."

"You came all the way to tell me that?" he said with an incredulous laugh. "How did you even know where I was?"

"A nurse at the hospital told me. I came to visit you, but you were gone." She gestured at his crutch, and she really wished that she could have a few choice words with the doctor who had discharged him. "How could they let you leave like that?"

"Duty calls. The airfield needs the extra hands."

Amy wasn't sure that she liked the sound of that. The airfield must've been short-staffed indeed if they needed an injured soldier like Laurie to return to active duty. She got the frantic urge to wrap him in a cocoon and stow him somewhere safe—away from the Nazis, away from the war, away from any danger that might stop him from ever coming home.

"I do appreciate you coming to see me off, but I'd better go find a seat," Laurie said. He nodded at one of the conductors, who was calling for the remaining soldiers to board.

You better get on with it, a voice whispered inside Amy's head, and she swore it sounded a lot like Beth.

"Wait! I never gave you your Christmas present," she said, grabbing his arm. She thrust the tattered drawing at him, refusing to let her courage wither this time around. "I made this for you. It was part of a bigger sketch, but it got a little ripped."

He eyed the paper. "A *little?*"

"Fine, more than a little!"

"But I thought you'd given up on art," he said, sounding perplexed.

"Can't a girl change her mind?" Her tone was probably too

abrupt, but she was so nervous that she thought she might lose her lunch.

He finally looked down at the drawing. "Is this me?"

Amy thought that she might shrivel up. Had she gotten so rusty that Laurie couldn't even recognize his own face? She almost snatched the paper from him and fled, but she had to see this through, no matter what he said. "Yes, it's you. With me. During our walk by the Thames." She was babbling now and unable to stop. "You know, the night that—"

"I got us tossed out of the Savoy," he finished for her. A rosy flush spread across his cheeks. "I think about that night a lot."

"You do?" she whispered.

His gaze lifted from the drawing to meet her eyes. "When I saw you in that ballroom, you know what I thought? That you were the most beautiful thing I'd ever seen."

Amy barely had time for his words to register before he curled an arm around her waist, pulling her close, and she gave a little squeak of surprise. His head bent toward hers, and Amy rose on her tiptoes to meet his lips, because he was taking a little too long for her liking.

Their kiss was heaven, sending tingles shivering down Amy's neck and straight into her toes. She could've stayed there for hours, for whole days on end, but she forced herself to pull away. There was so much left to say.

With her hands still looped around his neck she said, "I'm so sorry that I was such a crumb on Christmas. I did come to see you at the hospital that morning, but when I got to your room I noticed a letter in your hand. The one from Jo." Her confession stuck in her throat a little, but she had to get it out. "I read it, Laurie. I know I shouldn't have, but I did."

It took him a moment to understand. "The proposal."

She gave a little nod. "Jo never told me a thing."

"She didn't? I figured she would've said something to you and Meg." He swore under his breath. His arm was still anchored at her waist, but his grip had started to loosen. "I'm sorry you had to find out that way."

"You aren't mad?" Amy clasped her hands tighter around him, not wanting him to let go.

He shook his head. "No wonder you took off that morning. It must've been a shock."

"You could say that." Oh, how she wanted him to kiss her again, but she knew they had to broach this; there was no way forward except through. "I know that you and Jo have been close for years. I guess I always wondered if—"

"Can I explain what happened?" He took a small step backward but kept his hands on her hips, for which she was grateful. "Back in training over the summer, the guys in my unit were getting engaged left and right. You could've sworn there was something in the water—my buddy Herb even bought a ring for a girl he'd only known for a month—and I guess I got swept up in at all. I figured that I ought to buy a ring before I shipped out and since Jo and I had been pals for so long, I connected the dots that I should propose. I did care deeply for her, but I think I got that mixed up with love." He glanced at his shoes, looking embarrassed. "Thank God she said no."

"So you aren't in love with her?" Amy said, searching his eyes.

He grinned and kissed her on the tip of the nose before he

kissed her again on the mouth, ever so lightly. "I'd say that my heart is already spoken for."

Happiness zipped through Amy like a song, and she nearly jumped up and whooped, but that was when the train conductor motioned at Laurie to hop onto the last car.

"Looks like that's my cue," he said, reluctantly pulling away. "But listen. I'll come back to London on my next R and R. Or maybe you can get a pass and come up to Debden. It isn't far—"

"I can't, Laurie." Amy winced. "I got the boot from the Red Cross a week ago, and they're sending me home tomorrow."

"What?" Laurie choked out.

"It's a long story, but I fessed up to my supervisor about everything. I was tired of all the lying. You were right about that."

"Well, I'm sorry to be right for once," he said glumly.

Amy threaded her fingers through his, wondering how long until she'd be able to do it again. She was already dreading the distance that would soon separate them. "I'll write to you every day until you get back."

"You promise?"

She gave him a swat on his shoulder. "I think I've already proven that I'm a diligent pen pal."

"That you did. And hopefully . . . hopefully you'll be more than that." His voice went shaky. "Will you be my girl, Amy?"

In answer, she kissed him again, almost knocking him over in the process, and they broke apart only when the train whistled and started to move.

"Is that a yes?" Laurie said, grinning.

"With a capital *Y*!"

He squeezed her hand one last time before he hopped into the car with only seconds to spare. Amy waved and blew kisses until the train rounded the bend and vanished from her view. Even so, she lingered on the platform for another minute, touching her lips and giggling. Then she looked up at the winter sky, squinting into the sun.

Keep him safe for me, Beth, she thought.

And she turned around to go home.

Safe

If I had the power
to keep him safe, to keep you safe,
and Jo and Meg, Marmee and Father,
Mr. Laurence, Aunt March, John, Sallie and Doro
and everyone I've ever known who still lives on
in this messy world of pain and brokenness,
don't you think I would?

I can only watch.
But that's not nothing.
And it's not so different
from my role when I lived.
I bear witness.

I am with Laurie
each time he straps into a plane,
so that come what may, he won't be alone.

I sail with you across an ocean,
honor your courage as you face our family
and tell them what you've seen.

I see Jo for who she is.
See Marmee's life work.
Father's ideals.

I sit with Meg
at the kitchen table as she whips cream
with the focus of Laurie in a cockpit,
Jo building airplanes,
and see her work as no less important
for it sustains the ones who've been left behind.

CHAPTER 29

MEG

T he damned whipped cream would not peak.

It was January, John was back at Fort Monmouth, and 1943 stretched out before Meg, full of separation and sacrifice and worry.

She *wanted* to face it with good cheer. Her spirits had been high when John was beside her—while they went ice-skating, red-cheeked and behatted; while they'd eaten meatloaf for supper with his mother; while they'd gotten Cokes at Woolworth's and run into half a dozen students; and certainly while they'd necked in his Buick. She'd only cried the tiniest bit when they'd said goodbye.

But Meg couldn't help thinking that if it weren't for this blasted war, she'd be engaged. She'd be planning their wedding; she'd see John every day at school. They'd close his classroom door and sneak kisses in the far corner where no one could see. (He'd gotten even more handsome while he was away, and she could hardly keep her hands off him, to be honest.) Instead, he'd be shipping out any day now, and who knew if—*when*, she corrected herself, fiercely—she'd see him again.

Without John, the winter days were long and dark and lonely. Meg was happiest when she felt useful, and without the flurry of Christmas shopping and decorating and baking, she didn't quite know what to do with herself. Her magazines couldn't keep her attention. She'd read only a few pages of the Daphne du Maurier novel Marmee had given her for Christmas.

All she really wanted to do was lie in bed, eat the chocolates Amy had sent from Montreal, and cry.

That wouldn't do, so Meg was making a trifle. But the whipping cream refused to stiffen. What was wrong with it? What was wrong with *her*?

She threw the cream-covered spoon across the kitchen in a fit of pique.

It clattered against the oven, and a moment later Marmee poked her head into the kitchen. "Meg, what's the matter?"

When Meg tried to paste on a smile, her mouth slipped into a grimace. Stupid, traitorous face. "Nothing. Everything's fine."

She sounded like a petulant five-year-old.

"Oh, Meg." Marmee knelt to pick up the spoon and put it in the sink.

Somehow, just that—her mother picking up after her, selfless as always, her voice full of exasperation and love—absolutely undid Meg. She burst into tears, still clutching the Pyrex bowl of cream.

Marmee took the bowl from her, patting her on the shoulder. "It'll be all right, dear. I'm right here."

"But you *aren't*!" Meg burst out, staring down at the freshly waxed floor. "You're always off volunteering somewhere. I'm trying to keep a stiff upper lip, but I can't be cheery when every-thing feels so broken. I just *can't*!"

Marmee was quiet. Meg squirmed, embarrassed. "I'm sorry, Marmee. I wish . . ." She trailed off, remembering Doro's plain-tive words. *I wish I could be good like you, but I'm not.* They had echoed her own feelings perfectly. "I want to be selfless. I want to make sacrifices gladly. But I can't seem to manage it. I'm so lonely without Beth and Jo and Amy, and I already miss John, and I feel so alone. I get so angry at this damned war and at God for taking Beth away from us that I could just—just *spit*!"

Marmee looked stunned. "Oh, Meg, I'm the one who ought to apologize. I didn't realize you were struggling. I'm afraid I've done you a great disservice."

"What do you mean?" Meg stared at her.

Marmee sank into one of the wooden kitchen chairs. "I want my girls to think of others and do their part with good grace. But that doesn't mean you can't have *feelings*. You're human, Meg. Don't you think I'm angry sometimes, too?"

"I don't know," Meg said uncertainly. She sat down across from her. She had seen Marmee sad. Exhausted. Frustrated with her committees, sometimes. But if Marmee had ever felt the fury that was sweeping through Meg, that made her wish they'd kept those old German ornaments so she could smash them into bits, she was excellent at hiding it.

Perhaps Meg wasn't the only actress in the family.

"More often than you might think." Marmee fiddled with the sleeve of her collared blue wool sweater, her eyes downcast. "I'm angry with God, too. For taking my daughter. For a long while he and I were not on speaking terms, but now . . . I still don't understand his purpose in taking her from us. Your father's faith is unshakable, but mine is not.

"I'm angry all the time," Marmee continued. She stared down at the opal Pyrex bowl. "All those committees keep me from drowning in it. This blasted war. The last one was supposed to be 'the war to end all wars,' you know. And your father . . . he's long past forty-five. When he told me that he wanted to reenlist and serve as a chaplain, when I almost lost him the last time . . . I had some choice words for him, believe you me."

"You and Father argued?" Meg had never heard her parents raise their voices to each other.

"I shouted at him," Marmee admitted. "I even asked him not to go, at first. But he was steadfast. He felt it was his duty. I asked him to think of his duty to me, to his children. I'm not proud of it. But it was so soon after losing Beth, and I was afraid."

This revelation shook Meg: Marmee, afraid? Even in those terrible days when Beth was dying, Marmee had been their rock.

Meg was quiet lest she break the spell that had fallen over the kitchen. Marmee had never confided in her like this before, woman to woman.

"You must be afraid, too. For John. I'm awfully happy for you, my dear. But being young and in love and separated by a war . . ." Marmee bowed her head. "It's difficult. You aren't weak for feeling that way."

"Of course I'm worried for him, but mostly I'm terrified for us, that we'll never get our family back." It all spilled out of

Meg like a faucet had been turned on. Marmee's honesty had given her permission to speak freely. "We were so happy before. Maybe I could have stood losing Beth, but now Jo and Amy are gone, and there's this distance between us that was never there before. I tried to patch things up like Beth used to, but I—couldn't do it."

Meg braced herself for Marmee's disappointment. She had not been able to keep them together, and she blamed herself for it, and she expected that Marmee would blame her, too.

There were tears in Marmee's blue eyes. "Meg, no. That was never your responsibility to bear. Or Beth's."

Meg traced the scars in the old wooden tabletop with one finger. "She was always able to smooth things over somehow. When Amy and Jo were fighting, she could make peace between them. She never lost her temper and shouted and made it all worse."

Marmee smiled fondly. "Sisters fight. You'll make up."

"I don't know," Meg said, miserable. She stared down at her chipped red nail polish. "I bungled things with Jo when she needed me, and I don't know if she'll ever forgive me. She hasn't written me in months. Not once. And Amy—she used to confide in me, tell me all her little secrets, and now her letters are nothing but fluff. Mine are just as bad, because I haven't wanted to admit how lonesome it is here at home by myself."

Marmee put her hand over Meg's. "You aren't alone. I'm sorry it's felt that way."

Meg wanted to protest that it was nothing, that she was a grown woman. She shouldn't need her mother. But she did. A tear escaped, and then another.

"I thought you were angry with me, too," she sobbed. "Or

that—that you were so disappointed in me you didn't care what I did anymore."

"Of course I care what you do! I will *always* care what you do." Marmee got up and wrapped her arms around Meg. The comforting smell of Je Reviens enveloped her. When her tears trailed off, Marmee handed her an embroidered blue handkerchief. "I'm not angry with you, my Meg. Not one bit. It seemed to me as though you'd come into your own with your work, and you were going out with friends—"

"They weren't very good friends," Meg admitted.

Marmee didn't look surprised by that. "I never did like that Sallie Gardiner. But I didn't want to lecture you or give you the burden of unasked-for advice. I wanted to give you room to figure things out on your own. I thought you'd come to me if you wanted to talk."

"I—I didn't want to bother you," Meg murmured. They had been at cross-purposes, hadn't they?

"You're never any bother." Marmee smiled and sank into the other chair again. "I *love* to be bothered by my girls. You and I are alike in that, I think. I like to feel useful. To be needed. It's another reason why I've filled my days with all those committees, even though sometimes Barbara Lowell makes me want to scream."

Meg gave her a teary smile. "I know exactly what you mean."

"I thought you might. I haven't told you enough how proud I am of you, Meg. At Thanksgiving, I got to see firsthand your work with the Junior Red Cross. You're so good with those girls. And inviting the Scotts to Christmas—that was very kind. Dorothy obviously looks to you as a role model."

"I don't feel like anyone's role model." Meg felt bolstered, though, by Marmee's praise. "I'm so . . . well . . . imperfect. Look at me! I've been driven to tears by an *actual* trifle."

Marmee chuckled. "We all have our moments. It's all right to have an emotional fall-apart every now and then. And I'm happy to listen, my dear. I think it would do us both good to talk to each other about how we're feeling." Marmee stood up. "Now. Would you like some help with this whipped cream?"

Meg laughed. "Yes, please!"

They had moved the radio back to the kitchen, and Meg switched it on while Marmee grabbed her new apron.

"Give your sisters time," Marmee said. "They'll come home when they're ready, and you'll be here for them when they do. Things won't feel this bleak forever, Meg. I promise."

Imperfection

I was so afraid
the first time I played the piano
in Mr. Laurence's grand drawing room.

I never would have dared
approach the keys
had anyone been listening
and even so each imperfection
resounded through the room, the house,
across the street and into our own home
where I just knew you'd hear my flaws
and nothing else.

Isn't it funny
how we spend
so much time

    and there's so little time, my darlings

desperately trying
to be perfect
for the ones who'll love us
no matter what?

CHAPTER 30

MEG

Meg had just gotten home from school and hung up her gray wool trench coat when there was a rather timid knock at the door.

She flung it open to find *Amy*.

Her baby sister stood on the doorstep, wearing a double-breasted olive peacoat Meg had never seen before, a stubborn set to her chin that Meg was very familiar with, and a look of trepidation in her blue eyes.

"Amy! What are you . . . ? How . . . ? Why aren't you at school?" Meg asked, bewildered.

Amy blinked at her. "You didn't get the telegram?"

Meg ushered her in. "Come inside. It's freezing." Amy was carrying a battered-looking suitcase with the Red Cross emblem on one side. "What telegram?"

"Where's Marmee?" Amy looked around the parlor warily.

"She's at Mrs. Lowell's. She'll be home any minute," Meg said. "I'm awfully glad to see you, but why aren't you in Montreal?"

"About that . . . Actually, I was never in Montreal." Amy started fidgeting with the buttons on her coat, but she didn't take it off yet.

"What?" Meg stared at Amy. "Where on earth have you been?"

Amy drew in a deep breath and then let it out slowly. "The truth is that I joined the Red Cross and they sent me to London."

"London?" Meg gaped. "You've been in *England* this whole time?"

"I was perfectly safe! The Blitz was already over, and there were hardly any bombs while I was there," Amy said, rushing to reassure her.

Meg's face paled. "Hardly any bombs" was not the reassurance Amy thought it was!

"I wish you could've seen it. Do you remember how Beth and I used to pore over the entry on London in Father's encyclopedia? The Nazi bombers did hammer parts of the city, but there was still so much to do: plays and dances and shopping at Selfridges!"

Amy had been in *London,* shopping and going to plays and dances? While Meg was teaching five classes of junior English, grading papers till her head ached, sewing comfort kits, and weeding Victory Gardens?

"Well, doesn't that sound lovely." Her voice came out acerbic.

Amy's shoulders inched upward. "I'm making it sound like a real vacation, but it wasn't. The Red Cross worked us hard—harder than I've ever worked in my whole life. I got assigned to their new Clubmobile program, and we clocked in twelve-hour shifts. You should be glad that a whole ocean separated us, because I positively reeked of doughnut grease." Amy sniffed at her coat. "You can still get a whiff of it. Here, smell!" She held out the arm of her jacket.

"No, thank you." Meg scowled. "I thought you had to be at least twenty-two to join the Red Cross. How did you get around that?"

A guilty look slid across Amy's face. "I may have fudged that portion of my application."

"You lied to them. And to us. For *months*." Meg's relief at seeing Amy had melted into fury. How could she have put herself in danger *on purpose*? *Hardly any bombs*? Meg could not lose another sister. She absolutely could not survive it. None of them could.

"I know. I shouldn't have lied . . . but I had to get out of Concord," Amy said, a newfound iron in her voice. "After Beth died, I needed to leave all these memories behind." Her eyes flicked up the staircase toward the bedroom she and Beth had shared, where Beth had spent her final days. "And after that awful fight we had . . . I needed to figure out who I was beyond the tagalong baby sister."

Meg put her hands on her hips. How many evenings had she spent alone in this house, surrounded by memories of happier times? "Did it ever occur to you I might have liked to run away, too?" she demanded.

Amy blinked in surprise. "You? But you've never wanted to leave Concord."

"I didn't think I'd be here alone. You *left* me," Meg said bitterly. "You and Jo both. And you hardly bothered to write!"

Amy's words came fast. "Jeez, what do you want me to say, Meg? That I regret what I did? Well, I don't! These last few months have been exhausting, yes, and heartbreaking, but I felt like I was making a real difference."

"As a Doughnut Dolly?" Meg scoffed.

Hurt flashed over Amy's face, and Meg regretted her hasty words. She remembered how stung she'd felt when Jo had said she couldn't stay in Concord and plant Victory Gardens. Belittling Amy's work was every bit as unkind. They were all trying to do their part, in their own way. They were all a little selfish in their grief.

"It was more than that. *Much* more," Amy said defensively. "You should've seen the way the soldiers smiled whenever they spotted our truck. We helped them forget about the war, even if it was just for a little while. Beth would've been proud of me."

Meg took a deep breath. She hated the distance that had sprung up between them. She never wanted to be on the outs with Amy again—which meant she couldn't play the scolding big sister now. Amy had been an entire ocean away, doing the work of a grown woman, for months.

"I don't know what to say," Meg confessed. "But . . . I think . . . I'm rather proud of you, too. You've been awfully brave."

Amy drew back warily. "But you were so mad a minute ago."

"I'm still a little mad. And I don't condone lying. But I'd never have the courage to go all the way to London. You didn't know a single soul, and there were bombs falling, and—" Meg crushed Amy to her in a hug. "I'm just relieved that you're safe. I've missed you."

"Have you?" Amy scowled, not quite ready to forgive Meg yet. "Before I left, you and Jo were treating me like an outsider. Like a kid."

"Well, you were acting like one, pushing and shoving," Meg snapped. "And you were so mean about John. I love him, Amy, and he loves me. He makes me happy, and I want the most important people in my life to respect him. I don't think that's too much to ask, really."

Amy's expression softened. "You're right. It isn't too much to ask." She reached for Meg's hand and gave it a squeeze. "I'm sorry that I didn't give John a chance. I was being a real fathead about that, huh?"

"You were." Meg's voice was still a bit cool. She couldn't help feeling defensive of her lovely, clever, steady John. "John came home for Christmas on a three-day pass. When the war is over, he's going to ask me to marry him. And I'm going to say yes. I hope you'll be happy for me, Amy."

"I will be," Amy promised. Her eyes met Meg's. "I *am*."

"Thank you." Meg sighed. "I owe you an apology, too. I'm sorry for shutting you out. I didn't mean to be patronizing, or make you feel like . . . well, like you were still a kid. It's evident that you're not, and I'm sorry it took me so long to see it. I wanted to tell you what Jo and I were arguing about, but I couldn't betray Jo's confidence, and—"

"I know all about Laurie's proposal," Amy said.

"Jo told you?" Meg's heart fell. Had Jo and Amy been corresponding all this time? She sank onto the brown leather chesterfield.

Amy flushed. "No. If you can believe it, Laurie walked right up to my Clubmobile back in November. I was so surprised

370

that I dropped twenty cups of coffee on his boots." She chuckled softly at the memory. "He was recovering from an appendectomy, so we were able to explore the city together before he was called back to duty. But a few weeks after that"—she swallowed—"his plane crashed in the Channel and he was brought back to London."

"We heard that he had been wounded." Meg remembered her panic when she'd come home to find Mr. Laurence in the living room with that awful telegram in his hands. "Thank God you were there, Amy. I kept thinking of poor Laurie, all alone in that hospital, so far from home."

"You should've seen me race across London to get to him." Amy was looking down at her hands, threading her fingers together. "I visited him whenever I could, and he returned the favor as soon as he was feeling up to it. He got me the most wonderful Christmas present, too. It's in my suitcase."

"That was kind of him," Meg said. "I'm sure he was grateful to have a friend in London while he convalesced."

Amy's face seemed to turn pinker by the second. "I saw him off at the train station before he left for the airfield, and . . . Neither of us planned it this way—it all happened so quickly—but he asked me to be his girl, and I said yes."

Amy and Laurie? It was on the tip of Meg's tongue: *Jo's Laurie?* But she saw the vulnerable look on Amy's face and bit back the hurtful words. The truth was, Laurie had never been Jo's. She had never wanted him in that way. And now he was Amy's, and the nervous happiness on Amy's face made only one response possible.

Meg rose and hugged her sister again. "That's wonderful, Amy. Now we'll both be waiting for our soldiers to come home."

Amy squeezed her back, then pulled away and trailed her hand—which had been pale and dainty when she left but was now chapped and calloused and sporting a burn scar near her thumb—over the lid of Beth's piano.

"I miss her," Amy said.

"Me too. Every day," Meg said. "I hated feeling like I'd lost you and Jo, too."

"You haven't! At least not me. I'm back home for good. And Marmee will probably lock me in my room till I'm twenty!" Amy laughed.

Meg smiled. "Well, I'm glad."

"Have you heard from Jo?" Amy asked. "She hasn't written me at all."

"No. Marmee phones, but half the time Jo dodges her calls. They did speak on Christmas," Meg said. "Jo hasn't written me, either. I've written her dozens of times, but . . . I don't think she's forgiven me yet."

"And she says *I'm* the selfish one," Amy muttered, finally hanging up her coat.

"We're all selfish sometimes, aren't we? Jo needed me, and I wasn't there for her. I didn't understand," Meg said.

And she'd learned her lesson from it. To listen, not judge. To respect, not scold. To support her sisters, even if their choices weren't hers. She held Amy at arm's distance and looked at her, so grown-up in her olive blazer over a spotless white blouse and a matching olive pencil skirt. "Look at you. You're really not a kid anymore, Amy, are you?"

"You can call me *Captain* March, if you'd like," Amy teased.

"I most certainly will not." Meg laughed as a thought occurred to her. "Your letters—they were such fluff. The descriptions of Montreal felt like they were straight out of a guidebook. No wonder! You weren't ever there!"

Amy grinned. "I did crib them from a guidebook! It was the one I used when Flo and I first went to Quebec. I was starting to run out of museums I'd visited or cafés I'd eaten at, when—"

The front door opened, and Marmee came bustling in with a burst of frigid January air. She stopped on the threshold, the door hanging wide open, when she saw Amy standing there.

Amy hurled herself at their mother. "Marmee!"

Marmee caught her and wrapped both arms around her. "Amy! What are you doing home? I didn't think you had a school break."

Amy's cheeks went very pink. "It's a long story, and I'll tell you everything, but could we get a bite to eat first? I'm starved. The food on the ship was awful, and I've been dreaming about your chowder for months."

"On the ship? What ship?" Marmee raised her eyebrows.

Meg pulled the front door shut, then slung one arm around Amy and one around Marmee. "It really is a long story, Marmee. Why don't we all go into the kitchen, where it's warm, and have some trifle while Amy tells us about it?"

"I could eat a whole plate of trifle!" Amy said. Behind Marmee's back, she mouthed, *Thank you.*

As they headed into the kitchen, arm in arm, Meg remembered Marmee's certainty that everything would work out, that the rift between the three sisters would heal in time. Now here Amy was, on their doorstep, like magic. Her return had proved that they couldn't step back into their old childhood roles. They had lost too much—and perhaps grown too much. But they could move forward into a new sisterhood, one comprised of equals.

When she was ready, Jo would come home, too. And Meg and Amy would both be waiting.

Waiting

I'm waiting, too.
But take your time.

CHAPTER 31

JO

They wasted no time setting to work. Charlie shrugged off her coat near the radiator so it'd dry off, and Jo began to go through the notebooks on the fainting couch. She'd barely cracked the first one when there was a knock on the parlor door and Molly poked her head inside.

"Charlie, Mrs. Wilson wants to know if she should put out extra blankets in Peg's room."

"If my sister doesn't kick me out," Charlie said.

"Did you not inform anyone you were coming?" Jo scolded.

"I told you, I sent you a letter," Charlie insisted.

"You could've called."

"Jo, you never pick up your calls," Molly said innocently, and Charlie laughed.

"Vindication!" she crowed.

"Oh, shut up," Jo muttered. "You, Charlie. Not you, Molly," she added hastily when Molly looked hurt.

"I'll tell Mrs. Wilson that you'll need the extra blankets," Molly said, shaking her head fondly at them. "Are you hungry, Charlie? Ruth baked cookies this morning."

"Thanks. Maybe later," Charlie said.

"I'll leave you two to it," Molly said, the door swinging shut behind her.

"Was she mad when she came back from Christmas?" Charlie asked, her air much too casual and innocent to mean anything but deep care for the answer.

"Peg?" Jo asked, going for casual herself. "She was a little quieter than usual at dinner right after, I suppose. She's been spending a lot of time at the airfield."

"She probably misses Texas." Charlie sighed.

"She probably missed you at Christmas."

"Do you think your sisters missed you?" Charlie asked in return.

"Ouch." Jo scowled at her, but she found she couldn't stay mad as Charlie grinned.

"At least I called to tell my family I wasn't coming."

"Who's to say I didn't call?" Jo asked, stung.

Charlie raised an eyebrow. Jo had to stop herself from sticking her tongue out like a child.

"All right, I didn't call," Jo muttered. "But I took my mother's call the day after Christmas. I talked to her. And I sent gifts."

"Did you talk with the sister you fought with the most? Meg, right?"

"Yes, Meg," Jo said. "And no. We haven't spoken since the fight."

Charlie let out a whistle. "That's a long time, Jo."

"I tried, once," Jo said, compelled to tell her, not to defend herself but to offer some sort of proof that she wasn't still running. "But I failed."

"You could try again," Charlie suggested.

Jo opened her mouth to respond but was interrupted when the parlor door opened with a dramatic bang. Standing in the doorway was Peg, hair and eyes blazing as she took in her sister lounging on the rug.

Charlie leapt to her feet, and the two sisters stared across the room at each other, the silence looming between them. Jo was suddenly reminded of the hair pulling that Charlie had referred to and wondered if she was going to have to get in the middle.

"You're back," Peg said.

"You know me," Charlie said. "Always chasing stories."

Peg's eyes narrowed. "You're not—"

"No, you took care of that. I'm here for a different story. One on factory girls. My editor told me if I ever wanted to be considered as a war correspondent, I had to keep in line."

"And are you going to?"

Charlie shrugged. "I guess we'll see, won't we?"

"You are impossible!" Peg snapped.

"So are you," Charlie said.

"Momma cried when you didn't show up. You know how hard holidays are on her, after Harriet. And now with all the boys gone?"

"She would've cried more if I'd come home for Christmas and we'd fought the entire time," Charlie said.

"There'd be nothing to fight about if you didn't put your nose where it doesn't belong."

"You won, Peg," Charlie said in frustration.

"There's nothing to win here!" Peg practically roared at her sister.

Jo nervously got to her feet, wondering if an actual fight was imminent.

"You think Mary's death doesn't gnaw at me?" Peg continued, her eyes shimmering. "She was in my training class. I knew her. You think I didn't scrape together every spare bit of cash I had to send her family? I understand the way the world works, instead of hoping I can change it with a snap of my fingers and a few words."

"The WASPs started from an idea. You are who you are because of women's ideas and words, and how they fought for them."

"You just see the results, Charlie. Not the years of work behind it. The work Mary loved and believed in. I understand her sister's grief—if there was someone to blame for Harriet's accident, I wouldn't rest until they paid—but Mary's sister is not going to get what she wants . . . because what she really wants is her sister back."

"She deserves more than what she got," Charlie muttered.

"Don't all women," Peg said, shaking her head. "I love you, but your idealism is going to kill me one of these days."

"Don't say that," Charlie growled, crossing the room in a way that filled Jo with alarm, until she realized Charlie wasn't going for a punch or a handful of hair.

No, she was pulling her sister into a long hug.

"I won't forgive you," Charlie muttered into her sister's hair as Peg held her back just as tight. "You might've been justified, but so am I."

"You'll never admit you're wrong," Peg said, but she laughed, shaking her head.

"Rarely," Charlie said, pulling away from her.

Peg dabbed at her eyes, catching sight of Jo on the fainting couch. "Oh dear, Jo, I didn't see you there. I'm sorry you had to see that."

"Jo knows all about our tiff," Charlie said. "She's been nice enough to act as my confidante while I've been away. And she's helping me with my new article, so *shoo*. She and I have work to do."

"You're staying, then?" Peg asked, the hopeful note in her voice unmistakable.

"Yes," Charlie said, and her eyes slid to Jo as she said it. "I'm staying."

Charlie was true to her word. She stayed. Every evening when Jo returned from the factory, she found her in the parlor, notes and books spread out in front of her, a typewriter propped on Mr. Wilson's old rolltop desk after she got permission from Mrs. Wilson to put it there.

"I'm thinking of this part that you wrote about how a boardinghouse is like a family," Charlie told her, not even hesitating for a greeting when Jo came in, her hair still in her kerchief because she'd forgotten to undo it in the locker room.

With a groan, Jo collapsed on the parlor couch. "What about it?"

"Well, there are so many people who keep saying women working and living alone in places like this is dangerous or immoral and whatnot. But if you looked at any of the girls here . . . or Mrs. Wilson . . . it's not exactly a den of sin."

"Please, I beg of you," Jo said solemnly. "Tell Mrs. Wilson people think she's running a den of sin. I want to see her reaction."

Charlie laughed. "I think this should feel like more than a neat and pretty slice of life. I want . . . I don't know . . . to write an article where photos of the girls on the line feel just as normal as photos of them washing their stockings in the bathroom sink."

"Surely the public doesn't want to see stocking washing." Jo frowned.

"I think you underestimate the public's desire for pretty girls and anything related to their underpinnings." Charlie snickered, and Jo blushed at the thought.

"As long as it's not mine."

"I volunteer mine!" Anna called from the hallway, causing the two to laugh.

"How goes the article?" Anna asked, sticking her head in. As soon as the girls found out what Charlie and Jo were doing, they were all for it, which was good, because they needed interview subjects after Mr. Bates had given *Life* approval to let Charlie and a photographer trail the girls for a day on the factory floor. "I'm so excited for tomorrow! Do you think I'll get fan letters once my picture's everywhere?"

"Here's to hoping," Charlie said. "And, Jo, don't forget I want to see the locker room, too."

"Oh, that'll never happen," Anna scoffed. "They'd have to fix it up!"

"Maybe this is how we get them to," Jo said with a grin.

Anna's jaw dropped. "Jo March, you sly thing. That's brilliant! Shame them into doing it. Maybe we'll get an actual mirror in there. Ruth would give you her firstborn if that happened."

Jo snorted. "That's only a reward if one wants a baby."

Anna rolled her eyes. "My mother always says the girls who say they don't want any babies end up with a dozen. It seems like a threat every time she says it."

"It sounds like one," Jo said.

"Anyway . . . we're all going to see *Casablanca*. Do you two want to come?"

Jo and Charlie exchanged glances.

"We'll take a rain check," Charlie said.

"Molly's already sworn to see it twenty times, after all," Jo said.

"Talk about a threat," Anna said. "See you later, then. Don't worry. We all promise to get our beauty sleep. Not that some of us need it."

Anna closed the parlor door behind her, and Jo further slumped into the comfort and depths of the couch.

"Long day?" Charlie asked.

Jo nodded, closing her eyes.

"I can see that," Charlie added.

A shadow fell across Jo's face; she felt it rather than saw it, and when her eyes drifted open, Charlie was bending over her, a smirk on her face as she plucked at the knot at the top of Jo's head, where her kerchief rested.

Jo's heart leapt, and her cheeks flushed, her hand flying up to deal with the cloth, tangling with Charlie's fingers in the process. Slowly, she drew them away, letting Charlie do as she wished.

She untangled the knot, pulling the cloth free of Jo's head, and her hair, unkempt and frizzed from being stuffed in a kerchief all day, fell free.

"My tired, forgetful Jo," Charlie said, her smile fond, and Jo found that there were no lies to her words. She *was* forgetful when she was tired (some would say downright cranky).

And she was Charlie's.

Perhaps if she hadn't had such a long day, if her body didn't ache while her mind was still so alive, always rushing and racing—like writing to and with Charlie had triggered something in her—she would've been able to banish such a thought.

But she found she couldn't. And that maybe, she didn't want to.

She had run from so much. Perhaps it was time to start running to something.

"So, when are we going to see the fruits of all your labor?" Mrs. Wilson asked at dinner a week and a half later.

"We've just put the finishing touches on the article," Jo said.

"I have one final interview with Mrs. Harris at the factory for fact-checking, and then it's done," Charlie added between the clinks of silverware on china.

"All I want to know is what photos they'll use," Molly said. "I have a bet with Anna that I'll be in more of them than her."

"The photographer was definitely more sweet on me than you," Anna shot back with a laugh.

"I haven't seen any proofs from the photo shoot yet," Charlie said. "But my editor did mention in his telegram that they were pleased with the results. He wrote that there was a photo of Ruth that he was very moved by."

All the girls whipped to look at Ruth, who reddened.

"How did he even see you?" Molly said. "You were hiding from the photographer the entire time he was here!"

"I was not hiding," Ruth said. "I just . . . spent my time outside while he was here. But when he went out for a smoke, he saw me and . . ." She shrugged. "I'm sure it's nothing. And anyway, you should be more concerned if your picture is in the magazine, Molly. What if your family sees it?"

"What's this?" Mrs. Wilson asked, her arched eyebrows truly terrifying.

"Nothing, Mrs. Wilson," Molly said hastily, kicking Ruth underneath the table. "My father just thinks magazines and the like are frivolous. He wouldn't be pleased if I was in *Life*. He'd say it wasn't proper."

"We all need some frivolity," Mrs. Wilson said firmly. "Especially in these times."

"Hear, hear," Charlie said, raising her glass. "To frivolity. And to the girls of the boardinghouse. You've given me a great story to share with the world."

The musical tap of glasses against each other filled the air, and in the low light, Charlie's eyes sparkled at Jo across the table, making her feel like the water she was drinking was champagne instead.

As the girls dispersed after dinner, some to their rooms, some to the Friday-night movie, Jo found herself alone in the dining room, clearing up. The last two weeks had been a whirlwind. A magazine article was not like a short story or a novel.

There were word counts and directions and the weight of telling a real story, one about real people, living and loving even in the hardest times. The idea of Molly or Ruth or any of her friends reading the article and not liking it . . . the pressure was so much more when it was about them.

But instead of crumbling underneath it or fearing it, Jo found herself welcoming it.

Was it because she had someone to share the burden of it? Was it that simple?

(Had it been that simple all along?)

"I'll take care of these, dear," Mrs. Wilson said when Jo carried the rest of the dishes back to the sink for her. "I'm sure you want to spend more time with Charlie before she leaves."

Jo frowned. "Leaves?" she echoed. Charlie hadn't mentioned anything about leaving.

"Didn't she say?" Mrs. Wilson asked. "Well, you know her. Busy girl, that one."

"Yes," Jo said, her stomach sinking as she set the dishes down and left the kitchen.

Dread built inside Jo with each step she took toward the back door. Sure enough, Charlie was sitting on the edge of the porch rail, blowing blue smoke into the cold air.

"You're leaving?" Jo winced at how it came out, so strangled and desperate.

Charlie sighed. "Come sit." She patted the spot on the porch railing next to her.

Jo went, unable to deny her, even as her heart thumped.

"The telegram I got from my editor this morning wasn't just about our article. One of their war correspondents got hurt."

Jo's heart went from thumping to leaping, because she knew

what this might mean for Charlie. "Have they offered it to you?" she asked, breathless at the thought.

"They have," Charlie said.

Her face felt like it might split from the smile on it. "Oh, Charlie." Their fingers tangled together, their knees bumping as Jo squeezed Charlie's hands. "It's your dream. You'll be such an asset. They'll see it; they won't be able to deny it. You'll be able to do anything afterward."

"I can't believe it. The only thing I can think of is that they're worried I'll keep snooping in the States about Mary Nielsen—"

"So they send you over there," Jo said. "They seem rather cutthroat."

"Unfortunately for everyone, so am I," Charlie said. She held something out to Jo, who took it automatically. It was a card.

Jennifer Nielsen

"Mary's sister," Jo breathed.

"Just because I can't keep investigating, doesn't mean someone else can't start," Charlie said. "Jennifer lives just across the river. I told her you might call. And a package with my notes about Mary are on their way to the boardinghouse from my place in New York."

A thrill filled Jo. This was more than a lead. This was trusting her with something precious, a responsibility that she would not shirk. "I won't let you or the Nielsens down."

"I know you won't," Charlie said. "They're lucky to have you. I'm lucky—" She stopped, looking down at her feet, at the sensible oxfords that were scuffed from use. "Will you write to me?"

"Of course I will." Jo could feel Charlie's fingers trembling underneath hers. The look on her face—it sent a twisting sort of hope through Jo as everything seemed to fade in the heady silence that stretched between them.

"And will you . . . will you wait for me?"

It bloomed inside Jo: an answer to a question that had been pounding in her head since that first moment in the alley.

Is this how it's supposed to feel?

Yes.

Before she could answer, Charlie's fingers began to pull away from hers. Jo scrambled for them, clutching at them, drawing her that much closer.

"Was I wrong, Jo?" Charlie asked.

"No." The word came out in a rush. A denial that might start the rest of her life. "No, you weren't wrong."

Charlie's fingers weren't trembling underneath Jo's anymore. They were gripping hers, just as tight.

"Will you wait?" Charlie asked again.

It would've been easy to answer.

But it was braver to lean forward and push back the golden fall of her hair to kiss her.

She understood now that to love was to be brave. And more than anything, Jo wanted to be brave.

Jo stared at the phone.

She had been staring at it for a good ten minutes without moving. Her back was to the boardinghouse wall opposite of it, and she was grateful for the solidness because she felt a little faint. Her hands were sweating, and the ink on the paper she was clutching in them was in danger of smearing if she kept it up. Considering how long it took her to write the letter, smearing it seemed a shame.

She could hear murmuring.

"How long has she been like that?"

"At least fifteen minutes."

"Jo? Are you waiting for a call?" Molly asked.

"The phone book's right there," Anna added.

"Maybe we should give Jo some privacy," Ruth said, and Jo didn't have to turn around to know that the scoff sound was coming from Anna.

A whistle cut through the air. Peg removed her fingers from her mouth. "Ruth's right," she said. "Let's mind our own business."

Her friends scurried away—some downstairs to see if dinner was ready, and others to their rooms—and Peg shot Jo an encouraging smile.

"Good luck, Jo."

"Do you think I need it?"

Peg shrugged. "Those of us who have sisters need all the luck we can get. After all, sisters—blood and found—are blessed but complicated."

"Blessed but complicated," Jo echoed, her stomach twisting as Peg disappeared into her room, leaving Jo alone at the end of the hall. It was only a step or two to the phone, but the space still seemed uncrossable.

They've been needing you as much as you've been needing them. Charlie's reminder wound through her head like a river moving through the deep parts of a forest, cool and untouched by civilization, a place to just be. To accept.

She had turned on Meg for not understanding her when she had not understood herself. It had been unfair—to both of them. She had faulted her sister for not being able to always read her mind, when she had so obviously missed the signs of the changes going on in Meg's life. She had brushed away both her sisters, hurting Meg by ridiculing her choices and dismissing Amy like she couldn't be bothered with her, enforcing that terrible truth Amy had always believed of being lesser in Jo's eyes.

Jo had been selfish, wrapped in grief and her own fear of what not loving Laurie the way everyone expected meant, and she'd lashed out, a scorpion determined to guard itself, no matter the cost.

But even guarded creatures must leave the dens they've run and hidden in.

As she dialed, she thought of the little song with their phone number and address Beth had made up when Amy was little, in case she ever got lost and needed to call home. How did it go? Jo could remember the tune, but not the ditty Beth had composed.

Perhaps Meg would know.

For the first time in months, the thought didn't pain her. Because the phone was ringing, and instead of fear rising in her chest, it was something else: hope.

"Hello?"

A shaky breath. *Blessed but complicated, remember.* "Meg?"

"Jo?"

Her heart leapt.

"It's me." Jo licked her cracked lips. "I—I wrote you a letter. An apology. An explanation. I could've sent it, I suppose, but it would've taken days, and I just . . . Once I wrote it all down, I didn't want to wait another minute."

Silence followed, and Jo wondered if perhaps Charlie had been wrong. Perhaps her sisters had found themselves better off without her.

But then Meg, a strange creature in her own right, in her own way, took the olive branch Jo was finally able to extend. "Will you read it to me?"

Jo smiled, and trembling through her tears, she began.

To read.

To be.

ACKNOWLEDGMENTS

This book was born when Jessica posted on Twitter about a book idea she loved but found daunting: a World War II–era *Little Women* retelling where Jo, who is queer, works in a factory and Amy goes overseas to serve the troops and encounters Laurie. Joy suggested a collaboration: four authors could each write one of the March sisters. That was definitely less daunting! Caroline and Tess were soon on board.

We are all represented by Jim McCarthy and are so grateful for his encouragement, advocacy, and guidance along the way.

Our wonderful editor, Wendy Loggia, brought her enthusiasm for the original source material to our collaboration, and her energy has been infectious. Many thanks also to Alison Romig and Hannah Hill for their support and insights.

A book is always a collaboration of many people, even when it's not written by four authors. We are so grateful to everyone at Delacorte, including Casey Moses, Colleen Fellingham, Elizabeth Johnson, Tamar Schwartz, and artists Ann Chen and Louisa Cannell for their dedicated work in transforming the documents on our four computers into a beautiful book on shelves.

And finally, to Louisa May Alcott, whose deeply personal book has resonated with readers for more than a century. She was groundbreaking but was also constrained by her time. We hope she would appreciate the new directions we've explored while honoring her foundational work.

Joy (Beth)

Thank you to Jessica Spotswood for allowing me to barge in on your initial idea, and to Tess Sharpe and Caroline Tung Richmond for bringing so much to the collaboration. Thank you to Tehlor Kay Mejia for first suggesting Beth's sections should be written in verse. And thank you to my wonderful, book-loving family.

Caroline (Amy)

I'd like to thank my coauthors first and foremost—Joy, Tess, and Jessica—for their creativity, camaraderie, and amazing talent. Working on this project with you brought me so much joy during the dumpster-fire year of 2020. I also would like to thank Timothée Chalamet for inspiring my Laurie. There is a long line of actors who have played Theodore Laurence, but at least in my book, you really take the crown.

Tess (Jo)

My most grateful thanks to my coauthors—Joy, Jessica, and Caroline—for their joy, creativity, and faith throughout a chaotic year, when this wonderful project was such a guiding light. Thanks to my mother and Gramz, who brought Louisa and *Little Women* into my life so many years ago. And to every person who's ever read *Little Women* and thought *This girl is queer*. I'm right there with you.

Jess (Meg)

Thank you to my wonderful, talented coauthors, Caroline and Joy and Tess, for making this book I dreamed of bigger and more brilliant than I ever could have on my own. To my big-hearted, insightful critique partner, Tiffany Schmidt, even if she is an unrepentant Amy March apologist. To my summer research assistant, Avery Castellani, for all her help. To my best friend, Jenn Reeder, for always listening. And to my brilliant husband, Steve, for reading every draft, even if he still hasn't read *LW* and initially thought Marmee was the housekeeper.

ABOUT THE AUTHORS

Joy McCullough is a playwright and the author of the young adult novels *Blood Water Paint* and *We Are the Ashes, We Are the Fire,* as well as picture books and novels for younger readers. She lives in the Seattle area with her husband and two children.

Caroline Tung Richmond is the award-winning author of *The Only Thing to Fear, The Darkest Hour, Live in Infamy,* and *The Great Destroyers* and the coeditor of the anthology *Hungry Hearts* (along with Elsie Chapman). Caroline lives in Maryland with her family.

Tess Sharpe grew up in rural California. She lives deep in the backwoods with a pack of dogs and a growing colony of formerly feral cats. She is an author and anthology editor and has written several award-winning and critically acclaimed books for children, teens, and adults.

Jessica Spotswood is the author of the Cahill Witch Chronicles, *Wild Swans,* and *The Last Summer of the Garrett Girls.* She is the editor of the anthologies *A Tyranny of Petticoats* and *The Radical Element* and coeditor (with Tess Sharpe) of *Toil & Trouble.* Jess lives in Washington, DC, where she works for the Public Library.